GOD BLESS THE CHILDREN

Something was terribly wrong. Her eyes were fixed on the bedroom door in dreadful expectation, and when the handle began to turn, she could contain herself no longer.

"Jon, is that you?"

The fear was evident in her voice.

"Oh please say it's you."

Then the door opened wide and she saw it was— only a child. A boy. A handsome, beautiful, angelic boy. She could have kissed him.

"Where's Jonathan?" she asked.

The boy moved toward the foot of the bed. He said nothing.

Slowly he raised the pistol. As she opened her mouth to protest, the boy pulled the trigger.

Bantam Books by Charles Robertson

THE CHILDREN
THE ELIJAH CONSPIRACY

THE CHILDREN

Charles Robertson

Bantam Books · Robertson

BANTAM BOOKS
TORONTO · NEW YORK · LONDON · SYDNEY

THE CHILDREN
A Bantam Book / November 1982

All rights reserved.
Copyright © 1982 by Charles Robertson.
Cover art © 1982 by Max Ginsburg.
This book may not be reproduced in whole or in part, by
mimeograph or any other means, without permission.
For information address: Bantam Books, Inc.

ISBN 0-553-20920-5

Published simultaneously in the United States and Canada

Bantam Books are published by Bantam Books, Inc. Its trademark, consisting of the words ''Bantam Books'' and the portrayal of a rooster, is Registered in U.S. Patent and Trademark Office and in other countries. Marca Registrada. Bantam Books, Inc., 666 Fifth Avenue, New York, New York 10103.

PRINTED IN THE UNITED STATES OF AMERICA

H 0 9 8 7 6 5 4 3 2 1

*For my wife Ann
and children,
Jennifer and Scott*

THE
CHILDREN

Prologue

"He is very close to death," said the doctor to the man who, with him, hovered over the frail shape in the cot. "He won't make it to Houston."

The man's expression never changed, but, given news he did not wish to hear, he turned away from the doctor and the cot. Returning to his seat by the window, he buckled his safety belt without thinking, as he looked out at the Mexican landscape drifting by leisurely almost thirty thousand feet below.

Finally he spoke. "You mean to tell me that with all this"—he indicated with a wave of his hand the sophisticated medical equipment of the Learjet ambulance plane—"he's still gonna die?"

The doctor said nothing.

The man in the cot seemed terribly small, shrunken almost, as if the years had stolen mass from him. Tubes and wires ran from various parts of his body to an assortment of machines clustered around his bed. His ashen face was framed by long wispy gray hair and a sparse scraggly beard. The eyes were sunken and encased in dark circles. He had the look of a man who had wasted his life on alcohol and wantonness; but that was not true. He also had the look of a man who had lived his life in poverty. That was not true either. He was, in fact, the richest man in the world.

The doctor was anxious to avoid responsibility for the man's death. "I hope we're almost there," he said, breaking the silence that had fallen between himself and the man at the window. The man said nothing. The doctor plowed on. "I should have been called long before this, Bob. I can't be held responsible for . . ."

The other man—Bob—silenced him with a quick stare. Even in a three-piece suit he still had the rough-and-ready

1

look of the West about him. "S'nobody's fault," he said. "You know how he is. He wouldn't let us call anybody."

The doctor turned back to the cot, satisfied that he was not to be blamed. He traced the intravenous tubes running from the sick man's arm. One went to a thick plastic bag, another to a portable machine at the bedside. The doctor tapped the machine with his fingertips as if trying to determine how well it functioned. Without turning his attention from the machine he said, "A man shouldn't have to be comatose before his employees—his friends—call for medical assistance."

The hard look was back in Bob's face. "I don't know about you, Doc, but I just do what I'm told. When the man gives instructions, no matter how bizarre, you don't ask questions; you just do it."

The doctor opened his mouth as if he were about to speak but thought better of it and only nodded his head in affirmation.

The man in the cot was absolutely motionless. His face was gray, and without the machines monitoring his vital signs, it would have been impossible to determine if he were alive or dead.

The doctor shook his head again. "He's not going to make it."

"You've already said that, Doc. If you can't help him, I wish you'd just fix yourself a drink, sit down, and not say anything."

Looking at the array of machinery which surrounded the dying man, the doctor said, "We are wasting valuable time. Why is he being taken to Houston? This equipment is fine, but he should be in an intensive care unit at a full facility hospital. He should have remained in Acapulco. It was foolish to transport him to Houston."

Bob looked at the doctor with a gaze of infinite patience. "For the last two years, Doc, we have been under explicit instructions from the man himself that in case of a life-threatening medical emergency he is to be taken to Houston General. He has a private penthouse suite there that is held for his exclusive use."

"It won't do him any good if he expires before we get there. I hope you've done the right thing."

Bob's eyes narrowed. "Don't worry, Doc. I wouldn't do

something like this on my own. I called the president of the company this morning and told him the situation."

The doctor raised his eyebrows. "And?"

"He said you'd meet us in Acapulco and then we were to get him to Houston."

"Why was I never informed about this Houston plan? I'm his doctor."

"You are one of his doctors. One of three very well-paid doctors. Do you know that when we called, one was vacationing in England, one was at a medical conference in West Germany, and you were taking a weekend in the Bahamas? We lost a good three hours waiting for you to arrive."

The doctor cleared his throat. "We are not paid to be available for this kind of medical emergency. We are paid as consultants on a long-range basis and to be available to prescribe a course of treatment or to operate, should an operation be necessary. We are not emergency room doctors."

"Not at these prices."

"Are you trying to suggest? . . ."

"Doc, I'm not trying to suggest anything. I know it's not your fault that the man moves from hotel to hotel and from country to country. You can't be expected to be at his side every minute." He shaded his eyes from the glare of the cabin lights. "I think that this is one time when there were too many instructions to follow. We're all used to doing exactly what he says, no matter how crazy. You're probably right"—he shrugged—"we should have taken him to a hospital in Acapulco."

The doctor seemed relieved. "You more than anyone should appreciate how difficult it is to treat a man with his . . . shall we say, eccentric behavior."

The forward cabin door opened and the copilot poked his head in. "We'll be in Houston in twenty-two minutes. How's he doin'?"

The doctor shook his head while Bob said, "Make sure the ambulance is waiting on the runway."

After the copilot had returned to the cockpit, the doctor asked, "Why is it so important that he be taken to Houston? He could have received excellent care in Acapulco."

This was old ground and Bob showed his annoyance with a sharp, hard glare that forced the doctor to silence. "Doc, I've worked for the man for over twenty years and why he does what he does is usually a mystery to me. They say he's kept me on so long because we're two old cowboys who understand each other, but the truth is, I never really understood him at all. I only know that for the past four years getting to Houston has been the number one priority in case of emergency. He's been sick for quite some time, Doc, and every once in awhile he'd get a stab of pain and a strange look would come into his eyes. 'I think it's almost time for Houston,' he would say." There was great sadness in Bob's eyes.

The doctor tapped the machine again. "I think it's too late for Houston."

The temperature was in the nineties and the late afternoon sun sent waves of hot air wafting from the macadam runways of the Houston Intercontinental Airport as the twin-jet ambulance plane made its landing approach. An ambulance, siren blaring, red lights flashing, raced onto the runway as the plane touched down, and like a swan followed by a noisy duckling, the two cruised down the runway.

The plane taxied to a halt in front of a low building next to an arc-roofed hangar where other twin- and single-jet corporate planes were tied down. The door of the ambulance plane opened and the special ramp-stairway automatically began to descend just as the ambulance screeched to a halt. The back doors of the ambulance flew open and ejected two attendants with stretchers who dashed for the ramp, but before they could reach the first step, the doctor appeared in the doorway of the plane.

He held up his hand. "Don't hurry," he said. "He's gone."

The white-clothed attendants stopped, looked at each other as if awaiting new instructions, then slowly made their way up the short ramp into the plane. The doctor was about to follow when he saw a black Cadillac limousine pull up and stop next to the ambulance. A man wearing a dark suit and clutching a leather briefcase climbed out and looked to the doctor with what might have been hopeful expectation. When the doctor shook his head in response, the man's shoulders sagged visibly, and he reentered the limousine to relay the bad news to the two men seated in the back seat. They conversed quietly for a few minutes until they were joined by the doctor and the other man from the plane.

The rear door window glided slightly open.

"Afternoon, Mr. Colhoun," said the man called Bob.

"Hello, Bob," said a voice from within. "I don't want you to blame yourself for any of this. I know you did everything possible."

The doctor, standing in the heat at Bob's side, gave a small strangled cough.

After a brief pause the voice spoke again. "I know that you did everything medically possible, Doctor. He had been failing rapidly over the last few weeks. We tried to get him to come here sooner, but I don't have to tell you how difficult he could be."

"It's a shame," said the doctor.

A low chuckle emerged from the limousine. "You'll never know how much of a shame it is."

The doctor, unable to comprehend the laugh or the statement, nodded uncertainly, like a man pretending to understand a joke, and then looked at his watch as if remembering previous commitments.

Bob stepped forward, resting an arm on the door below the open window. He looked into the faces of the three men inside the limousine and said, "There's something I'd like to ask about this Houston plan of ours, Mr. Colhoun."

Colhoun stopped him with a wave of his hand. "Bob, you don't need or want to know any more than you know right now. It's over." His eyes narrowed slightly. "Believe me, you're better off. Why don't you go get something to eat? Maybe have a few drinks. Spend the night at the hotel."

"I left everything in Acapulco. I should get right back."

"Don't worry about that. Buy what you need here; charge it to the company. I want to see you tomorrow. We'll talk about reassignment."

Bob nodded. "Whatever you say, Mr. Colhoun."

"Run along then," said Colhoun with a smile. "One of the boys in the hangar will drop you off at the hotel and I'll see you in my suite tomorrow. I've got some business to discuss with our friends here."

The window closed and the meeting was over.

As the two men turned away from the limousine, the body from the plane was being loaded into the ambulance. Bob stood rigidly still, almost at attention. The doctor fidgeted nervously, anxious for the moment to pass. The three men in the dark sanctity of the limousine gave the body only a moment's notice, then turned quickly back to their discussion.

"What now?" said the lawyer. He was a fairly young man

with a long thin face and balding pate. His name was Jason Arnold.

Colhoun considered his reply very carefully. "First thing, of course, is that we protect our own interests," he said quietly.

Jason Arnold looked toward the third man in the car as if he were unsure whether or not he should continue in his presence. The third man, who was stern-faced and bearded, did not seem interested in any of the conversation. Arnold decided to continue. "But how?" he said to Colhoun. "I've got a legitimate will here in my briefcase. He left everything to that child. It's absolutely incredible."

Colhoun took a long cigar from a leather case in his jacket. He inspected the cigar carefully, rolling it in his fingertips, aware that Jason Arnold was watching his deliberation. Colhoun knew that Arnold was near hysteria over the problem of the will and that now, especially now, was a time for calm.

He lit his cigar and gave Arnold a reassuring slap on the knee. "Do you also have the covering letter that goes with the will?"

"Yes, but . . ."

"You have noted, of course, that the covering letter is written in his own hand."

Arnold only nodded.

"His instructions are quite explicit," said Colhoun softly; his voice was the essence of reason. "Unless I am completely satisfied as to the time of his death, the will is to be destroyed." He blew out a narrow stream of cigar smoke, which was instantly whisked away by the limousine's air filtration system. Then he turned to face Arnold. "I'm telling you now that I am not satisfied."

Arnold squirmed. "This is highly—" he searched for a word—"unusual. I'm not sure of the legality."

Colhoun shrugged. "I suppose we could test the legality in the courts, at a cost of millions of dollars. At which time of course we would almost certainly be accused of trying to deny a child his rightful inheritance. The media would have a field day with this." He smiled, revealing his too perfect teeth. "We would be assigned the role of the evil corporation; the boy would represent the defenseless public. It would be no contest. No matter what the legalities, popular opinion would force the court to bestow millions of dollars on that child. The litigation alone could tie up the corporation for years."

"What about the boy? What will happen to him?"

"Don't worry. He will be taken care of."

The lawyer shook his head. "I don't know about this . . ."

For the first time a note of intimidation crept into Colhoun's voice. "Do you doubt the authenticity of the covering letter?"

"No," said Arnold quickly. "I'm quite certain it's genuine. But . . ."

"Then there really is no need for buts, is there? The man has given his last order—from beyond the grave, if you prefer melodrama—and it remains for us to carry out that order."

Arnold, defeated, only nodded.

Colhoun displayed the barest trace of a smile. "The letter also states that all copies of the will are to be turned over to me and that I personally am to be responsible for their destruction."

"Yes."

"Do you have all of the copies with you?"

"Yes."

"Are you prepared, now, to hand them over to me?"

Arnold sat up straight in his seat. "The letter says I'm to do all of this if at the time of death you are not satisfied that certain conditions have been met. You could at least tell me what the conditions are, and why you are not satisfied."

Colhoun stared intently into the lawyer's eyes. It was a look that carried with it the full power and weight of his position and Arnold's left eye began to twitch under the strain. When the lawyer's eyes had been forced to turn away, Colhoun said, "I am not required to do so. I need only state to you that those conditions, which were communicated verbally to me, have not been satisfied. I, therefore, am not satisfied."

The lawyer said nothing.

"Let me put it to you another way," said Colhoun. "How much are you paid by the company to handle this aspect of the legal work?"

Arnold thought carefully. When he spoke his voice was defensive. "The amount is considerable."

"If that will is processed and the child is declared the legal heir to this fortune, we will all be out in the cold."

"Not necessarily. It is also possible that . . ."

Colhoun interrupted him with an explosive discharge of cigar smoke. "Come on! Be realistic. This will would set off the biggest legal scramble the world has ever seen. Every do-gooder in the country would want to make sure the boy's interests were protected. They'd all want their share, of course. I would instantly be dismissed by the board of directors for allowing such a thing to happen." He waved his cigar as if such an occurrence were only a minor concern. "You of course could no longer represent the company. I would think there is a clear conflict of interest here."

"I assure you," said Arnold quickly, "that your interests are my interests, Mr. Colhoun."

Colhoun's eyes twinkled. "That's very reassuring, Jason."

"It's only that this is so highly unusual."

"Everything about the man was unusual. Those of us who worked for him, and will continue to work for his corporation, accepted that as part of his genius."

Jason Arnold sat slumped in a corner of the cavernous limousine. "What now?"

Colhoun reached down to the floor and lifted a briefcase onto the seat between them. "You will take this briefcase, which contains copies of the will previous to that which you now hold, and place it in the safe in the suite in Acapulco."

Arnold's eyes opened wide in protest. "Acapulco! Why not let someone else take it there? How about Bob? He wanted to get back there."

Colhoun patted the lawyer's knee. "I think it's only fitting that this matter be handled by a company lawyer." He smiled. "A company plane is waiting for you now on the runway. The sooner this matter is taken care of, the better."

Sighing heavily, resigned to anything now, Arnold exchanged his briefcase for the one held by Colhoun.

"You are welcome to inspect the will to assure yourself of its authenticity," Colhoun said, clutching the precious briefcase in trembling fingers.

Arnold nodded with only partial interest. "Which one is it?"

Colhoun laughed. "It's will B-Fourteen. You drew it up yourself."

"B-Fourteen," said the lawyer, his eyes squinting as he tried to remember. "There have been so goddamn many of them." He shook his head. "He was always trying to leave somebody a fortune. Somebody'd do him a favor and he'd want to leave them a couple million dollars. I've made so many changes in his wills over the years that I can't remember all the details." He looked at his briefcase, now safely ensconced in the arms of Colhoun. "None of them was more bizarre than that one, though," he said, motioning to the briefcase. "Imagine leaving a multibillion dollar estate to a child, not even a relative! Why did he do it? For God's sake, why?"

"He didn't do it. Did he?" said Colhoun patting the briefcase on his lap. "He only thought of doing it. He was wise enough to empower me to make the final determination." Colhoun was tired; he wanted this conversation to end. "All you have to worry about now is that you deliver will B-Fourteen to the safe in Acapulco. Don't let that briefcase out of your sight for a minute."

Arnold remembered something. "B-Fourteen is the will that leaves most of the inheritance to the foundation, isn't it? We'd probably be better if that will were never found either."

Colhoun stopped short for a moment. "It's the best we can do. At least it leaves the company itself under the control of the present board of directors."

"We'd probably all be better off if no will were found," said Arnold. "The legal problems would be mountainous, but at least the board of directors would retain total control."

"It's a question of ethics, my boy," said Colhoun, staring sincerely into the younger man's eyes. "We can protect the company only to a certain extent. What price are we willing to pay to guard its interests?"

As Arnold nodded, Colhoun quickly looked away and took a telephone from a receptacle near his hand. "John," he said to the driver on the other side of the soundproof glass, "take us to the company hangar. There is a plane waiting for Mr. Arnold."

Arnold sighed quietly as the limousine moved forward on the short trip to the hangar. Look on the bright side, he said to himself. I'll spend the evening in Acapulco and be back early tomorrow morning.

The limousine pulled up next to a sleek, twin-engined corporate jet which displayed red striping over the white fuselage. On the tail, in large red letters, the company logo—HT—was prominently displayed. The two men shook hands and Colhoun watched as Arnold walked to the jet. He was the only passenger and as soon as he had boarded, the plane began to move slowly toward the runway.

As the plane taxied into position for takeoff, Colhoun turned his attention to the briefcase which still sat in his lap. He flipped open the brass clasps, opened the lid, and for just a moment inspected the contents. With what could only be described as loving care, he removed three identical documents, each backed by a light blue folder, and held the wills carefully in his hands, caressing the words with his fingertips as if he were a monk and these were sacred scrolls. As Arnold's plane picked up speed on the runway, Colhoun began slowly and methodically to tear the documents into very small pieces.

At the end of the runway the jet leaped into the sky, banked steeply, then flashed back over the company hangar, dipping its wings in salute as it passed over the black limousine, squatting beetlelike on the gray macadam of the runway approach.

Colhoun shut the lid of the briefcase as the plane shot past overhead. The fragments of the wills now enclosed, he drummed his fingertips on the side of the case.

"Good-bye, Howard," he said softly. "Good-bye, little boy." He tilted his head to look at the sky where the company jet was only a tiny speck vanishing in the haze, and hugged the briefcase to his body as if it were an adored child. With some trace of sadness he said, "Good-bye, Jason Arnold."

The third man spoke for the first time. "This whole thing could have been avoided if you people had just listened to me. If only . . ."

Colhoun interrupted him. "Doctor, when you're dealing with someone like the late Mr. Hughes, you can only do what he allows you to do." He smiled. "Or what you can get away with."

Jason Arnold was well settled into his comfortable seat when he finished reading will B-Fourteen. It was an awesomely complicated document but strictly legal. He was relieved that the matter had been settled amicably. Colhoun was right; it was better for all concerned—with the exception of the child, of course—that this will be discovered and not the other bizarre document. That will would have been contested in court by every possible heir. The legal fees and the time involved would have tied up the company for a decade.

He placed the will back in the briefcase, closed it, and swung the case into the seat next to him. He opened the case again. Except for the copies of will B-Fourteen, it was empty. He ran his fingers around the inside of the lid and behind the leather pouch that served as a holder for loose documents or pens or notepads.

With a quick shrug of his shoulders Arnold closed the lid and reached for the intercom button. "Russ," he said, speaking into the device on the cabin wall, "how much longer?"

"About twenty-five minutes, Mr. Arnold," replied the crackling voice. "I'm still out over the Gulf. In about ten minutes we'll make a steep turn to the right and begin our descent to the coastline. Everything OK back there?"

"Fine; thanks, Russ."

"There's plenty of liquor in the cabinet right in front of you."

The pilot heard the sound of the intercom click and then only part of a word from his passenger. At that moment there was a distinct thump as if someone had smashed a giant hammer against the fuselage of the plane, and the jet went into a shallow dive. The air pressure dropped and there was a roaring sound of rushing air in the rear compartment.

"Mr. Arnold," called the pilot as he frantically tried to battle the controls, but where Arnold had been, there was now only a gaping hole in the fuselage.

The dive steepened and the plane began to roll over on its back. The pilot's voice crackled into the empty passenger compartment. "I'm sorry, Mr. Arnold," he said calmly. "It looks like we're going in."

Chapter 1

It could have been midnight. It was in fact 8:40 A.M., but the light of day did not penetrate to the lower platform of the Fourteenth Street IRT subway station. The harsh glare of florescent lights reflected off the grimy, once white, tile walls and spilled onto the gray cement of the platform itself. Garbage everywhere. Above the head-high level of the tile, the walls were painted a tired excuse for beige. To the left and right of the platform, two dark holes devoured the debris-littered tracks that disappeared around a dimly lit bend.

The odors of New York were dominant—exhaust fumes, urine, tobacco, oil, and grease—but somewhere beneath them hung the sickly sweet, pungent smell of something indefinable.

Fred Romanello noticed little of this backdrop as he descended onto the platform from the upper level. Romanello was tall and gaunt, his eyes bulging from a face that even when clean-shaven, displayed a faint trace of shadowy beard. His slack-jawed look gave an impression of dullness that was belied by his quick, confident movements. As he moved across the platform to glance into the dark tunnel, he shifted his briefcase to his right hand and looked at his watch. He seemed oblivious to his surroundings, but was in fact acutely aware of the presence and position of every other person on the platform.

Only the mildly disturbing odor penetrated the indifference that Romenello presented to the world. It was an indifference that said, don't bother me; don't invade my space; don't approach me. He wore an air of imperturbability that was the required cloak of conduct for millions of New Yorkers. Even the lack of color in his clothing—brown slacks and shoes, tan raincoat—was intended to repel attention. This anonymity of person was a fairly common device to escape the realities of life in a city on the verge of anarchic breakdown.

13

A brief glance around the platform enabled Romanello to quickly categorize the waiting passengers. He arranged them in two groups: commuters and natives.

Commuters: The term itself was loaded with derision. He ignored them immediately. They were no possible threat. Their eyes darted back and forth nervously as they attempted to keep themselves apart from the others on the platform. Their most fervent desire was to reach the office without incident and then scurry home to some insular patch of green in Queens or on the Island. A commuter would walk to the end of the platform to avoid contact with anyone in his vicinity; Fred Romanello could avoid contact by making his features devoid of expression.

Don't touch anyone's eyes with yours, he warned himself. The eyes could look, but they must not touch. Touching brought vulnerability. What was required was a perpetual expression of boredom. Anything else was like a beacon to the predators—blood to the sharks—who inhabited the subterranean regions of the city.

The second group, natives, was more varied and potentially more dangerous. There were women who were on their way to work in the stores and offices of downtown Manhattan. They clutched their purses and clustered together in silent affirmation of their fears. There were the old who seemed constantly lost and bewildered. Society had raced beyond their comprehension, and now, as if in some ancient ritual, they had been abandoned to await their inevitable fate. Keep away from them, Romanello told himself. When the predator strikes, these are his first victims.

The rest of this group were to be treated with caution: the kids, full of loud noise and boisterous behavior, who could sometimes be dissuaded with a cold look but were best avoided; the young black men, with dangerous, unblinking eyes and dark angry faces, who were on their way to God-knows-where.

If there were danger, it would come from this direction.

Fred Romanello wore his mask of indifference like a shield. Years of practice kept him safe. His society in chaos, he lived by simple rules: Be alert. Show no interest or recognition. Show no fear.

Consequently, on this cold October morning in the Fourteenth Street station, Romanello, face expressionless, eyes without passion, waited for the uptown train. Only the sick-

ening odor broke through. It touched a part of his brain long
dormant and he found himself remembering the time he had
discovered a dead rat in the cellar of his father's house on
Freemont Avenue in Brooklyn. He was only ten, but his
mother had designated him to get rid of the rat.

The house was gone now. So was his father. Christ, I
haven't thought of that place for years, he said to himself.

No one spoke. As the expectation of the train's arrival
grew, the crowd shuffled forward in silence, all eyes directed
toward the tunnel, ears cocked for the first faint rumblings
from the tracks.

"Come along, children," said a woman's voice, shattering
the silence. "Keep in line, please."

Romanello turned in the direction of the voice and beheld
an unlikely sight. The woman was in her late fifties, tall and
well dressed, with an air of authority about her that immediately evoked unpleasant memories of teachers Romanello had
known. The children followed her in a double file and Fred
could barely suppress a smile. They were all boys; sixteen of
them, around eleven or twelve years old, he imagined, and
all were dressed as if they had just stepped out of an English
movie. They wore blue blazers with a patch over the breast
pocket, gray flannel slacks, white shirts with starchy-looking
collars, striped ties, and small caps with some sort of insignia
on the front.

The usually complacent New Yorkers were looking at
each other in amusement. Small smiles were beginning to
replace perpetual frowns and Romanello was amazed to see
that the stolid face of a young black man, whom he had
earlier singled out for watching, had broken into an aston-
ished grin. The man caught Romanello's glance and winked
as though the two were sharing a private joke.

"Right here will be fine, boys," the teacher said as the
boys filed past Romanello. The crowd fell back without its
customary protest as the boys took their positions near the
front.

As the boys stopped behind Romanello, the teacher's
voice lashed out like the crack of a whip. "Ronald! I expressly
instructed you to walk behind David, and now I see that you
are once again in front of David."

One of the schoolboys, presumably Ronald, wilted under
her withering gaze. "Yes, Miss Parsons," he said softly. "I am
sorry."

For a moment there was silence as everyone on the platform became involved in this small display of power, and then Miss Parsons spoke again. "Well?"

Without a word, the boys changed positions. "That's better," said Miss Parsons with a bright smile. "Now we shall just await the arrival of our train."

Class trip, thought Romanello. Immediately, visions of an endless list of boring trips to various city museums ran through his mind. Teachers always thought that kids were interested in that sort of stuff. Who wanted to see dead Egyptians, stuffed animals, or wax dummies of Indians paddling canoes? Only teachers.

Romanello leaned slightly forward, peering once more into the tunnel. Train's late, he thought with some irritation. Behind him he could hear the chatter of the schoolboys. At the head of the line, Miss Parsons stood erect and motionless, staring straight out across the tracks.

Romanello ran his eyes down the line of boys engaged in quiet but animated conversation. There was something about them, he thought. Something that was almost angelic. They were squeaky-clean and proper, and each had an aura of innocence that seemed out of place in the squalor of the subway platform.

One of the boys caught Romanello's stare and returned a dazzling smile. Caught off-guard by the warmhearted gesture, Romanello felt the corners of his mouth begin to move in response. He tried to stop himself, but the smile was infectious. He gave a quick grin in the boy's direction and, strangely unnerved by the experience, turned his attention back to the tracks.

A rumbling in the darkness heralded the arrival of the train and Romanello advanced on the platform as the crowd behind him moved up. A light appeared and the train burst out of the tunnel, brakes already screeching like chalk scraped across a blackboard.

As the waiting crowd maneuvered into boarding position, Romanello was jostled slightly. Suddenly he felt a strong push from behind. His first reaction was merely surprise and then shock and dismay as he was propelled outward across the tracks. With arms flailing to preserve his balance, Romanello was aware of the gasp of the crowd even above the intensified shriek of the brakes.

He landed between the tracks, on his feet, mind working

like a computer. Catlike, he spun around, avoiding the third rail, taking in the velocity and distance of the fast-approaching train and the height of, and distance to, the platform.

I can make it, he told himself, as he took one giant stride across the track. His hands were already on the shoulder-high platform, his right leg on the rail bent to propel himself upward as the train hurtled closer. He leaped, bringing himself up to waist-level, his left shoe digging into the wall to provide more lift as he swung his right leg up.

I can make it, he told himself, to drown out the scream of the train.

As if he could will himself to join the openmouthed faces above him, he looked up to the safety of the platform. It was at that moment that he saw the eyes—sixteen pairs of eyes that bore into his brain like icy, steel-gray needles—and the faces: cold, alien, venomous.

Above the sound of the brakes were other sounds, other voices. *Hurry, hurry. Oh God, hurry.* There were screams somewhere in the distance, the squeal of the train's brakes as metal scored metal, but the silence of the eyes and the darkness of the faces superseded everything.

The faces assaulted Romanello, and the eyes—large, luminous, demonic orbs—were a barrier he could not scale.

The screams rose to a crescendo and then Fred Romanello felt a hammer blow in the small of his back and he carried the image of the eyes with him into a dark tunnel of oblivion.

Eyewitness accounts of the accident differed. Some said that he never really had a chance, while others thought that he was going to scramble safely onto the platform but inexplicably paused at the last moment. "It was almost as if he'd changed his mind," said one witness. Some were sure that he'd been pushed but could provide no clues as to who might have done such a thing. A few were certain that he had jumped onto the tracks and then lost his nerve. "Tried to kill himself, then chickened out," said one bystander.

One woman, Elsie Matlock, age fifty-three, who was on her way to a cleaning job in a high-rise apartment in the East Eighties, said that she'd never forget the look on his face just before the train swept him away.

"Poor man," she said through choked sobs for the *Six O'Clock News.* "His eyes open wide and staring," she said into the camera while teenagers made faces in the background. "Just like,"—she paused, wiping back tears, groping for words—"just like he was staring into the gates of hell."

Chapter 2

The rain was almost torrential, driving all but the foolish to seek shelter in doorways and under storefront awnings. Clogged storm drains refused the sudden burden. Flooded streets became impassable barriers to the few pedestrians who still insisted on getting to work on time.

Although the sidewalks of Fifth Avenue were almost deserted, vehicular traffic plowed on, taxis sending out ribbons of spray to drench the few unsuspecting pedestrians. Some gave up and huddled together, waiting for the rain to subside; the more knowledgeable were able to make their way from the train or subway to their offices through the uncharted labyrinth of tunnels beneath the buildings and streets of New York City.

Jonathan Carruthers, lying in his bed sixteen stories above the tumult, was oblivious to the travails of those in the streets below. The wind hammered the rain against his bedroom window, and the noise, like the sound of marbles falling on a kitchen floor, stirred him from contented slumber. He opened his eyes and stared blankly at the ceiling, which was alive with the reflection of the rain on the window.

It was several moments before he recalled the woman in bed beside him.

For a second, while he tried to remember her name, he resisted the temptation to turn and look at her. He drew a blank, remembering only that she had been attractive and extremely cooperative. Turning to face her, he wondered if the morning's view would be as good as the remembrance of the night before.

She lay on her side, facing him, head resting on one bent arm, blond hair falling over one bare shoulder and partially obscuring her face. She was beautiful, he thought with a sudden, relieved smile, and then, just as suddenly, another thought wiped the smile from his face.

I've got to stop doing this. I've got to stop bringing these girls home.

His agent had pleaded with him at least a hundred times. "Jonathan, you're a celebrity. One of these bimbos is going to slap you with a paternity suit and the publicity alone could ruin you."

But it wasn't easy. He smiled as he looked at the girl, his eyes tracing the curve of her body beneath the single sheet that covered them both. In sleep she radiated innocence, and her deep rhythmic breathing seemed to suggest that she felt security and comfort here in his bed.

Carruthers did not brush the blond hair away from her face and give her some small touch of reassurance. Instead he slipped carefully from the bed so as not to disturb her, and, taking a robe to cover his nakedness, made his way quietly out of the room.

He closed the door softly behind him and walked through the large living room to the galley kitchen. From the refrigerator he removed a can of coffee and proceeded to fill the coffee maker on the counter.

As he counted out the scoops, his mind returned to the girl. He shook his head. I've got to stop doing this, he said, his lips moving with the words, but he did not say them aloud.

Being a celebrity in New York City made some things very difficult. Women, for instance, came at him from every angle. The girl who at this moment lay in his bed, was until last night a stranger to him—indeed, was a stranger even now. He had seen her at the network screening of a new miniseries scheduled for spring viewing and had assumed that she was with the network. Actually, she worked as a teller at the Fifty-fourth Street branch of the Chase Manhattan Bank. A cousin who worked in programming had given her a ticket to the preview.

Carruthers had seen her standing alone in the lobby of the theater and, drawn by her good looks, had engaged her in conversation. Sensing that she was suitably impressed with his star quality, he had invited her to sit with him during the screening and then to join him at the network party after-

ward. And then to return to his apartment for what he
euphemistically called a nightcap.

The girl, whose name was Lara or Laura or Lauren or
something, had of course been overwhelmed by all of this,
and ten minutes after entering Carruthers's apartment had
found herself naked and being led through the gamut of
sexual gymnastics that substituted for passion in the world of
Jonathan Carruthers.

But he had to be more careful. If one of these star-struck
bimbos ever decided to make trouble for him, it could be
very embarrassing. You have to treat them right, he thought
with a smile. A dozen roses, with a vaguely romantic note,
delivered by messenger the next day usually forestalled any
problems. Women were such incurable romantics. Any tender gesture was usually enough to satisfy their disappointment at not seeing him again.

Long before stardom in New York, Carruthers had been
a man who had a way with the ladies. Even in Des Moines
and Indianapolis, where he had worked before the network
brought him to New York in an attempt to bolster the sagging
ratings of the *Six O'Clock News*, he had always found the
time to cultivate his appreciation of beautiful things.

It was considered quite a gamble when the network took
this comparative unknown from the backwaters of Indiana to
anchor the evening news on the flagship station. Usual procedure dictated that the anchorman, who is to the news what
a star is to a motion picture, be brought along more carefully.
If he was successful, a fledgling anchorman moved to progressively larger cities until he arrived in Boston, Washington, Philadelphia, or Chicago. It was from one of those large
but still minor-league cities that the anchor was prepared to
make the leap to New York or Los Angeles. Even L.A. was
considered a step down from the big one. New York was
where it all happened, where the thousands of young, ambitious newspeople wanted to be. New York was mecca to
those who worshipped the eye that never blinks.

For years, the WNBC *Six O'Clock News* had run a
distant third to its two network rivals. In the previous five
years no fewer than seven new anchormen from the top
affiliates across the nation had been imported in an attempt to
improve the ratings. None of the changes had had any impact.
Weathermen were replaced with such frequency that

viewers were bewildered by the flurry of new faces. Local New York sports heroes were hired to do the sports segments and most performed so ineptly that the station became the laughingstock of the industry. But when professional sports journalists were hired to replace the incompetents, the ratings still did not show any improvement.

The program was mired, apparently permanently, in last place in the biggest advertising market in the country. One point in the ratings could mean several hundred thousand dollars a week in advertising revenue. The program was barely afloat, desperately awaiting the arrival of someone who could change its course.

Finally some inspired network executive decided to investigate the reports about a young anchorman at the network affiliate in Indianapolis who had steered that program out of the doldrums and into second place behind the strong CBS affiliate. Jonathan Carruthers was thirty-four and had been with WTHR in Indianapolis for two years. He had started with the NBC affiliate in Des Moines as a reporter on the police beat and had quickly worked his way up to a regular position on the evening news program. After less than a year with the station he had been given the anchor position on the eleven o'clock program, and soon thereafter he had become coanchor on the more prestigious six o'clock program, where he soon displaced all rivals for the anchor position.

After one year he moved on to the larger Indianapolis station where, in addition to assuming the anchor of the *Six O'Clock News*, he was made host of an all-news talk show that was shown on Sunday evenings. Jonathan Carruthers was on his way up, but it seemed that he was still a long way from the big time.

What he didn't know was that he had already attracted the attention of the network bosses, who in desperation were ready to make an almost unprecedented move.

Jonathan Carruthers was perfect for the job. He was movie star handsome—he had tried for almost five years to make an impression in Hollywood before turning to broadcasting—personable and harshly inquisitive. The network's own Q ratings, in which a positive or negative attitude of the public toward different TV personalities was rated, showed that Carruthers was thought to have integrity and credibility. His public felt that he was a nice guy who dealt with facts and really cared about his viewers. What his public didn't know, and what his Q ratings could not reveal, was that Carruthers was incredibly ambitious and would kick anyone aside who stood in his way to the top.

This, then, was the man brought in from the hinterland to lead NBC out of the wilderness of the New York ratings jungle. Jonathan Carruthers had been successful beyond anyone's wildest expectations. With the customary hoopla, the new anchorman had been introduced in May of 1979 to the New York audience. At first the ratings had shown only a barely perceptible rise, but over a four-month period the ratings had moved gradually but steadily upward. After six months on the job, Carruthers had moved his program into a virtual tie for second place with the CBS station.

Network executives were ecstatic. For the first time in years an action they had taken had shown positive results. There is nothing that network executives do quite so well as pat each other on the back, and the success of the *Six O'Clock News* was cause for much back-pounding in the upper levels of the RCA Building.

Carruthers was an unqualified success. He was described as a man with the public acceptance of Phil Donahue, the wit and appeal of Johnny Carson, and the accusatory style of Tom Snyder. Even with all these attributes his program's popularity began to level off until it seemed that it would be permanently mired in the number two spot, a distant second to the front-running ABC *Eyewitness News*.

Then something happened that put Carruthers and his news program over the top. Gale Anders, a rising starlet on one of NBC's new bounce and jiggle shows, was interviewed by Carruthers on the three-minute Celebrity Interview segment that he did on each news program. What ensued was instant fireworks.

Viewers could see the sparks between the two during the interview, and Carruthers concluded the segment by asking quite blatantly, on camera, what Anders was doing after the show. Just as blatantly, as she leaned forward to fill the screen with cleavage, the starlet quipped, "You can buy me breakfast."

The next morning at 9:20 A.M., an enterprising photographer who did some free-lance work for the New York *Post* snapped a photograph of Gale Anders as she left Carruthers's apartment building. The afternoon edition of the *Post* carried the photograph on the front page. Above the picture, in letters two inches high, was emblazoned the headline "Breakfast in Bed?"

The fact that Anders was married to a screenwriter who lived and worked in California, only added spice to the story. Carruthers moved from being a success to being a celebrity.

His ratings soared. Everyone was watching the *Six O'Clock News* on NBC. In a flurry of activity, the network raced to embrace its newest superstar, and Carruthers was signed to a lucrative, long-term contract. After a surprisingly successful stint as guest host of the *Tonight Show*, rumors flew that Carruthers was being primed as a possible replacement for Johnny Carson. His face appeared on national magazines, and gossip columns rarely missed mentioning his latest romantic escapades. Next to his desire to be the number one newscaster in America, they said, these romantic entanglements were his most pressing priority.

Carruthers became known in the industry as an incorrigible skirt chaser. In addition to his well-publicized romances with New York and Hollywood beauties, he was prone to one-night stands with women he happened to meet at parties, restaurants, bars, discos, or any of his other favorite New York City haunts.

Carruthers finished his cup of coffee and thought of the girl in the bedroom. He muttered to himself, this time aloud, "I've got to stop doing this," but with the remembrance of the girl and of the night before, his resolve began to crumble. He caught sight of his own reflection in the mirror above the bar in the living room. A smile crept over his face as he watched himself, knowing he was ready to return to the bedroom, and he shook his head slowly in resignation at his inability to suppress his desire.

On his way back to the girl he paused in front of his image in the hall mirror. "You're hopeless," he told himself.

As he slipped quietly back into bed, the woman stirred, rolling over onto her back. The sheet slipped down below her breasts, and Carruthers smiled appreciatively at the way they held firm and solid in this position. He reached over and traced a circle around her left nipple. The woman smiled and trembled slightly, her head moving slowly from side to side, and then she opened her eyes.

"Good morning," she said, adjusting immediately to what

should have been unfamiliar surroundings. Carruthers only smiled, his fingers kneading her breast.

Her hand snaked toward him under the sheet, brushed against his knee, then ran up his thigh until she found her target.

"Still plenty of life in you yet," she said.

He nodded in acknowledgment. "I've put coffee on. I thought we might have some breakfast before I have to leave for work."

Her face fell. "Can't we just stay in bed today?"

"The news never rests," he said with mock seriousness. "I have some people coming over this morning, and you have to be gone by ten."

She pouted. "Will I see you again?"

This was a question at which he had become expert. "Of course you will. Do you think that after last night I could ever forget you?"

He watched the smile return to her face. The girl sat up in bed, the sheets falling away from her body. She shook her hair, letting it fall into place behind her and then leaned back supporting herself on her elbows. Turning her face slowly toward him, she smiled over her shoulder. "Last night was . . . very nice."

"I thought so, too," he said, watching the steady rise and fall of her breasts.

"You're really something," she said, and Carruthers noticed with fascination that her nipples were growing erect. She looked down at her breasts. "Look what you're doing to me. . . . Are you sure you want me out of here by ten?"

Carruthers reached over and in one swift motion pulled the sheets from her body. She did not flinch. "Maybe we could stay just a little longer," he said, moving closer to her, letting their bodies touch.

Pulling her toward him, he kissed her. He placed a hand on her knee, and as he began to trace a slow path up the soft flesh of her inner thigh, the doorbell rang.

"Shit!" he said, and she, like a schoolgirl discovered in sin, whipped the sheets back up to cover herself. Carruthers almost laughed at the sight of her—eyes wide open, sheets pulled up to her neck, but the bell rang again and erased all thoughts of laughter.

"It's all right," he said, rolling out of bed and donning his robe. "Probably somebody selling Girl Scout cookies. Just sit tight and keep quiet. I'll get rid of whoever it is. Be right back."

He closed the bedroom door behind him and padded across the living room to the front door, opening it to reveal a small boy of about eleven, who smiled brightly as though he had some glad tidings to relate.

"Todd," said Carruthers not too happily, "this is a surprise."

The boy wore a school uniform: blazer, flannels, and cap, and carried an old-fashioned satchel-type briefcase. "Good morning, Jon," he said. "I hope I'm not intruding."

The boy's mother was a VIP or Carruthers would already have closed the door. Always aware of who could help him and who could not, he had carefully nurtured the boy's friendship. Right now Carruthers was on top and needed nothing from anyone. But next year? Five years from now?

Carruthers fought the impulse to turn his gaze toward the bedroom door. "Well, actually, Todd, I was just getting dressed to go out. You caught me as I was about to get into the shower."

The boy seemed genuinely upset. "I'm terribly sorry. It's just that I was wondering if you remembered that book you'd promised to loan me."

Carruthers's look was blank.

"You know," the boy went on, "the one we had that great discussion about last week."

"Oh, yes," said Carruthers. "Let me get it for you."

The boy followed him into the living room, and Carruthers noted with some annoyance that he had closed the front door.

"I'll tell you what," Carruthers said as he ran his fingers across the tightly packed shelves of the bookcase, "if you like the book, you can keep it." He wanted to be rid of the boy and this seemed an expedient method to send him on his way. "Any eleven-year-old who can enjoy heavy stuff like this deserves a bonus."

The boy beamed. "Do you mean it? Really? That would be awfully nice of you."

Carruthers wanted to ask the boy what kind of school it was that made him dress and act so . . . so what? so . . . un-American? So foreign? So unchildlike? He wanted to ask but, with more important things waiting for him in the bedroom, he decided to save the question for another day.

"Here it is," he said triumphantly, pulling a dust-jacketed

book from his well-stocked but largely unread collection. "I think you'll like this one."

"Gee, thanks, Jon," the boy said, eagerly accepting the prize. As he did, his adult composure seemed to crumble with the glee of his new possession.

Placing an arm around the boy's shoulders, Carruthers gently directed him toward the door. "After you've read it, let me know what you think about it, huh? I'd like to talk to you about it sometime."

Carruthers had taken two steps farther before he noticed that the boy had stopped his movement toward the door. Looking down at the floor he seemed embarrassed about something. He spoke quietly. "Jon, I don't want to be a bother, but could I ask you for one more favor?"

Carruthers was trying hard to hide his impatience. "What is it, Todd?" he said, forcing a smile.

The boy was almost shy now. "Would you autograph the book? It would mean a lot to me. Not just to be able to show the kids at school that you gave it to me, but . . . well"—he was flustered now that his admiration had been revealed—"I'd just like to have you sign it."

Carruthers was not unaffected by flattery. "Of course," he said, taking the book from Todd's hands. "Just let me get a pen."

"I have one in my satchel," said the boy, quickly placing the satchel on a chair and opening the top clasp.

Reaching in, he scrambled around, then pulled out a ballpoint pen. He thrust the pen at Carruthers. "Here," he said happily.

Carruthers took the pen, opened the book, and turned to lean on a table. "How shall I sign it? To Todd? To my friend Todd?"

The boy was silent. He reached inside the open satchel and withdrew a small twenty-two-caliber automatic that had been fitted with a silencer. With swift, purposeful strides, he covered the distance between himself and the man who was bent over the book. As he approached he raised it, arm outstretched to shoulder height. Sensing Todd's presence behind him, Carruthers turned his head slightly to look back at the boy. "So what should I say?"

Todd leveled the automatic as the turning motion of Carruthers brought his temple into contact with the barrel of the silencer. The older man's eyes opened wide in surprise at the touch of the metal and then the boy squeezed the trigger.

Carruthers's brain reacted in explosive alarm. For the briefest of moments it worked frantically, trying to reroute shattered circuits. But the damage was too severe, and his brain transmitted faulty signals to his extremities. As his left leg kicked out in a reflexive twitch, his right arm, in a convulsive movement, swept a glass figurine and a heavy ceramic ashtray from the table. Carruthers slumped forward, his head slamming hard against the table. One eye twitched spasmodically as his blood made a swift-running rivulet on the floor.

In the bedroom Lauren Masterson, who had been impatiently awaiting his return, was startled by the crash of glass and a loud thump that sounded as if a heavy weight had been dropped. "Jonathan," she called out and then slapped a palm across her mouth. She knew she was supposed to remain silent. When there was no reply, her fears multiplied. She wanted to go to the door but could not make herself get out of bed. She wanted to hide under the bed, but her fear was suddenly paralyzing.

Something was terribly wrong. Her eyes were fixed on the bedroom door in dreadful expectation, and when the handle began to turn she could contain herself no longer. "Jon, is that you?" The fear was evident in her voice. "Oh, please say it's you."

The door began to open slowly. Her throat constricted in panic and the blood pounded in her brain. In a thousand ways, New York had made her aware that this devastating moment might come, but she had never imagined the sheer terror of it. She was stricken, immobilized, her mind a useless jumble.

Then the door opened wide, and she saw that it was only a child. A boy. A handsome, beautiful, angelic little boy. She could have kissed him.

As her panic subsided, she gulped down deep breaths of air. She wanted to call for Carruthers, but her throat would not let her speak.

The boy, smiling broadly, approached the foot of the bed, both hands behind his back.

Finally she could gasp, "Where's Jonathan?"

The boy stood at the foot of the bed. He said nothing.

A small touch of fear crept back into her voice. "Did someone break something out there?" She squirmed a little, feeling very uncomfortable. Here she was, naked except for a single sheet, and this strange kid she didn't even know was standing at the foot of her bed without saying a word. She called out again, her voice cracking with the effort, "Jon, are you out there?"

The boy brought one hand out from behind his back and placed it on the bed. Catching her completely by surprise, he ripped the sheet away from her body. She gasped, instinctively trying to cover her nakedness with her hands, but the shock and the insult of this unexpected action banished her fear.

"Now, see here," she snapped. "What the hell do you think you're doing?"

In a silent answer, Todd revealed his other hand and raised the pistol. At first Lauren was dumbfounded; because of the bulk of the silencer she did not recognize the object in his hand as a weapon. But when she stared directly into the barrel her doubts vanished. She opened her mouth to protest, and the boy pulled the trigger. The bullet slammed into her forehead, driving her head back against the headboard. Her body struggled as if trying to move to a sitting position, and then she slumped loosely back, her chin resting on her chest. Her eyes and mouth were open in mock amazement at her predicament, and even though there was as yet no blood from the small caliber hole in her forehead, the pillow behind her was drenched in ever-widening deep red streaks.

The boy waited until there was no more movement and then walked around to the side of the bed. He prodded her in the right side with the barrel of the gun, and when there was no response, he poked her right breast. It shivered slightly and then was still. Todd looked at her without making a sound or a movement; then his hand reached out stopping just short of her breast. Suddenly he whirled and ran from the room.

Before he left the apartment, the boy went into the small study off the living room, and after a few moments emerged with a neat stack of manuscript pages, which he carefully placed into his satchel. Then he unscrewed the silencer and left the gun near Jonathan Carruthers's hand. He dropped the silencer and the book into his satchel, listened for a moment at the front door, opened it, turned the latch to lock, and finally stepped out. The door shut gently behind him.

Chapter 3

Jonathan Carruthers's death was a huge media event. The fact that the police termed it a murder/suicide only fueled the fires. The event pushed everything, including the death of the man in the subway, off the front pages of the New York tabloids. Flowers came from fans across the country; crowds lined up for hours for a glimpse of his coffin, and women swooned at the mention of his name.

The media loved it, and their coverage was unrelenting.

The media would also have loved a big New York or Hollywood funeral, but Maisie Carruthers, Jonathan's mother, insisted that his body be returned to his Idaho home. Dutifully but with some reluctance, the network returned the body to the family in Clearview, Idaho. At NBC's expense, it was shipped by a small chartered jet to the county seat at Arco, and from there driven to the Delmore Funeral Parlor in Clearview. To accommodate all the people and equipment necessary to cover such an event, the combined media chartered a commercial jetliner which landed seventy-five miles away at Idaho Falls, the closest airport able to take a jet of this size. From there, by chartered bus and rented car, the media entourage made its way to Carruthers's hometown, where they were greeted with shocked bewilderment by the citizens of the small community.

All those reporters and all those technicians with all that equipment had to do something while in Clearwater, and so just about every adult and many of the children of the town were interviewed about their reaction to the death of their town's most illustrious son. Unfortunately, most of those interviewed had never really known the man. Carruthers had left town three days after the graduation of his miniscule high school class and had returned only twice in twelve years. If he had had any friends in high school, they'd also left town.

Clearview, it seems, was not a place that provided much opportunity for its young people. People were born in Clearview and people died there, but anyone who didn't have to live there got the hell out.

Maisie Carruthers seemed bewildered too by the combination of her son's death and the media attention. She rarely said more than what a wonderful boy he had been. "So handsome," she repeated over and over as though certain that physical beauty reflected the inner workings of the soul.

Jonathan's father, Joshua, a quiet man with a weatherbeaten face beneath a gray crew cut, with gnarled, worker's fingers on his huge hands, was sullen and resentful of all of the attention. When a microphone was stuck in his face he looked as if he would like to bite it off. His only comment throughout the entire ordeal was, "Why don't you just leave us alone?" Needless to say, he was not very popular with the reporters, who felt that everyone should be willing to participate in the grand event.

Ultimately the TV and press people got around to doing what they like to do best, which is to interview each other. In this situation there was some justification. After all, there were so few people in Clearview, and fewer still who knew anything interesting about Carruthers. As it turned out, the media people, especially the television group, knew him better than anyone, although they too didn't know him very well.

In stark contrast with the day of his death, the day of Jonathan Carruthers's funeral was bright and sunny. Wispy clouds skipped across a clear blue sky above the small cemetery where his grandparents lay waiting in the chill Idaho soil.

And so, with the commotion of the media and the falsely hysterical mourning that usually accompanies the untimely death of any celebrity, Jonathan Carruthers was laid to rest in his home ground. In death he found more celebrity status than he ever could have sustained in life.

But what was he? What had he been?

The only media person in attendance who had worked with him and who really knew him put it most succinctly in an informal, off-the-record, off-camera interview at Clearview's only bar. "He was a real shit," she said.

Amid the laughter, someone said, "C'mon Shelley, we can't print that. The public doesn't want to hear that."

Shelley James nodded in agreement. "What do they want to hear?"

A voice from somewhere at the back of the crowded bar called, "How was he in bed, Shelley?"

An embarrassed laughter and then gradual silence moved across the crowd as Shelley tried to pick out the face who had called from the back of the room. Just before the silence became repressive she shot back her reply. "I didn't realize that *The Enquirer* had sent anyone to cover the funeral."

The room erupted in applause and laughter and hoots of derision aimed at the anonymous heckler in the rear. Mere mention of *The Enquirer* was enough to rally those reporters who considered themselves members of the legitimate press.

Almost every one of the many journalists crowded into the Dew-Come-Inn (bar, grill, and rooms to let) knew that Shelley James and Jonathan Carruthers had been lovers. Most had a sneaky suspicion, some a firm belief, that Shelley had climbed from copy editor to news reporter to coanchor of the late news because of that relationship. Privately, some were quite vocal in their assertions of how she had achieved her success. "On her back" was how it was usually phrased.

Those who knew her and those who worked with her, however, knew that Shelley James was talented and competent and that she had enough drive and ambition to move her to the top of any field. Shelley had graduated with a straight four-point-0-average from Northwestern University, where she'd majored in journalism. She had been editor in chief of the campus newspaper, *The Daily Northwestern*, and after graduation had worked as a reporter on a small, downstate daily in Alton, Illinois. There she had worked her way up from the society page to hard news, and in three years with the *Alton Sentinel* was nominated for two Pulitzers. Although she did not win the prize either time, her nominations made her a celebrity within the newspaper business and enabled her to step up to the big time with the *Chicago Tribune*.

After only one year at the *Trib*, Shelley made the jump into television. Hearing through the grapevine that a position was opening up on the news staff at WMAQ, one of the local network affiliates, Shelley prepared an impressive résumé. As an afterthought she included a small photograph of herself and sent the material to the station.

It was the photograph, of course, that got her the job.

Shelley James was twenty-six when she made the move to broadcast journalism, but she had the regal looks of a more mature woman. It wasn't that she looked older than her twenty-six years, only that she seemed wiser and more sophisticated than a twenty-six-year-old should be. She had high cheekbones, a straight nose, and full lips that always wore the hint of a smile suggesting that she knew something no one else did. Her face was a sea of cool sophistication, but her eyes were two blue islands that sparkled with humor and intelligence. Her face was beautiful, but it was the eyes that rescued her from the coldness that great beauty often brings.

She wore her wheat-blond hair shoulder length and straight in a style that was early seventies. On anyone else it might have been considered dated, but on her it was perfect.

Shelley was tall and slim, with the kind of figure that wore clothes well. At a formal affair she looked splendidly cosmopolitan; at a football game in bulky sweaters and blue jeans she could have been doing clothing ads.

Shelley James had grown accustomed to the fact that men stared at her. They always had, and she supposed they always would.

After receiving her résumé, the station manager had asked her to come to the studio to make a demo tape on which she read that day's news while sitting at the news desk on the set of the *Six O'Clock News*. A few days later she was invited for an interview with the producer of the program.

Alex Granelli was twenty-eight and considered the boy-wonder of the station. He was smooth and handsome and obviously on his way to the big time in the network news business.

"I must tell you," he said to Shelley as she nestled into the large leather chair in front of his desk, "that I'm very impressed with your qualifications for the job."

Shelley smiled. "I've worked very hard, and I think I can do a good job here at the station."

Granelli went on in the style of someone who only listens to his own end of a conversation. "With your looks, you're a natural for television." There was a slight pause here for reaction, but Shelley did not respond in any way. The producer continued. "I think we can find a spot for you on the midday news."

"That's great," said Shelley. "When do I start? I'd like to give my paper some notice that I'm leaving."

Granelli pondered for a moment. "We'll probably need a replacement by the end of the month. Why don't we have dinner tonight? We can talk about it."

Shelley flashed the sweet smile she usually reserved for the fix-ups her aunt in Evanston insisted on finding for her. "I'll tell you what. I'll give the *Trib* my two weeks notice today, and I'll start here on Monday the twenty-eighth. How does that sound?"

Granelli looked at his desk calendar. "That's fine. What about dinner?"

Still smiling, Shelley kept her voice level. "You said we could talk about it at dinner. We just talked about it and it's all settled."

Granelli coughed a few times into his fist, his face turning slightly red. "I'm not trying to . . . uh. . . . The dinner invitation had nothing to do with the job offer."

"Of course not. I understand that," said Shelley helpfully.

"I mean the offer is there, one way or the other."

"And I've accepted your offer."

Granelli, in the face of Shelley's detached, businesslike manner, was stumbling a little bit. "It's just that I thought it would be nice to get acquainted or something."

Shelley stood up and extended her hand. "Don't worry. We've got plenty of time to get acquainted when I start working here. Meanwhile, I've got a story to get finished for my paper."

She left feeling that she had not only started a new career, but had won a small victory in an old battle.

Granelli felt convinced that he had met someone who was going places faster than he was. He was right.

Steadily, Shelley moved up the ladder, quickly catching the attention of the network executives in New York. She became coanchor on the late news within a year, and six months after that, coanchor on the evening news.

On-the-job, as she had in college, Shelley had often found it necessary to retreat behind a facade of cool efficiency if she wanted to get anything done. When she was around, men invariably began to think of other things, and she was sometimes forced to be unfriendly just to preserve the normal work routine. The name usually used in private to describe her was Beautiful Iceberg.

At twenty-nine she made the leap to New York, taking a step down from her anchor position to that of reporter because she felt that she had exhausted her potential for advancement in Chicago. It was no secret that she had her eye on an anchor spot in New York, and with the networks moving toward the utilization of women in the anchor positions, Shelley felt that her chances were excellent.

But then came Jonathan Carruthers.

When he arrived on-the-scene, he knocked all schedules for advancement into a holding pattern. He quickly established himself as number one. He was *the* anchor. His popularity and ego were such, that he did not require, nor would he tolerate, a coanchor. It was obvious from the ratings' improvement after Carruthers's arrival that he was going to be around for a long time. Many young, aspiring anchors saw the writing on the wall and began sending subtle feelers to other stations.

On Carruthers's first day in New York a bevy of network executives introduced him around the newsroom. When they arrived at Shelley's desk one of them said, "And this is Shelley James, our resident Miss America."

Suppressing a sigh, Shelley extended her hand to Carruthers.

He grasped her hand firmly. "Nice to meet you," he said simply and moved on to the next desk.

It was somewhat refreshing not to be ogled or fussed over, but in this case it was, at the same time, mildly disappointing.

Carruthers was handsome in an almost indescribable way. He wasn't really good-looking, though he did have a certain rugged masculinity about him. Perhaps it was the way he projected self-assurance. Perhaps it was the solid competence that others attributed to him. Whatever it was, every woman in the room, and most of the men, were almost instantly impressed with his presence.

Shelley watched Carruthers being led around the room; the executives clustered around him as if he were a hot stove on a cold night. She saw the other women follow him with their eyes and realized that she was probably doing the same thing. She resolved to get back to work and not to gawk at him.

It was difficult not to watch the reactions of the others in the large room. Half the reporters and correspondents greeted Carruthers warmly, feeling, perhaps hoping, that he might bring some improvement to the station and thus prevent the mass firings that had been rumored for months. Others saw him only as a barrier to their own ambitions: If he succeeded, they could not advance. This group gave him big-toothed smiles and hearty handshakes, secretly hoping he would fall flat on his face.

Shelley James fell somewhere between these two positions.

She turned her attention back to her typewriter, mildly amused at her own reaction to his lack of attention. It was a new experience for her. Men naturally found her attractive but at the same time overwhelming. Some told themselves that she was too cold or too bright or too beautiful. Others felt that a prize like her was beyond their capabilities or must have already been claimed by someone more fortunate than they. Consequently, Shelley had relatively few romantic entanglements. A bright young corporate executive here and there, a young liberal congressman from Manhattan, and once a messy affair with a married network vice-president. The experience convinced her to stay away from married men; that particular decision probably cost her at least half her social opportunities.

Although she found it distasteful, Shelley had grown accustomed to the response of most men at the first meeting. Some were awed; some were vulgar; some stumbled over themselves trying to make a good impression. Very few did what Jonathan Carruthers did: He ignored her.

Some men instinctively know what it is that attracts beautiful women.

That night he called.

"Hi. Jon Carruthers. New kid in town, all alone in the big city."

Shelley felt a surge of excitement but at the same time disappointment. He hadn't seemed to notice her today, and that was interesting because it was different. But was he going to be like most of the men she met? She said nothing, forcing him to continue.

"I'm expected at a party with all the network bigwigs tonight. Sort of a let's-greet-the-new-boy-wonder party." Still she said nothing. "It's not required," he went on, "but I thought I'd like to take a beautiful female with me."

Shelley spoke for the first time. "Why me?" Her voice was chilly.

In the face of her coolness he went on with remarkable

aplomb. "I thought I'd start at the top and work my way down."

She found his self-assurance mildly stimulating. "Thank you," she said, "but I couldn't possibly go out tonight."

"Perfect! I'll get some wine and a couple of great steaks and we'll eat in."

"Wait a minute. What about the network people?"

"Let them find their own women."

In spite of herself, she laughed. "I mean what about the party?"

"I said I was expected. I didn't say I always do the expected. . . . What kind of wine should I bring?"

"Look, I'm very flattered," Shelley said, humor creeping into her voice, "but I think you'd better get to that party. I mean it's in your honor, your first night in the city."

"Then come with me."

"It's almost eight. I couldn't possibly be ready in time."

"Let them wait."

"I don't have anything to wear. . . ."

"Wear anything. It will be marvelous."

"My hair isn't . . ."

"It's beautiful."

Her protests were subdued into silence. Carruthers laughed, and she found his laughter endearing. "Look," he said, "at this very moment, we are probably the two best-looking people in New York. Why should we make everyone wonder when we're going to discover each other? Let's just go to the party and get the suspense over with. We'll have the wine and steaks tomorrow night."

They went to the party, and Carruthers was a smash with the network people. The next night, after the steaks and the wine, they became lovers. Shelley was surprised by the depth of his passion and the intensity of her own. Within two weeks she had moved into his apartment. They were happy for perhaps two months, and then Shelley recognized a barely perceptible chilling of the atmosphere. Jonathan started staying out late, occasionally inventing excuses for not coming home at all.

Finally, she asked him. "Is there another woman?"

He laughed softly, but his eyes never touched hers. "Baby, there are a lot of other women."

Shelley cried a little as she was packing, and Jonathan tried to explain things to her.

"It's not you," he said. "None of the others are as bright as you or as beautiful as you or as together as you. They don't even come close."

"Then why?"

He seemed at a loss. "They're different," he said, as if that explained everything. When he saw by her expression that she didn't understand he added, "I need variety, Shelley. You know, spice of life and all that old crap."

She shook her head sadly. "It's too bad. I thought we had something good going for us."

"We do. We do." He put his hands on her shoulders. "Look, I want you to stay." She looked up at him hopefully, and he went on. "As long as you understand that I need to bring home other women once in awhile. . . ."

She moved out from under his grasp. "That sounds rather sleazy to me," she said coldly. "I think I can do better than that."

Shelley James moved back into her apartment, and the next day told the executive producer of the news department that she was leaving the station.

"I've had another offer," she lied, "and I want to take the opportunity while I have the chance."

Art Spengler shot forward in his chair as if he had been slapped from behind. "Shelley, don't do anything hastily." He paused for a moment before going on. "We have big plans for you."

"I'm sorry, Art; I'm leaving."

Spengler got up from his chair and came around his desk. "I mean big plans, Shelley," he said, sitting on the edge of the desk. "And very soon."

Shelley's eyebrows went up. "Can you explain what you mean?"

He looked around his office as though checking for eavesdroppers. "Let's have lunch today and we'll talk, OK?"

Shelley nodded her agreement.

Over lunch, in whispered tones, Spengler told her that Carolyn Marshall, coanchor of the *Eleven O'Clock News,* was being replaced, and that Shelley was considered the top candidate for the job.

"We think a lot of you, Shelley. We're very impressed with your work."

Shelley's eyes narrowed slightly. "What's the problem with Carolyn? She's been on less than a year."

Spengler shrugged. "You know how it is in this business. The ratings have leveled off and don't seem to be going anywhere. . . . Channel Two just hired that new head from L.A. . . . We need a fresh face up front, Shelley."

"A fresh face," she said, shaking her head ruefully. "Is that what this is all about? A fresh face?"

"For Christ's sakes, Shelley," Spengler said, still in a soft whisper though his agitation was beginning to show. "You know the game. The viewer wants to see beautiful people up there." He looked around, then laughed quietly. "I started out as a reporter. Why do you think I got into the production end?" He touched the tip of his index finger to the tip of his nose. "On camera this schnoz looks like Mount Olympus. The face looks like a dry riverbed."

Shelley smiled. "It's a good face, Art. It has lots of character."

"Yeah, so did Lincoln's. . . . Do you think old Abe could get the anchor post on the *Six O'Clock News*?"

She saw his point and nodded her agreement.

"Anyway, Shell, I can't guarantee the job, but I'm recommending you, and I think you'll get it. That's why I want you to hang on and not rush off right now. I promise I'll let you know within two weeks."

"Thanks, Art." She squeezed his hand across the table, then her smile faded. "Does Jonathan have anything to do with me getting this job?"

"Not directly, no. He knows nothing about this."

"Indirectly?"

Spengler gave a half-nod. "He's getting to be a pretty important face around here and it's generally considered good form to have the top dog at least approve the choices in the other positions." He coughed in embarrassment. "Of course, with your relationship that should be no problem."

"There is no relationship, Art."

Spengler's eyebrows shot up, and he squirmed a little in his seat. "I don't see that as a problem," he said, but the certainty had gone out of his voice.

"If you're counting on Jon to give me a vote of confidence, you're wasting your time."

But she was wrong. If there was any vote of confidence needed, it was given. Shelley James became the coanchor on the *Late Evening News*, and once again her career was in high gear. Many people in the business assumed that

Carruthers had pushed for her to get the job because of their romantic involvement. The truth was that she had earned the position by virtue of hard work and, to at least some extent, good fortune. Her face just happened to be a more marketable commodity than any other face at the network, perhaps in the industry. But there were still those who believed that they, or someone they knew, had missed out on an opportunity because Shelley James had slept with the right people.

That was why the snide question from the back of the room at the Dew-Come-Inn in Clearview, Idaho, was no real surprise to Shelley. Such remarks, spoken and unspoken, had followed her for some time. She had learned how to adroitly parry such a question. But it was always there, hanging in the air like stale cigar smoke after a card game.

Shelley's quick retort had helped clear the air, and the reporters went on talking, drinking, laughing, and trying to find some new angle to the Carruthers story. For most of them it had been a long day of looking for something fresh to say about what many of them had come to call "the Carruthers mess." Everything that could be said had been said a hundred times, and yet their editors demanded more.

The public was insatiable. Lauren Masterson, the young woman who was presumed to have been killed by Jonathan Carruthers before he took his own life, had been quietly laid to rest after the newspaper attempts to sensationalize her life had failed. There was nothing much, besides her last moments, to sensationalize. She had already become merely the blond in Jonathan Carruthers's bed.

Journalists were forced to write new stories with old facts. Some were accused of creating stories with no facts. The situation reminded some of the old pros of the publicity surrounding the death of movie star John Garfield, who had apparently died of a heart attack while in bed with a beautiful young girl. The public had demanded more and more information about the case. Harassed editors had insisted that harried reporters provide new stories to satisfy the voracious appetite of the public. Finally, in desperation, some obscure but now legendary reporter had suggested a headline that summed up the feelings of every reporter in America. The headline read "John Garfield Still Dead."

"Maybe that's what we ought to do now," said the reporter from the New York *News*. Then with a wink to his colleagues in the print media he added, "Maybe the TV boys could turn it into a series for the new second season." He shook his head sadly while accepting the applause of his peers. "There isn't a damn thing else to say about this story."

Shelley James was not so sure.

Chapter 4

Someone else was not so sure either.

Mark Chandler was a newspaperman who three times a week wrote a column for the New York *News* which was syndicated in almost a hundred other papers across the country. He wrote on a variety of topics—politics, foreign affairs, sports—anything that caught his fancy. What caught his fancy this week was the fact that a man named Fred Romanello had apparently been pushed to his death in front of a subway train, but because a celebrity had killed some dopey blond and then himself, no one seemed to care about the poor jerk who had been crushed by the train. Ordinarily the subway death would have been front-page news in at least two of New York's newspapers, but because of the public's incredible clamor for news about the death of Jonathan Carruthers, the subway-death story had been relegated to page 13 in the *News*, and page 15 in the *Post*. By the next day it had been all but forgotten.

Chandler, disturbed by this series of events, had decided to write a column, not so much about the man who had died beneath the train but about the capriciousness of the public and of the news media which served it. Chandler had been doubly disturbed when he'd discovered that the body of the subway victim had not yet been claimed from the City Morgue where it still lay in chilling isolation.

On the day of Carruthers's funeral, Chandler wrote a second column which appeared in the morning edition of the *News*. The column began:

Today while Jonathan Carruthers is laid to rest surrounded by family, friends, and an adoring public, another man lies alone, his body unclaimed and apparently unwanted.

Chandler's column reflected the irony between the tremendous publicity over the funeral of Jonathan Carruthers, and the complete and total neglect of a man who seemed bound for Potter's Field. The column was sympathetic to the dead man and critical of the media—even his own newspaper—for their lack of compassion and distorted sense of priorities. Compared to the death of a celebrity, the death of an ordinary citizen was deemed unimportant by the media, claimed Chandler, and that judgment diminished the importance of all of us.

This particular column was an uncommon outpouring of moralizing for Mark Chandler, and even he was at a loss to comprehend his depth of feeling in the matter. Others would say that at forty-three, his father dead for five years and his mother terminally ill in a New Jersey nursing home, Chandler was beginning to feel intimations of his own mortality, but he himself rarely intellectualized such observations. Wisps of gray were beginning to spread through his thick dark hair, and the face that accompanied his newspaper column was of a much younger man—a photograph of himself taken almost ten years earlier. The photograph was the idea of his editor, who felt that the public would be more receptive to a younger face.

The face today was somewhat heavier and certainly more lined, but Chandler liked today's face better than yesterday's. His once angular, sharply defined features had been softened by maturity—a nose that had seemed too prominent over the years, apparently receded—and he had grown comfortable with the face that, every morning, stared at him from his shaving mirror. Perhaps this satisfaction was merely another manifestation of maturity, but Chandler felt that today's face showed more character and experience. Every day he told himself that he was going to update the picture on his column, but somehow he never got around to it.

He was tall and had once been slender, but now, even a fairly hectic schedule was not enough to contest the inevitable thickening around the middle. What surprised Chandler, when he let himself think about it, was the way that he had fallen into an easy acceptance of his vanished youth. It was not in his nature to wear the newest style in clothing or to learn the latest dance craze or even to frequent the in places in the city. He had never really thought of himself as growing older, but merely that the world and everything in it seemed to be getting younger. Reaching forty hadn't even been much of a shock. It just arrived and camped on his doorstep. His friends were amazed at how well he accepted his crossing over, and outwardly he was nonchalant about the whole process. Inside he could sometimes sense a rising panic.

Two years earlier his wife had divorced him and taken their daughter back to her parents' home in Pennsylvania. Hardly a day went by when he did not miss his child.

On the same day that Chandler's second column appeared in the *News*, his phone rang in his apartment on East Eighty-first Street. It was Chandler's editor at the *News*, Tom Sheehan, who informed him that he had a woman on the line who claimed to know something about the Romanello killing.

"She called the paper to talk to you," said Sheehan. "Do you want to speak with her?"

Chandler sighed. "Get her number for me, Tom, and I'll call her right back." He knew better than to give his private number to an anonymous caller.

He dialed the number. "Hello, this is Mark Chandler." There was no response. "From the New York *News*. You said you wanted to speak to me."

"Yes, I did," said a throaty voice.

"You said you had some information about the man who was killed in the subway."

"Well, yes." She didn't sound too sure.

"If you have anything to tell me, I'll respect your privacy. I won't use your name, if that's what you're worried about."

"That's not it."

"What then?"

He heard her take a deep breath before she spoke. "I was wondering if you could do me a favor."

Chandler was getting impatient. "What kind of favor?"

"I thought, maybe you could help me get Fred's briefcase back."

"Briefcase?"

"Yes; he was carrying a briefcase when he left here that morning." Her confidence was growing as she went on. "I gave it to him as a present. I'd like to get it back . . . it cost seventy-five dollars."

"Are you family or something?"

There was a long pause. "No, not family . . . just a friend."

"Are you going to claim the body? Or contact the family?"

She seemed bewildered by this double question. "No . . I don't know any family . . . I can't afford funeral expenses."

"But you want the briefcase," Chandler said, sarcasm and distaste dripping from every word.

She caught none of it. "It cost seventy-five dollars. You wrote such a nice story about Fred—just like you were a friend—I thought maybe you could help me get the briefcase."

"Why don't you just call the police and ask for it?"

She thought for a minute. "I'm afraid they'll make me claim his body. Like I said, I can't afford funeral expenses."

"Yes, I know you said that." Chandler was on the verge of being rude. "What was in the briefcase?"

"Oh, just some papers. He was working on a case. I don't care about the papers. I just want the briefcase."

Instinctively Chandler's news reporter's mentality took over. A small light began to glow somewhere in the back of his mind. He was on automatic pilot. "You said he was working on a case. What kind of work did your friend do?"

"Oh," she said, and the pride was evident in her voice, "Fred was an investigator. The papers in the briefcase were about the case he was working on."

Back to the briefcase, he thought. "An investigator? You mean like a private investigator or an insurance investigator?"

She was bewildered again. "I'm not sure."

"What kind of case was he working on?"

"I'm . . . not really sure. He never told me."

The small light grew dimmer, and Chandler stifled a yawn. "Look, I'll call the police and find out how you can get the briefcase back. Then I'll give you a call, OK?"

"Thanks, Mr. Chandler," and despite the voice she was suddenly very young. "That's excellent. Tell the police they can keep the papers. They're no good to anyone now that the guy is dead."

"You mean your boyfriend?"

"No. The guy he was working for. You know, that TV guy who killed himself."

Chandler said nothing for the briefest of moments. The light was blaring like a beacon. He tried to keep his voice steady. "What TV guy?"

"You know the guy. You wrote about him in your story. That Carruthers guy."

"You mean that Fred worked for Jonathan Carruthers?"

"Yeah. Isn't that something? Both of 'em dying on the same day."

"Do the police know that Fred worked for Carruthers?"

She paused, suddenly worried. "I don't think so. It's not illegal, is it?"

"No, of course not. I just wondered." In spite of his attempts to act normal, Chandler found his voice lowering to a conspiratorial whisper. "Listen. I didn't get your name."

"Jeanette."

"Listen, Jeanette. I'm going to find out about your brief-case, and then I'd like to come and talk with you."

"You'll bring the briefcase?"

"I'll try. I can't promise that I can get it, but I'd still like to talk with you."

She said nothing.

"I'm sure I can help you get the briefcase back."

"OK."

"Then give me your name and tell me where you live. I'll try to get back to you this afternoon."

Her name was Jeanette Nielson. She lived on Thirteenth Street near Third Ave., and as Chandler hung up the phone he had the rare feeling of exhilaration that came when he stumbled across some unexpected disclosure in a news story.

The Ninth Precinct sits amid a rubble- and garbage-strewn part of East Fifty-seventh Street on the Lower East Side of Manhattan. Thirty—even twenty—years ago its red brick front had been an integral part of a thriving Jewish neighborhood, but now the dominant language was Spanish, and the precinct house stood like a fortress seemingly more suited to the protection of the policemen inside, than the community around it.

Chandler parked his battered Pontiac and walked across

the street to the police station. Inside he showed his press card to the desk sergeant.

"I'm looking for Detective Colandro. I called earlier and was told that he'd be back by now."

"Yes, Mr. Chandler," said the sergeant with an over-politeness that Chandler was sure was precipitated by the press card. "He's upstairs in the squad room." He pointed a beefy finger. "Take these stairs to my left, and it's your first door on the left at the top of the stairs." As Chandler turned to go, the sergeant stopped him. "Hold on," he said, handing Chandler a yellow ticket that looked like an airport baggage check. "Tie that onto your jacket so that everybody can see you're a visitor."

Chandler nodded and proceeded to the stairs.

In the squad room he was greeted by Detective Colandro with a quick smile and a firm handshake.

"Hey, you guys know who this is?" said Colandro, turning to his colleagues, who seemed totally uninterested in the visitor. "This is Chandler, the guy from the *News*."

This seemed to wake them up. "How come you don't do sports no more?" asked one detective from behind his desk.

Chandler shrugged. "I like this better."

"Better than sports?" said the man, a look of amazement on his face.

Colandro directed him into an office at the back of the large room where they could talk with some degree of privacy. There were four chairs around a steel table and another table against the far wall.

"It's nice to meet you," Colandro said when they were seated, and Chandler heard the ring of sincerity in the man's tone.

Chandler was very aware that he was generally well liked by the police because it was felt that he treated them fairly. He saved most of his blistering attacks for the politicians and the judicial system, and policemen felt he was sympathetic to their plight. In addition, as a former sports-writer, he had enough of a down-to-earth quality about his writing that he could communicate with the average citizen. Being a sportswriter—even a former sportswriter—gave him a certain stature on the street. He wasn't really considered a writer. He was just a guy who happened to like sports and had been lucky enough to find a job that let him get paid for watching it. Chandler was often able to use this misconception to his advantage.

Colandro was short, dark, and wiry. He looked like a tough middleweight, which was just what he had been in the Navy.

"Whaddya think about the Giants this year?" he asked as he poured two cups of coffee from a Mr. Coffee on the bare table against the wall. "That kid quarterback looks pretty good."

"No running game," said Chandler, willing to play this male conversational ritual until more comfortable ground could be found. "Gotta have a running game if they're gonna do anything."

Colandro nodded a sad-eyed agreement. "So, what can I do for you?"

Chandler sipped his coffee. He did not wish to appear too anxious. "I'm still kinda bugged by this guy who was shoved under the train the other day. Inspector Downey over at Central told me that you were on the case and would be the man to talk to about it."

"Yeah, he called here awhile ago and said you'd be stopping by. Glad to do whatever I can."

There was no resentment in what he said. Most cops didn't take too kindly to superiors from headquarters who told them to be cooperative with reporters. Chandler had been through some rough interviews with policemen who had taken umbrage with what they considered to be outside interference. He didn't get that impression this time.

"Anybody claim him yet?"

"No. Still got him on ice. I thought after your article that somebody might call."

Chandler nodded. "I guess it's not really unusual, though." It was more of a question than a statement.

When Colandro spoke there was pride in his voice. "The man's Italian. You ever hear of an Italian without family?"

"What about personal effects?"

Colandro opened a manila folder that had obviously been placed on the table in preparation for this meeting. "Nothing to speak of—the usual—you know." He paused to extract a single sheet from the folder. "Here we have it. A wallet— twenty-two dollars . . . no credit cards . . . clothing . . . a watch—a Timex," he said with derision.

"Nothing else?"

"No; that's it." Colandro eyed the reporter carefully. "Why do you ask?"

"I got a call from somebody who said he was carrying a briefcase."

Colandro placed his cup on the table. He sat back in his chair, linking his fingers together behind his head. "Who told you this?" he asked as casually as he could. "A witness? No one said anything to me about a briefcase."

"Just someone who claims to have seen him earlier. They didn't see the accident."

Colandro shook his head. "It wasn't there when the uniforms arrived on-the-scene. If he dropped it, some scavenger probably walked off with it. We got people in this city who rob graves, so it doesn't surprise me when they don't wait for the corpse to get cold." He paused to let that sink in. "Maybe the creep who pushed him grabbed it before shoving him off the platform."

"That's always possible, I suppose."

"Anything valuable in it?" Colandro sipped his coffee, but kept his eyes on Chandler's reaction to his question.

"Not really. Just that the case was worth about seventy-five dollars."

Through Colandro's casualness, Chandler could detect the policeman's rising interest. "If this is true, it might put another slant on the case. What if he was carrying drugs? This could be a drug-related hit. Maybe your someone on the phone wants to know what happened to his merchandise."

"The caller didn't seem interested in the contents of the case."

Colandro smiled. "I doubt if he'd ask you to go to the police about a satchel full of heroin."

Chandler nodded but said nothing.

Colandro stood up, picking up the folder from the table. "Look, I know you newspaper people have a thing about sources, so I won't ask you who this mysterious caller was, but I want to warn you so that you don't get involved in something that's a bit over your head."

"I appreciate your advice. But don't worry. I've been around this town long enough to know better than that."

Colandro eyed him steadily. "The guy on the slab downtown had been around for a while too."

Chandler got up to leave and extended his hand to the policeman, who held onto it as he spoke. "If you get any more information from this caller, I'd appreciate it if you'd let me know."

Chandler immediately thought of the connection between the dead man and Jonathan Carruthers and hoped the guilt did not show on his face. "If I get anything," he said, "I promise, I'll let you know."

Chapter 5

Chandler parked his car on Third Avenue near a Hudson's Army-Navy Store that advertised clearance prices on a vast array of camping equipment, and then walked east on East Thirteenth Street. About halfway down the block he paused in front of a five-floor walk-up with basket fire escapes and marble columns flanking double front doors at the top of the stoop.

Chandler checked the address and started up the stairs.

Jeanette Nielsen answered his knock by calling through the closed door, "Who is it?"

"It's Mark Chandler." There was no answer. "From the newspaper. I'd like to talk to you." He knew that he was being scrutinized through the small peephole. He felt the sudden urge to straighten his tie, but he wasn't wearing one.

The door opened a crack, security chain still in place. Half a face was pressed against the opening. "You look younger," said the throaty voice. "I mean in your picture you look younger."

"It's the strain of standing in hallways," he cracked good-naturedly.

The door closed, and he had the feeling that she did not appreciate his joke, but he heard the jangle of the security chain and then the door opened wide.

Jeanette Nielsen was seventeen but could easily have passed for fifteen, and Chandler could not help the look of surprise on his face. He had been expecting a woman and instead had found a girl—a kid really. She had blond hair that hung in unkempt clumps to her shoulders, and large blue eyes in a face whose innocence was marred only by the cigarette dangling from her lips.

"Come in, Mr. Chandler," she said in the voice that belied her years, and Chandler knew why he had felt she was older. He found himself wondering how many packs of cigarettes a day it took to turn a kid's voice into that of an old woman.

She closed the door behind him and locked it again as if the motion were automatic. "In case you're wondering, I'm nineteen. Everybody thinks I'm younger." She said it as if she knew he wouldn't believe her lie but still felt obligated to tell it.

Chandler smiled. "I didn't think my surprise was so obvious."

She shrugged. "I'm used to it. It happens all the time." She seemed nervous. "I see you didn't get the briefcase."

He lied. "Maybe by tomorrow."

She made a face and for a moment he thought she was going to say, damn, or something like that, but she didn't.

The girl wore only a long T-shirt. On it was emblazoned the name of one of those rock groups that Chandler had never heard of. It was evident that she was not wearing a bra, and Chandler wondered if she was wearing anything else.

"I'm making coffee. Want some?"

Chandler nodded and she padded away barefoot to a small kitchen just off the living room. He watched her go. She was small but nicely built with good legs.

There was not much furniture. The place looked as if someone had just moved in—or was ready to move out. Chandler sat on a long sofa in front of a low coffee table. There was a chair that didn't match on the other side of the table. He looked around. That was about it.

Jeanette called from the kitchen. "What did you want to see me about?"

"I was wondering about your friend Romanello."

"What about him?" she asked, returning with two mugs of coffee. "I don't have any milk," she said without apology. "But I do have sugar."

He hated black coffee. "It's fine this way," he lied. He wondered if anything they had said to each other was true. She had lied about her age, and he'd lied about the purpose of his visit. Now he was even lying about the coffee. Was she lying about the reasons for her interest in the briefcase? Colandro's remarks about merchandise, and his advice about getting in over his head came back to him. The girl was obviously no physical threat to him, and he was sure she was alone in the apartment. Still, he was aware of a certain amount of nervousness in her actions. Perhaps nervousness was not the right word for it. She seemed fidgety.

"So what about him?" she repeated as she sat at the far end of the couch, crossing her legs in front of her and holding the bottom of the T-shirt down with one hand so that it covered her crotch.

"Well, if I'm going to get back your briefcase, I'm going to have to know a little more about him."

She reached over to the table for her coffee, the T-shirt riding up in the back exposing a brief view of her nakedness.

Chandler was fighting to keep his mind on the matter at hand. "Like what did he do? How long did he work for Jonathan Carruthers? And what was he investigating?"

"I told you he was a private investigator."

"You said you weren't sure."

Her face twitched. "I'm sure. He told me he was a private investigator."

"The police don't know anything about that. A private investigator would have to be licensed."

She thought about that, her face twitching again. "So maybe he bullshitted me. Guys have been bullshitting me all my life."

"What about working for Carruthers?"

"He told me he worked for him. Maybe that was bullshit, too." She wiped her nose with the back of her hand.

"Did he ever say what he was working on?"

She thought for a moment, then shook her head. "Only that he had to find some people. Look, I really wasn't that interested, y'know?" She lit another cigarette and took a long, deep drag. "You're starting to make me nervous with all these questions." The twitch was back.

Chandler gave his best reassuring smile. "It's just reporter's curiosity. Do you think you'd like to tell me a little about Romanello?"

She shrugged and sniffed.

"How did you meet him? Where was he from?"

Jeanette sipped her coffee. "He told me he was from the

Midwest. That's how we got together. I'm from the Midwest, too. He said he used to be in television out there somewhere . . . I forget . . . Des Moines, maybe. Said he was an investigator reporter, or something."

"Investigative reporter?" said Chandler helpfully.

"Yeah—maybe that was it. Anyway, he said he used to know the big deal TV guy out there."

"Carruthers?"

"Right. Worked with him a couple of times. That's how he got tied up with him this time. At least that's what he said."

"What brought him to New York?"

"Said he got bored out there and came East." She smiled sadly. "Lots of us get bored out there and come East."

"And you met him here," Chandler said, directing her carefully. She seemed less nervous now—more open. She actually seemed to enjoy talking, as if it had been a long time since anyone had bothered to listen to her.

She nodded. "I was working at a club here in Manhattan, and he came in one night. We talked and found we were both from the Midwest and kind of struck up a friendship. He came back a few times, then asked me to move in with him."

Chandler said nothing.

"He said he didn't want me working in that kind of place anymore."

Chandler nodded.

"Don't you want to know what kind of place?" she said.

"I can guess."

She was undeterred. "It was a massage parlor over on Eighth Avenue. You know, the kind of place where for twenty-five dollars guys can get a girl to give them a rubdown."

Chandler sipped his coffee. It was terrible.

Jeannette went on, seeming to enjoy the revelation. "For another twenty-five dollars you can get more than a rubdown." Her blue eyes sparkled. "Y'know what I mean?"

"I understand . . . Romanello didn't want you to do that?"

She shrugged. "He didn't want me to do it with anybody else. Anyway, I was getting pretty tired of giving blow jobs to old fat men, so when he offered to let me move in here, I said why not."

Chandler looked around the apartment. Other than the door leading to the kitchen there was only one other door.

"How many bedrooms?" he asked, instantly feeling incredibly naive.

She smiled, licking her lips. "One bedroom—one bed." She pouted her lower lip. "I had to pay for my room and board."

"Sounds like a warm relationship."

Jeanette Nielsen laughed, a throaty, womanly laugh that seemed incredibly misplaced coming from her childlike face. "I wanted out of that place, and he helped me. That's all."

"You don't seem particularly sad that he's dead."

She stubbed out her cigarette, immediately lighting another. "He was just a guy I knew, that's all." She was scratching her bare arms as if she felt a tremendous itch. "I'm sorry he's dead, but that's life. Right?" She thought that remark was funny and started to laugh again. Her nose was running a little.

"You thought enough of him to buy him a seventy-five-dollar briefcase."

She stood up very quickly as if the question had insulted her, then just as suddenly sat down. "Look, this isn't going to take much longer, is it?" She was scratching her left shoulder. "I've got to meet some people in a little while."

"Not much longer. You were going to tell me about the briefcase you bought him."

"He bought it himself," she said flatly. "I just want to get it back."

"Why? What's the big deal?"

She looked at him as though he were incredibly stupid. "So that I can sell it. I can probably get twenty or twenty-five dollars for it." She waited for him to say something. "I need the money. The rent on this place is paid up till the end of the month; then I'll have to get out. But I need money to live on until then." She made a twisted smile that made her face seem old. "I got some bad habits."

It was clear to Chandler now. The nervousness, the twitching, the scratching, the generally slovenly appearance. The girl was an addict. "You have no money?" he asked, remembering once again Colandro's remarks about merchandise and thinking that the evidence was beginning to mount in that direction.

"I've got some money," she said. "He left a coupla hundred bucks. I found it in with his shaving stuff . . . But that's almost gone," she added quickly.

Chandler calculated rapidly. Romanello had been dead for four days. He had left a couple of hundred dollars and that was almost gone. Any way he figured it, the girl was sporting about a fifty dollar a day habit.

"What about your family? Where are they?"

"Family?" She laughed her sad, deep laugh. "My mother married some creep when I was twelve. When I started to . . . y'know . . . develop a little, the guy wouldn't leave me alone. Christ, I had to take showers at my friend's house and lock my bedroom door at night. When I came home from school, I wouldn't go in the house until I was sure my mother was home." She lit another cigarette, her eyes fixed on the coffee table. "One night my mother went out to visit her sister. She didn't tell me she was leaving. The next thing I know this creep is in my room grabbing me. I didn't want to scream because I was afraid to wake up my kid brother down the hall." She stopped and looked into her coffee cup as if trying to find an answer in the brown scum floating on the top. "I did the best I could," she said softly. "I really did."

"Did you tell your mother?"

She laughed. "Sure. She slapped my face, called me a whore, said it was my own fault, running around half naked all the time." Her voice was full of sympathy. "She was afraid to throw him out. Afraid of being alone. Y'know what I mean? She was willing to put up with a creep like that just because she was afraid to be alone."

"So you left?"

"Not right away. I was too scared." Her voice was beginning to sound like a little girl's again. "About two weeks later she went out again, and he came up to my room. This time I didn't even struggle. I just took off my clothes and got into bed. I figured it was expected of me—maybe even my mother expected it. Why else would she leave me alone with that creep?"

Chandler could think of nothing to say.

"So, anyway, I packed a bag, stole some money from him, and got on a bus to New York."

"How old were you?"

"Fifteen."

Chandler shuddered visibly.

"I met a guy in the bus terminal here in the city who got me a place to stay and set me up in the massage parlor." She dragged on her cigarette. "I was very popular. Seems they like 'em young in the big city."

Her tale of horror had battered him into silence. What made it worse was knowing that she was one of thousands wandering around New York's seamier districts. But *they* were out there. This girl was sitting right in front of him. Take away the ubiquitous cigarette, dangling from the pouting lips; comb the unkempt hair and tie it back with a ribbon; put her in a dress with knee socks and loafers, and she could have been a typical teenager, probably a junior or senior in high school. She should be just finding out about things that were already too well-known to her. She should have been giggling with friends, worrying about homework, flirting with boys, going to high school football games. Instead she was hoping to keep herself off the streets until the end of the month.

"You married?" she asked.

"Divorced."

"What kind of a place do you have?"

"A nice place," he said, not realizing at first what she was getting at. It came to him in a flash. "It's very small, though," he said guiltily.

She looked into her coffee cup again and said nothing.

Remorse came rushing through him. The girl was crying out for help. He said only, "Look, when I get my hands on your briefcase, do you want me to bring it to you or should I just sell it for you? I think I can get more than twenty-five dollars for it."

Her eyes brightened. "Do you think you could?"

"Sure. I'll bet I could get fifty dollars."

"It *is* almost new," she said, her head bobbing up and down.

"I could even give you the money now. That's how sure I am."

Her eyes narrowed as she thought about that. "No. Wait until you sell it." She wasn't sure. "Do you think it will take long?"

"I know somebody right now who will probably buy it. Let me give you half now."

He could see her struggling with a calculation. She smiled. "That would be terrific."

His gesture wasn't much, he knew, but it had made him

feel better. He counted out twenty-five dollars. "Do you have any idea what was in the briefcase?"

She shrugged. "Just some papers."

"You actually see that it contained only papers?"

She nodded enthusiastically. "Oh yeah. I saw him put them in there before he left."

"A lot of papers?"

She lit another cigarette and made a gesture with her palm up. "I don't know what you call a lot. The briefcase wasn't full or anything. He put the papers into those . . . uh . . . folders."

"Manila folders?"

"Right. About a dozen of them. It made a little stack, about like this," she said, holding up her hand, forefinger and thumb about an inch apart.

Chandler leaned back on the couch, making himself comfortable. "Now I want to ask you something," he said, choosing his words carefully, "and before you answer I want you to remember that I'm not a cop and I'm not interested in seeing that anybody gets arrested. I'm only interested in finding out what happened. OK?"

She nodded but seemed puzzled. "Yeah. Go ahead."

"Was there any chance that Romanello was carrying anything illegal? Anything that someone might want to take from him? Even to kill him for?"

Jeanette turned her head to the side and looked at him with what appeared to be genuine puzzlement. "What could he have in there that someone would kill him for?"

"Heroin . . . cocaine."

Her face seemed to sag. "If he was carrying H, I would have known about it."

"Did he leave anything behind? Something that might indicate what was in the briefcase?"

"He took everything with him."

"Any notes . . . or anything?"

"Well . . ." She seemed uncertain.

"Anything!"

"He left a notebook, but there's almost nothing in it. I looked through it."

"Could I see it?"

Jeanette hesitated, then went to the bedroom. She returned with a small, cheap spiral notebook which she handed to Chandler. Many of the pages had been torn out, small

scraps of paper clinging to the wire spiral. At the top of the
first remaining page, Chandler saw the initials "J. C." and
what was obviously a phone number followed by another
three-digit number.

On the next page was a list of seven names; except for
the first and the last, each name was followed by a date. The
first four names had a small checkmark in the left column of
the page. The rest of the pages were blank.

"You said that Fred had to find some people?"

"That's what he told me."

Chandler turned back to the list.

The checkmarks indicated, perhaps, that the first four
names on the list had been found. The others, perhaps, had
not been found. That's a lot of perhaps, he thought.

He turned back to the first page. "Can I use your phone?"

Jeanette pointed to the kitchen. "It's a mess," she said as
he headed in that direction.

She was right. The small kitchen was a greasy clutter of
unwashed pots and dishes, but Chandler hardly noticed any
of that. He dialed the number from the notebook.

"NBC," said a cheerful voice. "May I help you?"

Reading from the notebook, Chandler said, "Extension
five-nine-one, please."

There was a pause. "I'm sorry, sir. That extension is not
in use at this time."

Chandler feigned puzzlement. "Oh, I see. Can you tell
me why?"

Another pause. Longer this time. "That extension belonged
to Jonathan Carruthers and has not yet been reassigned."

"Thank you," said Chandler, hanging up the phone.
Through the open doorway he could see Jeanette, indiffer-
ently sipping her coffee and puffing on her cigarette. Occasionally she would swipe at her nose with the back of her
hand or scratch her arms or legs. She seemed lost—almost
catatonic.

"Can I keep this notebook for a while?" he asked, reen-
tering the living room.

Without looking at him, she shrugged. "Sure, go ahead.
I don't need it."

He put the notebook into his inside jacket pocket. "I
think that's about it for now. I'll be in touch with you soon."

"You won't forget about the money, for the briefcase?"

"No, I won't. I can even give you some of it now. It's no problem."

Jeanette stood up, straightening out her T-shirt as she did. "No, I can wait."

"Are you sure you don't need the money now?"

"I'll get by," she said smiling. "For a few days anyhow." The smile was gone.

"Isn't there someone, somewhere? Some family you could go to?"

"Don't worry about me. I'll be OK. I'll find someone." She seemed very small and very young.

Chandler backed his way to the door feeling the need to do something but not knowing what. Should he report her to the Youth Bureau and have her sent home? What kind of life was this?

"Look," he said, struggling with the words. "You'll be all right here until the end of the month. I've got some contacts with the Youth Services. Maybe I can find something for you."

"Hey," she said smiling. "Don't worry. Something will show up."

Chandler left the apartment, saying only that he would be in touch. His thoughts kept running to his own daughter, now nine, living with her mother in Pennsylvania. He wondered what she was doing at that very minute and wished that he could hug her.

Jeanette Nielsen was probably right, he thought. Something would show up. Chandler was afraid of what that something would be. More than likely it would be someone who would use and abuse her, and when her usefulness was gone discard her like a worn-out rag to join the ever-descending ranks of the New York street population.

The Youth Services Bureau had to be better than that.

Chapter 6

After taping a three-minute funeral-site spot, which was rushed to the nearest affiliate station, KIFI in Idaho Falls, and then fed to New York, Shelley James and her crew parked their gear and headed back to New York to do her eleven o'clock newscast. Most of the media people were in a jovial mood on the return trip, but Shelley was quiet, almost morose. Those who noticed, attributed her demeanor to the fact that she had known Carruthers better than anyone else, had in fact been very close to him, and, perhaps, still loved him.

That was not, however, the reason for her perturbation.

Very few people doubted the official police version of murder/suicide in the Carruthers case, because almost everyone at the station recalled—and had since passed along this information to colleagues everywhere—that in the weeks before his death, Jonathan Carruthers had appeared to be a driven man. He was perpetually haggard and apparently exhausted, his behavior bordering on the hyperactive. This behavior attracted only scant attention when he was alive, but now, after the tragedy, it was easy to retroactively pinpoint the manifestations of some deep psychological problem.

"We should have known," was the common cry echoing up and down the sixth-floor offices in the RCA Building. "He acted like a man in trouble. But how do you know how bad the trouble is before it's too late?"

There was great wailing and gnashing of teeth in the NBC executive offices. They had lost one of their major talents and it was impossible to assign blame. How could the intense feelings of loss be diminished if responsibility could not be delegated to some hapless underling who could be dismissed? The hunt for a scapegoat was initiated immediately.

What disturbed Shelley James, however, was that she

could not bring herself to believe any of the current variations given as reasons for the tragedy. She did not believe the rumors of overwork and driving ambition sending a talented but sensitive celebrity over the edge of the psychological precipice. True, it had happened before, to Freddie Prinz and others. But Carruthers had none of their characteristics. He was, thought Shelley, about as sensitive as a block of granite.

She did not believe the heartbroken-lover variation. Why, she asked herself, would a man, at the top of his field, in the prime of his life, kill a girl he hardly knew and then kill himself? It made no sense. It was too pat. Besides, a heartbroken lover had to have a heart, and Shelley knew that Carruthers was only a doubtful qualifier in this category.

Consequently, Shelley could not believe the police version of the case as a murder/suicide.

In addition to all her doubts, Shelley also knew something that no one else seemed to know. She knew why Carruthers had been acting so strangely in the weeks before his death. He was exhausted because he was working night and day. After working all day at the studio, he was spending his nights working on some project—a book, an article, a news report—that only he knew about.

Because of the concern expressed around the station, Shelley had approached Carruthers three days before his death to ask him if there was any reason for his haggard appearance and manic behavior. Although no longer close, they had maintained a good working relationship. Rarely a week went past that Carruthers didn't bemoan the fact that he had been foolish enough to let Shelley get away. It was usually said in jest for all within earshot to hear, but both Carruthers and Shelley knew that there was a great deal of truth to his joke.

Consequently, Shelley's inquiry had come from genuine solicitude.

"Have dinner with me," he had replied, "and I'll tell you all about it."

She'd eyed him skeptically. Dinner with Carruthers usually meant a trip to the bedroom. "Jon," she said, "everybody around here is worried about you. I just want to know that you're all right."

He laughed and his eyes rolled to the ceiling. "Everybody's worried that the boy-wonder—the old meal ticket—is going down the tubes, eh?" His lips set into a sneer. "Without me they'd all be on the street looking for jobs. And this station would be back on the skids."

He caught her worried look. "Don't worry, Shelley. I'm just tired. I'm working hard, but it's nothing to worry about, it's . . ." His voice trailed off and he looked around suspiciously. He draped an arm around her shoulder and his voice dropped to a lower register. "Shelley, I'm on the verge of the biggest story to hit this country since Watergate, maybe since the Kennedy assassination." His voice was crackling with excitement. "And it's all mine. An exclusive, a scoop, whatever you want to name it. It's dynamite!"

Shelley turned to look at him. His eyes were practically dancing. It was just this kind of animation that had worried everyone. But then she saw something else, something that only one who knew him intimately could see. There was joy in his face.

"I mean it, Shell," he said. "It's dynamite."

"Your staff doesn't seem to know anything about it."

He smiled. "No one does. I've told you more than I've told anyone. But soon everyone will know." His eyes grew misty as though he saw an undiscovered paradise. Then he focused back on the present. "Until then, I'm not taking any chances. I don't want some ambitious bastard leaking my story to someone else." He smiled again. "It's almost too big to contain, Shell. That's why it's so secret." He shook her and said for the umpteenth time, "It's dynamite."

She was caught up in his excitement. "It must be, but you look exhausted."

"I'm working till four in the morning on this thing. I've got to finish before someone else breaks the story. I've given up sleep."

"No girls?"

He laughed. "I said I'd given up sleep. I didn't say I'd given up living."

"How long can you go on working alone like this?"

He paused for a moment, taking his arm from her shoulder. "I'm not exactly alone on this. I have someone—someone from outside the network—helping me with research."

"Do I know who it is?"

He was cautious. She could see that. "I don't think so. It's someone I worked with back in the Midwest. He's a good researcher."

They walked along the corridor together, not saying anything, both of them thinking.

At the door to Shelley's office, they paused. "I was worried about you, Jon. I'm glad it's something like this. I hope it's as big as you say it is."

"Bigger, Shell, bigger. This story is going to set the world on its ear. It's going to establish my credentials as a newsman, not just as some honcho who reads the news. Dan Rather would give his right arm for this story."

"I can't wait to hear it."

"Don't wait." He looked down at the floor. "Come back to me, Shelley. I miss you."

She was startled by this uncharacteristically frank admission. It may have been the first truly open thing she had ever heard him say. He had actually left himself vulnerable.

"I don't believe it," she said.

"It's true. Come back. Move in tonight."

"Jon, we both know it wouldn't work. You're you and I'm me."

He was serious. "It'll be different this time. You'll see. We'll work on this story together. I've got a stack of papers on my desk. You can read them tonight." He seemed almost childlike in his persistence.

Shelley raised her eyebrows in mock surprise. "You're going to share the biggest story since the Kennedy assassination?" She pursed her lips to show her skepticism. "That is probably the biggest line you ever fed me."

Carruthers smiled sheepishly. "Well, maybe I'd want most of the credit." He hastened to add, "But it's big enough for two. Shit, it's big enough for a hundred."

Shelley touched his cheek with her fingers. "I hope that it all comes true for you."

He knew this meant she wasn't coming back to him and as a defense against her rejection he assumed the mask of his old bravado. "You're missing a big chance, Shell. We could be the Lunt-Fontaine, the Steve and Edie of the news business."

"Probably more like Sonny and Cher," she said, smiling. "When does the world get to hear this great story?"

He was suddenly serious. "Soon. Another month maybe. As soon as I gather enough material I'm going to break it. I still don't have everything I need, but I'm close."

She again wished him luck. They promised to have dinner soon and Shelley wondered if maybe he had changed, if maybe she should go back to him.

It was perhaps this final thought that made the news of his death doubly shocking. She was shaken when she realized how close she had come to being the girl who was murdered in his bed.

Immediately upon returning to the RCA Building in New York, Shelley went to what had been the office suite of Jonathan Carruthers. She entered the outer office area where his secretary still sat at her desk, quietly reading a paperback novel. The once bustling office was deathly still.

Shelley broke the silence. "Hello, Gladys."

Gladys, startled, jumped and her book snapped shut. She looked up guiltily and put the book in an open lower drawer. "Hello, Miss James. How are you today?"

"Fine, Gladys. I see you haven't been reassigned yet."

The secretary made a face. "The rumor is that the new anchor will take over these offices. He has his own people, but I'm hoping I can stay on right here."

The new anchor was John W. Carlson, who had been promoted, at least temporarily, from the afternoon news while a major talent search was underway to replace the irreplaceable Jonathan Carruthers.

Shelley was all sympathy. "Don't worry, Gladys. I'm sure they'll keep you right here. Everybody knew you were Jon's right arm."

Gladys, a woman in her late forties who still sported the styles of her youth, seemed on the verge of tears. "I still can't believe it. I keep expecting him to barge in here, bellowing at everybody."

The two women were silent for a moment. Then Shelley patted the older woman on the shoulder. "I know how you feel, Gladys. I know."

"I think we were closer to him than anybody else," moaned Gladys.

Although not believing it for a minute, Shelley nodded in agreement. Then, figuring she had spent enough time in commiseration, she got to the point of her visit. "Has his office been cleared out yet?"

"His things are still in there. A lot is already in cartons." Gladys shook her head sadly. "It has to be cleared out by tomorrow afternoon." She looked quizzically at Shelley before asking, "Why?"

Shelley was as casual as possible. "Well, Jonathan had some notes of mine from a story we were working on together. I'd still like to do it for my eleven o'clock newscast. I wondered if you had perhaps run across the notes?"

Gladys shook her head slowly.

"Jon said," Shelley went on, "that he was going to get someone to do some research for us, maybe someone outside the station. I was hoping he might have given you a name so that I could get in touch with this person."

"He never mentioned it to me. Why would he get an outsider for research? He had plenty of assistants right here. What was the story about?"

"It was part of that abortion thing I've been doing," said Shelley, thinking fast. "He didn't mention anything to you?"

"No."

"Do you mind if I take a look through his things?" asked Shelley, tilting her head toward the closed door of Carruthers's office.

Doubt crept across Gladys's face. The request seemed like an intrusion into a sanctuary.

"I won't take long," said Shelley. "It is very important to me, Gladys."

The secretary could not resist this personal appeal. "Of course, Miss James. Go right ahead."

Carruthers's large corner office looked out over Fifth Avenue. It was one of the choice office locations on the floor and Shelley had always felt a certain amount of envy any time she entered this particular room. Her own office was less than half this size and had no windows. At this moment, however, the sight of the bare desk and empty, almost expectant chairs brought only a sense of sadness and loss.

Quickly, she looked through the near empty desk drawers and then turned to the cartons stacked on the floor. Carruthers's papers and personal effects had been encased in three cardboard file boxes that lay like miniature coffins on the plush carpeted floor. One contained plaques, photos, and awards, the kind of personal memorabilia that had only lately been displayed on the office walls and had now been replaced by rectangular patches of off-color empty space.

The two remaining cartons were only partially filled with manila folders and papers of one type or another. Shelley flipped through the papers without removing them from the cartons, occasionally pausing to take a closer look at a particular paper that happened to catch her eye. There was nothing of any real interest, at least nothing that had any bearing on the information she sought.

Shelley returned to the large teak desk which dominated the room. From the middle drawer she extracted an appointment book and flipped through the pages. She advanced to the day of Carruthers's death and then carefully began to work her way back. On the day of his death there was only one entry,

Meet R

and as she moved back through the book she noted that there were several similar insertions. In the six weeks prior to his death, Jonathan Carruthers had apparently met with this "R" at least four times.

Shelley continued to work back through the book until, eleven weeks before the final entry, she found a notation that gave her goose bumps. On the page, in Jonathan Carruthers's impeccably precise handwriting, she read, "Call Romanello," followed by a Manhattan phone number. But it wasn't the name or the number that made her flesh tingle with excitement. Just beneath that notation, in large lettering, written with a red pen and with a hand that was no longer precise, Jonathan Carruthers had scribbled the word,

Dynamite!

Shelley recalled how many times Jonathan had used that word to refer to his story. She was sure she had found it. She wasn't sure what it was, but she had found it.

She was looking through the rest of the appointment book when the office door opened. Shelley looked up, startled by the intrusion and feeling as if she had been caught committing some terrible crime. She slammed the book shut.

The woman in the doorway looked at her strangely, then smiled. "Why, Shelley. I didn't expect to find you here."

Shelley stood up. "Hello, Mrs. Gresham," she said. "I was just looking for some notes that Jonathan and I had compiled together." She felt her face flush.

Sylvia Gresham was the widow of the former chairman of the board of the parent corporation. As such, she was the majority stockholder in the network and still maintained an office in the building. It was said that she wielded more power than the present chairman and had been responsible for the hiring and firing of three board chairmen since the death of her husband, Raymond T. Gresham, five years ago.

Mrs. Gresham was in her sixties, tall and slender, and forged in steel. Her stare was rumored to have turned grown men into blundering adolescents. She sat down across from Shelley. "We all miss him terribly," she said, looking around the office. "He could have been a legend." Her eyes were moist. "He could have been the dominant personality in his field. But now . . ." Her voice trailed off, and she looked at Shelley. "I've been watching you closely," she said. Her voice grew stronger. "I think it's about time that we had a woman coanchor on the network news."

Shelley could not prevent the smile that crept across her face.

Mrs. Gresham smiled too. "Yes. You've got everything it takes to make it in this business. With your looks you could do anything, but you've also got brains . . . and talent."

"Thank you, Mrs. Gresham," Shelley said. "I appreciate that."

Mrs. Gresham stood up. "It won't be long, my dear. Just keep up the good work." She went to the door. "I hope you find what you are looking for," she said before she left.

Intending to copy the pages and return the appointment book to the desk later, Shelley slipped it into her shoulder bag and left Carruthers's office. Gladys looked up expectantly from her book, but Shelley merely shook her head and marched past.

Hardly able to restrain herself from breaking into a run, Shelley made her way back to her own office. Once inside, she removed the appointment book from her bag and dialed the number next to the name, Romanello.

A woman's voice answered, "Hello?"

"May I speak with Mr. Romanello, please?"

There was a pause. "He is not here," said a very tenta-tive voice.

"My name is Shelley James and I am a colleague of the late Jonathan Carruthers . . ." There was no response . . . "the TV newscaster?" Again nothing. "Mr. Carruthers informed me that he had a working relationship with Mr. Romanello and I would like to speak with him in order to reestablish that relationship."

"He's dead," said the voice bluntly.

"I know that," said Shelley misunderstanding. "I meant reestablishing the relationship between myself and Mr. Romanello."

"No—no," said the voice as if reprimanding a child. "Mr. Romanello—Fred—is dead."

Shelley, stunned, tried to stammer a question, but before she could force out the words from her paralyzed lips, the voice went on.

"He was killed the same day your fancy Carruthers blew his brains out."

Shelley was sufficiently recovered to respond. "I'm terribly sorry to hear that. Are you Mrs. Romanello?"

"No."

"Were you a friend?"

A pause. "I guess so. Look, I'm in kind of a hurry. I have to meet some people in a few minutes."

"Wait, please. Don't hang up. Just a few minutes . . . please."

The woman said nothing but she did not hang up.

"May I come and speak with you?" asked Shelley.

The voice was full of impatience. "I don't know anything. Besides, I spoke to one of your reporter people already."

Shelley was alarmed. "Who?" she asked sharply.

"The guy from the *News*."

"The *News?*"

"The paper. You know."

"Oh, the New York *News?*"

"Yes."

"Do you remember the name?"

"Sure. Chandler. The one who wrote the nice story about Freddie in the paper."

Shelley was puzzled, but this avenue seemed to be leading to a dead end. "I would still like to come and talk with you."

The woman sounded jittery. "Not today. I'm busy. I have to go out."

"Tomorrow then. Name the time."

"I suppose so." She didn't sound too anxious.

"Fine," said Shelley in her most positive tone, treating the meeting as a *fait accompli*. "Give me your name and address and just tell me when to be there."

Jeanette Nielsen gave the requested information to Shelley James, almost as much to get rid of her as anything else. She then quickly dialed a number and tapped her fingers nervously on the phone as it rang.

"Lester? . . . Jeanette. . . . Yes, I'm coming. . . . You got it? . . . Of course I got the money. . . . I said I got it, Lester. . . . I'm leaving now. . . . Don't make me wait, Lester. I need it. I really need it."

Chapter 7

Jeanette was in the kitchen making coffee when she heard a faint knock on her front door. Cautiously, she went to the door and called, "Who's there?"

A small boy's voice answered, "My name is Michael and I am a friend of Mr. Romanello's."

Jeanette looked through the peephole in the door and saw a young boy of about eleven or so. He was tall and slender and quite handsome in the innocent way of a preteenager. She opened the door, keeping the chain on, and gave the boy a cordial smile through the gap. "What can I do for you, Michael?"

The boy smiled back, a broad, beaming, open smile that dazzled her with its perfection. Jeanette could feel her own smile broaden. "Mr. Romanello," he said, "told me that if anything ever happened to him, I was to look in on you and see that you were all right." He held out an envelope. "He also said that I was to give you this."

"What is it?" she asked through the slit in the door.

"I don't know, but I think it's money."

Jeanette snatched the offered envelope from the boy's

hands and turned her back to the door. She ripped open the envelope and then smiled with juvenile pleasure as she counted six fifty-dollar bills.

As if embarrassed by her bad manners she turned back to the door and said, "Oh, excuse me, Michael. Let me open the door for you."

She did so and revealed the boy—even more handsome than she had first believed—standing there in gray flannel slacks and a gray, sleeveless V-neck sweater with a maroon tie knotted over a white shirt.

"You look so nice," she said with genuine sincerity. "Most of the kids around here dress like they're out collecting garbage." She was immediately aware that in her blue jeans and loose-fitting T-shirt, she probably didn't look any better.

"I just got out of school," said Michael by way of explanation as she beckoned him into the room and led him to a seat.

They sat on the sofa and for a moment there was an uneasy silence. Jeanette could think of little other than her sudden fortune and the boy seemed content to just look at her and let her make conversation. His bright, beautifully blue eyes never left her face.

Jeanette felt the eyes boring into her. If he had been older she would have been uncomfortable. "I must be a mess," she said, tousling her hair.

The boy said nothing, which only added to her growing sense of discomfort. The kettle whistled from the kitchen and Jeanette, momentarily rescued, sprang from her seat.

"I was just making some coffee for myself when you knocked. I don't have any soda or anything. I can give you some milk. It's fresh today."

"Coffee would be fine," he said, and when she stared he added, "It's all right, really. I like coffee. I drink it all the time at home."

Jeanette's face expressed her doubt, but she shrugged and went off to the kitchen and soon returned with two coffee mugs.

She placed both mugs on the table. "I made yours with lots of milk," she said, smiling hopefully.

"That's fine," he said without the trace of a smile.

Jeanette sat on the couch opposite him and for a moment neither said anything. She blew into her mug several times while Michael slowly sipped his coffee. Finally she spoke. "How did you know Fred?"

The boy leaned forward, placing his cup on the coffee table. He took a long time to answer. "Actually he was a friend of my father's. They worked together on some investigations."

Jeanette smiled. "Yes, Fred was very good at investigating things."

"I used to listen to Fred and my father talk about their cases for hours. It was really fascinating." He picked up his mug and sipped. "Did he ever tell you any of his interesting stories?"

"Why, sure he did," Jeanette lied, thinking that Romanello had hardly ever mentioned anything about his work. Most of his stories had been about women who had practically thrown themselves at his feet. She didn't believe much of what he had told her.

"Did he really?" said Michael. "I love to hear those stories. They're so fascinating."

He was smiling expectantly, encouraging her to proceed.

Jeanette squirmed. "Actually, most of his stories didn't have to do with his work. He really didn't tell me a lot about his work."

"Didn't he?" The boy seemed disappointed. "I would think that he would tell you everything about what he did. I often heard him say that you were closer to him than anyone, that you were the one person in the whole world that he could trust."

"Did he really say that?"

Michael nodded.

Jeanette made a face. "Boy, that sure doesn't sound like Fred."

"I'm sure he told you lots of things. You probably just didn't think that they were important at the time."

Jeanette spoke almost defensively. "Well, sure. We talked about things all the time."

Michael looked into his coffee. "Someone as beautiful as you should always be told what's going on."

"Why, Michael. What a little flirt you are. I'll bet the girls at school are just wild about you."

"I go to an all-boys school," he said sadly. "I really don't have much contact with girls."

"That's too bad. You should really be learning about girls now. You're very handsome, you know."

He beamed. "Do you really think so?"

"Oh yes," she said. "The girls are going to be crazy about you." Somehow this conversation reminded her of what she used to tell the johns at the massage parlor.

"I like girls," he said. "Some of my friends at school don't. But I like them a lot."

Jeanette watched his eyes. There was something there, lurking behind the blue, something indefinable that seemed terribly familiar. "You seem older," she said. "How old are you?"

He sidestepped her question. "I'm very intelligent. I have an IQ of one hundred seventy-five. I'm not really interested in most of the things that kids are into."

Without meaning to, Jeanette slipped into his conversational snare. "What kinds of things are you interested in?"

"You know," he said, "more adult kinds of things."

Although uncertain of his meaning, Jeanette nodded knowingly. "Oh," she said.

"I wish I had a friend who could talk to me about things." He turned shy. "You know. Someone who could teach me."

Jeanette was still uncertain but sensed in herself a growing uneasiness. She did not like the way this conversation was going. "Teach you . . . what?"

"You know . . . about sex and things."

Jeanette was on familiar ground now and her face hardened. "Perhaps your parents should tell you about it."

Michael edged closer. "Oh, I know all about it. It's just that I don't have any experience."

Eyes widening in amazement, Jeanette said, "You don't really think that I . . ." She stuttered a bit. "You're just a kid." She put down her coffee mug with a heavy clunk. "How old are you?"

"How old are you?" he retorted brazenly.

"Old enough that I don't have to make it with preteens for thrills." Her amazement had turned to anger.

The boy was very calm. "Fred told me what you used to do for a living."

Her surprise defused her anger. "He did?" She shook her head sadly. "Good for him. You know, I thought you were a nice boy, someone I could talk to, who wasn't going to give me a hard time, but . . ." She shook her head in exasperation. "Doesn't anybody in this town think of anything else?" She looked up to the ceiling as if expecting some answer, then got up quickly. "It's time to go, Michael. Thanks for stopping by, but I'm very busy right now."

He made no move to get up. "If I tell him to, my father would pay the rent here."

Jeanette laughed out loud at this absurdity. "Let's not be ridiculous, Michael."

"I have my own money. Lots of money. From trust funds." He removed his wallet from his back pocket and placed a fifty-dollar bill on the table. "That's for you."

"You are really weird—do you know that—really weird. What kind of kid does this? You are weird."

He slid the money toward her. "Take it."

She put her hands on her hips. "What do I have to do for it?"

Sensing a loosening of her resolve, his eyes brightened. "Just take off your clothes. Let me see what you look like."

"Forget it, Michael. Listen, kid," she said, with heavy emphasis on the last word, "I can get money any time I want. I don't have to stoop to cradle robbing." She was anxious to be rid of him. He was making her edgy. "You'd better get going. I have to go out. I have to meet someone very soon."

"Who, your connection?"

She stopped. "You know lots about me, don't you? Well, it's none of your business what I do. Just hurry up and go."

He said nothing. Instead he reached into his pocket and extracted a small, square envelope. He displayed it for a moment and dropped it on the table.

Jeanette's eyes stared. "What's that?"

"Guess."

Her eyes narrowed. "Where would you get it?"

"When you have money," he said simply, "you can get anything."

"Do you use it?"

He smiled. "No. It just comes in handy sometimes—like now. I can get it any time I want."

She was doubtful. "I'll bet it's not even real."

Carefully he folded back the corners of the small package, wet his index finger on the tip of his tongue, and dabbed it gently into the open envelope. He held up the finger with a white spot of powder on the end for her inspection. Jeanette knelt in front of him like a parishioner receiving communion and extended her tongue. He touched the powder to it. She tasted, closed her eyes, and smiled.

Jeanette took Michael's wrist in her hand and guided his still extended finger into her mouth. She held his hand there for a moment, sucking on his finger, then let him withdraw.

She opened her eyes to look up at him. "You can get this stuff any time you want?"

He nodded.

"And all I have to do is? . . ."

"Yes."

Still kneeling in front of him she pulled her T-shirt over her head. She was naked to the waist. Michael stared hard, his tongue flicking out to wet lips suddenly gone dry.

Jeanette leaned forward and gave him a hard, open-mouthed kiss, snaking her tongue into his mouth. "Sonny," she breathed into his ear, "you've just won yourself some dancing lessons."

She stood up quickly. Michael watched, fascinated by the jiggle of her breasts. "When I come back," she said, picking up the envelope from the table, "you're going to have the time of your life."

"Wait," he said. "Let's do it first." But she was already racing toward the bathroom.

She closed the door and Michael heard the clinking sounds as she gathered her paraphernalia. For some time there was silence. Then he heard her say, "Hang on, little man. Momma will be there soon."

Michael picked up the fifty-dollar bills that lay on the table and put them in his pocket.

Jeanette stood in front of the medicine cabinet mirror, syringe in her right hand, and grasped her tongue in the fingers of her other hand. Watching herself in the mirror, she lifted her tongue to expose the blue, veiny underside, then inserted the needle into the large vein at the base.

She felt the sharp prick of the injection, then the hot rush as the slimy liquid entered her veins. A hot, burning, indescribably delicious feeling raced through her body.

Oh, she thought, it's going to be a beauty.

Almost immediately, her chest was caught in a vice that began to squeeze with thunderous pressure. She opened her mouth wide but was unable to cry out or draw in a breath of air.

In a split second of instantaneous, horrifying recognition she was aware of what was happening to her.

She staggered back against the door; saw herself wide-eyed, openmouthed in the mirror; heard, above the roaring thunder of her heartbeat, the shattering glass as the syringe hit the tile floor. Her image in the mirror seemed more surprised than fearful and she formed the word "Michael" on her lips but no sound came. Then, incredibly, she actually felt her heart stop. The roaring in her ears ceased and was replaced by an immense and awful silence. The image of herself in the mirror faded to gray, then everything was red, moving to orange, and lights like flashbulbs were popping somewhere behind her eyeballs.

She never knew that she pitched forward, her forehead smacking against the hard porcelain sink before she sprawled face first on the cold bare linoleum tile of the bathroom floor.

Michael rinsed his coffee mug in the kitchen sink, drying it carefully before placing it in the open cabinet. He came back into the living room and listened intently for a few minutes, and when he was sure there was no sound, he made his way to the front door, being careful not to touch anything.

Chapter 8

There was no response when Shelley James knocked on the door of Jeanette Nielsen's apartment. She knocked again. Again, no answer. Shelley tried the handle on the door; it turned easily, and the door swung open to reveal an empty room.

"Are you there?" she cried from the hallway.

The apartment was eerily silent.

Shelley checked her watch and looked up and down the narrow hallway. She was right on time and debated whether or not she should go back downstairs and wait in the street for Jeanette Nielsen. Instead she decided to consider the unlocked door an invitation to wait inside. So, leaving the front door slightly open, she cautiously entered the apartment.

"Are you here?" she called again.

Something was wrong here. She could feel it. She began to feel that someone was in the apartment with her. Someone was watching her.

Shelley perched on the arm of the sofa. After less than a minute she checked her watch again. The feeling that she was being watched became intolerable.

She stood up. "Is anybody here?"

From her vantage point in the center of the room she could see directly into the kitchen. It was obviously empty. To her right was a partially opened door to what was apparently a bedroom. Shelley went to the door and pushed it open, revealing a dark, musty room with an unmade bed against one wall.

Turning away, Shelley edged open the next door, which struck something after moving only a few inches. Some hidden instinct told her not to push harder, but she could not resist. She placed her shoulder against the door, and with some effort was able to force open the door enough to fit her head through the aperture.

Shelley's eyes widened and her jaw dropped in mock imitation of the scene before her. Jeanette Nielsen's mouth was open as if gasping for her final breath, her eyes staring at some undiscovered secret. The woman, naked to the waist, lay chest-down, her face turned to one side. Shelley jumped back to close the door, momentarily trapping her head inside the doorway. Fighting panic she pushed the door open to allow her escape, then slammed it shut with a loud bang that echoed throughout the silent apartment and up and down the empty hallway. She was certain the sound would disturb the whole building and half expected to hear the commotion of shouting voices and running feet.

There was only silence.

Shelley backed away from the door, trembling violently and swallowing hard against a rising nausea. She fought to keep herself calm, but the urge to flee was intense.

The police—the police—the police. The thought kept running through her brain and she went to the kitchen phone, never turning her back on the bathroom door.

She knew that she had to call the police, but when she

picked up the phone she found herself, with fumbling fingers, dialing the number of the station.

"Get me the newsroom," she said, her voice already growing steady.

"This is Shelley. Get a camera crew over to Nine hundred East Thirteenth Street. I've got a dead girl here. Tell them to hurry. I'll meet them in the lobby."

Only then did she call the police.

The camera crew arrived several minutes before the police and was actually able to shoot the arrival of the first patrol car. The two uniformed policemen seemed bewildered to find themselves the focus of a TV camera crew and the small crowd that had inevitably been attracted by the tragedy. As they entered the building, the policemen appeared awkward and clumsy as though they were passersby who had been thrust on stage in the middle of a professional performance.

The cameraman, minicam on shoulder, scurried upstairs to find Shelley James with a microphone in her hand, standing in bright lights in front of the open doorway of the apartment. She was surrounded by gawking neighbors.

As soon as she was on camera, Shelley began to speak. "This is Shelley James with mobile camera unit two for WNBC News." At that point the policemen walked into camera range and entered the apartment. Shelley went on. "Less than one hour ago I came to this apartment to interview a young woman who had called me about a personal problem. I found her, just as the police are finding her now . . ."—she turned so that the camera could shoot, over her shoulder, the scene of the policemen forcing open the bathroom door—"lying in a pool of her own blood."

One policeman squeezed his way into the bathroom. The other stayed outside. After a brief conference the second policeman came to the door. "Excuse me," he said. "You'll have to back away from the door."

Shelley stuck the mike in his face. "Officer, what was the cause of death?"

The young policeman seemed startled by the question. Without looking at the camera or at his questioner he responded, "I think you'd better talk to Lieutenant Garvey when he gets here."

Shelley was insistent. "Can't you tell me how she died?"

The policeman was uncertain as to procedure here. Usually some senior officer would be in charge before the television people arrived. He began, "Well, she's got some bruises on her forehead, but I can't really say what caused her . . . death."

"But do you suspect foul play?"

He looked at Shelley as though she had suddenly donned a clown suit. "Lady," he began, as if he were going to say something obscene, but thought better of it. "It ain't my job to suspect anything. Talk to Lieutenant Garvey."

With that, he reentered the apartment and closed the door.

Within a few minutes of this minor altercation, Lieutenant Garvey arrived on-the-scene. When he saw the lights and television crew he shook his head and forced a thin smile. "The ghouls are here early today," he said through clenched teeth.

Shelley pushed the mike in front of his face but before she could ask one question, he barked at her. "You the one who called this in?"

She nodded and Garvey motioned with his head toward the apartment and his thumb toward the lights. "Turn off those lights and get in here." He smiled sweetly. "I want to interview you first." Garvey's eyes twinkled with satisfaction and Shelley had the sinking feeling that things would not go as smoothly as she had hoped.

Garvey was a short, heavy man with slicked back, thinning gray hair and a large, beefy face. He wore a cheap, dark blue suit that looked slept in.

After conversing for a few minutes with the uniformed officers, Garvey turned to face Shelley. "What happened here?" he asked in a tone that made it evident to Shelley that she would not receive the customary courtesies accorded to someone who reported a crime. She was obviously considered the enemy in the us-versus-them mentality that pervaded the New York Police Department.

Shelley was cool. "I don't know," she said, shaking her head. "I came here to meet with her and found her"—she motioned toward the bathroom—"in there."

Garvey considered this for a moment. "How'd you get in?"

"The door was open."

The lieutenant looked around the room. "You usually walk into empty apartments when the door is open?"

"I was invited, Lieutenant. I was supposed to meet her here. When she didn't answer my knock I tried the door. I assumed she had left it open for me."

Garvey lit a huge cigar, puffing billows of heavy smoke in Shelley's direction. He inspected the end of his cigar. "What did you want to see her about?"

Shelley hesitated. She had carefully planned what she would say when this question was inevitably asked. She did not wish to declare that she herself had initiated the meeting, nor did she want to mention the possibility of the connection with Jonathan Carruthers. Figuring that the best defense was a good offense, Shelley began. "Miss Nielsen called me yesterday to complain that the police were not doing anything to find the person who killed her boyfriend."

Garvey's eyebrows shot up. "Boyfriend? What boyfriend?"

"Mr. Romanello. The man who was pushed onto the subway tracks on Monday."

The policeman's face went blank for a moment, then screwed up into a beefy scowl. "Jesus," he said. "That was her boyfriend?"

"Yes."

He shook his head, his body visibly sagging. His face seemed to lose much of its ruddy color. "Isn't New York a wonderful place to live?" He spoke quietly, the belligerence gone from his voice.

Shelley sensed that the moment had come—for her to seize the initiative. "Was she murdered?" she ventured.

"No," he said, and when her expression seemed to question his response he added, "She wasn't murdered."

Shelley looked toward the bathroom where men were hovering over the body with cameras, plastic bags, and God-knows-what-else. She shivered. "What then?" she asked.

"Overdose." Garvey sucked on his cigar. "Your little friend OD'd herself on what was probably some very fine heroin. There's some very good merchandise being dealt around the city right now . . . from Iran I understand." His voice had taken on the monotone of a bored salesman discussing the latest fashions for the new fall season. "The merchandise is so good in fact that it occasionally provides the ultimate high." He flicked a thumb over his shoulder in the direction of the body on the floor.

Shelley said nothing. She wondered if the men standing over the body were ever going to cover its nakedness.

Garvey went on. "You got anything to add about what happened here?"

Shelley shook her head. "No, nothing."

They looked at each other, both wary of the other's capabilities. Shelley flashed her most dazzling smile. "And now that I've cooperated with you, Lieutenant, how about a short interview on camera? It'll only take a minute." She slipped an arm around Garvey's elbow and began leading him to the door. "Let's give the folks at home a little bit of that Clint Eastwood charm, huh?"

Garvey smiled, weakening at her touch. "OK, but it's got to be quick."

"Don't worry," said Shelley, still smiling as she positioned the lieutenant in front of the ever-ready camera.

Chapter 9

Sitting in front of his typewriter at which he had unsuccessfully attempted to compose a column that could make some sense out of the link between Jonathan Carruthers and Fred Romanello, Mark Chandler watched the Shelley James segment on tape at six o'clock and again, later, when she did her own newscast at eleven.

The spot was really intriguing: reporter on-the-scene of a tragedy before the police arrive, camera crew taping the entire procedure. It was the kind of spectacle that television does so well. No amount of newspaper reporting, no matter how well done, could ever hope to compete with the scene of the actual event unfolding on the screen. It would be like trying to write about Jack Ruby's murder of Lee Harvey Oswald. Why bother? Every living room in America had been witness to the event. Television gave the people what they wanted: murder, mayhem, tragedy, and high drama in the safety of their own homes.

Goddamn television, thought Chandler; it will be the end of us all.

He also thought that the ratings on Shelley James's late night newscast would be impressive, and he was right.

Chandler had been so stunned by the news of Jeanette Nielsen's death that he was unable to detect any other significance to the event. Later, after watching Shelley James live at eleven o'clock, he was certain that she had somehow made the connection between Jonathan Carruthers and Jeanette Nielsen's boyfriend. It was not in anything that Shelley said, but rather in what she did not say. She only vaguely referred to her reasons for visiting Jeanette Nielsen and as she did, her eyes dropped quickly to a printed page on her desk as if her story could not endure the scrutiny of the camera's eye.

Chandler sat up in his chair. "She knows," he said out loud to his cat, who eyed him disdainfully from her favorite spot near the radiator.

Shelley James and her story even made the front pages of the New York *News* and the New York *Post* the next morning. In a photograph culled from the videotape, Shelley was shown, mike in hand, standing before the apartment door. Vaguely in the background, shadowy figures in dark uniforms could be seen standing over an even more shadowy shape on the bathroom floor. Both papers made much of the fact that Jeanette Nielsen's boyfriend—roommate, they called him—had been killed just five days earlier. There was a largely unsuccessful attempt to portray Jeanette Nielsen as a bereaved lover who conceivably might have taken her own life.

What disturbed Chandler about the newspaper coverage was that, unable to compete for immediacy, the newspapers had resorted to first mimicking the television coverage by copying the videotape, and then trying to create some sort of soap opera melodrama out of the available facts to add a touch of sensationalism to a rather tawdry story. What they succeeded in doing was demonstrating their collective inability to contend on an equal basis with their broadcast rival.

Early that morning, after reading the stories and after an evening of considering the significance of the death of Jeanette Nielsen, Chandler called WNBC News, identified himself as a reporter and asked to speak with Shelley James. He was told that she would not be in her office until later and that if possible she would call him back. It seemed that reporters had been calling for interviews all morning.

When Shelley called in to her office she was told about the many requests. Once again, the announcer and not the announcement had become news. Shelley asked her secretary to run down the list of callers and when the secretary arrived at Chandler's name, Shelley stopped her, and, remembering Jeanette Nielsen's comment about Chandler, asked for his number.

Chandler was mildly surprised. He had not expected her to call back. At least not so soon. "Thanks for calling, Miss James. I understand you've been very busy."

"Yes. Reporters have been calling me all day and I'm going to be on the *Today* show tomorrow."

Chandler chuckled. "There's nothing we reporters like better than to make a celebrity out of one of our own."

"I suppose so," she said, laughing uncomfortably. "Now what can I do for you?"

The brief moment of social informality over, Chandler came right to the point. "I wondered if you could tell me why you went to see Jeanette Nielsen?"

There was a brief pause and then in a practiced tone Shelley repeated what she had said on her broadcast.

"That's the only reason?"

Shelley forced a chuckle. "Watch my program, Mr. Chandler. If there are any new revelations you can hear them there."

"If you were a cop or a politician, we reporters might claim that you were not giving us the facts we need in order to inform the public."

"I would never withhold facts from a colleague," said Shelley in mock seriousness.

"Why did Jeanette call you?"

"Jeanette? Did you know her, Mr. Chandler?"

"As a matter-of-fact, I did. I talked with her just a few days ago. It's funny, she didn't express any interest in goading the police into finding her boyfriend's killer then. In fact, she seemed rather blasé about the whole thing."

"Well, perhaps she saw me on television and felt she could confide in me. I'm sorry she wasn't able to do that with you."

Chandler decided to ignore this swipe. "Is it customary for you to follow up a lead like this? After all, you're the anchor. Don't you have ordinary reporters who usually do that sort of thing?"

"As I said, she felt she could confide in me." There was an awkward pause and then she went on. "Look, Mr. Chandler, I don't want to cut off a fellow member of the press, but I've been over this bit a hundred times today. I don't think we're covering any new ground with this line of questioning, and I am especially busy."

"I'd like to meet with you to discuss this further."

"I don't think that will be necessary, Mr. Chandler. What could we possibly gain by that?"

Time for trump cards, he thought. "Frankly, Miss James, I don't think you're telling everything you know about this case."

"Oh?"

"You're not even telling as much as I know about this case."

Silence.

"You haven't once mentioned Jonathan Carruthers in connection with this death."

Chandler could almost see her facial expression change and Shelley cleared her throat before answering. "I'm not sure I understand what you're talking about."

"Miss James, I don't think you went to that girl's apartment for the reasons you've given. I think you went to find out about her connection with Jonathan Carruthers."

"Well, you're quite wrong about that."

"Look, if you don't know anything about a link between these two, then why haven't you asked me what it is?"

She began slowly, "Perhaps because I don't believe there is any connection."

"I think we should stop kidding around here, Miss James. I know there is a connection and I don't think it was mere coincidence that led you to that girl's apartment."

Shelley said nothing.

Chandler continued. "Look, I'm going to have a late lunch over at McQueeny's on Forty-eighth and Madison. That's only about two blocks from your building. If you'd like to join me, I'll be at my usual table by the window. If not, I'm sorry that I took up so much of your time. It's been nice talking to you." He hung up without a good-bye.

McQueeny's was one of those eateries in midtown Manhattan that strove for the old neighborhood bar look: lots of polished brass and dark mahogany. Mock Tiffany lamps over each booth gave the place a kind of movie-set authenticity. McQueeny's, however, was too plush and too polished to ever really pass for a neighborhood bar. But if any doubts remained, one had only to look at the prices on the menu to realize that this was the Big Apple and not some small-town beer-joint.

Chandler was sitting in a booth by the window at what he had come to refer to as his table. The truth of the matter was that he usually ate a late lunch and McQueeny's was relatively empty at that time. Consequently, it was a simple matter for the maître d' to hold the table for him. But the waiters and the owner knew him by name and this, plus the fact that they did hold a table for him, gave him a feeling of importance and, yes, even a feeling of belonging. He never really asked himself why he ate in the same place—at the same table—every day, but after his wife had left him, he had felt the need for some kind of domestic stability. In a way, his daily lunch routine provided just that.

Lunch was usually Chandler's biggest meal. He took only coffee for breakfast and worked on his column until well past the regular lunch hour, then ambled over to McQueeny's for lunch and a few beers. Chandler often forgot what he had eaten for lunch the day before and sometimes found himself eating the same thing two or three days in a row. On at least three or four days of every week the luncheon fare was a cheeseburger and fries, downed with two mugs of draft beer and then apple pie and coffee for dessert. Dinner was often from the frozen food section at the market. Friends sometimes remarked that this must have been a distressingly monotonous meal plan, especially to someone who had been married for fifteen years, but the truth was that Chandler's ex-wife had never been a very enthusiastic or even reasonably competent cook. Food was not terribly important to him, and if asked, as he sometimes was at boring cocktail parties, what kind of food he liked, he usually replied, "Hot." People thought he was being funny and laughed at his quick wit, but he was serious. Gourmet food meant little to him; expensive restaurants were a waste of money, and exotic dishes were something to be inspected carefully before eating.

So it was that Shelley James found him over at his window table, finishing his last bite of the cheeseburger. Chandler had seen her approach McQueeny's from across the street, but aside from a small satisfied smile, he gave no

indication that he had noticed her. Shelley entered the restaurant, looked around, then spoke softly to the maître d',
who pointed out Chandler's table. As she approached, Chandler feigned watching the activity on the street outside his
window so that Shelley stood in front of his table for a few
seconds before he turned to notice her.

Shelley wore a brown tweed jacket over a yellow silk
blouse and tan slacks. A thin gold necklace was her only
adornment. Her features were sharp and defined as though
somehow more in focus than anyone else's. She wore no
makeup. Her hair was pulled back away from her face and, as
usual, although she seemed to give her looks very little
thought, the effect was spectacular.

Chandler felt his face flush with color. With some struggle, he suppressed the urge to breathe a silent whistle.
Instead he raised his eyebrows as if observing a perfect
stranger at his front door.

"Mr. Chandler?" asked Shelley, somewhat puzzled.

"Yes?"

"I'm Shelley James."

"Oh," he said in mock surprise. "I'm sorry. I didn't
recognize you. I don't watch much TV," he lied, "and I
wasn't sure you would come." He motioned her to a seat at
the table. "Would you like a drink?"

She hesitated. "Some white wine would be fine."

He gestured to the waiter who raced to the table, anxious for a closer look at this beautiful celebrity, and when
Chandler ordered her wine he detected a new look of respect,
replacing the usual easy familiarity, in the eyes of the waiter.
In fact, as Chandler looked around McQueeny's, all of the
help and most of the patrons had stopped whatever they were
doing to watch the couple at the window. The silence was
deafening. He wanted to lean toward her and say, "My
broker is E. F. Hutton and he says . . ." He realized, of
course, that they were looking at Shelley James. Had she not
been a TV celebrity she still would have attracted this kind of
notice. Her fame merely added to the intensity of the attention.

"Does this happen all the time?" he asked, indicating the
room with a wave of his hand.

She shrugged. "Sometimes."

They sat in silence for a moment until Shelley began.
"Well, Mr. Chandler, you seem to feel that we have something to talk about."

He sipped his beer. "I'm not sure. You didn't have much to offer in the way of information on the phone."

Shelley spoke carefully and deliberately. "I'm here."

Chandler smiled, realizing they were like two boxers, cautiously circling each other in the first round of a championship fight. Both were reluctant to show what they had until the other had demonstrated his capabilities.

"What I had in mind," he said, "was some kind of information exchange. I assumed that you, having had close contact with Jonathan Carruthers, might have some idea of what is going on here. I've already revealed to you that I'm aware of a connection between Jeanette Nielsen and Jonathan Carruthers. You, on the other hand, don't seem to agree, or are unwilling to admit that you agree. If we are going to share information, you'll have to convince me that you know something of value."

"Like what?"

"For instance, there is a third person who more directly connects the girl to Carruthers."

Shelley interrupted him. "Mr. Chandler, are you trying to establish some sort of sex-scandal story here?"

He sat back in his chair, shoulders sagging in disappointment. "Is that what you think this is all about? Maybe I was wrong. Maybe you don't know anything."

Shelley sipped her wine. "I know quite a bit, Mr. Chandler," she said evenly, her blue eyes boring into him. "I just don't know what you know."

"Then tell me about the third person."

"I suppose you must mean the poor-departed Mr. Romanello," she said casually.

Chandler shrugged. "You could get that from today's newspaper. Everybody knows that her boyfriend was killed last week."

"Does everybody know that her boyfriend worked for Jonathan Carruthers?"

His eyes widened and he leaned forward again, acknowledging her information with a nod. "OK. Now we're getting somewhere. Does anyone else know about this?"

She shook her head. "Not that I'm aware of."

Her hands on the table were incredibly graceful, her fingers long and slender. It was difficult for Chandler to concentrate with her sitting within arm's reach of him. He rubbed his eyes as if to block his view of her. "Let me ask you one thing," he said, looking out into the street. He paused dramatically and turned to stare into her eyes. "Do you think Jonathan Carruthers killed himself?"

She spoke without hesitation. "I don't know."

Chandler slowly shook his head. "I don't think he did. We've got four people dead: Carruthers, Lauren Masterson, Fred Romanello, and Jeanette Nielsen. It's too much of a coincidence for four people, linked to each other, to be killed in such a short time."

"What do you know about Romanello?" she asked.

"That he was being used as an investigator—perhaps researcher would be a better word—for Carruthers."

"And Jeanette Nielsen?"

Chandler eyed her with suspicion. "I seem to be doing most of the talking here. So far you haven't given me very much. You tell *me* about the girl."

Shelley smiled. "There really isn't very much to tell. I doubt she was involved in any way in what they were looking for."

"Then why was she killed?"

"Who said she was killed? The police report says that she overdosed."

"Come on," he said impatiently. "We've got four deaths. A murder/suicide; a mindless, random 'accident'; and an overdose. We've got four people who in one way or another were involved. We have to go on the premise that these deaths are not what they seem. Otherwise we're just indulging in an exercise in futility. If Carruthers really did kill himself and that girl, if Jeanette Nielsen really did OD, if Romanello really was the victim of some random selection by a maniac, then what do we have?" Without waiting, he answered his own question. "Other than a grotesque series of coincidences, we've got nothing, absolutely nothing."

"It's possible that that is what happened," she said calmly. "Maybe it is just, as you put it, a grotesque series of coincidences."

Chandler slumped back in his chair with a long sigh of exasperation. He watched Shelley as she sipped her wine. She was distractingly beautiful and he found himself thinking that the curve of her nose was probably as absolutely perfect as the curve of a nose could be. He could easily have spent the rest of the hour just looking at her, but he forced himself to continue.

"New York is a terrific place to eliminate a group of people. Murder happens so often here it's commonplace. The police don't attach any particular significance to a single killing, and they certainly don't connect one killing with another." He saw that she was watching him with some skepticism. He tried to speak as calmly as he could. "Look, I'm not one of these people who believes in the conspiracy theory of history. I mean, I really believe that Oswald and Sirhan and Ray were just crazy people who acted on their own imbecilic impulses. I don't think there was a conspiracy of rightists, leftists, industrialists, bureaucrats, or anyone else involved in those deaths. But those were isolated assassinations involving nationally famous people; here, with the exception of Carruthers, these people are nobodies."

"Then why do you think they were killed?"

"Because they knew something. I think someone is trying to prevent the release of whatever information Carruthers and Romanello were collecting."

"What about the women?"

Chandler shook his head in frustration. "I don't know. I don't think Jeanette Nielsen really knew anything. She may have been eliminated just to make sure. I can't be positive about that."

"And what about the girl with Carruthers?"

"Lauren Masterson? As far as anyone has been able to determine, Carruthers never met that girl before the night he is supposed to have killed her. I think she was just unlucky enough to be there on the night somebody decided to get rid of him." He gestured with his palms upward. "Wrong place at the wrong time."

Shelley nodded in agreement. What Chandler had said had struck a responsive chord. She had never bought the story of Jonathan Carruthers's death. It hadn't made sense to her. She knew Jonathan too well to believe he could ever commit such an act. He was too self-assured, too egomaniacal, too damn selfish to ever consider killing himself.

Chandler went on. He was getting caught up in his story. "I think that Carruthers was working on something—a news story, perhaps an exposé of some kind—and Fred Romanello was hired to help him gather whatever information he needed. On the morning they both died, Romanello was on his way to meet Carruthers, carrying a briefcase full of papers about this story. I know that much is true because

Jeanette Nielsen told me so. After Romanello's death, that briefcase and whatever information it contained disappeared."

For the first time, Shelley's eyes were alive with interest. Chandler had articulated her own unspoken doubts and she felt a growing sense of excitement that perhaps her reaction to this story had been right all along. She had been too close to it to make a truly objective judgment, but Chandler had given form to what she had tried to dismiss as paranoia.

Her mouth formed a smile as she leaned forward. "Mr. Chandler, I think we're onto something here."

"We?" he said with a sarcastic chuckle. "So far you haven't said very much. You haven't told me anything I don't know. You haven't even told me why you went to see Jeanette Nielsen."

She took a deep breath. "You're right. I went to see Jeanette Nielsen because I discovered that Fred Romanello and Jonathan had been working together. I wanted to find out what they had been working on."

Chandler slapped the table with his palm. "I knew it. I think there's a huge story here." He looked around the restaurant and then lowered his voice. "I took a chance on you because I was sure you knew something. You're closer to the Carruthers end of it than I am. You knew him well. At least, that's what I'm told."

Shelley raised her eyebrows at this last remark, but there was no malice in his expression.

Without noticing her look, he went on, "I'm hoping that you can provide some clue as to what they were working on. If we knew that, we would probably know who had them killed."

She shook her head. "I can only tell you that you're right about the story angle. Jonathan was working on something, something that drove him like a crazy person over the last month of his life. It was an absolute compulsion. He acted like a man possessed. That's why many people believe the suicide story."

"But you know different."

She smiled sadly. "Yes. He confided in me when I asked him if everything was all right. He told me he was working on something that would establish his credentials as a legitimate newsman. It was a story he described as 'dynamite.' Something that would 'knock the world on its ear.'"

"The world?"

"Yes," she nodded emphatically. "Those were his words. He felt it was that big."

"But he never told you what it was?"

"He offered to. He wanted us to get back together again." She paused for a moment, selecting her words with care. "We had lived together for a while; he wanted me to move back with him, said we could work together on the story."

"Too bad," Chandler said, shaking his head. "If you had gone back to him, we'd know the answer to all this."

Her face was devoid of expression. "If I had gone back, Mr. Chandler, I probably would have been the young lady killed in his bed." She spoke in a calm, deliberate tone but the effort was obvious.

Chandler dropped his eyes from hers. He knew this was not the first time this thought had occurred to her. "I'm sorry," he mumbled. "I wasn't thinking."

For a moment they sat in silence, the thought between them like an unexploded bomb that neither wanted to touch. Finally, Shelley said, "Do we go to the police?"

"We could," he said tentatively. "What do you think?"

She smiled. "I think we're sitting on one hell of a story here—Jonathan said it was the biggest story since the Kennedy assassination—and I'm not about to turn it over to every reporter in town." She extended her hand across the table. "Mark," she said, using his given name for the first time, "I think we're going to have to work together on this one."

Chandler took her hand and was surprised by the strength of her handshake. "Shelley, you've got yourself a partner. Where do we begin?"

"If we can get into Jonathan's apartment, I might be able to find out what he was working on."

"Do you think it's in there?"

She nodded. "I spoke with him just two days before he died. He told me that he was working on a manuscript in his apartment. I've already been through his office at the studio and found nothing, so I'm sure his work must still be at his home." She fumbled in her pocketbook, finally producing a key. "I have the key to his apartment," she said, displaying it with what Chandler thought was a suggestive smile, "but the apartment has been sealed by the police. You can't get near the place."

"Wait a minute! If what we are looking for is in the

apartment, don't you think the police would have already found it?"

"Would they have any reason to look through a stack of papers sitting on his desk?"

He was doubtful. "Maybe. Maybe not."

Shelley's eyes narrowed and suddenly he could see the steel in her. "Look, I know that manuscript was there. The police haven't found it or we'd have heard something about it by now. So how do we get into that apartment?"

"I can arrange it," said Chandler quietly.

"How?"

He smiled. "I'll ask the police to let us in."

She sat back in her chair. "You seem to be a rather resourceful person, Mr. Chandler." As she sat back, her tweed jacket fell open and Chandler was painfully aware that beneath her silk blouse she was not wearing a bra.

"A minute ago you were calling me Mark."

She nodded. "Mark."

He fought to keep his eyes level with hers, but watching her was giving him a gnawing ache in the pit of his stomach. "I do have a few connections that I can count on in this town." He felt like a bumbling schoolboy.

She smiled, apparently oblivious to the effect she was having on him. "When can we do it?"

"I'll try for tonight. When can you be free?"

"I've got my eleven o'clock show to do. Any time after that."

"OK," he nodded. "I'll try to set it up for then."

Shelley stood up. "Come to the studio. We can leave right after the broadcast."

They said good-bye and Chandler, along with everyone else in the restaurant, watched her leave. When she reached the door she turned and looked back at him. "Tonight," she mouthed silently, gave him a conspiratorial wink, and then was through the door and gone.

Chandler returned to his beer aware that every man in the restaurant was watching him, envying him, perhaps even hating him a little. It felt good. They didn't have to know that tonight was a working arrangement and not what they were all so sure it was. He looked up with a small, confident grin, to find that no one seemed to be watching him. Shelley James was gone; the show was over.

He nursed his beer for some time, remembering how

she had looked as she'd sat just a few feet away. He realized that behind that incredibly beautiful face was a tough, hard-headed, competent news reporter. He was sure that her looks had misled a lot of people. Many, dazzled by her beauty, would probably tell her things that they would never tell anyone else. With a start he realized that he had just done the same. He had told her everything he knew while she had told him hardly anything. She had confirmed the fact that Carruthers was working on an important story, but he had already suspected that.

Chandler shook his head, more bemused than angry that he had fallen victim to her looks like a hundred unsuspecting politicians who had bared their souls to this dazzling woman. He knew what they had all been thinking: Anyone this beautiful must have been given the job because of her looks. She could not possibly be a real threat. That's what they thought until she lowered the boom. Even when one was aware of her capabilities it was difficult to get past the barrier of her looks. Those eyes invited you to intimacy, invited you to share your secrets. Chandler wondered if the open jacket was part of the routine.

He almost slapped a palm to his forehead. I told her everything, he thought. How can I be sure she won't release the story herself and just leave me out in the cold?

He reached for his wallet to pay his check and in his inside jacket pocket felt the notebook. The notebook! He grinned. He had forgotten about Fred Romanello's notebook and the list of names. Maybe he had been a little too dazzled by her, but he had held something back.

He sighed and slouched back in his chair, distractedly watching the passersby on the street. At least, he thought, I've still got something left. At least I didn't tell her about the list. That will just be my little secret until I can find out what the lady really knows about all of this.

Chapter 10

Inspector Brian Downey of the New York Detectives Bureau sat behind his desk listening to the voice on the telephone while making faces at Mark Chandler, opposite him. Every few seconds he would grunt some kind of reply into the receiver and jot down a note on a small pad. After a few minutes he put a hand over the mouthpiece and said with a sigh, "D.A.'s office—this could take forever."

Chandler smiled and shrugged. There was not much else he could do.

Downey was almost fifty and was almost a pound overweight for every year he had lived. Beneath a thinning thatch of hair his face sported a red, beefy, blue-veined nose that was testimony to too many trips to the bar rail. When Downey was off duty, his face was like soft, pliable putty. But on duty the putty was hard, set into solid granite.

Right now the face was hard as he spoke into the phone. "How the hell was he supposed to have a lawyer present when he confessed?" he snapped, his face turning crimson to match his nose. "When my men broke the door down he was standing with the gun in his hand. He's lucky they didn't pump ten rounds into him right then. The guy's sister told the officers that he had shot his wife . . ." He listened for a moment. "Then he admitted that he did it. What were they supposed to do, put their fingers in their ears?"

Downey looked at Chandler. He was shaking his head in disgust. "Look. Tell Legal Aid that if that's what they want, they'd better put a lawyer in every apartment in Manhattan. What should my men say, 'Don't shoot; your lawyer's on his way'? . . . I don't think you can say we prejudiced the case, but if we did, that's too bad. . . . We just arrest them; your job is to put them away. . . . Yeah, sure. Later."

Downey slammed down the receiver. "The world's going

crazy, Chandler. Sometimes I think we'd all better head for the suburbs."

Chandler laughed. "What would you do in the suburbs, Downey?"

Downey shrugged. "Christ. I don't know."

Chandler and Downey were friends who shared a few drinks and caught a few ballgames together three or four times each year. Like many newspapermen, Chandler found that it made good sense to cultivate the friendship of a policeman or two. He did have several friends in police precincts throughout the city, but Downey was not that kind of friend. There was a genuine camaraderie between the two that transcended the usual professional relationship. Downey too was divorced, and that gave the two men additional reason to be close.

"My son told me to thank you for the tickets, Mark," Downey said, changing the subject. "It was a really great game."

Chandler shrugged and smiled as though it were nothing, even though he had wanted to see the Giants and Cowboys himself. "Glad you enjoyed it."

Downey looked away as if embarrassed. "I want to thank you too," he said. "I'm not as close to the boy as I'd like to be. He looked at Chandler. "You know how it is."

Chandler nodded. He did indeed know how it was.

"The tickets give me a little status with the kid, y'know, and it's a great way to spend some time with him." Downey was quiet for a moment, and his beefy face was sober as he pondered his fate. Just as quickly the smile was back and the mass of flesh moved upward. "I should have listened to my mother," he said, laughing. " 'Marry an Irish girl,' she said. 'They won't leave you no matter what you do to them.' " He shook his head as he remembered. "My mom knew me better'n anybody."

"I've got two tickets for the Eagles next week," Chandler said. "I don't think I can make it. I have to be out of town. Maybe your boy would like to see that game too."

Downey beamed. "He sure would. The kid is Giants crazy." He looked at his hands, fingers spread. "I don't know why, though. They haven't had a decent team since . . . since Tittle." He raised his eyes to Chandler's. "Back in . . . Christ, when was it?"

Chandler shook his head. "Long time ago."

Downey nodded, his eyes misting over a moment as though remembering fallen kings and lost battles. "Long time ago," he repeated. He clasped his hands together in front of him on his desk. "Christ," he said. "Everything makes me feel old."

They both laughed self-consciously at his admission.

Downey changed the subject. "How'd you make out with Colandro?"

"He was very helpful, but there just isn't anything there. I think I got a bum lead on that one." He hated lying to Downey.

The detective nodded. "So what can I do for you?"

"Brian," said Chandler hesitantly, "this one's a little touchy."

Downey responded with a shrug, and when Chandler wavered he said, "So? Go ahead. Ask."

Chandler plunged in. "I need to get into Jonathan Carruthers's apartment."

His eyes narrowed and Downey said nothing for a brief moment. "Why?" he asked simply.

Chandler was prepared. He looked down at the floor sheepishly. "I've got myself this new girl friend"—he looked up quickly to catch Downey's reaction—"and it seems that she went out a few times with Carruthers. She tells me that she left something in his apartment and would like to get it back."

"All the valuables—money, jewelry, and the like—are being held over at Properties. She'd have to submit a claim form. . . ."

"It's nothing like that," interrupted Chandler. "Nothing valuable." He was deliberately vague. "It's just something personal. She'd rather not have it fall into the wrong hands."

"Oh," said Downey with a knowing smile.

"When do you want to get in?"

"Tonight. Midnight."

Downey sighed. "We've got a uniform on the door round-the-clock. I'll find something for him to do for an hour. You better be out of there by one."

"No problem, Brian. Thanks." Chandler stood up.

Downey got up and moved with him to the door. "Let's get together for a drink one of these days. We haven't been sloshed together in a long time." He gave a smile that radiated across his beefy face. "You can tell me about your new girl friend."

Chandler smiled. "Sounds good, Brian. Let's do it soon."

Downey opened the door and just as Chandler turned to leave the policeman said, "Top drawer, right-hand side of the bedroom dresser."

Chandler looked puzzled.

Downey nodded knowingly. "What you and your girl friend are looking for? It's in the top drawer, right-hand side of the bedroom dresser."

Downey closed the office door, leaving Chandler in a state of bewilderment.

Chapter 11

It was after midnight when Shelley and Chandler were able to get away from the WNBC studios. They took a taxi to Carruthers's building, the driver concentrating more on watching Shelley in the rearview mirror than on driving.

"You that lady on TV?" he asked, with words that actually sounded like, "Youdatlayonteevee?"

"Yes," said Shelley. "I'm that lady on TV."

"Whatch you alla time."

"I'm so glad to hear that," Shelley said, icicles dripping from every word.

The driver was undeterred. "Dat was sump'n how you beat da cops to dat dead chick."

"All in a day's work."

That was basically how it went for the remainder of the brief trip to Carruthers's building.

After escaping from the cab, they went directly into the building through plate glass doors that left them in a small enclosure with mailboxes and an intercom system. A second set of doors barred their way into a larger foyer.

With a smile, Shelley produced a key and they entered the larger area. The foyer was luxuriously appointed: gold carpeting, leather sofas, and an excess of greenery everywhere.

Chandler was about to say something about the room, but Shelley silenced him with a finger to her lips and a thumb motion in the direction of a door to the rear of the foyer.

"Doorman," she whispered and put her finger back to her lips again.

Chandler shrugged and followed Shelley to the elevator.

They stepped out on the sixteenth floor and, with Shelley still leading, made their way down a plushly carpeted hall to Carruthers's apartment. At the door, Chandler stepped forward and, ignoring the posted signs which said: Police Crime Search Area—Keep Away, used his key on the police lockbox.

The door to Jonathan Carruthers's apartment opened easily and Mark Chandler and Shelley James slipped quickly inside. Chandler closed the door quietly behind them and Shelley flicked on the light switch. They stood silent for a moment, aware that they were in the presence of death. Something terrible had happened in this room and they could both feel it.

Finally Chandler spoke. "Where is the room where he did his work?" he said, softly interrupting Shelley's reverie.

She pointed to a door to the left, but when Chandler took her arm to move in that direction she resisted. She seemed rooted to the spot. His eyes questioned her, and finally, after taking a deep breath, she led the way.

Shelley opened the door and without stepping across the threshold, reached around the door frame to turn on the light. A lamp by a deep leather chair illuminated a small room, which was dominated by a large desk in front of the window.

The desk top was clear.

"It's not there," said Shelley. "The other day he told me it was sitting right on his desk."

Stepping into the room, Chandler said, "Check the drawers. Maybe he put it away."

They did so, each opening and closing the drawers on opposite sides of the desk. Shelley opened the long middle drawer, lifting and peeking under the folders.

She shook her head. "Nothing."

"You're sure you searched his office at the studio?"

"Yes, I'm sure," she said sharply, giving him a look of annoyance.

Chandler ignored her petulant manner. "Maybe he put it somewhere else in the apartment."

Shelley shook her head doubtfully.

"Well, at least let's look around," he said, leading her back into the living room.

They stood without speaking, Shelley's eyes down to the floor, Chandler's eyes darting around the room.

"Check the bedroom," he said, moving toward the bookcase against the wall. "I'm going to look behind these books."

Shelley did not move. Chandler reached the bookcase and was in the process of feeling behind the bottom row when he noticed she was still there.

"Aren't you going to check the bedroom?"

She shook her head rapidly. "I can't go in there."

"Why not?" he started to ask. "OK, I'll check the bedroom. You look behind the bookshelves."

The bedroom was large and sparsely furnitured. It contained only a platform bed with built-in night tables and a large dresser next to the door.

The bed was rumpled, a huge brown stain covering almost the entire pillow and the upper third of the sheet. Chandler wrinkled his nose in distaste and began his search. He went through the closets and night tables, finding nothing resembling the manuscript that Shelley had described.

He then moved to the dresser, remembering Downey's parting words, and opened the top drawer on the right-hand side. Inside he found a Polaroid camera and a stack of pictures. He could not resist looking, and was amazed to find a procession of photographs of nude young women in various poses. Most of the pictures had been taken in this room. He wondered if Shelley James's picture was here.

Shelley's voice startled him. "Did you find anything?"

Quickly he replaced the photos in the drawer. "No, nothing," he said guiltily.

Shelley stood outside the door, just out of view. "Is it terrible in there?"

Chandler looked at the bloodstained bed. "Not too bad. You can come in."

"No, I'd rather not. There's something I want you to see out here."

Chandler joined Shelley in the living room where she stood facing the bookcase.

"Did you find anything there?" he asked.

"No, but look at the bookcase. Do you notice anything unusual?"

He looked for a moment then shook his head.

"Look carefully," she said. "Tell me what you see."

He sighed. "OK, I see a bookcase crammed with books from top to bottom."

"Yes. Go on."

"So crammed, in fact, that except for one shelf where there is a gap and a trophy, it looks like it would be difficult to remove a book."

"Yes. Go on."

Chandler looked at Shelley with a crooked smile. "Look, Miss Marple, if you've discovered something in that bookcase, you'd better tell me because I've told you as much as I can see."

"Look at the books!" He did and she continued. "They're all about show business: Movie stars, movies, television, TV stars, old TV shows."

"Not all," said Chandler, moving closer so that he could read the titles. "This row is different. These seem to be medical texts of some kind."

"Exactly."

"Exactly what?"

"This must be what his story was about. He must have been doing some kind of medical exposé."

Chandler was doubtful. "What kind of medical exposé could be bigger than the Kennedy assassination?" He looked at some of the titles. "I can't even tell what this stuff is about. It all looks pretty technical." He turned back to face Shelley. "Maybe he just liked this stuff. Maybe it relaxed him to read medical texts. You'd be surprised at what some people do for recreation." He was thinking of the stack of photos in the bedroom.

"I lived with this guy for three months. I never saw him read a book."

Chandler grinned suggestively. "Maybe with you around, Shelley, he didn't have time for reading."

She gave him a cold look that wiped the smile from his face. "He never read any of these books. He ordered them by the yard."

Chandler looked puzzled.

"He measured his bookshelves and ordered enough books to fill them." She laughed. "It used to be a joke between us.

He had so many books on a shelf that you couldn't get them out. The only thing he was interested in was show business, but he didn't even read about that. He just owned the books."

"What does all this prove, Shelley?"

She slumped into a chair. "I don't know. When I lived here, *all* the books were about show business. Now there is a shelf of medical texts." She paused to let him follow her.

"OK. So suddenly he takes an interest in the practice of medicine."

"There's something else, too," she said. "Look at that shelf with the medical texts. . . ."

He did and shrugged. "So?"

"It's the only shelf that isn't packed with books. Not only that, but there's a gap in the middle."

"Maybe he took a book out of there."

"Did you find a book around here?"

"No."

She bit her lower lip and her eyes darted around the room. "Why didn't he just close up the gap between the books? All he had to do was move the bookend."

"Shelley," Chandler said in exasperation, "no one killed him for that book."

She gave no sign that she'd heard him. "I'd love to know the name of that book."

"Maybe it was overdue at the library and they sent a hit man to get it back."

Her face flushed in irritation as she snapped at him. "You can be a real pain in the ass, you know that? I listen to all your ideas about this thing and I'm willing to give you the benefit of the doubt. I have one suggestion and you treat it as a joke. I'm not sure we can work together on this."

"All I meant was . . ."

"I'm not saying somebody killed him for the book. I'm just saying that something is out of place here. I knew Jonathan better than anyone else did." She shot him a defiant glare. "And I'm telling you there is something about those books that is out of character for him. . . ."

"Maybe there was a book there, maybe there wasn't. But even if there is a missing book, the chances are, it doesn't mean anything."

Again, she didn't seem to be listening. She spoke almost to herself. "The bookstore might be able to get me a list of the books he ordered. I can check it against the list of the books in the bookcase and then I'd know which one is missing."

"You mean *we* can check it, don't you? We still have a working partnership here, don't we?"

She stared at him, her eyes suggesting nothing. Finally she smiled weakly, a smile that did not represent much confidence in their working relationship. She motioned with her head toward the books. "Make a list of them."

Chandler did not move. He eyed her carefully for what seemed like a long time. Both knew that this was a critical moment. They had had a brief falling-out and now part of the reconciliation was a struggle for primacy. Chandler was instinctively aware that she had decided to be the dominant partner in the relationship and just as instinctively he rebelled against the idea.

When he spoke his voice was very deliberate. "Who first caught on to the connection between Romanello and Carruthers?"

She seemed puzzled. "You did."

"Who actually talked to Jeanette Nielsen?"

She was beginning to get his drift. "You did," she said, her lips set in a hard line.

"Who got us into this apartment?"

She glared at him without answering.

He went on. "What have you brought to this story?"

Shelley didn't answer, so he continued. "I'll tell you what. You had the idea about a manuscript that is nowhere to be found. Now you've got an idea about a mysterious book that may or may not be missing."

She was silent, her face locked in anger.

"In other words," he said, "you haven't brought very much to this story. Without me you've got a big zero."

"Meaning?"

"Meaning we can help each other. But don't get the wrong idea. You need me more than I need you."

Shelley pulled herself erect, chin up. She really was beautiful, he thought.

"I'm not so sure how much I need you," she said.

Chandler smiled like a man holding a straight flush. "Then why did you bother to meet me at McQueeny's today?"

She shrugged. "I was interested in what you had to say. Why are you telling me all this?"

"Because I want you to make your own damn list of books."

"Talk about chauvinism," she said with a short, derisive laugh. "You've been ordering me around since we got here. Go do this. Now do that. But that's fine, right? That's the way it's supposed to be. Big boss man speak, woman obey. Right?" She wasn't laughing anymore.

"We'd better get out of here. If we're going to have an argument, someone might call the cops."

"We're not going to have an argument," she said quietly, "and I want to get my 'damn list' before I go. You might not think it's important, but I do."

Chandler shook his head. "Wait a minute," he said and disappeared into the bedroom. He returned a moment later with the Polaroid camera.

"Where did you find that?"

"It seems that Carruthers liked to take pictures of his bedroom encounters. We can use it to take a picture of the bookshelf. It'll save time. We've got to get out of here; we've been here too long already."

"Will it take pictures that close?" she asked as he moved to the bookcase.

He aimed at the books. "Sure. It's one of those sonar jobs that focuses itself." He snapped one picture and then a few seconds later snapped another. "One each," he said, smiling grimly. "Just in case we're not working together anymore."

Chandler turned to face her but Shelley was looking toward the bedroom. "Does he have pictures of lots of women in there?" she asked, without looking at him.

"Yes."

Her head moved only slightly. "What happens if the police find them?"

"I'm sure they've already found them."

"Will their existence ever be revealed to the public?"

"It's hard to say. Sometimes that kind of thing has a way of getting out."

"Let's destroy them," she said. "I wouldn't want people to remember him for stuff like that. I wouldn't want his family to find out about it."

"I don't think we can destroy evidence. The police know it's here and they'd soon know that we've been here. What could anyone say, anyway? That Carruthers liked sex? Maybe he was a little kinky."

Shelley said nothing. She didn't look at him; her eyes were still on the bedroom door.

Chandler coughed. "If, however, you wanted to look through the pictures and . . . remove any that you . . . uh . . . personally . . . would be reluctant to have revealed, I think that we could take that chance."

Shelley shook her head, and then it dawned on her what Chandler was trying to say. She tilted her head to the side. "Do you think that any of those pictures are of me?"

"I didn't say that."

"But you think that that's what I'm worried about?"

He raised his hands in protest. "I don't know what you're worried about."

"Jonathan might have taken snapshots of all the chippies he brought to his bed, but he never took any pictures of me. You got that straight, Chandler?"

He nodded somewhat meekly.

"I was concerned that newspapers might sensationalize something like this if they got a hold of it. Some of the gossip rags would have a field day. Your paper, of course, would never do anything like that," she said.

"OK, OK; I apologize. I was just trying to be helpful."

Now that she had him on the defensive, she was reluctant to let it go. "Wasn't it your paper that said the mayor was a closet homo?"

"I said I was sorry. Lighten up, huh?"

Shelley took the developed prints from his hand and looked at them closely. The book titles were clearly visible. She handed Chandler one of the copies. "Here, you might need this."

He started to protest but she turned away. "Put that damn camera away," she said, "and let's get the hell out of here."

This time he did not protest her command.

Chapter 12

Shelley James stood outside, admiring for a moment the scholarly ambience of Milbourne's Bookstore on East Eighty-fifth Street. The name of the proprietor was printed in large gold-leaf lettering on the front window and again in smaller letters on the plate glass insert on the heavy, oak door. Rather than the typical bookstore pyramid of current best-sellers, Milbourne's window displayed only a complete set of Dickens, which stood in a simple bookshelf row as if to say that this was how books were meant to be displayed. Next to the books was a small, discreet sign: First Edition, Enquire Within.

Milbourne's Bookstore was only two blocks away from Jonathan Carruthers's apartment building and was the third bookstore that Shelley had visited that morning. As she entered, a small bell above the door announced her arrival and the proprietor looked up with a polite smile from the book he was reading. Anthony Milbourne was in his late sixties, tall, slim, and aristocratic in bearing. There were those who were certain that he had once owned and operated a bookstore in his native London before moving to New York. In fact, he was born and raised in Queens.

"Good morning," he said in the clipped tone that was neither London nor New York. The antique railroad station house clock that hung on the wall showed that it was almost 10:30. "My name is Anthony Milbourne and I hope I can be of some service."

Shelley, mesmerized by the place, smiled a vague greeting. It was like a visit to another era. The ceilings were high and ornately sculpted with baroque paneling. The walls were lined with books and tall ladders to enable the staff to reach those volumes perched on the shelves near the ceiling.

"I don't think you've been here before," said Milbourne,

noting Shelley's neck-straining glances. "I would not have forgotten such a beautiful young lady."

Usually that kind of remark made Shelley wary, but coming from Milbourne she somehow felt that she could accept the compliment in the spirit in which it was given. "Thank you sir," she said. "This is certainly an interesting bookstore you have here."

Milbourne smiled and nodded. "I'm afraid we find it difficult to compete with some of the more modern stores, so we have stopped trying. I sell classics, first editions, and fine books of all descriptions. I also buy and sell collections."

"No best-sellers, no paperbacks."

"Of course." He pointed to the rear of the store. "Best-sellers on the tables, paperbacks on the shelves. Upstairs we have more of the same, as well as the usual remainders and sale items." Milbourne seemed almost embarrassed by this revelation. "It helps pay the rent," he offered as an apparent apology. Then the smile returned to his narrow face, spreading deep wrinkles everywhere. "May I help you with anything in particular?"

"Actually, I'm looking for information about a specific book and hoped you might be able to help me."

Milbourne tapped a finger to his temple. "My dear, you've come to the right place. Many scholars come here for information about works of reference or literature, and I am proud to say that I am often able to provide some assistance. What is the name of this particular book?"

Shelley hesitated. "I don't really know."

Milbourne made a face, then smiled politely. "That will make the search somewhat more difficult."

"Perhaps I should explain."

Milbourne nodded patiently.

"I am—or was—a friend of Jonathan Carruthers, and I am trying to find the bookstore where he purchased his books." What Shelley didn't say was that Carruthers had once described the bookstore and its proprietor as dusty old relics. "From a description he once gave me, I'd say that this might be the place. Unless I'm wrong . . ."

"Say no more, my dear," said Milbourne, his eyes alive with pleasure. "This is indeed the place you seek. I was responsible—if responsible is the correct word—for Mr. Carruthers's collection."

Shelley heaved a sigh of relief. "Can you tell me anything about the collection? His taste in books, perhaps?" She was deliberately unrevealing.

"His taste was rather parochial," Milbourne said tactfully. "As you are probably aware, most of his books were about his own profession. I provided, at his request, of course, a small library of works about motion pictures and television. Many of those works, I am embarrassed to say, are merely picture albums about those who have worked in those media, although I did manage to provide him with several scholarly works about the art of the motion picture. As I recall, one or two of those were reasonably valuable, and if your inquiry is in regard to the value of his collection, I would be glad to quote current prices for those works. Unfortunately, most of his books are worth very little. As a collection, it could have been put together from the special sale racks at any bookstore. Many are "remainders," or even special printings that were never meant to sell for their cover price."

Although he struggled to control the gesture, Milbourne was unable to prevent a slight wrinkling of his nose, as if he detected a faintly foul odor. "Mr. Carruthers seemed more interested in filling space than in providing a safe haven for works of literature."

"I'm not really interested in the value of his collection," Shelley said. "What I am interested in is the sudden change in his"—she didn't want to say taste—"interests?"

"You mean about the medical texts?"

"Yes," said Shelley, her excitement growing.

"Rather strange, I thought. But then I just assumed that he was doing some research for a segment on his news broadcast. It all seemed out of character for a man of his—interests, I think, was the word you used." Milbourne obviously didn't want to say taste either.

"Can you tell me anything about those books?"

Milbourne thought for a moment. "Mr. Carruthers gave me a list of titles one day and asked if I could provide them. They were not, of course, the kind of books I usually carry, but I told him I would try. I was able to acquire most of them for him."

"You said he gave you a list?"

"Yes."

"Do you still have that list?"

Milbourne shook his head. "I returned Mr. Carruthers's list when I delivered his books."

Shelley's heart sank. Her disappointment showed.

Anxious to help, Milbourne hurried on. "I don't have Mr. Carruthers's original list, but I do have my own list of those books that I was able to acquire—if that is any help to you."

Shelley's smile lit the room. "That is exactly what I need." She took a list of titles from her coat pocket. "I would like to check this list against your list. What I am looking for is a book that is on your list, but not on mine."

If Milbourne wondered why she needed this information, he was too polite to ask. "Please come with me," he said and led Shelley to a small office in the rear of the bookstore. The office contained a desk, a chair, three old-fashioned wood file cabinets and, across the rear wall, a row of glass-encased bookcases. Most of the books in these cases were leather bound, many with gold leaf titles.

Milbourne saw Shelley's eyes widen in admiration when she saw the books. He smiled. "I keep my favorites in here. Some of them, as you might imagine, are quite valuable. They're for sale, of course, but I hate to part with them. It's like sending a friend to live with someone else." He touched the glass gently with his fingertips as if he might draw sustenance from the treasures within.

"There's nothing like a fine old book," he said, peering through the glass. "The craft of the bookbinder, the skill of the printer, and the genius of the author." His smile was accompanied by a small sigh. "A book is all of our civilization, all of our history, all of our knowledge, wrapped up in one small package."

He turned back to face Shelley. "Pardon me. I do tend to run on and I'm sure you have business to attend to."

"That's quite all right. I admire your appreciation for your profession. As a matter-of-fact, someday I'd like to interview you for my television show."

"You're in television too?" Milbourne shook his head. "I'm embarrassed to say that I don't watch very much television." He smiled shyly. "I read a lot."

"I'm on at eleven o'clock every night."

"Oh, my gracious. I'm in bed by that time. But I will make a special effort to watch your show. You are a remarkably lovely young woman." Milbourne turned his attention to one of his file cabinets. "Let me see if I can find that information for you."

"Perhaps you could tell me something about Carruthers's latest acquisitions," said Shelley as Milbourne rummaged through his file.

"You mean the medical texts?" he asked, looking back over his shoulder.

"Yes."

He paused over the open file drawer. "It's not really my area of expertise, of course—I deal primarily in classic literature—but from what I could gather from the titles of the works, most of them seemed to be about the brain and the nervous system."

"The brain—the human brain?"

Milbourne shrugged. "Have you ever tried to ascertain the subject matter of a medical text by reading the title? Most of the titles are longer than Pound's poetry . . . and just as vague."

Shelley nodded. "Yes. I have the list here, and I still don't know what the books are about."

With a grunt of agreement Milbourne returned to his search. "Here we are," he said, extracting a manila folder with Carruthers's name written across the top in a fine, neat hand. "I must organize my filing system," he said softly to himself, before removing a single sheet of paper from the folder and handing it to Shelley. "This, I believe, is what you are looking for."

Shelley took the paper and saw that it contained, in addition to Carruthers's name and address, a list of books which had been ordered in his name. After every title but the last, there was a small red checkmark and a date.

As Shelley ran her eyes down the list, Milbourne said, "You'll notice that most of the books in Mr. Carruthers's collection are not on this list. I was able to provide many of the entertainment volumes he required without special ordering; as I said, most of them could be found on the discount tables at any large bookstore. Only those books requiring a special order appear on the list. Consequently, you'll see only a few of the movie and television books. I spent a considerable amount of time finding some of the books on the early days of filmmaking." He shook his head. "I don't think Mr. Carruthers cared much one way or the other, but I wanted to add a little value to his collection. After all, he did pay me quite well to put it together."

"I'm sure he appreciated your efforts, Mr. Milbourne," Shelley said. "He was quite proud of the volumes you acquired for him."

Milbourne seemed gladdened by this white lie and went on. "All of the medical texts are on the list, as I had to have them specially ordered."

"What are the checkmarks and the dates?"

"When I receive a book that I have ordered, I place a checkmark after the title. The date is the date the book is picked up by the customer or delivered by me."

"I notice the last title has no checkmark."

Milbourne smiled sadly. "No; Mr. Carruthers ordered that one only a day or two before his death. It has not yet arrived."

Shelley compared her list with that which Milbourne had given her. The titles were long and replete with medical terminology. She turned to Milbourne, who stood quietly like a butler in an English movie. "Perhaps you could help me," she said, and he moved forward obediently, anxious to be of assistance. "I really hate to bother you," Shelley went on. "I've taken up so much of your time already."

Milbourne waved aside her protests. "I'm glad to be of help." He glanced to the door. "If the bell rings, I'll have to go back outside, but until then I am at your disposal."

Shelley gave him her best smile—the one that had resulted in broken hearts in at least four states—and Anthony Milbourne was visibly moved.

"I'm going to watch that show of yours tonight," he said. "What station is it on?"

Shelley laughed. "Channel Four. Eleven to eleven-thirty." She gave him back his list. "Now here's what I'd like to do. I'll read the titles on my list, and I'd like you to check them off on your list. Then we can see what's left. OK?"

"Of course," he said, moving to his desk. He sat down, found a pencil, and then looked up at her. "Proceed."

With Milbourne seated, pencil poised, Shelley began reading the titles on her list. Even with her experience in reading text on the air, which often contained unpronounceable names from the far corners of the globe, Shelley found herself stumbling over the terminology in a few of the titles. "These are really something!" she said.

"Yes," said Milbourne as he checked off a particularly troublesome title. "You can always tell the strength of a profession by how clearly it communicates its ideas to the general public."

They both had a good laugh at that and continued working down the list until finally Shelley said, "That's it. What's left?"

Milbourne handed her his list. Other than the last, undelivered book, only one other book had not been checked off in Milbourne's meticulous penmanship. Shelley copied the title and author's name onto her own list. As she copied, she read the title out loud. *"The Neuroscientific Significance of Chemical Imbalance in the Nature and Function of the Human Brain."*

As strange as it seemed, Shelley felt that this was not the first time she had seen this title. She let her eyes run down Milbourne's list to the most recently ordered book. The titles were the same.

Her eyes narrowed in puzzlement. "This book is the same as the one ordered last week." She handed the list to Milbourne. "Why would he order two of the same book?"

Milbourne studied the list and scratched the tip of his nose before answering. "As I recall, he said he was going to give the first copy to someone—a friend, I think."

Shelley's eyes narrowed and she shook her head slowly as she read the title again. "Who would you give this to?"

Milbourne remembered, his face brightening with the pleasure of being able to recall such an insignificant detail. "A young friend," he said. Those were his exact words—'a young friend.' "

The puzzled look was still on Shelley's face. "A strange gift to give someone, don't you think?"

Milbourne took exception. "If a person is interested in the subject matter, no book is a strange gift. I've had people order much more unusual books as gifts. Yes; I can assure you of that."

Shelley shook her head, her disbelief turning to a reluctant acceptance. So that was it. That was why the book was missing. Carruthers had given it to someone as a gift. Her big clue had turned out to be nothing more than a ribbon-wrapped surprise. She said, "He must have been dating a nurse with delusions of grandeur," in an attempt to lighten her spirits, but she felt defeated.

She had been sure there was some significance to the missing book, sure that this had been the clue that would reveal the mystery of Carruthers's death. This is what it had come to: nothing! She had never considered the obvious: The book was missing because he had given it away!

Chandler had been right. It was nothing. He had called her Miss Marple. He was right again. She had tried to turn Carruthers's death into an Agatha Christie mystery and her attempt had left her with pie on her face. What would she call it? The Case of the Missing Book? She could hear that bastard Chandler laughing at her right now.

She was furious for allowing herself to be taken in by her own faulty deductions. Nothing was ever like it is in books or in the movies. Any cop would tell you that. No one clue ever caught a killer or uncovered a motive or solved a crime. No one ever called all the suspects into the drawing room and revealed intent, means, and finally, as all the light went out, leaving the audience on the edge of their seats, the murderer.

Shelley thumped her palm on Anthony Milbourne's oak rolltop desk. "Dammit," she muttered as he watched her curiously. She wasn't sure if she was angrier about wasting her time on a false lead or about the reaction she expected from Chandler when he found out that her big clue had been a big nothing.

So who said he had to find out? was her next thought—the only consolation.

She extended her hand. "Thank you, Mr. Milbourne. You have been most gracious and extremely helpful."

"I am glad to have been of some assistance, although it seems evident that you were unable to find whatever you were looking for."

She nodded glumly. "Yes," she said, looking around the room. The leather-bound books, oak desk, and antique paneling gave the room the feeling of a Victorian study or a miniature drawing room from an old English movie. "It's too bad," she said with a brave smile. "This would have been the perfect place to solve a murder."

Mr. Milbourne escorted her to the door, assuring her that he would watch her television broadcast that evening. At that moment the news broadcast was far from her mind. As an afterthought, she gave Milbourne her card. "When that books arrives—the one Jonathan ordered—please send it to me."

Milbourne waved his hand back and forth. "It's not necessary, Miss James. I can send it back. There is no need . . ."

"No. Please. I want you to send it to me. I really would like to have it."

Milbourne shrugged and said he would be glad to send her the book when it arrived.

Shelley felt that buying it was the least she could do for all his trouble, but wondered what the hell she would do with *The Neuroscientific-Whatever-It-Was* when she got it.

Maybe it would be an interesting decoration for her coffee table.

Chapter 13

At the same time that Shelley James was pursuing her only clue, Mark Chandler was attempting to decipher the only piece of evidence he had not revealed to her. With the list of names he had acquired from Jeanette Nielsen safely ensconced in his inside jacket pocket, Chandler went to the News Building on East Forty-second Street. After saying hello and talking briefly to the receptionist at the front desk, he signed in with the guard stationed in the lobby and then took the elevator to the basement level where the newspaper had its reference section. The sign on the open door said Morgue, and Chandler walked in to find a vast array of library shelves, standing like long lines of dominoes, and, blanketing one wall, a row of filing cabinets.

All large metropolitan newspapers and most prominent suburban ones, maintain elaborate libraries of reference material for their reporting and editorial staffs. These reference sections contain all back issues of the newspapers, current issues of magazines and other papers, encyclopedias, almanacs, and various reference works, as well as clip files on any number of subjects. But the best-known function of a morgue, and the function from which it derives its name, is the compilation of information for obituaries of the famous and near famous. Obituaries are prepared and constantly updated on the premise that even the famous do not live forever and that a newspaper should be prepared to quickly deliver information about the life of the recently deceased.

A newspaper morgue is often the bottom rung of the journalistic ladder. Newly hired reporters begin their careers down in the bowels of a newspaper building, gathering and rewriting material for the obituary file. For older reporters, an assignment to the morgue can be a preliminary warning to seek other employment. Only when the death of a famous person seems imminent, does the activity in the reference section approach the frenetic pace that is a customary aspect of most journalism, and even then much of the excitement of the news-gathering process is somehow missing.

For this reason most reporters consider an assignment in the morgue to be somewhat akin to a stopover in purgatory. In short, the morgue is a nice place to visit, but, even though it is a vital and necessary part of the modern newspaper, no one wants to work there.

Chandler approached the young woman who sat at the first desk clipping an article from a magazine.

"Hello, I'm Mark Chandler. I write a column for the paper?" This last was a question because Chandler used the morgue so infrequently that he did not know any of the personnel and was quite sure they did not know him.

The young woman smiled. "Of course, Mr. Chandler. What can we do for you?"

"Well, I'm not really sure, but I have a list of names and I'm trying to discover if there is any connection between these people." Realizing that it was a rather vague proposition and that he had not phrased his request particularly well, he added, "Do you understand what I mean?"

Doris, who was small, blond, and rather pretty, frowned. "You've got some names and you'd like us to find out if they are linked in any way to each other?"

"Exactly. Do you think it's possible?"

She made a face. "Anything is possible, Mr. Chandler. Why don't you let me see the list and we'll take a shot at it?"

Chandler handed over a copy of the names from the notebook, which he had copied on a three-by-five-inch file card.

The woman took the list, looked at it for just a second,

then raised her eyes to look at Chandler. "These are only last names," she said, making faces again.

"I'm afraid so," said Chandler with a helpless shrug.

Doris Melton shook her head. "That is going to make it rather difficult." She was looking at the card. "These are rather common names and I'm willing to bet we have several listings under each. Without first names we will have to run down all the info in the files on each of them. With all the cross-referencing involved"—she looked up—"that could take some time."

She waited hopefully for Chandler's response.

He grinned apologetically. "I thought it might."

It was not the response she had wanted, and realizing that he was insisting on proceeding, she made another face.

By this time Chandler didn't think she was quite as pretty as he had at first. She seemed to spend much of her time with her face screwed into an uncomely mask.

Doris bit her lip and shook her head as if Chandler had presented her with the terms of an unconditional surrender, and then she began to read the names out loud. "Hughes . . . Arnold . . . Taylor . . . Watson . . . Coleman . . . O'Brien . . . Dr. Harrison . . . Jefferson." She looked up. "Waspy group," she said without humor, and then studied the list, her eyes narrowing in concentration, as if the answer lay somewhere on the card. Suddenly her face brightened. "I've got an idea," she said cheerfully, and Chandler knew she had thought of someone to hand this task to. Miss Melton picked up her phone and dialed a number, giving Chandler a happy wink as she waited. Her face was pretty again, but Chandler had the feeling that she would probably spend her entire career down here in the morgue.

"Hello, Allan," she said into the phone. "It's Doris. . . . Fine and you? . . . Listen, I have someone here,"—she struggled to remember—"Mike Chandler,"—Chandler winced —"he's a columnist with us and he has a rather interesting problem that you might be able to help with." She briefly described the situation, then concluded with, "I'll send him right over."

Hanging up the phone she gave Chandler his file card, happy to be rid of him and his request. She pointed to the door in the far corner of the stacks. "Go through there and take a left. Allan Greenfield might be able to help you. His office is the second door on the right."

Chandler took his card and mumbled an insincere word of gratitude, but Miss Melton had already turned back to her clippings.

Allan Greenfield greeted Chandler with an enthusiasm that in contrast to Miss Melton, was almost overwhelming. "It's *Mark* Chandler, isn't it?" he asked, shaking Chandler's hand. "I thought Doris said Mike and I wasn't sure it was you. I read your stuff all the time. I like it a lot."

Chandler, never very good at accepting compliments, mumbled a thank you.

Allan Greenfield was young—middle twenties, Chandler guessed—with sharp features that made him seem alert and ready for whatever came his way. His hair was a tousled sandy brown, and he wore an impeccably laundered blue, pin-striped shirt and a dark blue tie. Chandler was immediately envious of his trim, narrow waistline.

Greenfield's office turned out to be not an office at all, but a large room with several computer banks lining one wall. On three tables in the center of the room sat the computer terminals that were obviously the focus of attention. To one side stood an empty table. A tweed jacket hung over one of the chairs drawn up to it.

"How are things out there in the world of journalism?" asked Greenfield as he led Chandler into the room. "I hope you remember the password to get you back upstairs; otherwise, you might be down here with us for a decade or two."

"How long have you been down here, Mr. Greenfield?"

"Call me Allan," he said, squinting as if trying to calculate a very large number. "Eight months, three weeks, and two days," he said.

Chandler gamely struggled to suppress a laugh. "That doesn't seem all that long."

Greenfield's eyes opened in disbelief at such an incredible statement. "Have you ever tried hanging by your thumbs for almost nine months. It's like being pregnant with no prospect of delivery—or should I say, deliverance?"

"I'd be glad to deliver any messages to the outside world, if you'd like."

"Just contact my mom and tell her I'm OK. Tell her to send thermal socks and some more of her fruit cake. She hardly visits anymore."

"It can't be that bad down here," said Chandler, laughing. Greenfield backed against the wall and stretched out his arms in the position of crucifixion. He let his head roll to one side, his mouth open in mock agony. "Actually," he said through twisted lips, "you get used to it after the first three or four months. I hardly feel the spike wounds at this point. Mostly it's just"—he stopped for a moment, arms falling to his sides, and the manic smile slipped from his face—"mostly it's just boring."

He looked directly into Chandler's eyes and the older man could feel his impatience. "You know," Greenfield continued, "when I was in junior high school Woodward and Bernstein were giving it to Nixon. *That,* I said to myself, is what I want to do. I started an underground paper in the eighth grade, accusing the principal of misusing school activity funds, and damn near got expelled." He smiled with the recollection. "But it was fun."

"Was he misusing funds?"

Greenfield dismissed the thought with a shrug. "Probably." He went on. "Then it was high school editor, college editor. You know, the whole journalism bit. I could have walked into a good spot in a small paper. But no, I wanted the Big Apple." He shook his head. "I thought this would be only temporary, but"—he waved his arms to indicate the room—"here I am."

Chandler's tone was consoling. "Eight months isn't forever. When I started, it seemed that I spent more time than that just getting everybody coffee."

Greenfield's eyes brightened. "Where did you start?"

"Sports department. I was a sportswriter before I started my column."

Greenfield didn't seem very impressed by this particular avenue to success. "I'm not much interested in sports," he said.

Anxious now to get on with his business, Chandler made no comment. He cleared his throat a few times then said, "I'm told that you can help me."

Greenfield seemed noncommittal. "Maybe. Doris told me you had a problem. Why don't you fill me in?"

"It's simple, really," said Chandler, handing Greenfield the list. "I want to know if there is any connection between these people."

Greenfield shot him a questioning glance.

"It's important for a column I'm working on," said Chandler in response to the look. "I'll know how important if you can come up with something."

"And you know nothing else about these names? Are they men or women? Rich or poor? Americans or Europeans? . . ."

Chandler could offer nothing.

"Well," said Greenfield, "I see that one is a doctor. That's something at least." He motioned Chandler to a chair. "Sit down and I'll show you what I'm going to try."

Both sat down in wooden chairs at the empty table. Nearby was a smaller table with a single computer console and TV viewing screen perched on top.

"What I've been doing for the last several months," said Greenfield in a very businesslike tone which made Chandler think that this must be how the young man explained his job to his superiors upstairs, "is attempting to computerize a lot of our reference material. If a reporter comes down here looking for material on, let's say, military dictatorships in various parts of the world, we can punch it up and the material will be exhibited on the screen. Anything the reporter needs can be duplicated on the printer, and he can take it with him. He won't have to cross-check references for everything or pull out twenty-five different folders out of the files. It's all here on type ready for recall."

Chandler was impressed. "You do all this by yourself?"

"No. I just select the material to be programmed. We have a team of secretaries who type the material into the computer banks. We also compile an index to facilitate recall."

"Very interesting."

Greenfield shrugged. "It's been going on for years. There's so much material that I doubt if we'll ever catch up." He smiled. "I hope to be long gone from here before we get close."

Chandler pressed on. "You said these items are indexed? The names on my list are obviously not going to be found in any of your indexes." He looked seriously at Greenfield. "So how can you help me?"

"It's still possible. The computer has a random access to all of its information. If, for instance, a name is included with some reference material and we want more information on that person, we can bring that information together simply by typing the name into the computer and punching the Random Access key. It's the same principle that some police departments use in order to find additional information about criminals whose crime record might otherwise be separated in various police departments across the country. You know, arrest a guy for shoplifting in Manhattan and then find out he's wanted for murder in Chicago. The computer is able to bring all the related material together and display it on one screen."

Chandler nodded. "Is that going to work for me and my list?"

"It's a long shot," said Greenfield honestly. "The computer isn't really programmed to deliver information about random groups of people. If these names are prominent enough, that some of them appear together in the files somewhere, or if there is some other interconnecting material, we might get lucky. But the biggest 'if' is whether or not any such material has been programmed into our computers. Your names might be sitting out there in our files, but if we haven't put the material into the computer, the search will give us nothing."

"What you're trying to tell me is there isn't too much hope of finding anything."

"Exactly. With this kind of information—just last names and nothing else—the chances are very small. And if we draw a blank and you have to go to the files out there . . ." He indicated the outside stacks with a thumb aimed back over his shoulder. "It'll take you forever."

"I understand," said Chandler. "Let's give it a try."

"Yes, *mon capitaine*," said Greenfield, a little of his exuberance returning as he moved to the computer keyboard. "First we'll try the most obvious approach. I'll just type in all the names and ask the computer to find the area of connection." He began to type and the letters appeared on the television screen. "It's the most obvious plan, and unless you've given me the names of eight of the Supreme Court justices, it's the one least likely to succeed."

When he finished typing the names, which now appeared in a column on the screen, Greenfield turned to Chandler and with a mock German accent said, "Ve musst be very careful now zat ve don't oferload ze reactor pile. One mistake und mankind iss doomed." He pressed a single key, then scurried behind Chandler as if seeking shelter from an imminent explosion. The screen went blank.

"Rudy is thinking," said Greenfield in his normal voice.

In a flash the screen came alive again. The eight names reappeared and in capital letters just below was the caption INSUFFICIENT DATA.

Greenfield shrugged. "So much for technological wonders. But that's what I expected. Now, let's try your Dr. Harrison here. I pick him because his is the only name with any other information attached. At least we know he's a doctor."

Chandler nodded as Greenfield began to type in the name. Again the screen went blank, but this time the name returned to the screen almost instantaneously, and Chandler felt a sudden thump in his chest as the computer began to display a message on the screen.

THIS NAME IS NOT PART OF MY PROGRAMMING AND DOES NOT APPEAR IN ANY OF MY INFORMATION CIRCUITS.

"Surly son of a bitch, isn't he," said Greenfield, gesturing to the viewing screen. "Well, that eliminates our friend Dr. Harrison. He may possibly be in our regular files and not yet included in the computer files. "Or," he sighed, "we might have zero info on him. He could be a veterinarian in Larchmont for all we know."

"This is going to take awhile, isn't it?" said Chandler.

Greenfield nodded. "With this kind of input, old Rudy might be searching for weeks. Let me show you what I mean. I can run down each name the way we did with Harrison, but I know what I'll get. The computer will punch up a listing of everybody in the files with that last name. If you want to pick one at random, I'll show you."

"Try the first name."

"Hughes," said Greenfield. "OK, Rudy, let's give old Hughes a try." He typed the name, punched a key, and waited for the screen to light up. When it did, there were more than thirty names listed on the viewing screen.

"I see what you mean," said Chandler morosely.

Greenfield went on. "We've got everything here from Charles Evans Hughes to Howard Hughes. Now what I could do, is request an individual printout for any—or all—of these names. Then I could repeat that process with the rest of the names on your list. What we'd probably wind up with is something that looks like the *Encyclopedia Brittanica*. We need some limiting factor: occupation, age, nationality. Something!"

Chandler thought for a moment and shook his head. "I guess it was too much to hope for." He extended his hand to Greenfield. "Thanks. You've really been helpful, and I appreciate your time."

"Maybe if you're ever asked to recommend a bright, eager, young reporter for a job upstairs, you'll remember me."

They shook hands warmly.

"I'm sure you'll be out of here in no time," said Chandler. "And if there's anything I can do to help, I promise you I will."

As they reached the outside corridor Greenfield said, "I'll tell you what I can do. I'll put old Rudy on a random search. That means that when he's not busy with other things he can put the names together in randon combinations of two, three, or four—or whatever—and try to connect one of them to another, rather than all of them together."

"I suppose it's worth a try," Chandler said without much conviction.

"I'll also take a look for our Dr. Harrison in the regular files on the odd chance that he's there and hasn't been fed into the computer. I'll let you know what I come up with."

"I don't want you to take up too much of your time with this thing. I'm not even sure how important it is."

"It's got to be more important," said Greenfield, laughing, "than anything else I do around here."

Chandler gave Greenfield his home phone number and the two parted in good spirits. Chandler left feeling that he had met someone with enough drive, ambition, and personality to get somewhere as a reporter. He made a mental note to mention Greenfield's name to his editor.

Back at the computer terminal Alan Greenfield said, "I'm very disappointed in you, Rudy. You just blew a chance for me to make some points with the outside world." Lately he had taken to talking to the computer as though it were a real person, another reason why he felt that he had to escape from this prison.

"I really had much more faith in you than that," he said. "I thought you'd come up with something." He sat staring at the screen in silence for a moment while Rudy stared back. Greenfield typed in a coded number combination on the keyboard and the word POLITICS appeared on the screen, followed, almost immediately, by the expected INSUFFICIENT DATA. He typed another number combination and BUSINESS appeared above the eight names.

After an expectant pause, again the words INSUFFICIENT DATA.

"I know you're in there," said Greenfield. "If only I had

the right key." He opened a thick book on the table and ran his finger down a long column of number combinations. "OK, Rudy old boy," he said as he typed in the code numbers from the book, "we're going to try a little random search. When you're not too busy you can do some independent detective work on these names."

Greenfield finished typing the code, waited for an acknowledgement from the computer, and then pushed the START SEARCH key. The screen went blank.

Rudy was thinking.

Chapter 14

As usual, the Forty-ninth Street studio of WNBC was a bustle of activity. Even four hours before the six o'clock broadcast the newsroom was in what was often referred to as "controlled chaos." Cameras, cables, lights, and other equipment, were everywhere. Technicians pushed past reporters struggling to complete assignments before deadline. On camera, announcers read through copy, stopwatches in hand, timing length to the second. Everyone seemed to be yelling at everyone else.

Last year, some bright-eyed executive had decided that the program should be broadcast not from a studio setting but from the newsroom itself. It was reasoned that viewers were tired of stiff cardboard personalities sitting behind elaborate formica desks. What this executive had in mind was something like the set of *Lou Grant:* desks, reporters, typewriters, action. What the viewers really wanted to see, the thinking went, was the news in process—reporters working, teletypes clacking, news in the making. What the viewer got to see, of course, was nothing of the sort. By the time the broadcast went on the air, most of the work was, of necessity, completed. Those reporters who were required to sit in the background while the show was on the air had already finished their assignments for the day and were merely window dressing. The ones who did get to make regular appearances on camera usually mugged it up in the background as though they were working on some headline event. Most wrote letters to girl friends and mistresses; some typed grocery lists; one was working on a novel. The set was absurdly sterile and a far cry from what it looked like when it was in use as a newsroom, but the producers had decided correctly that the public would never accept the idea that important information could come from such chaos, and so the newsroom that wasn't a newsroom became a regular feature of the *Six O'Clock News*.

In an odd way, most of the personnel found the prebroadcast confusion somehow stimulating, and there was no question that it added an air of excitement and immediacy to the proceedings. As the hour approached six, the excitement grew, and each reporter labored to complete his assignment and then get his desk in order before the camera lights went on. One of the producers, another of the many fugitives from Broadway who had made their way into television, would call out as the time approached, "Two minutes to showtime."

And that's what it was. Showtime. It was Broadway. It was Hollywood—only the men were better looking and the women were more capable.

Although it was exhilarating, the confusion could sometimes get in the way of clear thinking; so whenever Shelley had a tough story to work on or a difficult problem to solve, she took refuge in her small office near the rear of the studio. Today, she had gone there almost immediately to study the list she had made of all the pertinent information on the death of Jonathan Carruthers. She didn't have much. Everything fit onto a single page in a small notebook.

At the bottom of the list she had written in large letters, MISSING BOOK. Now, after her return from Milbourne's Bookstore she took a red pen and crossed out that final entry with two short, quick strokes.

What was left, she had to admit, was almost exclusively information she had been given by Mark Chandler. Her only positive contribution had been the definite knowledge that Carruthers had been working on an important story. But

Chandler had assumed that that was the case; her information had merely corroborated what he already knew.

Damm it! She'd known Carruthers; yet this Chandler—a newspaper reporter—knew more about the case than she did. She squeezed her eyes shut and shook her head, hoping to block the self-doubt that was rising in her. Somewhere in the back of the broadcast journalist's mind resided a hidden fear that whispered an unspeakable uncertainty. Newspaper reporters are real reporters, the voice said. Television reporters are highly paid imposters.

Shelley knew—and had almost convinced herself—that this was nonsense, but at moments of stress she sometimes felt that newspaper reporters had kept the faith while she and her TV colleagues had sold out to the big buck. Although many television reporters made much more money, were instantly recognized on the street, and were given preferential treatment by politicians and bureaucrats because of the power of their medium, they still had feelings of inferiority in the presence of print journalists.

Shelley thought about Chandler and realized that other than the fact that he wrote a syndicated column and had been a sportswriter, she didn't know much about him. Sportswriter! Why the hell should I feel inferior to a sportswriter? she wondered. He probably got his information in the locker room at Madison Square Garden.

Shelley smiled, remembering that one of her first assignments in New York had been a postgame interview in the locker room at Yankee Stadium. It had been at the time when feminists were charging that women were being denied equal opportunity in broadcasting by not being allowed access to locker rooms. When the courts ruled that this exclusion was indeed illegal, one brilliant network executive had thought it would be a great idea to send the best-looking female reporter they could find into the locker room after a game. Shelley had been the unanimous selection. Of course, all the network affiliates and independent stations had thought of the same idea, and there were more than a dozen women reporters in the Yankee locker room that night.

One of the Yankees had allowed himself to be interviewed wearing only a towel around his waist, and naturally during the course of the live interview one of his more exuberant teammates had ripped the towel away from his body. None of this, of course, appeared on camera, so Shelley had gamely continued the interview as a group of Yankees clustered around laughing like drunken schoolboys. Finally Reggie Jackson had stepped forward, fully clothed, and had gallantly stood between Shelley and the nude player. She had gratefully continued the interview with Jackson.

The players soon tired of such hijinks, most of them wanting nothing more than to shower, dress, and go home. As soon as the novelty of the female in the locker room had worn off and the feminists were satisfied that their point had been made, the practice was discontinued.

Anyway, that had been her experience with sports and athletes, and it hadn't left her with what might be termed positive impressions. So how did this sportswriter Chandler get more information about the case than she?

Thinking about that threatened to set off another round of self-disparagement. Instead, she picked up the phone and dialed an inside number. The ring was answered almost immediately.

"Nancy?" Shelley said. "Are you busy right now?" She listened, smiling a little. "Can you come over to my office? I'll put on some coffee. . . .Tea then. I've got something I want to ask you."

Nancy Kelly was in her late twenties and attractive in a sober, refined kind of way. Her short dark hair, large intelligent eyes, and regular square-jawed features projected the kind of competent sincerity that producers felt the home viewer expected in a female reporter. Nancy played to this image with the man-tailored suits and horn-rimmed glasses that she wore on camera, but Shelley and nearly everyone else at the studio knew that the image was not the reality. Nancy Kelly was actually fun-loving, happy-go-lucky, and often rather spacy—attributes that were not eagerly sought in the world of television news reporting.

Nancy had been with the *News* for almost four years before joining NBC eighteen months ago, and she was proving to be a competent and hard-working part of the news team. She liked the recognition of working in television, and her enjoyment showed in the enthusiasm that she brought to her work.

She slipped easily into a chair in Shelley's office. "What's up, Shell?"

Shelley smiled and poured Nancy's tea. "Sugar?"

"Do I look like I need more calories?"

In truth she looked as if she would never have to worry about her weight, but because the TV camera added the appearance of an extra ten or fifteen pounds there was a constant battle in the newsrooms to stay below what might otherwise be called optimum weight.

Shelley sat behind her desk, dunking a tea bag into her cup.

"Rumors are flying like crazy, Shelley," said Nancy, smiling mischievously.

Shelley looked puzzled. "What rumors?"

"That you're being considered to replace Jonathan on the *Six O'Clock News.*"

Shelley shook her head. "Well, it's news to me. No one has said anything."

"One of the cameramen told me he overheard Mrs. Gresham giving you the big buildup to the production people on the show."

"I'll believe it when I hear it myself," said Shelley.

"Don't forget where you heard it first." Nancy laughed. "What did you want to see me about?"

"I had lunch the other day with a columnist at the *News.* Mark Chandler?"

"Oh," said Nancy smiling, "did he ask you to say hello?"

"As a matter-of-fact he did," Shelley fibbed. "I was wondering if you could tell me anything about him. We're working on the same story and there's a possibility that we might have to work together for a while. What kind of a guy is he?"

"What do you want to know? Personal or professional?"

Shelley sipped her tea. "Professional," she said, placing the cup on her desk. "But anything you can tell me would help. I really want to know how reliable he is."

"Absolutely," said Nancy without hesitation. "He's a nice guy, Shelley. In fact, maybe a little too nice."

Shelley frowned. "I don't get it."

"I'm sure he told you that we went out a few times a couple of years ago, right after he broke up with his wife."

Shelley sipped her tea and nodded another lie from behind her cup.

"You should have seen it, Shell. When he broke up with his wife there were at least a dozen women at the paper who went after him. It was awful." She laughed and shook her head. "Like sharks drawn to the smell of blood."

"But you got there first," said Shelley, smiling.

"No, it wasn't like that. I had an advantage."

"Advantage?"

"Yes. Chandler is crazy about baseball. He can go on for hours talking about it."

"And you just happen to love baseball, too?"

"No," said Nancy, shaking her head emphatically. "My father used to pitch for the Red Sox back in the forties. He wasn't a star or anything—he only won three games in his whole career—but when I happened to mention to Chandler that my dad had enjoyed his sports column and told him that my father had once pitched for Boston"—she shrugged—"he was suddenly interested. Turns out he was a big Red Sox fan. Even knew who my dad was. Anyway, that's how we started going out. It was a rough time for him. His wife had just left him and taken their daughter to Pennsylvania. He missed her—the daughter I mean—a lot."

"Did you ever meet his daughter?"

"Once. We took her to the zoo. She was about seven then. Nice kid." Nancy's eyes grew wistful. "I sometimes think that the timing was wrong for Chandler and me. At another time—who knows?" She left this last remark hanging in the air as she sipped her tea.

Shelley said nothing, and Nancy Kelly resumed her monologue. "Of course it wasn't for lack of effort on my part. I made it perfectly clear, as they used to say, that I was available for more than drinks and casual conversation."

"And?"

"He was a little slow on the uptake. I mean, a girl shouldn't have to say, 'I want your body, honey.' Y'know what I mean? He used to like to talk about his daughter, have a few drinks, eat dinner. He even liked my cooking. Now that's rare!"

In spite of herself, Shelley asked, "So what happened?"

Nancy smiled. "I thought this was strictly professional, Shell?"

"I'm sorry, Nancy. I didn't mean to be so damned nosy."

"I'm only kidding, Shelley. I don't mind telling you." Nancy sighed a little before she went on. "When we got to the bedroom part of the relationship, he was very nice, but I think he had the guilts because his marriage was breaking up. You know. When we were going out, he wasn't divorced yet—just separated. I always got the feeling that he felt he should be doing more to keep his marriage together."

"What about his wife?"

"I never met her. He never talked about her. Anyway, he was a very nice guy. I liked him a lot. Still do. Not like that anymore, but I still like him. I don't think he was ready to fall into any kind of permanent relationship. Maybe he's ready now." Nancy eyed Shelley with the kind of look that is usually reserved for viewing an abstract painting.

"What's that look for?" asked Shelley.

"I don't see you two as an item."

Shelley laughed. "We're not 'an item.' We just might be working together—that's all."

"It's just professional then?" Nancy's eyes were dancing with humor and there was a trace of sarcasm in her voice.

"Strictly professional," said Shelley.

"That's good because I don't really think he's your type."

Shelley smiled. "And just what do you think my type is?"

Nancy Kelly flashed her biggest smile. She was enjoying this. "Oh, Robert Redford, maybe. Or Burt Reynolds. Maybe Paul Newman. But only for something casual. For something really heavy, I think Clint Eastwood would be more your type."

"That's your fantasy," said Shelley, shaking her head, "not mine. Besides," she said shrugging, "you know as well as I do that if you meet two guys at a party who look like Robert Redford and Burt Reynolds, they'll probably leave together."

Nancy made a face and nodded in sad agreement. Then the furtive smile was back on her face. "Maybe you and Chandler wouldn't be such an odd couple after all."

Bouncing out of her chair Nancy looked at her watch. "Hey, I've got to get back to work. Tell Mark I said hello. He's probably at McQueeny's right now having lunch." She smiled at the memory. "Cheeseburger and fries. He loved my cheeseburgers." She wobbled her right hand back and forth like a wounded bird gliding to a landing. "My fries weren't so hot though. Maybe that's what did it." With a cheerful wave she was gone.

Shelley checked her watch and thought about Chandler. She wasn't sure why she had asked Nancy Kelly over to her office and then let her run on about a lot of personal stuff. All she had really wanted to know was how reliable Chandler was. Could she trust him? Last night she and Chandler hadn't parted on very good terms. She had resented the fact that he had made light of her contribution. But, she thought, apparently he had been right. Her missing book theory had been a false lead, and now she felt foolish about her passionate recital of its possible significance. He had called her Miss Marple and made her angry. Not being taken seriously always made her angry. She had had quite enough of that.

Yet there was no doubt that she needed something from him. She checked her watch again.

Chapter 15

In the middle of biting into his cheeseburger, Mark Chandler looked up in surprise to see Shelley James standing next to his table. He was so taken aback that he could think of nothing to say. He stared at her, his mouth full. All of his shrewd contrivances of yesterday had deserted him.

Shelley broke the silence. "Mind if I join you?"

Chandler mumbled through his food and motioned her to a seat. He took a long slug from his beer mug to clear his throat. "What brings you here?"

Shelley slipped her arms out of her long, quilted overcoat. "Would you believe me if I said that I just happened to be in the neighborhood and thought I'd stop in for a beer?"

Taking his cue, Chandler asked, "Would you like something to drink?"

"I'd like some lunch. I haven't eaten."

Chandler waved to the waiter. "Good cheeseburgers," he said and resumed eating.

"Good God," said Shelley. "I hope they can do better than that."

She settled for a chef's salad and white wine, and when the waiter left with her order they sat without speaking, Chandler could not think of anything to say and she took his silence for stubbornness.

Again Shelley broke the silence. "You were right."

"About what?" he asked in a tone that implied that since

he was usually right about most things, she had better be more specific.

She could feel her anger rising and already regretted her decision to come. "About the missing book. I checked it out this morning. It seems that it was missing only because he gave it to someone as a gift." She showed Chandler the piece of paper on which she had written the name of the book. He raised his eyebrows but said nothing. "He even ordered a replacement for himself," she said. "So my big missing book theory turns out to be not so terrific."

Chandler didn't seem to be listening. "Did you find out who he gave it to?" he asked as he downed his last morsel of cheeseburger.

"No."

Chandler lit a cigarette. He was still looking at the title. "Who the hell would you give a book like this to as a gift?"

The waiter returned with Shelley's order and the conversation was interrupted for a moment as he placed a large bowl in front of her.

"Look at the size of this thing," she said to Chandler as the waiter retreated. "I hope you can help me with it."

"I don't eat anything that hasn't been thoroughly saturated in animal fat," he said. "My stomach rebels at the thought of any food considered to be healthy."

She pointed to the cigarette in his hand. "I'm sure that's good for you too."

"Didn't anyone ever tell you that they won't let you work on a newspaper in New York unless you smoke two packs a day." He took a deep drag on his cigarette and expelled a long narrow stream of smoke. "It's part of a reporter's uniform. An ashtray with stubbed butts and stale smoke rising to the ceiling is considered as essential to a reporter as a typewriter. Who can write without the taste of a good cigarette?"

Shelley wrinkled her nose. "Who can eat with the smell of one?"

"Sorry." He stubbed out the offending cigarette and placed the ashtray on the empty table behind him.

Shelley stabbed at her salad. "Aren't you going to ask me why I'm here?"

"I did already. You said something about passing by and stopping in for a beer."

"I was only kidding."

"I figured that," he said.

"You're angry with me."

Chandler's expression went from blank to quizzical. "About what?"

"About last night—at Jonathan's apartment."

He shrugged. "I thought you were angry with me. I didn't know I was angry with you too."

"I was just a little upset that you didn't take my idea very seriously. That's all."

"And you were right. Your idea was as good as anything I've come up with. I shouldn't have treated it so lightly."

"Can we just forget about it? I was wrong about the book and you were right. Maybe we could just start over?"

Chandler squinted and sipped at his beer. "I've been thinking about what you said, though. I was starting to think that maybe the book wasn't such a dumb idea after all."

"Thank you very much," said Shelley frostily.

He winced. "I didn't mean that the way it sounded. I didn't mean that you were dumb. I just meant that the idea." His voice trailed off. "Maybe I'd better just shut up."

Shelley nodded in agreement. "I hope you write better than you talk, Mr. Chandler."

He shook his head. "If this is a reconciliation, it's not going too well, is it?"

The ice was broken. Shelley smiled at him and they both laughed. "It *was* a dumb idea," she said and they laughed even more.

Chandler looked around the room, noting that the waiters and many of the customers were watching the beautiful woman at his table. Stan, the owner and maître d', gave him a wink and the high sign. It was all he could do to prevent himself from winking back.

Shelley seemed oblivious to all this attention. "Look, Mark," she said, "I came here today to tell you that I want to keep working with you on this thing. I know that most of the information so far has been yours, and I don't have anything to add to what you already have, but I knew Jonathan and I know the people he worked with. I think I can help you . . . I think we can help each other."

Chandler wasn't so sure how much help she would be, but he knew that it would be nice to have her around. The admiring glances of the men in the restaurant had convinced him of that. "OK," he said. "We can still work together. Just one thing. I don't want to get scooped on the *Eleven O'Clock News*. I do the story first in my column."

"That's a promise. You get first crack in print; I get exclusive TV coverage."

"Agreed." They shook hands rather clumsily and he held her hand longer than he felt he should have.

"And I promise," she said, extracting herself from his grip, "no more dead ends like the missing book theory."

"This case is full of dead ends. I just had my own this morning." He pulled the notebook from his jacket pocket. "I got this from Jeanette Nielsen. It belonged to our friend Fred Romanello." He opened it to the page with the list and handed it to Shelley. "It might not have anything to do with this, but then again . . ." He shrugged. "Recognize any of the names?"

Shelley read the list carefully. She shook her head. "No, could be anybody. Any first names?"

"You're looking at everything I've got on the names. This morning I had my paper run a computer check on them. The computer came up with a big zero. Not enough information to go on."

"That's not surprising."

"The point is," said Chandler, lifting a piece of lettuce from her bowl, "there are lots of dead ends in this story: Lauren Masterson, Jeanette Nielsen, the missing book, this list. In a way, even Jonathan Carruthers is a dead end. I don't think we're going to find out what he was up to. He was such a public figure that we should already know what he was up to, if we are going to find out at all."

"Who then?"

He spread his hands, palms up.

"Romanello," she said. "If we can find out what he was up to."

"I think you might be right. Romanello could be the key to this."

She thought for a moment, her fork poised over her salad. "Have the police been able to trace him at all? Where he came from, what he did?"

"No. So far he's a blank."

"If he was Jonathan's researcher, they may have worked together before Jonathan came to New York."

"And Jeanette Nielsen told me that Romanello had once worked with Carruthers somewhere in the Midwest. If we can trace back through the places where Carruthers worked, maybe we can come up with someone who knew Romanello."

Shelley frowned. "Then what?"

"Who knows? Maybe we'll get lucky. Maybe it will lead to another dead end. But right now we've got nothing else to go on."

Shelley put down her fork. She had hardly eaten anything. "I'm going back to the station. I can easily check on places where Jon worked. I'll call those stations and ask if anyone remembers a Fred Romanello." She slid out of the booth and slipped on her coat. "Call me tonight. Better still, come to the station after my show. We can have a drink somewhere and talk." She opened her purse to pay her bill but Chandler stopped her.

"I'll take care of the check," he said with a gallantry he did not feel.

Shelley laughed. "Chandler, if you knew how much money I make, you wouldn't be so anxious to buy me lunch."

"I can imagine," he said without much humor. "Why don't you just put me down as old-fashioned."

Shelley shrugged. "I owe you one. See you later."

She was gone as suddenly as she had appeared.

Chapter 16

Shelley spent most of her afternoon on the telephone. First she called WRTV in Indianapolis, but no one there had ever heard of Jonathan working with a Fred Romanello. From there she worked her way back in reverse chronological order through the different television and radio stations where Jonathan Carruthers had worked: KHTV in Houston, WHO-TV in Des Moines. The stations grew progressively smaller and more rural in a direct reversal of Carruthers's meteoric rise to success and stardom in New York City. But at each station the response was always the same. "Of course we remember Jon—he got his start here—but we don't recall any Fred Romanello."

It had been another long shot, Shelley knew, but with this one there had been at least a reasonable expectation of some success. But once again she found herself getting nowhere. By the time she had made her final call to a small radio station in Fillmore, Utah, where Jonathan Carruthers had taken his first step on the ladder to the summit of his profession, Shelley James was all but willing to concede defeat.

Her last call was as fruitless as her first. Shelley sat at her desk, pretending to read over a news story for that evening's broadcast. Actually she could think of nothing else but her search for some scrap of evidence that would link Romanello to Jon Carruthers. All she had was the Nielsen girl's claim that the two men had worked together, and the fact that Jonathan himself had told her that he had been working with a man he had once worked with before. Was it the same man? If Romanello was that man, if he had worked with Jonathan before, someone had to remember him.

She had assumed that Romanello had worked in broadcasting in some capacity. After all, Jonathan had said he had "worked with" his researcher. But now she began to fear that working with, did not necessarily mean working on the job together. Perhaps Romanello had done the same kind of independent work for Jonathan in the Midwest that he appeared to have been doing in New York. He may have been behind-the-scenes and unaffiliated with any of the stations that Jonathan had worked for. Why, she wondered, would anyone work with, and pay for—out of his own pocket— an independent researcher when the company provided for any number of young, willing, and aggressive researchers right in the newsroom? The answer came to her almost as quickly as the thought: because then Carruthers would not have to share any of the glory. No one at the station would ever have to know that anyone other than the great man himself had uncovered the scandal or the crime or whatever it was that was revealed. This scenario certainly fit the personality of the egomaniacal Carruthers.

If this scenario were true, how would she ever be able to link the two men?

She found herself recalling what Chandler had said: "Maybe we'll get lucky."

The phone rang. It was Doug Mason, the station manager at WRTV in Indianapolis. Shelley had made her first call there and talked with him several hours before.

"Shelley," said Mason, "I've been thinking about this Fred Romanello guy you're trying to locate."

It was impossible to keep her voice steady. "Yes, Doug. Have you found anything?"

"I'm not sure, but after I talked with you I cast my mind back. We had a reporter here right around the time that Jon left us to go to New York. He did some features and investigative stuff for us. Worked with Jon a couple of times, as I recall."

"Was it Romanello?"

"No, the guy's name was Al Román, but hear me out on this one. I remembered that we had hired this guy on Jon's recommendation. Seems that when Jon was at KHTV in Houston this guy worked at a radio station there. I called our personnel department and asked them to send me Roman's file. The name listed on his sheet is *Alfred* Roman. Your guy called himself Fred; do you think we might be talking about the same person?"

"Do you have a picture?"

"Yeah. Thin face, kinda dark. Think it's him?"

Shelley could feel the excitement pulsing through her. She struggled not to let it show. "It's possible, Doug. Will you send me a copy of that file? It might help."

"Sure thing, Shell. Can you tell me why you're looking for this guy?"

Thinking fast, Shelley said, "I'm trying to help the NYPD trace a John Doe. It may or may not be this Romanello."

Mason gave a low chuckle. "It wouldn't surprise me if it was our friend Al Roman."

"Why do you say that?"

"Well, I probably shouldn't say this, but he was kind of a sleazy character, if you know what I mean." Shelley said nothing and after a brief silence Mason explained. "Not only did he investigate stories like drugs, prostitution, and organized crime, but I got the feeling he enjoyed being mired in that kind of muck. Jonathan thought he was a good investigative reporter—and maybe he was—but whenever he was around, I felt like he was going to contaminate the room with some kind of disease. He was just a creepy character. I don't know if I'm making myself clear, or if I should even be saying these things, Shelley, but that's just the reaction a lot of us around here had."

"What happened to him?"

"About two months after Jon left, we got rid of him. He got himself involved with some elements that we felt were detrimental to the integrity of the station. Covering sleazy news is one thing; but being sleazy is quite another. You know how it is in this business, Shelley. You have to be able to project integrity. The man just didn't have it." Mason gave a soft laugh. "When we fired him, he said we'd be sorry someday. Told me that he had a story that was going to make him a giant in the industry."

Shelley's pulse quickened. "Did he ever tell you what it was?"

"No; he was very secretive about it. I doubt if he really had any story." He laughed again, his voice crackling over the long-distance wire. "It wouldn't make any difference. He was the kind of guy who could uncover the identity of the second gunman in Dallas and no one would believe him. If he had claimed Nixon was guilty, the public would have refused to accept the resignation. He just had no integrity, Shelley. We had to have someone else do his stories on the air."

"Someone like Jonathan Carruthers?"

Mason said nothing for a moment, then said, "Yes, Jon did a few of his stories. But a newsman has to be able to do his own stuff, Shelley. This Roman wasn't that kind of person."

"I think you might have found my man for me, Doug. It sounds like we're talking about the same guy." Shelley was imagining what Romanello must have been like. Thoughts of Jeanette Nielsen jumped into her mind. "I'd appreciate it if you could get those files and a photo out to me right away."

"Sure thing. I'll send them by telex immediately. By the way, when are you gonna visit us out here in the heartland?"

"When I do, Doug, I'll buy you a drink."

"So that's him," said Chandler, looking at the photograph that Shelley handed him across the table.

"I think so," she said. "Maybe you could check with the morgue for a positive identification."

Shelley sipped her drink as Chandler scrutinized the photograph. They were seated in a small booth in a bar across the street from the studio, where most of the station personnel came to unwind after a long exhausting day. It was almost midnight.

Chandler stared at the photograph of Al Roman as if he could read the thoughts behind the heavy-lidded eyes. He turned the picture over. "What is this, a telex?" he asked.

Shelley nodded. "The whole package, photo and file, came over the wire from Indianapolis just a few hours ago," she sighed. "I called every damn TV and radio station from here to Idaho and got nothing. Would you believe this is from the first station I called?"

"Good piece of work, Shelley."

She smiled, happy that he thought so. "Lucky. Lucky that Indianapolis called me back."

He agreed grudgingly. "We make our own luck." He placed the photograph back on the table and picked up the rest of the file. "OK. We've got this. Now what does it tell us?"

Shelley slid across the seat so that they could both look at the page at the same time. She pointed to some figures. "Not only did they work together at WRTV in Indianapolis, but in 1976 they both worked in Houston. Jon was at KHTV and Roman was at radio station WKMZ."

Chandler shrugged. "But did they know each other?"

"Al Roman got his job at WRTV on Jon's recommendation."

"If I can verify that this is Romanello, one of us will have to go to Houston to check him out. According to his file he was there for three years. There must be people down there who knew him and . . ."

A grin spread across Shelley's face.

Chandler stopped. "So, tell me. Why the big smile?"

"I'm way ahead of you, Chandler. I called WKMZ right after I got this file. Talked to the station manager. He remembers Al Roman all right. It seems that our friend Al married the station manager's sister"—her eyebrows went up—"who was all of seventeen at the time."

"Mr. Roman or Romanello seems to like his women on the young side," said Chandler.

Shelley nodded. "Seventeen-year-old wife: Jeanette Nielsen wasn't much older than that either. Anyway," she went on, "about a year after the marriage, Roman walks out on his wife. Leaves her with a baby. The station manager sounded pleased when I mentioned that his brother-in-law might be dead."

"Have you talked with the girl—Mrs. Roman—yet?"

"No. I wanted an official verification of the ID before I told her the bad news."

"Or the good news," said Chandler.

"Well, it's good news for the brother-in-law. Maybe not for the wife."

Chandler nodded and looked at the photograph again. "I'll get a positive ID tomorrow morning."

Shelley looked at him. "Then we can both fly to Houston tomorrow afternoon." It was almost a question. "I have the weekend off," she added.

Chandler thought for a minute, looking into her eyes. He nodded. "Houston it is."

Chapter 17

"Good morning, Rudy," said Allan Greenfield as he entered the small space that he called his office.

Rudy sat quietly on the table in the center of the room, its one large, nineteen-inch eye staring intently at his human colleague.

Greenfield flicked a switch on the keyboard and the computer screen glowed dimly with a hazy half-light. "Find anything for me on our little problem, Rudy?" Allan asked as he punched in the search code he had programmed into Rudy the day before.

Without any fanfare, the screen flashed to life as Rudy displayed the fruits of his search. Greenfield's blank expression turned to openmouthed surprise as the display appeared. The first two names from Chandler's list appeared on the screen, each followed by the data that Rudy had uncovered. The screen was filled with information.

Greenfield's eyes narrowed, an expression of puzzlement on his face. His mouth was dry as he quickly scanned the screen. He pushed another key and a second display appeared.

Again, two names were listed, followed by the background material collected by the computer.

Greenfield, his heart pounding, moved closer, his face illuminated in the dim glow of the screen, each eye reflecting in miniature a copy of the ·computer screen before him. "Holy Christ," he said softly, his eyes widening as he read.

Mesmerized, Greenfield pushed a third key and again the display changed. This time the screen was only partially filled. After the first name were several paragraphs of information, but after the second name, O'Brien, the computer said only, "INSUFFICIENT DATA."

Quickly, Greenfield punched the fourth key and the next display appeared on the screen. It was similar to the last. For the seventh name on the list—Dr. Harrison—there was insufficient data, but for the eighth—Jefferson—background material was listed in detail.

Greenfield pushed the REVIEW INFORMATION key and watched as the computer ran through the data one more time; then he switched to HOLD and the screen went blank. Eight names, he thought. Information on six, insufficient data on only two. Chandler would be pleased that he had found this much.

When he pushed the REVIEW INFORMATION key again the screen sprang to life and in monotonous cadence began switching from one display to the next. Allan blinked with each data change, and in time the relentless rhythm of the computer became his rhythm. His pulse and respiration rate seemingly slackened to the pace of the blinking screen, which continued to beat with metronomic regularity.

Lost in thought, Allan sat staring at the screen for what seemed like hours. Finally, he reached into his breast pocket and withdrew the card with Mark Chandler's phone number. With great force of will he moved away from the computer and picked up the phone. He dialed. "Mr. Chandler? . . . Allan Greenfield. . . . I'm fine, thanks. . . . I've been looking for that information you requested. . . . There's nothing in our files on this Dr. Harrison. . . . Nothing in the computer either. But—he paused, his eyes returning to the glowing screen. The flashing was like a silent alarm bell—"but I'll keep trying," he said. "No, the computer hasn't come up with anything else yet. . . . Yes, we knew it was a long shot. . . . Well, I'm glad to help out. I only wish I could have come up with something for you. . . . Good-bye, Mr. Chandler."

Slowly, almost delicately, Greenfield hung up the phone. "Rudy," he said as he approached the computer, "I want you to print up a copy of this information and then you're going to forget you ever laid your beautiful eye on any of this."

With the touch of a button, Rudy's display terminal went blank and then, with blind obedience, the print machine began to type.

One by one, Greenfield tore off the sheets as they emerged from the printer. He read each as it appeared, nodding his head in satisfaction. "Rudy," he said, turning the printer off when the fourth sheet was in his hands, "you've done a good job today and I think we should both take the rest of the day off. I feel a slight chill and I think I might be coming down with something." He punched several buttons and then the ERASE MEMORY key.

Rudy sat quietly, and Greenfield with genuine affection, patted the top of the display screen. "I won't forget you for this, pal. I'm taking you with me to the top."

He folded the four pages carefully, in halves and then in quarters, and slipped them into his jacket pocket. He looked around the room as though he were viewing it for the last time and then with the hint of a smile—before he remembered that he was supposed to be feeling ill—he left, closing the door behind him.

Rudy sat quietly, his cyclopean eye fixed on the door, his integrated micro-processor circuits wiped clean of their most recently gathered information. Rudy had quite simply forgotten what he knew.

The Pan Am terminal at John F. Kennedy International Airport was, as usual, bustling with weekend travelers. Inside the domed concrete roof Chandler awaited the arrival of Shelley James. He sat on his suitcase in front of a staircase that faced the information booth. Above the booth hung the huge arrival/departure board and Chandler noted that their flight was scheduled to leave for Houston in less than ten minutes. With a peevish shake of his head he recalled that Shelley had promised to meet him at the terminal thirty minutes before flight time.

Travelers entered the terminal through the automatic doors on both sides of the information booth, and each time one of the doors opened, Chandler's eyes expectantly sought Shelley's arrival. Finally she marched in, looking, in her long fur coat and dark glasses, as if she had just completed a fashion layout. Behind her, pushing a luggage cart containing three large, bright blue, matching suitcases, came the same porter who had sneered derisively as Chandler had carried in his own single suitcase.

Shelley stopped, coat open, one hand on her hip, the other raising her dark glasses to her forehead, as she scanned the terminal. The pose and the gesture were so classic that Chandler was sure it must have been rehearsed. Probably a grand entrance at Elaine's, he thought. Rehearsed or not, people noticed her.

Chandler stood up and with his palms upward to the turtle-shell ceiling, a gesture that was half-exasperation and half-supplication, drew her attention.

"Sorry I'm late," she said when she had made her way over to him. "I got tied up at the studio and had the damndest time getting out."

Chandler shrugged and pointed to her luggage. "How long are you expecting to be away?"

Shelley shook her hair and threw her head back. "When you're a star," she said, laughing, "wardrobe is everything." Her eyes were full of humor. "One never knows what one will need."

Chandler said, "You must be a bit hit with porters and bellboys."

The porter—who knew a good tipper when he saw one— was still in attendance. His face was impassive, but his eyes drilled holes in Chandler's chest.

Shelley patted Chandler gently on the cheek. "If I dressed like you, Chandler, I wouldn't need luggage. I could travel with a shoebox."

He sputtered a protest. "This is my best jacket."

"I'm sure it is," she said, taking his arm. "It was probably lovely when you bought it." Shelley looked at her watch. "Let's get going. We don't want to miss the plane." She handed the porter a five-dollar bill. "Would you take Mr. Chandler's bag," she said, "and escort us to the gate."

The porter eyed Chandler with a mixture of malice and envy before heading for the departure gate. Shelley, still holding Chandler's arm, led him after the disappearing porter.

"What's the matter with this jacket?" he asked, fingering a lapel.

"Don't worry," she said reassuringly. "I doubt if anyone in Houston will notice."

Chapter 18

The first thing that Allan Greenfield did when he got back to his apartment was to call his girl friend, Julie Loonin. She was surprised to hear his voice, and even more surprised to find that he was at home.

"I thought you were working today," she said.

Greenfield chuckled. "I went in, but I didn't feel well, so I came home."

"Oh,"—she sounded concerned—"are we still on for tonight?"

"Sure, I'm fine. I'm not really sick; I just wanted to get out of there. What are you doing?"

She thought quickly. An afternoon with Allan usually meant only one thing. "I was just about to go out shopping. I have to pick up a few things."

He ignored her response. "Come on over. I've got something important to show you."

She sighed heavily. "Allan, we can spend the whole night together. You'll have plenty of time for whatever you've got in mind."

"For once," he said, laughing, "I'm not even thinking about sex. I've really got something important to show you." She said nothing. "I want your advice."

"All right, Allan," she said, her voice betraying her reluctance although she was flattered that he wanted her counsel rather than her body. "I'll be there in about twenty minutes."

*   *   *   *

Julie pulled up the sheet to cover herself as Allan came out of the bathroom. He winked at her and she mustered a fair impression of a contented smile as she took a long, deep drag on her cigarette. Allan, naked, slipped back into bed, his feet cold against her legs.

She did not turn to face him; instead her eyes were fixed on a small smudge on the ceiling. She had lost count of the number of times in the past few months that she had found herself inspecting that smudge while Allan grunted in her ear.

"That was very nice," he said, moving closer so that his body fit around hers.

As sincerely as she could manage she said, "Yes, it was," but what she was thinking was that this relationship had gone about as far as it could go. Maybe it was time to strike off in a new direction before too much time was invested. There was a new young man at the office who had been eyeing her appreciatively lately. He was fairly good-looking, seemed bright, and had a nice way about him. Why not? This looked like another dead end.

Julie Loonin was twenty-six years old and a graduate of New York University. She worked as a copywriter at BBDO and made over thirty thousand dollars a year. She was good at her job and was moving along at a fairly comfortable pace in her profession, but all that her mother wanted to know was when was she going to get married.

"Mom," she would plead during their weekly talks on the phone, "I'm doing fine. Nobody worries about getting married anymore."

Her mother would tut-tut and add the obligatory, "A single girl should find herself a husband."

Sometimes during these conversations, which, although her parents lived in Queens and Julie in Manhattan, were conducted as though the distances were transcontinental, Julie would laugh; sometimes she would get angry; but mostly she would plead for her mother not to be so old-fashioned. Yet even as she protested, she knew in her heart, in a place so deep that she could not exorcise the thought, that her mother was right. She also knew that only a lifetime of not so subtle propaganda had made her feel that way. But even knowing how she was being manipulated, could not erase her sense of failure. Her greatest fantasy was not to imagine her wedding day or the day some indefinably handsome young man would slip a diamond ring on her finger, but to imagine herself on the telephone with her mother. "Hey, Ma," she would say very casually and without hint of the bombshell to follow, "guess what. I'm getting married."

Instead she lay naked between the sheets in the bed of a man who had never once even intimated that theirs was anything more than the most casual relationship. She liked Allan, and sometimes even his lovemaking was passable—occasionally his intensity made up for his crudity—but she had just about given up hope that their relationship would ever progress to more than companionship and a roll in the hay. A nagging thought that plagued her more and more lately was the remembrance that twice in the past four years she had lived with men who had broken off their relationships and shortly after gotten themselves married. She didn't intend to have that happen again.

Her relationship with Allan Greenfield seemed to have become one of convenience. She wanted someone to take her to dinner and the movies; he wanted someone to take to bed. Allan seemed satisfied. She needed something more.

Allan watched her staring at the ceiling. In profile, he thought happily, she was damned good-looking. Her nose was turned up at just the right angle and her lips, full and thick, recalled talents that sometimes took his breath away. Her arms were outside the sheets, pressing the material firmly against her breasts, and he wondered if he could make her nipples show through by nibbling on her ear.

"What was so important?" she asked, shattering his reverie. She wanted to add that she hoped this encounter wasn't it, but didn't.

"I wanted you to see something."

She corrected him. "You said you wanted my advice."

He reached for her, tangling his fingers in her hair. "Oh, yeah. That too."

Julie sat up holding the sheet tightly in front of her. "I'm going to get dressed," she said. "I give much better advice when I'm fully clothed." She flashed him a quick smile so that he would not feel rejected and hopped out of bed. Allan watched her appreciatively as she gathered her clothes from the chair by the bed and went into the bathroom.

"You can stop watching the engine now," said Shelley. "I don't think it's going to fall off."

Chandler turned his face away from the window, slightly embarrassed that she'd read his mind. "You never know," he said. "I just want to be prepared."

She shook her head and laughed. "If you're the first to notice it, don't tell me. Sometimes ignorance can be reassuring."

"You're right about that."

They were seated in the first-class smoking section of the wide-bodied DC-10. Shelley had insisted that they fly first-class and Chandler, knowing full well that his paper would only pay for a coach ticket, if they paid at all, had agreed only if she would sit in the smoking section.

Shelley had shrugged aside his objections to going first-class. "You've got to travel first-class," she said, "if you want people to think you're with a first-class news operation."

"Sure," said Chandler, looking at his ticket. "The *News* will probably make me pay the difference between this and bus fare to Houston."

It wasn't until they were about to enter the boarding tunnel that Chandler had noticed the distinctive tail assembly of the DC-10. "Oh, Christ," he said.

"What's the matter?" asked Shelley. "Forget something?"

He shook his head. "Do you know what kind of plane this is?"

Her eyes widened. "No. Should I?"

"DC-Ten," he whispered, as if afraid the name might start a panic among the other passengers.

Shelley stared at him, waiting for the rest of his explanation.

"DC-Ten," he repeated. He stopped, forcing those behind to walk around him to proceed. "It's a terrible plane. Engines fall off. Doors fly open."

He looked around as if someone might be eavesdropping. "I did a column on this plane once, even before the Chicago accident. I told my readers not to fly on it. Said they should make other arrangements if they found themselves booked on it." He shook his head sadly. "I can see the inscription on my headstone now: Here Lies Mark Chandler— Too Dumb to Heed His Own Advice."

"Could we talk about something else? You're starting to make me nervous," said Shelley.

Shelley took him by the arm and propelled him forward. "Don't worry; I'll tell them to make sure the doors are locked."

Chandler's eyes had remained riveted on the wing engine during takeoff; only after they had been airborne for several minutes did he turn and give Shelley a very weak smile.

Shelley gave him a reassuring pat on the hand and he returned to his vigil. She shook her head, her eyes going to the ceiling in an expression of exasperation. Men, she thought. If I live to be a hundred, I'll never figure them out.

Chandler lit another cigarette. "I'm going to have another drink. Want one?"

Shelley waved her hand to clear the smoke-filled air. "No, thanks. How many cigarettes are you going to smoke on this trip?"

He smiled sheepishly. "I'll probably run out before we get to Houston." He stubbed out his cigarette in the ashtray. "I'm sorry," he said manfully. "I won't smoke anymore, I promise."

He began to whistle in mock cheerfulness.

"I think I'd rather have you smoke," said Shelley.

"I'd feel better if it was built in Japan," he said. "Ever notice that the doors on Japanese cars always seem to fit better than the doors on American cars?"

Shelley placed her hand on his. With just a slight trace of sarcasm in her voice she asked, "Would you feel better if I held your hand?"

"Actually," he said. "I think that would make me feel a lot better."

When the plane landed routinely in Houston, Chandler was the only first-class passenger to break into spontaneous applause. The other passengers eyed him skeptically and the stewardess who had served him his drinks skewered him with the look she usually reserved for those male passengers who liked to rub against stewardesses as they passed in the narrow aisles.

"If you kiss the ground when we get off," said Shelley, "I'm going to belt you one."

Chapter 19

Over coffee in the kitchen Allan watched as Julie read through the four pages of the computer printout that he had given her. Occasionally she raised her eyes to look at him over the top of the page. He watched her with an expectant smile on his face, awaiting the inevitable moment of shocked recognition.

It did not come.

She finished and placed the printouts back on the table. "So what's this all about? All I see here is some background info on some dead men and the names of their wives and kids."

"Don't you get it?" he asked incredulously. "Look at the pattern on those sheets."

She spread the sheets apart on the table, looking from one to the other. "What pattern? I don't see any with the first two, nothing with the last three, maybe—just maybe—with the middle three." She gathered the sheets into a single pile and drummed her fingers on the table as if challenging him to continue.

Allan snatched the papers from under her fingers. "Look," he said impatiently as he again spread the sheets on the table. "Just look at this." He watched her until her eyes settled on the pages.

"OK," he said, pointing to the first sheet. "On this page I've got two names. One of them is Howard Hughes. You remember him?" he added sarcastically. "The other is Jason Arnold, who happens to be—or was—Hughes's personal attorney."

Julie nodded brightly as if interested in these revelations. She did not wish to antagonize him unnecessarily. He was obviously excited by this information.

Allan went on. "On the day that Hughes died, his attorney, Jason Arnold, died in a plane crash. A legitimate Hughes will has never been found, unless," he added, "you believe that gas station attendant in Utah."

Allan touched his index finger to a line on the page. "Now, see where Hughes was heading when he died?"

Julie nodded. "Houston," she said, smiling.

"Right. And Arnold's plane left Houston and went down somewhere in the Gulf. No wreckage was ever found."

Suppressing the desire to give a skeptical shrug, Julie nodded agreeably.

Allan turned his attention to the second page. He pointed to the name at the top. "Taylor. Multimillionaire oil tycoon. One of the wealthiest men in Texas—in the whole country."

Julie nodded.

Allan said, "Look where he died."

"Houston."

Allan raised his eyebrows and smiled knowingly, but Julie interrupted him. "Allan, I'm willing to guess that a lot of the oil people in Texas live in Houston. And when they die, I would assume that most of them die there."

She pointed to the next name. "Look at this. Watson." She read the full name. "Winthrop T. Watson . . . from one of the oldest and wealthiest families in Maryland. Family money in chemicals and South African gold." Her finger stabbed the sheet. "He died in Switzerland."

Greenfield's voice was steady. He was disappointed that she had not yet seen the reason for his excitement. "Read the personal histories," he said. "Especially the later years."

Julie read on, talking as she did. "Both died in their middle sixties. Watson from a heart attack. Taylor, a stroke that left him comatose for several weeks. Both were widowers who had recently remarried. Both had also adopted sons before their deaths."

She looked up. "Read on," said Greenfield.

She shrugged. Her eyes moved from one paragraph to the next, collating the information as she went. "Both left the bulk of their estates to the newly adopted sons and a sizable chunk to the new wives. Both wills were contested by the families but held up in court."

Allan smiled as if he knew something. "Read the next page," he said, moving it in front of her.

Again, she read out loud. "Coleman, Forbes R., billionaire New York financier." Her eyebrows went up. "These are all heavy hitters." Allan's look of impatience sent her eyes scurrying back to the page. "Died in Switzerland." Her eyes raced through the information, dancing from line to line. "Had been divorced for eight years . . . remarried five years before his death . . . adopted a son shortly after his second marriage . . . left the bulk of his estate to his adopted son and cut off most of his other relatives." Julie's eyes narrowed. She looked up at Allan, then back at the page. "The family contested the will, but it was ruled valid in court."

There was nothing after the second name, O'Brien. Julie looked up at Allan, who quietly slipped the last page in front of her. "Forget Dr. Harrison," he said. "No information. But read the next one."

"Jefferson," she said. "Jefferson, Lawrence T. Computers . . . Started his own company in 1957 . . . reputed to be one of the world's wealthiest men." She stopped for a moment, puzzled by what she saw. "This guy is still alive," she said, looking up at Allan.

Allan nodded. "Go on."

"He's sixty-three years old . . . twice divorced . . . recently remarried and"—her eyes narrowed—"adopted a son soon after his marriage." She leafed back through the other pages. The information was virtually the same on all of them.

Allan sat back, his hands clasped behind his head, a look of smug superiority on his face.

"OK," said Julie, counting her thoughts on her fingers. "We've got five very rich men here. Four of them are dead. Two of them died in Houston. Two in Switzerland. With the exception of Hughes, all of them remarried, adopted a son, and—in the case of those who died—left all their money to the new wife and the adopted son." Her head shook back and forth as she stared at the sheets. "It's all very interesting, Allan. But what the hell does it mean?"

Allan leaned forward, pausing for a moment before he spoke. "I think my computer-friend, Rudy, is trying to tell us that somebody killed these people. Somebody killed these people for their money."

Julie sat straight up as though she had been slapped. Her eyes opened wide to register her incredulity. "Allan! You can't deduce that from this information. Besides, look at the other names. Jason Arnold doesn't fit any of the patterns and you have absolutely nothing on O'Brien or Harrison." She smiled, trying not to be too harsh. She felt as if she were taking a toy away from a child. "Hughes has only a rather tenuous connection with the others; Jefferson is still alive; which leaves you with only three names." She looked quickly at the sheet. "Watson, Coleman, and Taylor, who seem to fit what you call a pattern."

He seemed crushed that she had not been able to recognize the importance of what he had seen. Trying to soften the impact of her reaction, she reached across the table to touch his hand, but he pulled away, sitting, shoulders slumped, hands beneath the table.

"Allan," she said softly. "I know how desperate you are to make a name for yourself, but I just don't want you to write something you can't support with evidence. Your computer could gather random lists of names of lots of people who had died in similar circumstances. That doesn't mean they were murdered."

He lifted his eyes from the table. "My computer didn't pick these names at random. They were on a list that was given to me by a reporter at the paper. He wanted me to find a connection, and I did."

"The computer did," she corrected.

"Whatever. The connection is there. These are all very wealthy men who remarried, adopted children, then died, leaving their money to the child."

"When you say it like that it doesn't sound very unusual. It probably happens all the time."

"But not with these kinds of people. We're talking really big-time money here. People like Howard Hughes."

"Not Hughes," she interrupted. "His only connection is that he died in Houston."

Allan sighed. "Right. Right. But his will was never found, and his lawyer dies the same day he does. Doesn't that suggest something to you?"

"But what does it prove?"

"It doesn't *prove* anything," he said curtly. "It needs more investigation. But it seems obvious—at least to me—that some very rich people are dying in very similar circumstances."

"You're right," Julie said. "And if I read in the newspaper tomorrow that Lawrence T. Jefferson has died and left all his money to his new wife and newly adopted son, maybe I'll start to believe there's something going on here. But until then . . ."

"If I wait that long, someone else will write the story."

"Do you realize, Allan, that if what you are suggesting is true, these very rich men would somehow have to be persuaded to marry younger women—"

"Happens all the time," he interjected.

She went on, undaunted. "Then adopt a child; then change their wills to leave the estate to the new wife and child?"

"Stranger things have happened."

"But why the child? If someone is arranging this, why not have the new wife inherit all the money?"

"I don't know," he said honestly. "Maybe the child is necessary so that the will will stand up in court."

"So what you are suggesting is that someone somehow gets these men to marry women who will go along with this . . . plan?"

"Right . . . maybe someone arranges for these men to meet young and attractive women."

Julie chuckled. "That sounds like the easy part. How do they arrange to get them to adopt a child, not to mention explaining why they want them to? Then how do they arrange to have them change the will? It's crazy. How would you ever get anyone to go along with such a scheme, or get anyone to believe that it's happening? I know that it appears to be more than coincidence, but it just doesn't make any sense."

"Look," he said, and she saw his determination. "Something is happening here—I can feel it—and I'm going to find out what it is . . . This could be a big story—a giant story."

Julie nodded without much enthusiasm. "What does the reporter think of this?"

"Who?"

"The reporter, the person who gave you the list."

A look of embarrassment spread over Greenfield's face and he mumbled an inaudible reply.

"What?"

He exploded. "He doesn't know anything about it." His embarrassment had made him angry but only for a moment. He added somewhat sheepishly, "I didn't tell him what I found."

Julie was amazed. "Why not?"

He looked at her as though the word "moron" was stamped on her forehead. "You don't get it, do you?" She stared blankly. He went on, "This could be my chance to get the hell out of the dungeon and into what I really want to do."

"By stealing someone else's story?"

"I didn't steal it," he said defensively.

"Don't you think this reporter might be a little suspicious when he reads his story with your by-line? I don't think that will help your career much." Allan was silent. "What's his name anyway?"

He eyed her with mistrust.

"Don't worry," she said sarcastically. "I won't tell on you."

"Chandler."

"The columnist?"

"Yes."

"So what's he going to say when you write that story?" She mimicked a man's voice to answer her own question. "Nice piece of work, Allan." She looked away. "You'll probably get fired."

"I'm not going to write the story. Someone else will write it. Chandler will never know."

"Who?"

He shrugged noncommittally, but then his need to share his idea overruled his reluctance. "You ever hear of Andrew Petersen?"

"The Washington columnist?"

"Right. This thing is right up his alley. He's got an investigative team and he's always breaking big stories like this. He's got more inside information than anyone in the country."

"So what are you going to do? Call him and say you've got a story you think he should do? What will that accomplish for you?"

"I'm going to sell it to him," he said softly, tentatively, as though he had not yet thought it all the way through.

Julie couldn't keep the revulsion from her voice. "Sell it!"

Allan broke in quickly. "Not for money. For a job."

"A job?"

He nodded, some of his enthusiasm coming back. "He's the biggest thing in Washington. He could get me a job with the *Post*"—he snapped his fingers—"like that. Or maybe even a job as one of his investigative researchers. He doesn't do all that stuff by himself, you know."

"No. He just takes all the credit."

"Julie," he said, and she could feel the pain in his voice, "I'm desperate. I want a real job. I want to get started doing what I know I can do best. I'm dying in that morgue. I want out of there."

She felt sorry for him. Sorry because for the first time she realized how pathetic he was. "I understand," she said soothingly, because that was what he wanted her to say. He didn't want her advice; he wanted her forgiveness.

Allan wore a wounded smile. "I know it's not the ethical thing to do. I know it's Chandler's story, but he doesn't know what he's got. When I called him, he said it wasn't that important anyway." He clenched his fists, and when he spoke the muscles in his jaw rippled. "And I need it. I need it."

Julie reached over and tousled his hair affectionately. "I know you do," she purred. "And it's all right."

Allan grabbed her wrist and kissed the palm of her hand. "I knew I could depend on you," he said. He turned her wrist over and kissed the back of her hand. "You're not in any rush to go anywhere, are you?"

Julie sighed, her eyes went to the ceiling. "Allan, you're incredible."

Grinning like a schoolboy, and still holding her by the wrist, he led her to the bedroom. "I'm going to call Andrew Petersen today," he said. "But it can wait till later."

Chapter 20

Lawrence T. Jefferson sat behind the large oak desk in his paneled study carefully reading the medical report in the manila folder in front of him. The report was his, and the news was not good. What he read was a verification of his own doctor's opinion. Lawrence T. Jefferson was dying.

Although expected, the news was a bitter blow, and his wide shoulders were slumped in disappointment. He was a tall man in his early sixties, but with barely a touch of gray in his thick wavy hair. His eyes, usually a penetrating blue, were clouded in apprehension, and the forceful, jutting jaw was somewhat slack as his hopes faded with each paragraph.

He finished the report, closed the folder quietly, then sat for a moment without motion or thought. Slowly he swiveled his chair around so that he could look through the French doors behind him to the rolling Virginia hills that lay beyond. He loved that view—had had this house built here on this spot so that he could always enjoy the symmetry of this lush, green panorama. Always! He almost laughed. "Always" suddenly seemed like a word without meaning, a cruel joke some sadistic linguist had perpetrated on the psyche of man. There is no always.

He turned his chair back to his desk, straightened his shoulders, and took several deep breaths to clear his head. Gingerly, as though he were handling a bomb, he picked up the offending folder and relegated it and its contents to the security of the locked, lower desk drawer.

Jefferson picked up the phone and pushed one of several buttons. "I'd like to see Mr. Owens now."

Almost instantly there was a soft knock on the door and after a momentary pause the door opened and Francis Owens entered. His eyes darted around the room taking in the subdued elegance of the leather furnishings and the mahogany paneling before finally alighting on the man behind the desk. It was the first time that Francis Owens had ever been admitted to Mr. Jefferson's private study and he felt like a serf summoned into the presence of his lord. If he had been wearing a hat, he would have removed it and wrung it in his hands to demonstrate his subservience.

"Good afternoon, Mr. Jefferson, sir," he said, barely refraining from a short bow.

Jefferson nodded and motioned Owens to a chair in front of his desk. Owens approached the chair, then hesitated, waiting for a verbal command before sitting.

"Sit. Sit," said the older man impatiently.

Francis Owens was thirty-four. He was tall and gaunt with large, protuberant eyes and a hooked nose. He feared, and was in awe of, the man on the other side of the desk, sensing that Jefferson, for one reason or another, despised him. He was quite wrong. Lawrence T. Jefferson neither despised nor admired Owens; he was hardly aware that the man existed.

"You've brought your report with you, I trust?" said Jefferson.

Owens displayed the manila folder, which was already damp from his perspiring palms. "Yes, sir."

"Then tell me, how is the boy doing?"

Owens opened his folder. He had prepared a fifteen-page, typed, single-spaced report. "Mr. Jefferson," he began as he had rehearsed, "your son is a remarkable young man. The testing that I have done, and which I suggest should be verified by independent sources, suggests that his IQ is in the one hundred fifty- to one hundred sixty-range. He is bright, attentive, hardworking, and at the same time a remarkably well-balanced individual. David is the most able student it has ever been my privilege to teach."

"What about his progress in specific areas?"

Owens smiled as he flipped a page. "Presently, he reads at the fifth-grade level and his mathematical aptitude is at least three years above his grade level. He is particularly interested in science, where he is—"

"And how old is the boy?" interrupted Jefferson.

Owens stopped, his mouth open in midsentence. He stammered, "Your son is . . . is five, of course, Mr. Jefferson."

"I know that," said the other sharply. "When will he be six? When is his birthday?"

Owens's eyes bulged. "In June. Your son will be six in June."

Jefferson nodded, quietly calculating. "Go on."

Owens returned to his folder, droning on interminably about the boy's abilities. Jefferson seemed to be paying only scant attention. He interrupted again, "Have you been spending time on the history of the family?"

"Yes, Mr. Jefferson. As per your instructions, your son has become well acquainted with the contributions that the Jefferson family has made to the region and to the nation." Owens smiled again, showing perfect white teeth. "I personally have read to him excerpts from your father's autobiography and he is particularly interested in the many newspaper and magazine clippings about you, Mr. Jefferson."

Jefferson nodded. "That's good." He seemed pleased.

Sensing fertile ground, Owens continued. "Your son admires you and your accomplishments very much, Mr. Jefferson. I believe he wants to be just like you when he grows up. He has told me—"

Jefferson silenced him with a wave of his hand. A dark cloud seemed to have passed across his face. "Thank you for your report, Mr. Owens. I appreciate the job you are doing with the boy. You realize of course that next year he will be attending school, to be with other boys his age."

"Yes, of course, sir."

"Then keep up the good work. Work him hard. I want him to be ready."

Realizing his audience was over, Owens stood up. Jefferson did not offer his hand, nor did Owens dare to presume that much. As he turned to leave, his employer spoke. "Send the boy in to see me now. I'd like to speak with him."

Owens backed out of the room mumbling obsequiously, his head nodding profusely in an odious approximation of a bow.

A few minutes later there was a timid knock on the heavy oak door. "Enter," said Jefferson and the door swung open to reveal a small boy who was neatly dressed in a white shirt and gray slacks. The boy had dark, well-groomed hair, dark, luminous eyes, and the face of an angel. He advanced into the room and stood in front of his father's desk. He did not speak, but his eyes devoured every facet of his surroundings.

"Sit down, David."

With some difficulty, the boy climbed into the leather chair which was still warm from the sweating presence of Francis Owens.

"Well then," said Lawrence Jefferson, unsure as to where to begin this infrequent conversation. "How have you been getting along?"

David's eyes never left his father's face. He sat back, hands folded in his lap, legs dangling from the chair. "Fine, sir."

"Your teacher tells me that you are doing well with your studies."

David nodded and his father squirmed under the scrutiny of the boy's eyes. Perhaps it was the discomfort of not being able to engage the boy in conversation. Perhaps it was the knowledge that he had never felt any particular kinship with this boy and the additional knowledge that the boy was probably aware of that. Whatever it was, the boy had always made the father vaguely uncomfortable. There was now, and had always been, something particularly unsettling about this boy: the large eyes, the long stares, the uninterrupted silences. Perhaps, thought Lawrence T. Jefferson, it was because he was not really a boy at all—at least not like any boy he had ever known. He was intelligent, to be sure—wiser than his years could justify—and he was incredibly handsome; but there was no joy in him, no spirit. Jefferson shook his head sadly, admitting that he himself was at least partly to blame for this. He had left the boy completely in the hands of his wife. He had been simply too busy and, quite frankly, not terribly interested in raising another son—an adopted son at that.

"What are you reading now?" he asked.

"*Tom Sawyer*, by Mark Twain." The boy waited for comment and when there was none he went on. "His real name was Samuel Clemens, but he called himself Mark Twain when he wrote books."

"You like books and reading, don't you?"

"Yes," the boy said.

"It's time to start thinking about school for next year."

David smiled.

"Does that make you happy?"

"Yes, sir."

"Why is that?"

"I'd like to have other boys to play with."

"Next year you'll be going to school in New York. There will be plenty of boys for you to play with."

David's expression clouded. "Is that far away?"

"Yes," said Jefferson without a trace of gentleness in his voice.

The boy swallowed. "Will Mommy be there with me?"

"Your mother will visit you often. She will be with you as often as she can."

David looked down at the carpet, his legs swinging. He looked up at his father, then back down.

"What is it?"

The boy cast a furtive look at his father and then again looked away. "Will . . ." he started, then stopped.

"Go on. You may ask."

"Will you visit me?"

The question was so unexpected that Jefferson was taken

completely by surprise. It had never occurred to him that the boy would care one way or the other. For a moment he was so flustered that he was unable to answer. Finally he spoke. "Would you like me to visit you?"

The boy's eyes opened wide, dancing in the reflected light from the French doors. "Oh yes, Da—father."

Lawrence T. Jefferson felt his eyes sting and grow damp and he was not sure whether it was for the boy or himself. "I will . . . be with you"—he paused, searching for the right word—"always."

Chapter 21

"So how did the wife take it when you told her her husband was dead?" Chandler asked. They were seated in the back seat of a taxi on their way from the airport to their hotel.

"She cried," said Shelley, almost in amazement. "This guy walks out on her; she hasn't heard from him in something like four years, and she cries."

"I have been told that women can be unpredictable," Chandler said straight-faced. "What else did she say?"

"Well, she wanted to know if we were positive. I told her that his ID had been confirmed by the personnel photo from Indianapolis. I also told her the NYPD would be getting in touch with her pretty soon. Actually I thought they would have called before I did."

"The wheels of justice," said Chandler, "ain't in no hurry."

"Well, I hated to be the one to break news like that."

He squinted at her. "You do it every night."

"What?"

"The *Eleven O'Clock News*."

Shelley wrinkled her nose. "That's different."

"Only in degree."

Shelley gave him a long, hard look. "Thanks, Chandler. I needed that."

They rode the rest of the way in silence.

At the hotel Chandler took charge of the bags and paid the taxi, while Shelley went to register at the main desk. The bellhop placed Shelley's three new suitcases on a trolley, then inspected Chandler's beat up suitcase carefully before picking it up. There were Yankee and Met stickers on the sides from when he had traveled as a sportswriter with the teams.

"You a ballplayer or sumpin'?" asked the bellhop.

"Yeah, I'm Pete Rose. Doncha reconize me?"

The bellhop, a tall reed-thin black man, looked at Chandler carefully. "Shee-eet," he said laughing. "You Pete Rose, I'm Nolan Ryan."

Chandler followed the bellhop into the hotel. Both men were still laughing. He came up behind Shelley, who was signing a room card at the reception desk. "Did you get us a nice room, sweetheart?"

The young woman behind the desk jerked her head up from the form she was filling.

Shelley looked at Chandler with bemused disdain. "I got us two rooms, Chandler."

"When are you ever going to get over this shyness of yours," he said, then turned to the desk clerk. "Two weeks we've been married and still it's separate rooms."

The young woman's eyes narrowed as she realized that Chandler was putting her on. "The rooms have an adjoining door," she said helpfully.

"Perhaps tonight we can sleep with the door open, sweetheart?"

"Over my dead body," said Shelley as she headed for the elevator.

Chandler shrugged at the desk clerk and the bellhop shook his head. "Seems like," he said, looking at Chandler, "Pete Rose goin' to strike out tonight."

Shelley was hanging some things in a closet when Chandler knocked on the adjoining door. "Come in," she called. "It's open."

He entered and looked around. "Nice room. Just like

mine." Shelley merely nodded and continued hanging up her clothes. Chandler said, "I've already finished unpacking."

"I'm not surprised," she said, without turning to look at him.

He was squirming a little, straining to make small talk, but Shelley was not being very helpful. "What do you have in all those suitcases?" he asked.

She turned slowly to face him. "Did anyone ever tell you it's not polite to ask a woman what she has in her suitcase?"

"Sorry." He wasn't sure if she was serious or not. "I don't know what came over me. I must've had too much to drink on the plane."

"Actually," she said, "if you must know, one bag is filled with my Fredericks of Hollywood lingerie collection."

He was glad that she had made a joke. "I figured it was something like that. Want me to help you unpack?"

"No," she said laughing, but then the silence came between them again. Somehow, being in a hotel room together did not seem to be conducive to conversation, and Chandler realized that he had been straining to be funny in order to conceal a strange kind of embarrassment he felt in being here with her.

Shelley was finished, but kept arranging and rearranging the clothes in the closet. Chandler sat down in a chair at the window and stared out at the street below. "We should have gotten a lower floor," he said.

"Why's that?"

He shrugged. "It's a long way down in case of fire."

Shelley finally closed the closet door. "You're going to make me a nervous wreck," she said. "First it's the plane. Now it's the hotel. I can't figure you out."

He said nothing.

"Call room service if you want a drink," Shelley said.

He scrunched up his face. "Good God, no. If I have anything else to drink, I'll sleep until Monday."

"You hold it pretty good," she said. "You were really knocking them back on the plane."

He shook his head and smiled sheepishly. "I don't usually drink like that. If I drank like that on the ground, I would pass out. Somehow on a plane it doesn't affect me. It just helps me calm down."

"You really do hate flying, don't you? I don't think I ever saw anyone quite so nervous."

Chandler looked down at the carpet. "I was in a plane crash once. It still bothers me."

"I'm sorry," said Shelley. "I didn't realize. What happened?"

He laughed a short, twisted laugh and said, "Nothing much. It just crashed; that's all."

She could see he didn't want to talk about it, but she couldn't resist the ultimate question. "Was anyone killed?"

He nodded his head slowly several times. "Maybe I will have that drink," he said, reaching for the phone. "You want one?"

"Yeah. Why the hell not?"

Shelley watched him as he sipped. He had said hardly a word since room service had delivered the drinks. He sat on the edge of the chair looking toward the window. When he wasn't sipping his drink he held his glass in both hands between his knees.

Shelley rambled on, talking about anything she could think of, talking for the sake of hearing her own voice. He mumbled only an occasional response.

"You OK?" she asked him.

He looked up, nodded, and took another sip from his glass.

"What do you think we should do first?"

He seemed puzzled.

She went on. "Should we visit the wife first? Or should we go see the loving brother-in-law."

Chandler shrugged noncommittally.

On impulse Shelley went to him and placed a hand on his shoulder. "If you want, I'll go see his wife. She's expecting us today. You can stay here and rest up. Tomorrow we'll see the brother-in-law." Surprising even herself, she kissed him on the forehead.

Startled, Chandler looked up into her eyes. "No," he said. "Let's go see her together."

Shelley nodded and smiled and then went to her dressing table where she took a brush and proceeded to brush her hair in long, quick strokes.

Chandler watched her as she worked. He saw her both real and reflected in the mirror, and sought inperfections in either view. From behind her golden hair hung to just shoulder length he followed the line of her body down to the cloth of her skirt, stretched tight over her behind and on down to her long, perfectly muscled legs, to her delicately thin ankles. In the mirror he saw her face, apparently lost in dreamy thought, as she gently stroked her hair. Only someone as beautiful as this, he thought, could turn the simple act of combing her hair into an incredibly elegant performance.

Shelley continued brushing. Out of the corner of her eye she saw Chandler's reflection watching her in the mirror. She smiled and tossed her head to one side, knowing how good her hair looked as it swung back and forth. She pouted a little, checking her lipstick, and ran her tongue across her lips to moisten them.

Chandler looked away. He took a mouthful of Scotch. Don't do this to yourself, he thought. Everybody who comes near this girl must get smitten. Don't let it happen to you.

Shelley turned away from the mirror. "I'll call the wife and let her know we're on our way. Then we can get going."

Chandler raised his glass. "Any time you're ready."

The wife turned out to be a small, dark-haired woman in her early twenties. She wore her long hair pulled straight back in a ponytail revealing a face that was—if not beautiful—strikingly attractive. Her loose-fitting dress could not conceal the amply rounded body beneath.

Chandler was surprised. He had expected to find a dowdy, abandoned wife, someone who had been left for a younger, more attractive woman. Instead he found himself in the presence of a young, very attractive woman who seemed in perfect control of herself.

Shelley was the first to break the silence. "We're very sorry about your husband, Mrs. Roman," she said as the woman admitted the two visitors into her apartment.

The apartment was small. It was the kind of apartment with a tiny kitchen in one corner that could be hidden behind a screen. Directly across from the entry hall was a door that led to the bedroom. The living room was neat, but things seemed somehow out of place, as though everything had been hurriedly arranged a few minutes before the visitors had arrived.

The woman smiled as if Shelley had said something funny, but in her eyes there was only sadness. "I hardly think of him as my husband anymore. I don't even use his name. I started using my own name again a few months after he left. It's Devereaux. Karen Devereaux. Please call me Karen."

They sat down, Chandler and Shelley on a couch and Karen Devereaux on a chair across from them. Chandler began by asking, "How long were you and Al Roman married before he . . ." He stumbled over the words.

"Before he walked out on me?" Karen Devereaux smiled. "About a year." She noticed that Chandler looked away as she answered his question. "Don't worry; I'm not embarrassed by it. I always knew that we were not destined for a long, happy marriage. We could have just lived together, I guess, but I'd been through that a couple of times. When I got pregnant, I was the one who wanted to get married. I thought it would bring a little stability to our relationship. Knowing the kind of person that Al was I didn't expect permanence."

Shelley jumped in. "What kind of a person was he?"

Karen Devereaux thought for a moment. "Pretty ordinary guy, I guess. Except"—at this point her eyes drifted to the corners of the room—"he always seemed to be looking for something."

Shelley and Chandler spoke at the same time. "Something?"

"Yeah. Something. Y'know? Something extra. As if whatever he had wasn't enough. He was always looking for the angle, a way to break out of his rut. It used to bother him that he didn't seem to be getting anywhere in broadcasting. He wanted to get into television. He said that's where the big money was. But he couldn't get a break. He didn't have the look."

"The look?" asked Chandler.

"Y'know, the look. He wasn't pretty enough." She looked directly at Shelley. "He said that TV was filled with pretty people, women *and* men, who got their jobs not because they were good but because they had the look." She smiled and said to Shelley, "You work in TV. Right?"

Shelley coughed a little. "I'm afraid so," she said with an embarrassed smile.

"I thought so. You've definitely got the look." She looked at Chandler. For a moment there was a long silence.

"Newspaper," he said. "I don't work in television."

"I didn't think so."

Chandler laughed. "No look?"

"Afraid not. But don't let it bother you. You look OK."

Shelley coughed an interruption. "If I might get back to asking you about your husband."

Karen Devereaux didn't seem to be paying any attention to what Shelley had said. Instead, she was staring at Chandler, a small flicker of a smile dancing on her lips as if she had just thought of something that was very pleasing. Finally she turned to Shelley and said, "Let me ask you something." Shelley nodded. "Why do you want to know about Al?"

Chandler broke in. "Although your husband's death was apparently the result of random violence, we have reason to suspect that he may have been, for some reason, picked out of the crowd."

Karen Devereaux's eyebrows went up. "Oh," she said.

"Yes," said Shelley, anxious to get back into the flow of the interview. "We think he might have been murdered." She watched Karen Devereaux for any change in expression. There was none. "That doesn't seem to shock or surprise you."

Karen Devereaux shrugged. "I suppose not." She took a cigarette from the coffee table and offered one to Chandler, who accepted, and then, almost as an afterthought, she offered one to Shelley, who refused. Chandler produced a lighter, and as he lit her cigarette, Karen Devereaux held his hand for what Shelley thought was an inordinately long time.

Shelley was beginning to feel like a fifth wheel. "Why wouldn't it surprise you that your husband was murdered?"

Karen blew a long stream of smoke in her direction that Shelley pretended to ignore. "He was always getting himself involved with an assortment of shady characters, most of them small-time hoods and the like. But a few months after we got married, he got himself involved with some heavy hitters."

"Heavy hitters?" asked Shelley.

"Big-time hoods," explained Chandler.

Karen Devereaux smiled at him and nodded. "He got involved with some Vegas gambling people. He used to fly up there all the time."

"Did he take you with him?" Chandler asked.

"No. He had other diversions there." She shrugged. "I knew what was happening, but by that time I didn't really care anymore." She gave Chandler a slow smile. "We all have our diversions."

Shelley jumped in quickly. "But you said you wouldn't be surprised if your husband was murdered. Why not?"

"I think he knew too much about those people. That's why he ran off. That's why he disappeared."

"He told you that?" asked Chandler.

She hesitated. "No, not in so many words, but that was the gist of it."

"Did he tell you what he knew?"

"No. But he became very friendly with some of the Hughes people."

In the back of Chandler's brain a small red warning light began to glow. "Hughes?"

"Howard Hughes." She smiled. "You have heard of him, haven't you?" Both reporters nodded dumbly and Karen went on. "Al became friendly with some of those guys. Not Hughes himself of course. He never laid eyes on him, but through his gambling connections he did get to know some of the Hughes people. That's where he got the information that put him in danger."

Chandler leaned forward, his interest suddenly sparked. "Did he tell you what it was? This information?"

She laughed. "He wouldn't tell his own mother. He only told me that it was about Howard Hughes's will."

Chandler and Shelley waited for her to continue. She stubbed out her cigarette in the ashtray and removed another from the pack. Chandler again lit her cigarette. "Anything else?" he asked finally.

She shrugged. "He said that when Hughes died his will would create a sensation." She looked from one to the other to emphasize her point. "And he got that information from one of Hughes's lawyers, the guy who wrote out the will."

Shelley said, "But there wasn't any will."

Karen smiled knowingly. "That's right."

"So where is this lawyer now?" asked Chandler. "Why didn't anyone talk to him?"

"The day that Howard Hughes died, his lawyer was killed in a plane crash."

Chandler and Shelley looked at each other. "The same lawyer who drew up the will?" said Chandler.

"Some coincidence, huh?" said Karen Devereaux, the knowing smile still playing on her lips. "The richest man in the world dies; his lawyer is killed on the same day; and no will is ever found."

"There must have been other lawyers."

Karen nodded. "*They* didn't draw up the will. Of course his chief executive officers denied that any of his lawyers had ever drawn up a will of any kind."

"Wait a minute," said Shelley. "I'm not sure I understand this. Exactly what do you think happened here?"

Karen Devereaux looked at Shelley with only thinly disguised contempt. She then looked to Chandler as if to ask, "Where did you get this dummy?" She said, "It sounds to me as if someone in the Hughes corporation didn't like where the money was supposed to go, so after Hughes died they got rid of the will and the lawyer who wrote it."

Chandler asked, "Do you know the lawyer's name?"

"Sure. It was Arnold. Jason Arnold."

Shelley asked a few more questions but Chandler seemed to have lost interest in the inquiry. He was preoccupied and in a hurry to leave. As they headed for the door Shelley asked one last question. "Did your husband ever work with Jonathan Carruthers here in Houston?"

Karen Devereaux laughed derisively at the mention of the name. "Jonathan Carruthers used my husband like he used everyone else. He made a name for himself by using material that my husband had uncovered." She shook her head sadly. "Al put stories on the radio and nothing would happen. Then Carruthers would do the same stories on TV and get all the publicity."

"But did they ever work together?"

"Carruthers was everything that Al hated about television. Pretty boys without brains or talent. I don't think he ever worked with him."

Shelley forced a smile. "Perhaps not," she said as she and Chandler left the apartment.

Chandler was still quiet when they got back to the car they had rented. "What is it?" asked Shelley.

"Hughes and Arnold. Those are the first two names on my list." He looked at her. "Maybe we're finally starting to get somewhere."

"Yes, but where are we getting?"

Chandler had no answer.

They drove north on the Eastex Freeway. Shelley seemed more interested in the construction, proceeding at boomtown pace in downtown Houston, than in their interview with

Karen Devereaux. She wouldn't admit it to anyone but herself, but she was disturbed that the interview had seemed to go over and around her. Chandler had asked most of the questions and received most of the answers. As Chandler drove across town, Shelley looked up at the tall buildings lining the streets. "I don't know if I'd put much stock in what that woman says," she said casually, still looking up at the buildings as if New York didn't have such skyscrapers.

Chandler chuckled. "She didn't seem to like you very much, but I thought she was a very charming, straightforward young woman."

"If I hadn't been there she'd have had your pants off in the living room."

"That's what I mean. Very charming and straightforward. I may have to go back and interview her by myself. I think I can get more information out of her that way. It's all in the technique, Shelley. You just have to know how to conduct an interview."

Shelley stewed silently.

Chandler said, "When are we going to see the brother-in-law?"

Shelley looked at her watch. "Tomorrow. It's getting late."

"Do you want to stop someplace and get something to eat, or should we eat at the hotel?"

"I forgot to tell you. I'm meeting someone for dinner."

Chandler couldn't keep the surprise from his voice. "Who?"

"One of the anchormen at our affiliate here in Houston. He's an old friend. I talked with him before we left New York and we made arrangements to have dinner. It's partly business, partly social."

Chandler tried to keep his voice light and cheerful as if he were not deeply disappointed. "Oh," he said glumly.

"You don't mind, do you?"

"Why should I mind?" His own voice reminded him of his daughter's valiant effort to be brave when he told her of her parents' impending divorce.

"I should have told you, I guess. It didn't seem important at the time, but now that I think of it, it does seem rather rude to bring you all the way to Houston and then tell you to have dinner all by yourself."

"You didn't bring me to Houston, and I don't mind

having dinner by myself." He hated the way his voice sounded. I'm going to start whining in a minute, he thought.

"Why don't you join us for dinner?"

"No thanks. I'm sure I can find some diversions on my own."

"Come on," she said. "Don't be silly. You can join us."

"Look, it's not like we're together or anything. We just happen to be working on something at the same time. You go to dinner with your anchorman and I'll see you later."

They rode in silence for a while with Shelley watching him out of the corner of her eye. She knew he was disappointed that they would not be together at dinner, and that gave her a surprising feeling of elation. She turned a little so that she could watch him. His face was without expression, his jaw set, mouth closed, eyes intently on the road. It was a good face, she decided, strong, intelligent, and . . . caring. She watched his hands, close together at the top of the steering wheel. There was strength in those hands, and for just the briefest of moments she felt the impulse to place her hand on one of his.

"Will you be back in the hotel tonight or should I expect you back sometime in the morning?" he said.

"Don't be a pain in the ass, Chandler."

"Just checking."

Chapter 22

Andrew Petersen was America's leading political columnist. His thrice weekly column, *Dateline D.C.*, was carried in over a thousand newspapers in the United States and in many foreign capitals. He was forty-five years old and grossly overweight. It was said—usually safely out of earshot—that he was boorish and overbearing. It was also said that he combined the tenacity of a bulldog and the curiosity of a cat with the ethics of a pit viper. To those who did not work for him, or fear his wrath, he often displayed charm and a sharp wit; but for those whose great misfortune it was to cross his path in some professional capacity, the results could be disastrous. It was rumored that the turnover rate was so great on the Petersen staff that one Washington reporter, with an ear for metaphor, had likened the columnist to a snake who sheds his skin every two years.

Petersen could destroy careers and reputations with a word. In the backstabbing, bureaucratic climate of Washington, D.C., this power made him even more effective than he might otherwise have been. In the futile hope that when their turn came, he would treat them with a modicum of mercy, people fell all over each other to give Petersen inside information about coworkers and politicians. His accusations were often so general and painted with such a broad stroke that those on the periphery of scandal were often damned with those who truly deserved exposure. The secretary who unknowingly cashed the checks from an illegal source was condemned along with the congressman who spent the money. The Air Force colonel whose job it was to fly congressmen, senators, and businessmen on all-expense-paid junkets, was condemned along with the generals who arranged the trips, and the politicians and businessmen who accepted such favors.

Andrew Petersen had reached his position of power after replacing the originator of the *Dateline D.C.* column, Ty Jackson, one of Washington's most respected reporters, who had met his untimely death in an automobile accident. After Jackson's death, everyone in Washington wondered which of the five top researchers would take over the successful column. To the surprise of almost everyone, the parent syndicate awarded the prize to Petersen, who, although hardworking and competent, had been the junior member of the team that had supplied most of the column's stories. The others resigned, miffed that their junior colleague had been chosen over them, and were subsequently replaced by a younger, more aggressive—some would say obnoxious—group of researchers who, if Washington veterans were to be believed, did not demonstrate the same maturity of judgment that had characterized the previous research group.

The word in the capital was that *Dateline D.C.* now went for the fast, sensational, headline story, rather than the in-depth, investigative study that had been the column's forte for over twenty years. The general public, however, had responded to the new sensationalism with a ravenous appetite. The column's popularity had increased immeasurably in the seven years that Andrew Petersen's photograph and by-line had adorned its logo, and he was generally acknowledged to be one of the most powerful and influential journalists in the nation's capital.

On this quiet evening in Georgetown, he sat at his favorite table in his favorite restaurant, his fork hovering over the remnants of a huge sirloin steak. As was his usual practice, he had eschewed any salad or vegetable, choosing to accompany his meat with only large quantities of good wine. He dabbed at the corners of his mouth with a napkin, checking his watch as he did so. He hoped that this Allan Greenfield, whom he had promised to meet, would be at least a few minutes late so that he could finish his dinner.

Petersen did not like to engage in conversation while he was eating and unless he was invited to one of Washington's many dinner parties, he usually dined alone. He preferred cocktail parties to dinner parties because then he could eat before arriving. Eating was serious business to Andrew Petersen and he coveted food the way some men covet money. He ate, elbows on the table, knife and fork in hand, ripping his meat apart and stuffing huge portions into his mouth. As he chewed, his arms formed a protective shield around his plate, as if he feared that some scavenger might seize its contents.

He liked to think as he chewed and at this moment he was wondering about this irritating young upstart who had insisted upon a personal audience. Usually one of Petersen's staff-researchers handled this sort of thing, but Greenfield had been adamant: He would speak only to Petersen himself. Ordinarily this kind of demand would be ignored and the caller would be told that he could peddle his story elsewhere, but this one had been different. He had intimated that this story had something to do with Howard Hughes and his missing will. Hughes still held some mysterious appeal for the American public, and stories about him and his fortune were always very popular with Petersen's readers. It was the kind of story that sometimes led to a magazine feature in *Esquire* or *Penthouse* or *Playboy*, and Petersen enjoyed the additional notoriety that such exposure could bring.

Somewhat reluctantly, therefore, Petersen had agreed to allow this young hotshot to meet him at Mario's Restaurant at precisely eight o'clock. That would give Petersen time to finish his dinner and then have his coffee and a cigar while Greenfield told him what was on his mind. This way, if he were not interested in what the young man had to say, he could just get up and leave without ruining his dinner.

At the stroke of eight, Petersen shoveled the last piece of meat into his mouth and shivered with satisfaction, knowing that his repast had been undisturbed. As the columnist flushed the last morsel down his gullet with a very nice California burgundy, Allan Greenfield entered the dining room. Greenfield had sounded hungry on the phone and now, as he searched for Petersen, his eyes darting to every corner of the room like a beast of prey, the columnist knew that this was his man. He smiled as he pushed his plate aside and dabbed his napkin to his corpulent lips.

Waiting until Greenfield's eyes had found their target, Petersen beckoned the young man toward his table. When Greenfield extended his hand, the older man reluctantly offered him a limp handshake, as if he expected the younger man to kiss the back of his hand. As far as Petersen was concerned, that act would have been indicative of their relationship: Petersen the monarch, king of the by-line, and this lowly reporter who wanted an audience with the great one.

"Be seated," Petersen commanded, indicating the single chair opposite his own. "I was just about to have my coffee. Perhaps you would care to join me?"

"I'd rather have something stronger."

Petersen ignored this presumptuous remark and motioned to the waiter. "Two coffees please, Walter. I'll be leaving very soon, so perhaps you could bring my check." He stared at Greenfield so that the import of his remarks would not be lost.

"This won't take long," said Greenfield; then he gave a slow knowing smile that Petersen did not care for. "But when you hear what I have to say, you won't be in such a hurry to get going."

Petersen raised one narrow eyebrow. He wasn't used to such insolent behavior on the part of supplicants. This new generation, he thought, no respect for anything. "Go on," he said. "You have five minutes of my time."

"Before I tell you anything," said Allan, "I think we should discuss price."

Petersen allowed the barest trace of a sneer to cross his lips. "We never pay money to informants. It taints the news-gathering process with the odor of subornation."

"I'm not talking about money."

Petersen squinted in momentary puzzlement.

"What I want," Allan continued, "is a job."

"A job?"

"Yes. You've got connections throughout the newspaper business. I want you to get me a job."

"I thought you had a job. Didn't you say you worked at the *News?*"

Allan's face contorted in disgust. "That's not a job. It's a prison sentence."

Petersen's smile was a red slash across his pallid features. "How impatient all you young men are today. I did my time in the mines, you know. Doing research work and watching someone else get the credit."

"I've had enough of that. I want out now."

Petersen shrugged. "If I wanted to, I could have you working at the *Post* tomorrow, or just about anywhere else."

Allan smiled. "That's the ticket."

"I said, if I wanted to." He paused for a moment as the waiter returned with the coffee. "It would have to be quite a story in order for me to expend that kind of effort."

"Effort? You could do it with a phone call."

"That's true," said Petersen, smiling. "It's not a physical effort we're talking about here. I have learned, over the years, that when one is owed favors, it is rarely to one's benefit to ask for them. Today's favor is tomorrow's obligation. I'd rather have someone owe me a favor then do a favor for me. If I ask someone to give you a job, he doesn't owe me a favor anymore. Understand?"

Allan nodded and Petersen went on. "So if I'm going to relinquish a favor, it has to be worth it."

"This is worth it."

"We'll see." Petersen picked up his coffee cup and checked his watch. "You've already used up most of your time, young man; I think you'd better get on with your story." He sipped from his cup, extending a fat pinky in a grotesque attempt at gentility.

"What guarantees do I have that you'll get me the job if I tell you my story?"

"None," said Petersen. He placed his cup back on the saucer before proceeding. "You've probably heard lots of things about me: how I am totally unethical, a scavenger, a destroyer of careers, a real bastard." Allan did not protest the accuracy of these remarks and Petersen smiled. "They're all true," he said. "But there is something else you should know." The smile faded from his face as he spoke, "I did not get where I am today by neglecting my sources. If my sources want confidentiality, they get it. You want a job. If your story is worth it, you'll get it."

Allan nodded, satisfied that Petersen would keep his word. "OK," he said, taking the computer printouts from his inside jacket pocket. "Here's what I've got."

Petersen said absolutely nothing as Allan told him the story. He sat motionless, his face an impassive mask, showing neither acceptance nor rejection, as Allan traced the relationships and patterns that he had deduced from the computer's information.

Finally Allan was finished and the two men stared at each other over the table. "Well," said Allan, breaking the silence, "what do you think?"

Petersen drummed his fingers on the table. "Quite a story, if it's true." He paused while his fingers continued to drum. "If it's true, it worth everything you say."

Allan beamed.

"But," said Petersen, wiping the smile from Allan's face, "we don't know if it's true."

"But the evidence——"

"Is purely circumstantial." Petersen pointed to the computer printout. "Do you have another copy of that?"

Allan hesitated for just a fraction. "No," he lied.

Petersen shrugged. "I'll need that if I am to verify this story."

"How?"

"I'll put my team of investigators on it, the best team of reporters in the country. If there is any truth to this fantastic allegation, they will find it."

"Why not let me work with them?" asked Allan, hopefully.

Petersen shook his head very slowly. "No," he said. "You would be trying to prove that your story is true. My people will be trying to prove that it is not. You have a personal stake in proving the truth of this story. I find that that often makes a reporter ignore important facts. I never allow a source to participate in an investigation." He pursed his lips. "We may ask you to supply additional information or to verify some of the questions you have raised." Petersen reached for the printout. "I'll have this copied and return the originals to you."

Allan hesitated.

"Does anyone else know about this story?" asked Petersen.

Allan lied again. "No." For a moment he kept his hand hovering protectively over the pages, then with the barest hint of a sigh he allowed Petersen to take them.

"Don't worry," said Petersen, folding the papers and putting them into his inside jacket pocket. "I'll get back to you within the week on how the investigation is going. It shouldn't take long."

"And my copy of the printout?"

Petersen smiled. "Of course. Give me your address and phone number. I'll have your original in the mail to you on Monday."

Allan scribbled the information on a notepad, ripped out the page, and handed it to Petersen who slipped it into his pocket without looking at it.

The columnist studied Allan's face carefully. He could read the younger man's mind. "Don't worry," he said. "You'll get your reward. There's no need for me to trick you on this. You'll just have to trust me."

Allan had never met anyone who appeared less trustworthy than Andrew Petersen, but he knew he had no other choice. He nodded.

"One thing," said Petersen. "I demand absolute exclusivity. No one else even knows anything about it, understand? If I do this story, it will be an Andrew Petersen *Dateline D.C.* exclusive. If anyone else knows about it, or even thinks that the story came from outside my organization, our agreement is off."

Allan nodded but his face showed his puzzlement.

"Call it ego if you wish, but I want people to think my investigative team uncovered this story. I don't want it known that this story walked in the door and plopped itself on my desk—or should I say dinner table?"

"Whatever you say, Mr. Petersen. It makes no difference to me. Just so long as I get my job."

"Very well then. Run along, my boy. I'll be in touch with you within a week." He smiled. "If your story is accurate, you can begin making plans to move to another newspaper."

"The Washington *Post* will be fine," said Allan.

"No problem. I'll call Ben Bradlee next week." He gave a beaming, almost lecherous smile, revealing brown-stained teeth. "He owes me lots of favors."

Allan rose from his chair and both men shook hands in mock cordiality.

Petersen ordered another coffee and sat staring into space for ten minutes after the young man had left his table. Finally he looked up and signaled the waiter who had been anxiously hovering near his table.

"Telephone," he said absently, and when the phone was brought to his table he quickly dialed a local number. "It's me," he said. "Yes, I just spoke with him. . . . No, he doesn't know very much. He's only scratched the surface." He listened for a moment, nervously fingering his empty coffee cup. "I might be able to dissuade him by telling him that I was unable to corroborate his information. . . . Yes; you're probably right." He reached into his pocket and removed the small piece of notepaper that Allan had given him. "If you feel it's necessary. . . . His name is Allan Greenfield and he lives at Four eighty-six West One hundred fourteenth Street in New York City. I'll leave it to you to decide. . . . I wash my hands of it then." Petersen took a deep breath. "Make sure you tell them that I did my part."

The phone went dead in his ear and Petersen felt foolish as he feigned a good-bye. He got up from the table and it wasn't till he noticed his waiter that he remembered that he hadn't paid his check. He sat back down and counted out the money, leaving, what was for him, an inordinately large tip. Knowing what he had done a few minutes before gave him a compulsion to be generous.

As he got up he recounted the money on the table, and took back a dollar.

Chapter 23

Chandler sat in the stuffed chair in his hotel room, his feet up on one of the twin beds and a bottle of Scotch perched nearby. The TV set was on and he found himself staring mindlessly at some game show where a row of women, pulled from the audience, jumped joyously at the prospect of being able to give the right price for a microwave oven while the announcer blared, "Charlene Hobson, c'mon down!"

He shook his head, got up, and changed the channel. Richard Dawson yelled, "Survey Says!" and Chandler switched off the set. Big Saturday night in Houston, he thought.

With the set off he could hear the sound of the shower running in Shelley's room. He tried not to think about that. He poured himself another good dollop of Scotch and sank down into the chair. The sound of the shower was everywhere. He closed his eyes and let it envelop him. It was impossible not to think of Shelley in there.

He realized he was already halfway to being totally inebriated. Not the kind of fall down drunkenness that comes to the casual drinker who has a bit too much, but the mellow mind-dulling drunkenness that comes with an all-day drinking binge. He hadn't done this in years—not since the breakup of his marriage. He was feeling sorry for himself and couldn't remember if he was drinking because he felt sorry for himself or he was feeling sorry for himself because he was drinking. Thinking about the woman in the shower in the next room didn't help much. If he closed his eyes he could picture her—hair tied back, wet, soapy—.

Stop it!

He got up and turned the TV back on, loud, and watched two families trying to guess how a hundred people in California had answered questions about various topics. He was amazed that not one of the hundred had listed *Thirty-Nine Steps* as one of Hitchcock's films and felt immediate kinship with the disappointed man who had given that as an answer. He guffawed out loud when one of the contestants claimed that New England was an American city where the residents spoke with an accent.

It was all nonsense but it helped him ignore the sound of the shower next door.

On TV Richard Dawson was kissing everyone good-bye when there was a knock on the door between the two rooms.

"It's open," Chandler called out.

Shelley stood in the doorway. She wore a brown tweed jacket over a tan skirt and silk camisole. Her hair was worn up, revealing small, gold pendant earrings. Chandler released his breath slowly as he watched her.

"Last chance to join us," she said. "I'm ready to leave."

He forced a smile. "No, thanks. I'm having company." He raised his glass in mock salute.

"Have you eaten anything?"

"Maybe later."

She went to the mirror above his dresser and made some minor adjustments to her hair, watching him in the glass. "We're having dinner here in the hotel, so if you want to join us later for a drink . . ."

"Don't worry about me. I'll be fine."

She smiled. "You could always call your little friend, Karen Devereaux. I'm sure she'd be glad to hear from you."

He pretended that the thought had never occurred to him. "I've got the feeling that Miss Devereaux is never wanting for male companionship."

"You're probably right about that," said Shelley, turning away from the mirror. She faced him. "How do I look?"

Chandler wanted to say something like "magnificent" or "marvelous" but somehow the words would not come. Instead he shrugged and said, "You look pretty good."

Shelley put her hands on her hips and tilted her head to one side. "Pretty good?" She turned again to look at herself in the mirror. "Pretty good? Maybe I should start all over."

As she went to the door, Chandler called her name. She turned to face him, an expectant smile on her face, and for a moment their eyes met across the space of the room. Then Chandler looked down into his drink. "Never mind," he said.

Her hand on the doorknob, she stood there waiting. "What is it?" she said. Her voice was soft and soothing.

Chandler looked up. "You look fabulous," he said very quietly.

Her smile filled the room, and for one desperate moment Chandler thought she would come to him. "That's more like it," she said as she opened the door. "I'll see you tomorrow." She winked, closed the door behind her, and was gone.

Chandler held his ice-filled glass against his forehead. He closed his eyes but the vision of her framed in the doorway remained riveted in his mind. "Forget it," he said out loud.

*   *   *

Chandler was getting hungry. He looked at the half-empty bottle of Scotch and his stomach rumbled a protest against further intrusion. He thought about where he would eat and, knowing that the real reason for his decision was his desire to see whom Shelley was with, he decided against room service.

He got himself cleaned up a little and pulled on his jacket. On his way to the door he inspected himself in the mirror and was not pleased by what he saw. His face seemed puffy and bloated, forcing his eyes into small slits suspended above large bags. With a thumb and forefinger he forced his eyes wide open, revealing the red veins running like bloody tributaries across the whites of his eyes.

"Look like something the cat dragged in," he said aloud and headed downstairs.

Taking a seat at the end of the long curved bar, Chandler saw that the dining room was on the other side of a low partition. The room was fairly large and dimly illuminated. Chandler told himself he was inspecting the plush decor, red and gold velours and rich, dark mahogany, but he knew that he was looking for Shelley. From the other side of the partition he could hear the soft murmur of the mingled conversations and the occasional clatter of the silverware from the kitchen.

Then he saw her. She seemed framed in the soft spotlight, radiantly beautiful, more visible than anyone else in the room. Her companion was leaning across the table animatedly telling some obviously hilarious story, and Shelley's laughter came drifting across the room. The storyteller was young, perhaps as young as Shelley, but with the mature good looks of a typical anchorman. He was too handsome to be old, and too seasoned to be young, and Chandler found himself vaguely disturbed that Shelley seemed to be enjoying his company so much.

The bartender snapped Chandler from his reverie. "Would you like something, sir?"

For a moment Chandler had forgotten why he had come downstairs. "Let me have a beer." Then it came to him. "Can I get something to eat?"

The bartender nodded.

"Cheeseburger and fries?"

The bartender's grimace told Chandler he had made the wrong selection. "What then?" he asked.

"Roast beef sandwich or—"

"That's fine. I'll take the roast beef with an order of fries on the side."

Nodding, the bartender jotted down the order, gave Chandler a mug of beer, and then retreated to the far end of the bar.

Chandler returned to his vigil. This time he watched Shelley and her anchorman in the mirror behind the bar, feeling voyeuristic as he casually sipped his beer while keeping his eye on the reflected images. The anchorman was still telling his stories and Shelley seemed to be enjoying herself immensely. At one point the young man reached across the table and covered Shelley's hand with his. Chandler noticed that Shelley made no attempt to withdraw her hand.

Chandler looked at himself in the mirror, amazed at how remarkably sad his face looked. If she takes him up to her room, he said in silent conversation with his own image, I won't be able to sleep thinking about the two of them next door.

The bartender placed Chandler's sandwich in front of him and he ordered another beer. As he took his first bite, he noticed in the mirror that a man was standing at Shelley's table.

Shelley was not aware that anyone else was there until she noticed that the anchorman was looking up at someone. She looked up too and saw a leering face hovering over her.

"You're Shelley James, aren't you?" the face said drunkenly.

"Yes, I am," said Shelley cautiously, a smile frozen on her face.

"I knew it," said the intruder, breaking into raucous laughter. "I'm from New York. I watch your show all the time." He stuck out his hand. "I'm Tom Halleck."

Reluctantly, Shelley took the offered hand. "Thank you, Mr. Halleck," she said saccharinely. "This is Jeff Cannondale of—"

"Call me Tom," said Halleck, ignoring the introduction. He held on firmly to Shelley's hand. "You're really something; you know that? I always say you're the best-looking woman in television."

"Thanks," said Shelley, trying to extricate her hand from Halleck's huge paw.

Halleck held on. "Look. I'm down here in Houston

doing a little business and I've got some friends over at my table—big shots from Houston, y'know. I want you to come over and say hello. I told them you were big stuff up in New York."

"No, thanks. We've finished dinner and were just getting ready to leave."

"Just for a few minutes. Have a drink with us. Whaddya say?"

Jeff Cannondale said, "Look, friend, we were just—"

Halleck threw him an ugly look that stunned Cannondale into silence. "I'm talking to the lady," he said menacingly. "Nobody asked you . . . 'friend.' "

In desperation Shelley began looking around the room, hoping the management would somehow be aware of her plight and offer assistance. It was at that moment that she saw Chandler, weaving his way around tables, heading in her direction. She wasn't sure whether she was relieved or embarrassed by his presence.

Cannondale started to get up, but Halleck actually pushed him back down in his chair.

Then Chandler was there, standing next to them.

"Evenin'," he said in what he hoped was a reasonable approximation of a Texas drawl. "I'm Lieutenant Buford Mapes of the Houston Police Department, and I was wonderin' if you folks were havin' a nice time in our beautiful city."

If Halleck was fooled by the phony drawl, he did not allow it to deter him. He turned on Chandler, his face ugly with anger and drunkenness. He pointed a finger at Chandler's face. "Listen here, Tex. Why don't you just get the fuck out of here and mind your own business?"

Chandler's eyes met his, a small flicker of a smile on his face. When he spoke his voice was very quiet and all trace of the phony accent was gone. "If you don't take that finger out of my face, I'm going to break it off and stuff it up your nose."

Halleck's eyes widened as if triggered by some minor explosions in his brain, and while Chandler continued to stare at him, he seemed to consider his options. With a snarl, he decided that it wasn't worth the trouble. "The hell with all of you," he said and staggered off to his anxious companions.

"Thank you, Sheriff," said Shelley without much sincerity.

Cannondale seemed flustered by all of this. "Yes, thank you . . . uh . . . Lieutenant? . . . I'm sorry I didn't catch the name."

Shelley stepped in. "This is Mark Chandler of the New York *News*. I told you we're doing a story together."

Cannondale was now even more bewildered. "Oh. I see." He gave an insecure laugh. "Would you join us for a drink then?"

Again Shelley jumped in. "The sheriff was just going to put his horse in the barn. Isn't that right, Sheriff?"

Chandler tipped his imaginary Stetson. "Anything you say, ma'am." He nodded to Cannondale, who seemed puzzled by all of this, and then walked back to the bar, feeling every eye in the dining room boring into his back. At the bar he found that his roast beef sandwich had disappeared.

The bartender gave him an apologetic shrug. "I didn't realize you were coming back," he mumbled, his mouth full of what Chandler suspected was roast beef. "Should I order you another?"

"No." Chandler paid his bill and as he waited for his change he saw in the mirror that Shelley's table was empty.

Chapter 24

The morning light streamed across the room, slashing at Chandler's brain like a light saber. He groaned as he pulled the covers over his throbbing head to protect his eyes from the rapacious glare. His eyes, even closed, were two portholes through which the laser blasts of sunlight seared the fabric of his brain.

In his semidrunken half-sleep he tried to reconstruct the events of the previous evening, but most of what he remembered was that he had somehow made a fool of himself in the dining room. He recalled strolling purposefully to the rescue like some latter-day Gary Cooper, but he also remembered slinking away in partial disgrace. In between those two events there seemed to have been an altercation which had ended successfully on his part, but for some reason, the damsel in distress did not seem particularly pleased with his intervention.

I didn't think I was that drunk, he thought. But from the way his head throbbed he now assumed that he had been.

There was a sharp rap on the adjoining door and Chandler mumbled something from behind the sheets. Then he heard the door open.

"I hope you're alone," said Shelley as she came into the room.

Chandler peered out from the sheets. "I think I am."

Shelley wore a bright orange Adidas tennis warm-up and dark blue Nike running shoes. Her hair was tied back and there was a sweatband around her forehead and a white towel around her neck.

"What are you doing?" asked Chandler, eying her outfit.

"I've been running. I run every day." She patted her forehead with the towel. "And how is Wyatt Earp this morning?"

"Was I really that bad?"

He shouldn't have asked. Shelley spun on him with surprising anger. "Yes; you were. You embarrassed me, and you embarrassed Jeff."

"Jeff? Who the hell is Jeff?"

"Jeff Cannondale, the man I was with. He would've handled it if you had given him a chance."

Chandler nodded, the effort making him wince. "Oh yeah, Jeff. I guess I was mistaken. I thought Jeff was going to have to go to the bathroom to get the load out of his pants."

"That's just what a lug like you would think."

"A lug!" He looked at her in disbelief. "A lug!" He laughed. "I haven't heard that one in years. Are you sure you don't write a boxing column on the side?"

In spite of herself, she felt a grin on her face. "You really are a pain in the ass, Chandler." There was no anger in her voice now.

He could only nod in agreement. "I know it."

"I must admit," she said, "that there was a certain amount of drama in your sudden appearance. John Wayne to the rescue. And when you threatened to stick that poor man's finger up his nose, I thought I'd die." She was laughing now and Chandler was beginning to feel better. "Where did you ever hear that one?"

"I once heard two guys arguing at the Garden during a

Ranger's game. One guy stuck a finger in the other guy's face and the other one said he'd break it off and stick it up his nose. I thought it was a great line."

"What happened?" she asked.

"When?"

"At the Garden?"

"The first guy broke the second guy's nose . . . and knocked out a couple of his teeth."

"Oh," said Shelley. "Works like a charm, huh?"

Chandler sat up. He was naked to the waist. "It isn't often that you get to be a hero to a damsel in distress at such minimal cost."

"You were lucky. That jerk could have broken your nose. Then what would you do?"

He pinched his nose between thumb and forefinger. "I'd probby talk like diss."

Shelley laughed and Chandler propped his pillow behind his back, then reached for his cigarettes on the night table.

Shelley made a face as he lit up and inhaled deeply. "How can you do that first thing in the morning?"

He inspected his cigarette closely. "Tools of the trade."

Shelley shuddered. "I have a pot of coffee in my room. Want some?"

Chandler grinned. He was feeling suddenly very bold. "I usually have my coffee in bed."

"You're not naked in there, are you?"

He peeked under the sheets to be certain. "No."

"Then you can get up and get moving." She walked toward the open doorway. "We have an appointment to meet the station manager at WKMZ in an hour. If you remember, he's your little flower child's brother. So you'd better get your butt out of bed." She smiled. "Help yourself to the coffee, I'm going to shower and get ready."

She closed the door behind her.

Ron Devereaux, the station manager, turned out to be much older than his sister. Chandler was sure that there was at least twenty years' difference and the attitudinal gap was just as obvious. Where the sister had been laid back and accepting about her situation, the brother was angry and resentful.

"I don't know why she married that creep," he said, chomping on a soggy cigar, his chubby face already red with anger. "I told her he was no good. I even told her to live with him if she had to, and I don't go for that kind of nonsense. God knows she lived with enough men before that creep came along. I don't know why she had to marry him."

"Maybe," said Shelley, "she loved him."

Devereaux sneered. "Love? Love had nothing to do with it. She was just a kid. She's still a kid." He shook his head sadly. "She was attracted to his"—he groped for the word—"shady character." He turned to Chandler. "Women are funny," he said as if Shelley were not in the room. "They like men who are different, who live outside the law. That's the way this Roman guy was."

"Outside the law? In what way?"

"I don't mean he was a criminal or anything. He didn't have the guts to be a criminal. It's just that he associated with underworld elements. You know, the Vegas gamblers, hustlers, pimps. He was always with those people."

Chandler said, "Maybe he was just doing his job as a reporter."

Devereaux made a sound like air escaping from a tire. "Reporter! He was never a reporter. He was an eavesdropper, that's all. He relished being in the company of criminals. I bet that's why they got rid of him. He knew too much; so they got rid of him."

"Wasn't he also a friend of Jonathan Carruthers?" asked Shelley.

Devereaux made another derisive noise. "There's another one. He may have been a big deal in New York, but he didn't impress me very much. These TV guys don't know the first thing about reporting. Somebody else does the work, they just read the copy."

Shelley was about to say something but Chandler interrupted Devereaux's diatribe before she could speak. "Didn't Roman ever work on a big story, maybe with Carruthers?"

"Not for me he didn't. He was always full of big talk, but that's all it was."

"Big talk about what?"

Devereaux laughed. "His big Howard Hughes story. He told everyone from here to Las Vegas that he had a blockbuster story about Howard Hughes. For a while I even believed that he might have something. He got in tight with some of the Hughes people so I thought he might have some inside info."

"And?"

"And nothing. Hughes died and there was no story. Suddenly he couldn't get close to the inside group anymore."

"So he never told you what this big story was about?" asked Shelley.

Devereaux looked at her, letting his eyes run over her body. "Lady," he said, "every reporter in Houston has at least one Howard Hughes story that he thinks will make him famous. Most of the stories are based on rumor or fabrication and can't be corroborated. Howard Hughes stories are to reporters what fish stories are to fishermen." He chuckled. "It's always the big one that got away." Suddenly he was serious. "You might ask my sister. She might know something."

"We did," said Shelley. "She doesn't know much more than you do."

Devereaux's face grew dark. "Who is she living with these days?"

"We don't know anything about that," said Shelley. "She was alone when we saw her."

"Well, she won't be alone for long; I guarantee you that. That girl is just a . . ."

Chandler broke in quickly to avoid an angry detour. "Mr. Devereaux," he said, taking out his list of names. "Do any of these names mean anything to you?" He omitted the first two and began to read, "Taylor. Watson. Coleman. O'Brien. Dr. Harrison. Jefferson."

Devereaux shook his head. "No. Can't say that they do."

"Are you sure?"

Devereaux's face was impassive and Chandler continued his probing. "Is it possible that any of these names might have meant anything to Al Roman?"

"Read them again." He listened carefully as Chandler read through the list again. At each name, Devereaux would shake his head. "Could be anybody, I suppose," he said when Chandler had completed his reading. Then Devereaux squeezed his eyes shut as if he were trying to recall something. "Maybe this Taylor is Clinton Taylor of the oil Taylors here in Houston. Caused a big splash a few years back when he died and left most of his money to his wife and young son. Cut off the rest of his family. The boy was adopted, if I remember correctly."

"What makes you think that this might be him?"

"You asked if any of these names might have meant

anything to Roman. Well, he covered that story for us."
Devereaux shrugged. "It's just a thought."

"None of the other names mean anything to you?"

"They're just names. Could be anybody."

Shelley stepped in. "Do you think we could get a copy of
that story?"

Devereaux said nothing. He did not look pleased.

"The one that Roman did on Taylor?" she asked.

"I suppose," said Devereaux without enthusiasm. "We
have file copies downstairs. Take awhile to find it, though."

Shelley fumbled in her purse. "Here," she said handing
him her card. "Send it to me at NBC." She flashed her
biggest smile. "I'd really appreciate it."

Devereaux looked at the card as if it were inscribed with
some disgusting message.

"We'd consider it a professional courtesy," chimed in
Chandler helpfully.

Devereaux nodded reluctantly. "OK."

Chandler looked at Shelley, "Anything else?"

"I don't think so," she said and they both stood up.

"Thank you, Mr. Devereaux," she said, "You've been
most helpful."

Devereaux did not get up. "I don't know how, but if I
have, I'm glad." He didn't look glad. "If you see that sister of
mine, tell her to stay out of trouble, y'hear?"

As they were leaving, Devereaux came to the door of his
office and called down the hall, "Let me know when they
bury that bastard Roman. I want to celebrate."

"Nice guy," said Chandler quietly as they made their
way to the street.

"This place seems full of nice guys," said Shelley, looking at her watch. "If we hurry, we have time to get our bags
and catch the noon plane back to New York."

Chapter 25

"Where have you been?" asked Allan Greenfield when Julie Loonin finally answered her phone. "I've been calling you all morning."

Julie deliberated before answering. "I've been out running, Allan. I've been doing a lot of thinking."

He didn't like the sound of that. He never really pictured Julie doing much thinking. "Thinking about what?"

"Just thinking," she said cautiously. "Thinking about us."

"What's to think about?" As he spoke he was watching himself in the living room mirror.

"That's what I mean. What *is* there to think about?"

"Look," he said, "I'm sorry about not being able to make our date last night, but you know how important this thing is to me. You knew I had to go to Washington. I had to see Petersen as soon as possible."

"It's not last night, Allan. And it's not Washington. It's lots of things."

He shifted gears. "Y'know I almost came back to New York last night—I missed you that much—but it would have been too late. I didn't want to bother you." What he didn't say was that he had met a woman at the airport and they had spent the night at the airport hotel. "But I really missed you," he said.

Julie avoided responding to his remark. She didn't want to lie but didn't want to tell the truth, so she said nothing.

Allan was struggling to break the somber mood. "Hey, it's Sunday. Let's do something together."

"Like last Sunday?"

"What about last Sunday?" Allan said.

"What did we do last Sunday?"

He thought for a moment. "We went to the museum."

"Before that," she said, her voice breaking.

"You came over. You brought the *Times* with you." He was happy that he was able to remember.

"Yeah, and we got into bed and read the paper. Only you wanted to have sex between sections."

He made a face at himself in the mirror. "I thought we had a good time," he said. He was pained that apparently she did not agree.

"Allan, my idea of a good time isn't giving somebody head while he reads the sports section."

Allan Greenfield realized that he was close to losing what he considered a very good thing. He thought carefully about what he would say next. "Julie," he began slowly, "I know that I've been kind of crazy the last few weeks—months even—but it's because my job has been driving me nuts. The only thing that has kept me from going off the deep end is you. If I didn't have you, I don't know what I'd do." He paused for a moment to let that sink in. Just as he sensed that she was about to speak, he said, "But things are looking brighter now. I talked with Petersen last night and he offered to get me a job with the *Post*."

"That's in Washington, Allan."

"Yes. But I told him I wasn't interested in leaving New York right now. I told him there was someone here I couldn't leave."

Julie was silent for a moment, then she took the bait. "What did he say?"

Allan smiled. "No problem. If I wanted to stay here he could get me a job with the New York *Post* or even the *Times*."

"Can he do that?"

"Of course he can." Allan laughed, knowing he was safe now. "This is one powerful man, Julie. He can do anything he wants."

After a long silence, Julie said, "That's all well and good, Allan, but you still haven't told me what I want to hear."

He winced. "What's that?"

"You haven't told me that you love me."

He watched himself in the mirror. Without a trace of inflection he said, "I thought you knew that."

She said nothing and he knew it wasn't enough.

"Julie?"

"Yes."

"I love you."

He heard her sigh. "And I love you too, Allan."

They both laughed and she said, "Things are going to be better for us now, Allan."

"I know," he said with all the sincerity he could muster while making faces in the mirror.

"When do you want me to come over?"

"Right away," he said hungrily.

"I've got the paper," she said coyly. "I can bring it with me if you haven't seen it."

"Terrific," he said. "I'll see you in a little while."

He hung up the phone and winked at his reflection. "Don't forget the sports section," he said out loud.

Julie Loonin kicked off her sneakers and slipped out of her bright red jogging suit. She dropped her underwear, bra, and socks into the laundry hamper and took a fresh towel from the shelf. She was exhilarated from her conversation with Allan. This could be it, she thought; this was as close as he had ever come to making something permanent of their relationship. Sure, she'd had to coax him a little, but he had finally admitted how he felt about her. He hadn't mentioned marriage exactly, but it had been on the tip of his tongue—or almost, anyway.

She stepped into the shower and let the warm spray envelop her. Her muscles relaxed, the tension draining from her body as she reveled in the warmth. She closed her eyes, stood stock-still, and allowed the water to surround her in its steamy warmth. Under her watery canopy she felt refreshed and revitalized, as though a tremendous weight had been lifted from her shoulders.

Her thoughts ran to what she would say to her mother if Allan proposed to her. This was an almost daily fantasy that never failed to depress her—but not today. She went over in her mind, as she had a thousand times, what she would say and how her mother would respond. In her fantasy her father always took the phone away from her mother, who was by that time too engulfed in tears to continue. He too would be choking back tears as he told her how happy he was. It was usually at this point that the sheer nonsense of her daydream saddened her. It was here that she usually realized her fool-ishness. She always knew that, bright and ambitious as Allan was, he was not the kind of man with whom she envisioned spending the rest of her life. He was too immature and self-centered. She made more money than he did, and her possibilities for advancement were better than his. Her fantasy always ended with the realization that what she really wanted was not so much to get married—especially to someone like Allan Greenfield—but merely to please her mother.

Today, as she submerged herself in the sweet release of the all-encompassing water, she was able to tell herself that such rationalizations were no longer necessary. All such thoughts had been sour grapes; she knew that now. There was no need for them anymore.

Julie stepped out of the shower, wrapping herself in the big, fluffy towel she had bought in Bloomingdale's. She had paid too much for the towel, but it gave her a feeling of luxury, of being pampered, and that was what she wanted. She toweled herself dry, rubbing until her skin tingled, then fastened the towel around her. After removing her shower cap she shook out her hair and it tumbled to her shoulders. She decided to leave it wild today.

Wiping a clear circle in the steamed bathroom mirror, she inspected her face closely. What she saw pleased her. Her eyes were large and brown with a look that she knew could be melancholy or seductive. She inspected her eyebrows to make sure she had tweezed away every trace of their relentless attempt to join forces. She ran a finger down the line of her nose, feeling for the all but invisible bump that she was sure was the first thing about her that people noticed, but still thankful that she had inherited her father's nose instead of her mother's. *That* nose would have made a mockery of her other assets. She puckered her lips and aimed a kiss at her reflection. Her lips were full and thick and framed in the perpetual pout that since the age of fifteen had made her aware of her sex appeal.

Stepping out of the bathroom, Julie threw the towel on her unmade bed. On the way to her dresser she passed the full-length mirror on the bedroom door and stopped to admire herself. She straightened her posture, causing her breasts to lift up and out. They were, she thought, touching them lightly, still firm although too large for her small frame, but Allan professed to love them dearly. In fact, none of the men she had ever known had ever expressed a desire for anything smaller.

Christ, she thought as she let her eyes run down the length of her reflection, if I were only five or six inches taller.

Then everything would be in perfect proportion. Maybe then I wouldn't have to starve myself or go running in the park to maintain my figure. Even with the running and the dieting she felt that she was a little too plump, just a little too well rounded. Cursing her mother's cooking and the childhood admonition to "eat, eat," she ran her palm across her stomach, which was flat, but managed to find a pinch of excess poundage.

With a final look and a reminder to herself to keep her shoulders back and her back straight, she rummaged through her dresser looking for her best underwear. She selected a new pair of beige bikini briefs with a delicate border of lace and with a defiant peek in the mirror rejected the idea of wearing a bra. She slipped a matching beige camisole over her head and then surveyed the effect in the mirror.

"Look out, Allan Greenfield," she said to her reflection. "I'm on my way."

Allan was also in the midst of preparation for Julie's arrival. His preparation consisted of a quick shower and shave and the application of deodorant and some aftershave that Julie had given him last Christmas. Thinking about Julie, he had started to get an erection while shaving so he had reluctantly decided to put on some underwear beneath his robe. He had planned to be naked under his robe when Julie arrived and to explain that he had just come out of the shower, but an erection peeking through the folds of his robe would almost certainly disclose his deception.

He went around his small apartment picking up some of the clutter and closing the shutters that separated the kitchen from the living area. Knowing that Julie would want to make him lunch afterward, he decided not to clean up the kitchen. It gave her pleasure, he thought, to pick up after him, so why do the breakfast dishes?

Allan went into the bedroom and pulled down the shade on the single window that looked out on the fire escape and then adjusted the lighting to what he felt was suitable illumination for the coming tryst. He pulled up the covers on the bed, smoothed them with the flat of his hand, then folded back the top to reveal the two plumped pillows.

He was standing in the doorway inspecting his handiwork when he heard the knock on the door. Instinctively he looked at his watch to gauge if Julie had had enough time to get here. His wrist was bare, but he was certain that it could not be Julie.

"Who is it?" he called.

There was no answer.

"Who is it?" he called again as he walked to the door.

"Messenger service," came the muffled reply.

Allan's eyes narrowed as he digested these words. His relatively brief time in New York had made him naturally suspicious of any unexpected knock on his door. There had been several robberies in this building in the past month alone and just last year an elderly woman tenant had been murdered on the floor above him.

"Message for Allan Greenfield from Washington, D.C.," added the voice.

Allan's eyes opened wide in surprise. Petersen! he thought. He's already contacting me about the story. He pressed his eye to the peephole on the door and looked through. In the hallway, in fishbowl distortion, stood a tall, black man in a dark blue uniform and cap. In his hand he held what appeared to be a thick brown envelope.

Feeling foolish, as he always did in these situations, and knowing that he would not have been so cautious had the man been white, Allan asked, "Do you have identification?"

"Yes, sir," said the man as if used to such indignities. "I'll hold it up to the viewing hole if you like."

He held an ID card and the envelope in his left hand and held both close enough to the peephole so that Allan could see them. The distortion from the glass was too great for Allan to actually read the card, but he could see that the picture was of the man in the hall.

What Allan did not see, as he pressed his eye to the peephole, was that almost simultaneously with the motion of raising the card and the envelope, the man, who had blocked Allan's view of him with the envelope, had reached into his coat with his right hand and removed an automatic fitted with a short barreled silencer. As Allan peered at the ID card, the man raised the pistol to within two inches of the door and aimed just below and to the right of the peephole.

When he squeezed the trigger, the bullet penetrated the door and entered Allan Greenfield's face one inch below his left eye. It shattered his cheekbone and, traveling in an upward direction, drove the razor-sharp shards of bone in an explosive pattern throughout his brain, then exited near the small bald spot that Allan had been able to conceal by meticulous grooming each morning.

The force of the blow drove Allan back from the door and dumped him on the carpet in the middle of the room. He was clinically dead before he hit the floor.

Without any sense of urgency, the black man in the hall returned his weapon to the holster strapped beneath his left armpit, put the envelope and ID card into his jacket pocket, then looked up and down the hallway. All was quiet. The only outward sign of what had happened was a small hole in the door a few inches below and to the side of the peephole.

The man removed a small ring of keys from his pocket, inspected the lock on the door, and selected a key. On the second try the key slid into the lock. He then inserted a long, narrow sliver of steel into the lock, jiggled the key, twisted the picklock, and felt the locking mechanism release. He turned the key and the door was opened.

The hallway was still quiet as he stepped inside Allan's apartment. He closed the door softly behind him and inspected the inert form on the floor. If he felt any surprise that Allan's body had landed so far from the door, his face did not register the thought. Without touching the body he was able to determine that no further action was needed. He looked around the room before deciding where to begin.

On the way over to Allan's apartment Julie's step was light and bouncy. The sun was shining and the weather was unseasonably warm. She had worn her long, down coat as protection against the expected chill but now because of the mild temperature she left it open. Under one arm she cradled her pocketbook and under the other she held the Sunday *Times*.

It was warm; it was Sunday; she felt alive and vigorous. Damn! she said to herself, I feel sexy today.

Her breasts, heavy and pendulous, heaved and fell in cadence with her stride. Normally she would not have allowed this to happen. She would have crushed her coat closed, pinning her breasts against her chest. But not today. Her breasts were part of her rhythm today. They rose and fell, unfettered as her spirit, her nipples caressed by the silky fabric of her camisole.

She crossed 110th Street at Columbus Avenue and walked

along Morningside Avenue at the perimeter of the park. The streets were quiet. She drew a few stares from a couple of men she passed, their eyes like magnets drawn to the lodestone of her dancing breasts, but she kept her eyes straight ahead and plowed on.

Near 112th Street a woman walking her dog gave Julie an envious look and Julie wondered for a moment what it would be like to be no longer young. The dog approached Julie, its tail wagging in a sign of friendship, but the woman yanked viciously on the dog's leash and pulled it away.

Julie crossed back across the street at 114th Street, walking past a row of mostly closed or abandoned stores. Some were boarded up with plywood; others sat ominously empty. In the dark shop windows she watched herself, her reflection disappearing and reappearing as she marched past.

She smiled at herself in the glass, feeling her desire grow as she saw herself as others saw her. She felt her nipples grow erect and the halos around them blossom like flowers.

Knowing Allan, he would be ready for her when she got there. He would be coy as if sex were not the only thing on his mind, but she could always tell from his first deep penetrating kiss that he was anxious for her. This usually annoyed her and made her feel used. If he could only be patient; if he could only bring her along slowly instead of galloping ahead of her.

She smiled. Today she was ready. She would surprise him. She remembered what she had said earlier about his reading the paper while she made love to him. She hadn't meant to hurt his feelings. Today she would make it up to him.

In her mind she rehearsed what she would say when she got to his apartment. Imagining that he was in bed waiting for her, she would open the door with her key, go to the bedroom, and throw the *Times* on the bed next to him. Then she would give him a sexy smile and say, "I thought you might enjoy reading the sports section."

Thinking about it, her mouth went dry and she ran her tongue across her lips to moisten them.

Finally she came to Allan's building and paused for a moment at the foot of the steps that led up to the front door. Julie looked up at Allan's bedroom window—the shade was already drawn—then took a deep breath and started up. She opened the door and entered the small vestibule that led to the inner door. Although that door was supposed to be locked, it was, as usual, wide open. She ignored the call boxes—most of them were inoperative—and headed for the stairs. She wanted to barge in on him anyway.

The man in Allan Greenfield's apartment did not enjoy making this kind of mess, but he wanted to be sure that the killing appeared to be a typical New York City robbery with homicide. As he dumped the contents of Allan's drawers quietly on the floor so as not to make any unnecessary noise, he carefully sifted through the belongings to make sure there were no photocopies of a printout he had been told to look for. Methodically he worked his way through the bedroom, dropping the contents of closets and dresser drawers on the floor. In a shoe box in the closet he discovered five twenty-dollar bills and with the barest trace of a smile he put the money in his pocket and kept searching.

In the top drawer of the bedroom dresser, where Allan had kept his laundered shirts, the man found what he was looking for. A smile creased his dark features as he unfolded the papers and recognized that this was what he sought. He didn't know what it was and he didn't care; he only knew that finding it was worth an extra thousand dollars to the people who had sent him here. He looked at the list of names and information, and then with a soft shrug, refolded the papers and went to the living room.

Satisfied that he had achieved his purpose, the man slipped the photocopies into his jacket pocket and went to the front door. Without a second look he stepped over the body of Allan Greenfield, who lay on his back, eyes wide open in surprise, in a rapidly expanding pool of blood.

The man listened at the door for a few seconds, then swiftly exited, his hand on the gun inside his jacket. He knew that if anyone appeared at that moment he would have to kill. The hallway was hushed. He closed the door quietly and started for the stairs. Halfway down he tipped his cap to an attractive young woman who was on the way up. He stared at her, knowing that this would cause her to look away. Later when the police questioned her she would remember only that he had been black and wore some kind of uniform.

After leaving the building, he turned left and walked along 114th Street. His pace was unhurried. He turned left on Riverside Drive and then in the middle of that block approached a black limousine parked at the curb. The limousine had dark-tinted windows, so dark that from the street it was impossible to tell if anyone was inside, but at his approach the curbside rear window glided open.

"Well, Anthony?" said a deep voice from within.

"All taken care of," Anthony said, reaching inside his jacket and removing the photocopies. He gave the papers to the man inside and walked around to the driver's side of the limousine.

As he started the car and drove away, he noticed in the rearview mirror that his employer was reading the copied printouts. He was a man in his middle to late fifties with silver-gray hair and patrician features. Seated next to him in the back seat and equally interested in the contents of the pages was a young boy of about eleven.

On her way up the stairs Julie saw a black man descending. The man stared at her and she felt a sudden shiver; for the first time that day she pulled her coat closed to cover herself. But the man's eyes did not leave her face. Instead he stared—a cold, hard, expressionless stare that she would never forget—directly into her eyes. Julie looked quickly away, noting only that he had a small, light-colored scar beneath his right eye. This would be the only detail she remembered when the police questioned her. Even under the hypnosis of a police expert she would remember only that he was black, wore some kind of uniform, and had this small scar.

Later she would come to believe that she had felt some chilling foresight of doom, but that was only after the fact. Actually, she was smiling as she slipped by the man on the stairs and continued on up to the second floor.

Very quietly, so as not to alert Allan, she slipped her key into the lock and opened the door to the apartment. At first her brain registered only surprise at the formless shape lying on the floor, but then her eyes focused on Allan's wide staring eyes and the pool of blood and her breath left her.

Julie stumbled back into the hallway, driven by a primitive need to evade the horrifying tableau. She gasped for air, but her lungs were incapable of expansion. Her throat seemed permanently constricted.

She didn't remember screaming. She remembered only fighting for air, struggling, as in some terrible nightmare, to swim to the surface where she could breathe. But her screams alerted the neighbors, who cautiously, one by one and with some reluctance, opened their doors to find this terrified woman pleading for help.

When the police arrived they found the neighbors clustered around Allan Greenfield's door, and Julie, who had refused to take refuge in anyone's apartment, sitting on a kitchen chair that someone had brought out into the hallway. A neighbor, Mrs. Estrella Ramirez, had placed a blanket around Julie's shoulders and was trying to comfort her. In spite of her heavy coat and the warmth of the day, Julie shivered uncontrollably and when the first policeman tried to speak with her, her teeth would not stop chattering.

Chapter 26

The last rays of a red sun were glistening over the granite block skyline of Manhattan as the 747 approached Kennedy International Airport. From above, the city seemed to glow in a blood-red hue as acres of glass reflected the glowing sun, fracturing the light into a million images.

Shelley turned away from the window and spoke to Chandler, seated next to her. "It's quite a sight. The city looks beautiful from up here."

He did not look. "I'm sure it does," he said without conviction.

Shelley patted his hand, which clung to the edge of the armrest. "Next time we go away," she said, "maybe we'll try a bus."

Chandler shook his head as if mystified by his fear. "When I covered the Yankees and Mets I used to fly all the time. I never really liked it, but it didn't bother me that much. Now . . ." he let his voice trail away. He could feel his heart thumping in his chest; his palms were clammy, and sweat beaded on his forehead. He was having trouble breathing.

Shelley squeezed his hand sympathetically. "Maybe you should have had that drink."

Chandler closed his eyes. "We'll be down soon."

Leaving her hand on his to comfort him, Shelley watched him as he breathed rhythmically to quell his panic. She could not help feeling disappointed in him. A small voice within her whispered that this was not how it was supposed to be.

They took a taxi from the airport to Shelley's apartment on East Eighty-seventh Street between Park and Madison, and Chandler helped her bring her bags inside. "Come on up," she said. "I'll make some coffee." And while the doorman pretended to be busy with something, Chandler left his bag at the desk and carried her bags to the elevator.

Shelley's apartment was on the thirty-fifth floor of a thirty-six-floor building and Chandler was suitably impressed as they entered. There were large expanses of windows on two sides, the front looking out over the city to the south and the right side looking over Central Park. The apartment had one large central room which served as living, sleeping, and dining quarters. It also had a small, modern galley kitchen and a study.

Chandler put down the bags and looked around. There were mirrors everywhere. The room seemed huge. "You own this palace of mirrors?" he said.

Shelley nodded. "Yes. You like it?"

"I guess I'm in the wrong end of the journalism business," he said.

Shelley laughed. "You, if I recall a famous quote correctly, do not have 'the look.' "

"For this," he said, sweeping an arm around the room, "I'd consider plastic surgery."

"Make yourself comfortable. I'll put on some coffee," said Shelley, disappearing into the kitchen.

The main room of the apartment was platformed into three distinct sections. The lowest encompassed the entrance and dining areas. These were on the same level as the kitchen. One step up was the living area, composed mainly of a huge, abstract print, L-shaped sectional couch, and large mahogany coffee table. Just beyond the couch was a sliding glass door leading to a terrace. Behind the couch and one further step up, was a queen-size bed covered in a quilt in the same pattern as the couch. The ceiling above it was covered in mirrored tiles.

Chandler went up the steps of the platform and edged

cautiously toward the windows. From there he could look all the way down Park Avenue. Lights were coming on over Manhattan and the city began to twinkle like some gigantic Christmas tree. From this height there was no dirt and grime and ugliness, and the city looked like that magical place that those who had only seen it in photographs, imagined it must be. Chandler edged closer but the height had a dizzying effect and he was forced to retreat to more solid ground.

Along the wall nearest the bed was a row of bookcases. Chandler browsed through the shelves, hoping to be able to tell something about Shelley by her collection. The list was too eclectic: art, literature, nutrition, biography, and a small collection of Agatha Christie. He smiled, recalling that he had called her Miss Marple when they were looking through Carruthers's books.

On the same wall, bracketed by the bookcases, was what appeared to be a working fireplace, and Chandler found himself imagining what it would be like to snuggle up in bed with Shelley, with the fire crackling and the Manhattan skyline twinkling outside the window.

"Forget it," said Shelley's voice, shattering his reverie and causing him for just an instant to wonder if he had been thinking out loud. She held a coffee mug in each hand.

"Forget what?" he mumbled, feeling as if he had been caught peeping into her bedroom window.

"You can't tell about me by my books."

She put the coffee on the low table in front of the couch. "You were trying to figure me out by looking at my books, weren't you?" Before he could answer she laughed. "You can't do it."

Chandler shrugged. "Maybe not." He pointed a thumb up at the mirrored ceiling above the bed. "But what about those?" He smiled wickedly, arching his eyebrows. "What can I tell from that? It's a nice touch, Shelley. I didn't expect mirrors."

"Before you get any ideas, Chandler, they were installed by the previous owner. I tried to remove them when I moved in, but it would have meant redoing the entire ceiling. So I just left them."

Pretending not to believe her, he held up his hand as if to quiet her protests. "Hey, whatever you say is all right with me, Shelley. You don't have to explain anything to me."

She rolled her eyes. "Jeez, you're a pain in the ass." By now, it was almost an endearment.

Taking her coffee, Shelley walked to the glass door that led to the terrace. "Let's go out here," she said, sliding back the glass.

Involuntarily, Chandler took one step back from the door. "It's just fine in here," he said quietly, sitting down on the couch.

Shelley looked at him strangely for a moment, a mixture of disappointment and understanding on her face, then stepped out onto the terrace. The city sprawled below her like an architect's model of some futuristic city of lights. This view had never seemed real to her; it was too magnificent, more like the skyline backdrop used on television news shows. But she never tired of, or became complacent about, the view. This was New York, the seat of all the power that mattered to her, and standing here she felt that she was on top of the Big Apple.

In the rapidly fading light she could still pick out the landmarks. The Chrysler Building, graceful and elegant in a cluster of more functional boxlike buildings; the Pan Am Building, squatting ponderously atop the nobility of Grand Central, like youth newly triumphant over an old warrior; and the Empire State Building, which, though no longer the tallest building even in New York, was still her favorite. It had an elemental grandeur, a primal magnificence that no number of twin-towered trade centers could surpass.

Reluctantly, she came back inside and closed the door. "You're missing a great view," she said.

Chandler shrugged. "Too cold."

"Or too high?"

He looked at her with a shame-faced smile. "That too."

Shelley looked at him. "You're not afraid of the dark, are you?"

He laughed good-naturedly. "Not as long as I've got my teddy bear with me."

Shelley leaned against the glass door, watching him over the rim of her cup as she sipped her coffee. There was something about this man that was both appealing and disturbing at the same time. He was attractive in a mature-not-really-good-looking kind of way, but he also seemed to be a mass of fears and phobias. She found his personality attractive but his petty fears somehow repugnant, as if those fears were in some way contrary to her definition of what a man should be like. Her imaginary man was nothing like Chandler. He did not have to be handsome—she herself knew too much

about the pitfalls of beauty to consider that as a criterion—
but neither could he be . . . how could she put it? . . .
"cowardly" was the word that came to mind, but seemed too
strong. Even though Chandler had made a mess of things in
Houston, he had tried to rescue her from that drunk, she
reminded herself. That was something.

He lit a cigarette as she watched him. There were no
ashtrays on the table.

"You smoke too much," she said sharply, surprised at
the feeling in her voice.

"I know."

"Then why don't you quit?"

He shrugged, his eyes searching for an ashtray. Shelley
did not help him. "It's bad for you," she said, and he made a
face as if he didn't much care about that. "It's a rotten habit,"
she continued. "I'd like you a lot better if you didn't smoke."
Her face was serious.

Chandler raised his eyebrows and inspected his cigarette
carefully. He held it away from him as if it had suddenly
become distasteful. "If you could find a suitable receptacle, I
think I could give up smoking right now."

They both laughed and Shelley handed him a ceramic
dish. He stubbed out his cigarette and Shelley sat at the
other end of the couch.

"How do you think our investigation is going so far?"

"So far, not too well. We don't seem to be any closer to
understanding what happened than we were before our trip
to Houston."

She nodded in agreement. "At least we have some leads
on a few of the names: Hughes, Taylor . . . what was the
other one?"

"Arnold. Jason Arnold."

"That's something," she said hopefully. "Tomorrow I'll
try to get some more information on this Taylor."

"We don't have much else to go on. Unless something
else turns up, it looks like a dead end."

There was silence between them for a minute, then
Chandler stood up. "I'd better get going. I've got a column to
write and I'm sure you have things to do."

He was hoping that she might stop him but she stood
and walked him to the door. "Will you call me?" she said.

"If anything turns up, I'll call you."

"What if it doesn't?"

He looked puzzled.

Shelley smiled. "You could call me anyway. We're friends, right?"

"Sure," he said. "I'd like that."

Shelley touched his arm as he opened the door. As he turned back to face her she kissed him, a quick peck on the cheek. In surprise, Chandler stumbled back, tripping over her suitcases where he had left them at the door, and almost fell out into the hallway.

Shelley winced. "That's not the usual reaction I get when I kiss someone."

Chandler pointed a finger at his chest. "Mr. Suave," he said. He took a brief bow. "I taught Fred Astaire everything he knows." With that he turned and headed for the elevator, his face red, ears burning. He did not look back.

As soon as Shelley closed the door he lit a cigarette and took a long, comforting drag.

Chandler's apartment was, as usual, cluttered with the debris of several days' newspapers, dishes, and other signs of renewed bachelorhood. The place smelled faintly of kitty litter, and if he expected a welcome home from his cat, he was disappointed. The cat, Samson, was sprawled on the windowsill and turned to peer over his shoulder when Chandler entered. Seeing that it was only his master, Samson yawned and returned to his vigil.

"Mrs. Terrell been feeding you?" he called to the cat, who still ignored him. Chandler went to the kitchen and inspected the empty food dish, took a can from the counter, and placed it in the electric can opener. At the sound of the machine, the cat appeared magically at his feet, caressing him in joyful ritual.

"Faithful friend," said Chandler, wondering if cats understood sarcasm.

While Samson ate, Chandler called his answering service. "Any calls?"

"Yes," said the woman and gave him a brief list of numbers. "One of them," she said, "has been calling since yesterday. I told her you wouldn't be back until this evening, but she just kept calling. Called not half an hour ago, too. She seemed very anxious to talk with you." The voice seemed concerned. "I promised her you'd call her first."

"Did she give you a name?"

"Yes. Her name is Julie Loonin."

"Did she say what she wanted?" said Chandler, wondering if he knew this person.

"Well," said the voice haltingly, "she wasn't making too much sense. Something about a list of names and a"——she paused as if reluctant to say the word; finally she spoke—"a murder."

"A murder?"

"That's what she said."

Julie looked terrible. Her hair was uncombed and there were dark circles under her bloodshot eyes. She and Chandler sat in a corner booth of the West End Bar across the street from Columbia University. The main room was cavernous and dimly lit by amber lamps suspended above each booth. There was a row of booths along each side wall and a large U-shaped bar in the middle. One step up from the bar area was another room, dotted with round tables, where food was served. That room was crowded with Columbia students who preferred not to test the fare at the university cafeteria.

After explaining to Chandler on the phone why she wanted to speak with him, Julie had gone to the West End and waited in the last booth of the main room. Behind her she could hear the boisterous laughter of students in the smaller room. Some were having a late dinner, others just a few beers and some company. To Julie they appeared incredibly young and appallingly carefree. It seemed to her that she could never have been quite so young, although most of the people in that room were only six or seven years younger than she, or that she could ever have been so unaware of the vicissitudes of life.

When Chandler entered, Julie spotted him right away; he was easily the oldest person in the place. She waved until he noticed her and approached the table. He sat with her and told her how shocked he had been to hear about Allan. Told her that even though he had met Allan only once, he had been impressed with the young man's drive and ambition. "It's this city," he added sadly. "The savages are taking over."

Julie, her eyes weary and damp with the promise of more tears, looked around the room as he spoke. Chandler was anxious to get on with what had brought him here and said, "You mentioned that this had something to do with the list I had given Allan."

"Yes," she said haltingly, fighting for words. "Allan found the information you wanted."

A waitress appeared and Chandler ordered a sandwich and beer for himself and another coffee for Julie. He turned back to Julie. "But he told me that he couldn't find anything."

"I know, but he . . ." Her eyes drifted from his and Chandler knew that she was about to tell a lie. "He checked the computer again,—later—and he found what you were looking for."

Chandler watched her carefully and wondered why she was lying. "What did he find?"

"The people you were looking for. The people on the list."

Chandler felt an instant flush of excitement but it was tempered by the gnawing feeling that this woman was not telling the truth. He took out his notebook and flipped it to the page where he had written the names. "Who are they?"

Her eyes opened in surprise as if he had asked her to perform a magic trick. "I don't remember them," she said. "I only saw the list once."

"You don't remember any of them?"

"Howard Hughes was the first name." Her eyes narrowed. "Then his lawyer. I don't remember the name."

Chandler nodded. Whatever her lie was, it was not about the names.

"What I *do* remember about the names," she said, "was that most of them were very wealthy and no longer living."

The waitress came with the order and Chandler took a bite of his sandwich. He chewed slowly, watching Julie, thinking about what she had said.

"If I read you the other names, do you think you might be able to remember anything about them?"

She nodded, then modified that with, "Maybe."

Chandler looked at his list. "Taylor," he said.

Julie thought for a moment, closing her eyes, picturing the printout on Allan's kitchen table. She saw Allan's finger pointing at the sheet, his voice explaining what was there. This name was on the second page. "He's one of the dead ones," she said, her eyes still closed. She opened them. "He died in Houston. I think he was in oil."

"Do you have a first name?"

Again, she squeezed her eyes shut, then shook her head, angry because she could not remember. "I can't remember. I only saw it once. Winston, maybe."

Chandler shook his head. "How about Clinton?"

"That's it," she said, excitement in her voice. "Clinton Taylor."

"Next name," said Chandler. "Watson."

"That's Winston."

"Winston Watson?"

She made a face. "No. That's not right." She smiled. "Winthrop. Winthrop Watson. That's it. He's dead too."

Once triggered, her memory proved formidable, and Julie was able to recall most of the information that Greenfield's computer had found. She remembered about the wives and the adopted children and the unusual wills each man had left. She told Chandler about Allan's theory that the men had been murdered to rob them of their considerable fortunes. If Chandler thought there was any credence to that theory, he did not show it and Julie added that she had told Allan that his evidence had been merely circumstantial.

As she spoke, Chandler made notations in his book. "Is that it?" he asked when she seemed to have finished.

"That's it," she said with a quick forced smile.

Chandler had the intuitive feeling that there was more. There was something else, he was sure, that this young woman was not telling him. He put down his pen, closed the notebook, and looked directly into her eyes. "Is there anything else you can remember, something you may want to tell me?"

Julie could not meet his eyes. "No," she said, looking down at the table.

Chandler struggled to hide his skepticism. "Do you know where the computer printout is now?"

She looked up at him. "No." She forced herself to maintain eye contact. "He had two copies. One, I assume, he took with him. The other was in the top dresser drawer in his bedroom. I saw him put it there on Saturday, but I don't know what he did with it. It's not there now." She shook her head, trying to block out the memory. "The whole place was ransacked."

"You said he took one of the copies with him. Took it where?"

Julie reacted to his question as if he had slapped her. Her eyes opened wide, and when she opened her mouth to speak, the words seemed stuck in her throat. Chandler knew that the lie was here. Finally Julie found her voice. "He took it on a job interview."

Chandler's eyes narrowed. He said nothing.

"He wasn't going to use the story," she added quickly. "Just use it as an example of the kind of investigative work that he could do." Her voice was almost pleading. "He was desperate to get a fresh start."

Chandler remembered the desperation. He sat back in the booth, a long sigh escaping his lips. So that was it. That's what this was all about. Allan Greenfield was using his story—was going to steal it. He had told Chandler that he had found nothing but then had tried to peddle the story to promote his career. Now that he was dead, his girl friend wanted to set things right. She wanted to give him his story back but was reluctant to reveal Greenfield's true intentions. Chandler's only hope now was that this punk kid Greenfield hadn't blown the whole story.

"Who did he take the story to . . . on this interview?"

"A man named Petersen—in Washington."

"Andrew Petersen?"

"Yes. He met with him Saturday night."

Chandler's eyes closed in pain. That was the worst thing she could have said. He knew Petersen only by reputation. The man was a vulture, a weasel, a man with no ethics. The fact that the story was stolen from another reporter would mean nothing to Petersen.

Julie saw the expression on his face. "Is it that bad?"

"If Petersen has my story, I might as well forget it." He shook his head in disappointment. "Are you sure that Allan went to him? You're sure he gave him the list?"

She wanted to be helpful. "I don't think he gave him your story. Alan said he'd use the story only as an example of what he could do. I don't think he intended to give Petersen your story."

Sure, thought Chandler, his jaw set in a hard line. This ambitious son of a bitch would have sold his mother to get ahead. Maybe they had him stuck in the morgue at the *News* because they were afraid to let him out. If he had turned over the list to Petersen there was probably an army of investigators crawling like cockroaches over everything. It was only a matter of time before they broke the story. The only bright spot, and it wasn't much, was that they didn't know that Jonathan Carruthers had been involved. That bit of sensationalism would send Petersen scurrying to his typewriter, salivating like a hungry jackal. By the time his column hit the streets, every paper in America would pick up on the story and Petersen would be accepting accolades from all over. Without knowing about Carruthers, maybe Petersen and his pack of ghouls would try to do some honest investigation before breaking the story. If that happened he was ahead of them. Maybe he could still bring it home before they could.

Julie searched his face. "I'm sorry," she said. "I know that Allan shouldn't have done what he did. I tried to tell him." She shrugged helplessly. "That's why I wanted to see you. I wanted to make sure you had your story back."

"Thanks," said Chandler, taking her hand across the table. "I appreciate it." He smiled at her, genuinely thankful. She was trying to right a wrong that was not of her doing. Even in the midst of her grief she wanted to make things right, to undo, even a little, what Greenfield had done. Perhaps, thought Chandler, she didn't want Allan Greenfield to face his final editor with a mortal sin on his head. He squeezed her hand. "It was nice of you to tell me."

She didn't say anything, but now, at least, she could look him in the eye.

"What will you do now?" he asked her.

"I'm getting out of this town," she said quietly. "It's not safe. I feel threatened. Every time I see a stranger I ask myself, is this the one who will kill me?"

"You can't think like that."

Her eyes blinked rapidly. "Allan never had more than twenty or thirty dollars on him at any one time. Who would kill somebody for that kind of money?"

"You can't let it get to you," said Chandler without conviction.

She looked into his eyes. "It did already," she said and looked past him to the street outside.

Chandler could think of nothing else to say. It had all been said before and would be said again. None of it would help.

Chapter 27

Chandler's first thought when he left the West End was that now he could call Shelley and tell her about this latest development. He crossed Broadway near the Columbia bookstore, exhilarated, not because he had some new information on his story, but because he had a good excuse to call Shelley. When that thought registered, he forced himself to stop and think for a moment, and standing in front of the iron railing gate which served as the entrance to Columbia, he conducted a monologue with himself. The story is first, he said. Don't let this woman make you forget that.

He continued the monologue as he walked to the subway entrance just north of the gate. This story is mine, he told himself. All the important evidence is mine. I'd be a fool to share this latest information with someone who has contributed nothing, especially someone who has the opportunity to broadcast the story any time she decides to. If she finds out about Petersen, she might panic and decide to get the story on the air before anyone else. She could do the story and take full credit. He knew that with one easy decision, Shelley could relegate him to the background.

His imagination was running wild now and he pictured her at the Emmy Awards, looking absolutely radiant in her Halston gown and clutching her golden statuette. "Oh, yes," she was saying, "I'd like to thank all the little people who helped me with this story: my producer, my camera crew, and"—a long pause—"my research assistant, Mark Chandler. Without him this award might not have been possible."

As he descended the steps to the subway platform, Chandler wondered if perhaps he should break the story in print before anyone else could. At least that way he could garner some of the credit. But credit for what? So far he had a rather spectacular-sounding story about the possible murder of a prominent TV celebrity and the deaths of some very wealthy men. But spectacular sounding was all it was. Chandler knew that he was falling prey to one of the worst journalistic diseases: scoop mentality. The idea was not to write the best, most informed, most complete story, but to be the first to break the news. Because the reporter who first reported a story was often lionized in his own profession, this mentality sometimes led to misinformation and misrepresentation. Chandler wanted no part of that.

On the subway ride downtown, he sat, rocking with the motion of the train and trying to ignore the stares of a four- or five-year-old boy who seemed to find something about Chandler fascinating. The boy's mother sat across from Chandler, reading a paperback book which she held in one hand while she clutched her son by the belt with the other. The boy, effectively snared in his mother's grasp, could only watch the world go by, and his project for that part of the evening was to watch the funny man who sat across from him on the subway.

Chandler made faces, both happy and sad, at the boy, but the child never changed his expression. He observed the man across from him with the relentless persistence of a research scientist watching the programmed activities of some laboratory animal. The boy stared at his selected subject, as only a child or a mass murderer could: without pity or remorse, never blinking.

Finally Chandler was forced to turn away. He read the magic marker signatures by which city youths declared their existence to a generally uncaring world. Graffiti was plastered on every available space in the subway car's interior. Glancing once again in the boy's direction, Chandler saw that he was still the object of implacable scrutiny, so he turned his attention to the advertising in the curved panels in the top corner of the car, duly noting the expected obscenities that someone had added to the hemorrhoid ads.

He forced his thoughts back to the story. His story. It was ironic that now that he had most of the names and a possible, although improbable motive for the deaths of several of those listed, it appeared that the story might no longer be exclusively his. If Greenfield had indeed turned it over to Petersen, it was just a matter of time before that vulture broke the story in his column. Chandler knew that Petersen would print the story before he had all the details—he didn't care much for details. Then when the story was out in the open, everyone would be after it. Petersen, of course, would take credit for breaking the story and make it sound as if he had known all along what the end result, if any, would be.

Angrily, Chandler slapped himself in the thigh and the boy's mother looked up sharply from her book and pulled her son a little closer. The boy, as though innately certain of eventual victory, was unperturbed by Chandler's apparent anger. He continued to stare, while the mother, probably convinced that the man opposite her was a typical semideranged patron of the New York subway system, tightened her already firm grip on her son's belt.

Ignoring them both, Chandler turned away, watching the dimly lit emergency lights on the tunnel walls flash past as the train rattled and wobbled its way through the labyrinthian subway system. He cursed himself for allowing Allan Greenfield access to his story, knowing full well that he could not have guessed what the young man would do with the information once he found it. Dammit! He should have known. He knew as well as anyone else the old axiom: Never trust anyone with your story, especially another reporter. With Greenfield, he could have added another desperate reporter.

But now the kid was dead. Killed by some lousy punk for a few measly dollars. Death itself was bad enough, but death without meaning or reason was too awful to contemplate.

He let his thoughts go back to Shelley. What should he do about her? He should cut her loose and carry on with the investigation himself. Doing that, however, might create more problems than it would solve. She could immediately go public with the story, although he doubted she would do that with the facts that were available, and ruin it for him. The other problem was that the story was his only link to her, his only excuse for seeing her, and he wanted to keep seeing her. He shook his head. Fool, he thought. She probably doesn't even know you're alive, and you can't get her out of your mind. She was in almost every thought, and last night in Houston he had woken in the middle of the night, wondering if she had returned to her room. He had listened at the adjoining door, half expecting, half dreading that he would hear voices in passion, but there was only silence. He had drifted off into sleep, picturing her in bed with the anchorman.

Sometimes he would imagine situations and conversations in which he was invariably witty, suave, and masterful. The Shelley of these daydream dramas, playing her assigned part, was always impressed and usually, after some agonizing hesitation, fell into his arms declaring that she was nothing without him.

He hadn't done this since he had fallen in love with a cheerleader in his senior year in high school. She, too, had been bright, vivacious, and beautiful, and she too had been barely aware that he was alive. The only thing they had ever shared was his algebra homework, which she shamelessly, and in firm belief that it was her God-given right, copied every day. Other than those tender moments when Chandler had slipped her his homework across the aisle between them, his cheerleader rarely acknowledged his existence. She had married the captain of the football team about three hours after graduation.

When Chandler had fallen in love with the woman who eventually became his wife, there was of course the exhilaration of love, but it was a mature and growing relationship. After several months they had known that they were in love and decided—mistakenly, as it turned out—that they wanted to spend the rest of their lives together. What he felt for Shelley, he decided, was closer to what he had felt for that cheerleader. He was, he acknowledged sadly, at forty-three, in the throes of an adolescent crush.

And why not? She was one of the most beautiful women he had ever seen, much less ever known. And he enjoyed being with her. That settled, he knew that he had to include her in the latest information just to have an excuse to talk with her again.

He got off at Sixty-sixth Street, leaving behind the staring child and clutching mother, and walked up to ground level. As soon as he arrived home he checked his watch. It was 10:30. Probably too late to call, but what the hell.

Shelley answered with a husky grumble and for a moment Chandler thought he had the wrong number.

"Shelley?"

"Who's this?"

"Mark." He waited. "Chandler," he added, just in case.

"What's up?" Her voice seemed far away.

"I didn't wake you, did I?"

"As a matter-of-fact . . ."

"I'm sorry. I didn't think that you'd—should I call back tomorrow? It's only ten-thirty."

"Did you call to tell me the time?"

"No," he said, suddenly wondering if she were alone. He pictured her in bed, head on the pillow, phone to her ear, looking up at herself in those ceiling tiles. In his picture she was nude beneath satin sheets and there was someone there in the bed with her. "I'm not interrupting anything, am I?" he asked foolishly.

She laughed. "Other than sleep, no."

"I mean, I can call you back, if this is a bad time." He winced. He was handling this as if he were calling for a date to the prom. The suave, macho man of his daydreams was nowhere in sight.

"This is a marvelous time, Chandler," she said sarcastically. "Now why don't you tell me why you woke me up and are babbling incoherently on my telephone."

"Well, I've got good news and bad news," he began.

She interrupted him. "Can we skip over the comedy routine and get right to it. I had a long, tiring weekend and some of us like to get to bed early."

"OK," he said. "I've got the identities of the people on the list."

"You do!" She was suddenly alert.

"Well," he admitted, "most of them."

"How?"

"That computer kid at the paper that I told you about?"

"You said he found nothing."

"Well, apparently he came up with more than nothing. I just got back from meeting with his girl friend and she told me what he'd found."

"Girl friend?" Shelley seemed puzzled. "What does she have to do with it?"

Chandler sighed. "It seems that the kid, Greenfield, got himself killed earlier today."

"Oh my God. That's awful. What happened?"

"Someone broke into his apartment. They must have thought he was out. He wasn't, and they killed him. And that's not the only bad news." He was embarrassed and a little ashamed because he had not thought of Greenfield's death as part of the bad news.

"What else?"

"It seems that Greenfield was a little bit overzealous when he came across the identities. He decided, on his own, that there was some kind of conspiracy to kill these people. He figured he had a hot story, so he tried to peddle it elsewhere."

"He did!" She sounded surprised at the audacity of this. "You mean he was actually going to sell our story?"

Chandler ignored the "our" in her question. "Yes. I think he was hoping to catch on with another outfit and figured he could impress them with this story."

"How impressed would they be if they knew he had stolen another reporter's story?"

"I don't think this person would care."

"Who is it?"

"Andrew Petersen."

"Oh shit," she exploded in exasperation. "Not him."

"I'm afraid so."

"You mean Petersen has the story now?"

"I don't know what he has or what he knows."

Shelley didn't say anything for a moment, then, "We've got to find out."

"Find out what?"

"How much he knows. If he has the story, it's as good as dead for us. He'll ruin it."

"What can we do?" said Chandler helplessly. "There's no way to know what he has until he breaks it in his column."

"I'll call him," said Shelley.

"Call him?"

"Yes." She seemed sure of herself. "I know him. I've met him several times. I even interviewed him once."

"What good would that do? This guy is a vulture. Do you think you can talk him into staying off this story?"

"Maybe not. But I can find out what he knows." She chuckled huskily. "He's hot for my body. He drools when I walk into the room. It's positively disgusting." She made a face as if Chandler could see her. "He is one of the most obnoxious men I have ever met, but I think I can find out what he knows. I'll call him first thing tomorrow."

"All right, but do it carefully. Maybe he doesn't know anything. Let's not turn him on to something he doesn't have yet."

"Don't worry," she said. "I know how to handle him."

I'll bet you do, thought Chandler. "There's something else I want you to do," he said. "Take down these names and see if you can come up with anything on them tomorrow." He waited while she got pen and paper, then read the names on the list. "Clinton Taylor, Winthrop Watson, Forbes Coleman, and Lawrence Jefferson."

"That's it? What about the others?"

"We've got the first two—Hughes and Arnold, but O'Brien and Harrison are still blanks."

"I'll get on it tomorrow," she said. "I'll run through our files."

"Do it yourself," he said. "Don't let someone else get involved."

"Don't worry. I'll call you tomorrow after I talk with Petersen."

"All right. Now go back to sleep."

Shelley hung up and lay back in bed. He's done it again, she thought angrily. He's come up with more info and so far I've got nothing. Everything seems to fall his way and I just go along for the ride. She felt as if she were holding onto the story by her fingernails. She wanted to contribute something, something that would make her feel like an equal partner in this collaboration. Something that would make Chandler aware that she too was a good reporter.

Shelley whipped the sheets aside and saw her body reflected above. She was naked. She drew her legs up to her chest and wrapped her arms around them, hugging herself. Resting her cheek on her knees, she thought about Chandler. He had done a good job on this story and always seemed to be in the right place at the right time. So far she hadn't helped much and she was beginning to wonder why he was sticking with her on this one.

She watched herself as she ran her hands down the backs of her thighs, enjoying the fact that her skin was still creamy soft and without wrinkles.

"Soon enough," she said out loud to her image in the mirror. "How many good years have I got left?"

Chapter 28

That morning, Chandler put on his coffee and went out to pick up the paper. By the time he came back the coffee was percolating and he poured himself a cup and sat in his chair by the window, leafing through the newspaper. He knew what he was looking for, and when he came to the story about the death of Allan Greenfield he paused, sipping his coffee before he read, as if reluctant to continue.

Finally he began the story, his head shaking sadly as he read. Seeing it in print somehow confirmed the truth of this senseless tragedy. It was a fairly straightforward story with a standard headline and lead for this all too common kind of incident, and Chandler sighed as he noted the page and length of the article. Five inches on page 16, he thought. Is this how we all end up?

He continued to read, and then something at the bottom of the article made him stop, his coffee cup halfway to his mouth. The last line of the article stated, "Police refused to categorize the murder as the result of a robbery in progress, stating only that the case was still under investigation."

He read the line again. It was tantalizingly ambiguous. What did it mean? Did the police feel that Greenfield was killed for some other reason? Or did it merely mean that they refused at this point to confirm the motive for the killing?

The alarm bell in Chandler's reporter's instinct was buzzing. There was something incomplete in the article that vaguely disturbed him. It was like an indefinable odor. He couldn't pinpoint what it was; but he didn't like it anyway.

He read through the entire article again, hoping to discover something he had missed, but except for that last line there was nothing out of the ordinary.

Chandler glanced through the rest of the paper, but the other stories, even the sports, held little interest for him today. He let the paper fall to the floor and for a long time sat in his chair, staring blankly at the window. He recalled that Julie Loonin had told him about a second copy of the printout. She even knew where Allan had put it. Now it was missing. Had he moved it again to some other place? Or . . . No! What he was thinking was ridiculous. He picked up the newspaper, went to the phone, and called Inspector Downey, sipping his now lukewarm coffee as he waited to be put through. "Brian," he said when Downey picked up the phone, "how's it going?"

Downey chuckled. "Seems like I just talked to you a few days ago, Chandler. You must be hot after something."

"No—nothing like that, Brian. It's about this kid Greenfield who was killed Sunday afternoon."

"Over on One hundred fourteenth?" said Downey.

"Right. I knew him; he worked at the paper. There's something about the report in the paper that bothers me a little."

"Like what?"

"Well, the report said"—and he read from the paper— " 'the police refused to categorize the murder as the result of a robbery in progress, stating only that the case was still under investigation.' What does that mean?"

"Means just what it says. The investigating officers haven't completed their inquiry, so they're not closing the door on anything yet."

"Do you think I could talk to the investigating officer?"

"I could tell him that you want to talk to him." Downey did not sound encouraging. "No guarantee that he will want to talk to you."

"I understand," said Chandler. "But I'd appreciate it if you'd ask. Tell him I'll meet him for lunch, or dinner, depending on his schedule."

Downey gave a deep rumble of a laugh. "That ought to get him."

It was an old joke between the two of them. Both knew that good contacts must be nurtured and provided for. In police work, as in newspaper work, it was essential that contacts be promoted and protected. The police took care of their sources—paying some, protecting others—but, for some reason, when they themselves were the source of information they were expected to divulge everything they knew without consideration. The typical reporter, especially a TV reporter, wanted to know everything that the police knew. In fact, he usually screamed foul if the information were withheld. And he always walked away without a word of thanks, as if the information was his by virtue of his exalted position. Chandler had always considered the police source in the same way that the businessman considered a potential customer. If someone had some information that Chandler wanted, he had found that lunch or dinner was probably the best way to get it. There was no hint of bribery or unethical behavior; it was merely an ordinary business relationship. Chandler felt that the police had the world's worst job and that the least he could do was treat them with the respect they deserved. And if someone gave him information that proved to be particularly useful, then the source might find himself the recipient of a couple of tickets to a Knicks or Rangers game.

"I'll get back to you," said Downey. "Where will you be in about an hour?"

"I'll probably be here at home. I've got a column to get ready for tomorrow."

As soon as he hung up, Chandler went to his typewriter. He had been working on a series of columns about tenants who were being displaced when their neighborhoods were upgraded. In neighborhoods all over the city, older buildings were being renovated and remodeled. The surface scenario, covered in most of the news reports, was about the revitalization and renewal of previously depressed areas of the city by this sudden influx of the middle and upper class, who had only recently been fleeing such neighborhoods in droves. Now these same groups were renovating brownstones and rescuing entire areas of the city from the typical urban blight that would follow their exodus.

But Chandler had looked beneath the surface story and found the typical New York story of exploitation and neglect. Residents who had lived in these neighborhoods for years, and who had, in effect, performed a holding action by remaining when others had fled, found that they could no longer afford to stay. Residents who had circled their wagons and held off the savages until the cavalry arrived found that the cavalry moved in and sent them packing. Rents soared; purchase prices rose to absurd levels, and the original neighborhood residents—the elderly, the marginally poor—had to take another step down on the economic ladder.

Even though he had the information, the words were not

coming easily. His mind was on other things: the names on the list, Allan Greenfield's missing printout, and Shelley James. Shelley's image was always there, running in and out between other thoughts. He saw her face and her body everywhere.

He thought about calling her but decided against it. She had said she would call. He would wait. When the phone rang he jumped at it and was disappointed when it was Brian Downey.

"Name's Bellman," said Brian. "Says he'll meet you today at one at Angelo's Pizzeria on One hundred first Street."

Shelley was amazed that talking with Andrew Petersen on the phone was almost as repulsive an experience as talking with Petersen in person. She could hear his wheezing breath coming in short gasping pants as he told her he was "so-o-o-o pleased" that she had called.

Petersen had come on the line almost immediately when his secretary told him who was calling. "I was just talking with the secretary of state," he said boastfully. "But I told him I'd get back to him." His voice dropped to an obscene whisper. "I'd rather talk to you anytime."

Shelley gagged. Everything the man said sounded like an indecent proposal. She fought the impulse to hang up. "Andrew," she said sweetly, "how are you?"

"I'm just fine, my darling," he said. "What can I do for you, or with you, or to you?"

Forcing a laugh, Shelley went on pleasantly. "Andrew, you old lech; don't you have enough girls in Washington to keep you busy?"

"There are plenty, my dear, plenty," he said, his voice cracking, and Shelley wondered if he was fondling himself. "None of them, I'm afraid, is quite as beautiful as you."

"The reason I called, Andrew," said Shelley, rushing into her prepared statement, "is that I've got a minor problem with a research assistant and I was wondering if you could help me."

"Anything, my dear. Anything."

"Well, this young man was helping me research a story I'm working on and I'm afraid he might have tried to peddle my story on his own."

Petersen chuckled. "Such a naughty boy . . . But how can I help you?"

Shelley paused. "I think he might have come to you."

"Me!" Petersen sputtered in amazement. Then it came to him and he closed his eyes, wishing that this was not happening. "Who was this person?" he went on as casually as he could, but Shelley had already detected the change in his voice.

"His name was Allan Greenfield. Unfortunately he was killed in a robbery attempt yesterday, so I can't confront him with my questions."

"Oh dear me. That is terrible."

"Did he bring my story to you, Andrew?"

Petersen was trying to think. "He came to see me . . . on . . . Saturday, I think it was. He was looking for a job—rather pushy young man, if I remember."

"What about my story, Andrew?"

He tried to organize his thoughts. His brain was racing wildly and sweat beaded on his forehead. He didn't want to say the wrong thing. "I don't remember anything about any story, Shelley. I didn't really give him much time, I'm afraid. He wanted a job and I told him I couldn't help him. He left. I think he was quite angry."

"Are you sure he didn't give you anything on my story?"

"Positive."

Shelley's voice dropped in register to her most seductive tone. "I've been doing a lot of work on this story, Andrew. It could be a big one for me. I'd hate to think that I'll read about it in your column next week . . . That would be a rotten thing to come between such good friends." She was deliberately coquettish, knowing that he would be unable to resist her.

Surprisingly, he said in a flat monotone, "I can assure you, Shelley, that I have no intention of writing your story—whatever it is—in my column. And that's the absolute truth."

"Thanks, Andrew. That makes me feel a lot better. I'd hate to put everything into this story and then lose it."

Usually, on the few occasions that it was necessary for Shelley to communicate with Petersen, he managed to say something repulsively suggestive at parting. The last time, at a press banquet in Washington, he had asked, with his usual leer, "When is the nation's most powerful columnist going to get together with the nation's most beautiful reporter?" With twinkling eyes and a broad smile, Shelley had replied, "The day after you win the Pulitzer for public service, Andrew."

This time, Petersen seemed anxious to get off the telephone. "I hope I've been able to put your fears to rest," he said. "And now I think I'd better be getting back to work."

Shelley was surprised by his simple good-bye, but grateful that she didn't have to deal with his customary double entendre. As she hung up the phone, she thought that perhaps Petersen was turning over a new and less loathsome leaf. She laughed and said out loud, "Not that dirty old creep."

Andrew Petersen, his head in his hands, stared at the phone on his desk. This was too much. He couldn't go on like this. It was getting too risky. First Carruthers, then Greenfield, and God knows how many others. And now Shelley James. Was any secret, even this one, worth such immense risk? It was too big a secret to hide forever. They couldn't just continue eliminating everyone who knew. Sooner or later too many people would know. They couldn't just kill everyone . . . or could they?

Slowly, reluctantly, he dialed a private number. When he heard the voice on the other end he said, "This is Petersen. I just had a call from Shelley James, the newswoman at NBC in New York." He waited but there was no comment. "It seems that the story our little friend, Greenfield, tried to sell me, belonged to her. I'm not sure where she got it. Maybe from Carruthers. They were an item once." He listened as the voice asked another question. "I don't think she knows any more than Greenfield knew, but she did say she's been doing a lot of work on this. I said I knew nothing about it. That Greenfield had told me nothing. He only wanted a job." He listened again, his face ashen, his thick lips trembling. "Is that necessary? Can't you use her? She could be helpful. She has a very good position now, and she could be advanced to a position of even greater responsibility. I know it's risky but quite frankly I'm getting very nervous about all of this violence. I don't think you can go on like this. How many people are you going to eliminate before someone finds out?"

Petersen listened to the voice, his eyes wide with fear. "I know it's not for me to worry about such things," he said, "but I just want you to know that I don't think you can go on like this." He nodded several times in rapid succession. "Yes. . . . Of course. . . . You know you can count on me." Then the line went dead, leaving him holding the phone to his ear and mopping his brow with a handkerchief.

Detective David Bellman looked at his watch. "I gotta be back in half an hour," he said, letting Chandler know the limits of their meeting. He was thirty-five years old, already graying at the temples and suffering from a spreading waistline. His face was chunky and open and he had a wide mouth and a quick, ready smile.

Chandler shrugged an agreement to the time scale and looked around Angelo's Pizzeria. It was fairly typical of the genre: formica tabletops, gray linoleum floors, and exposed ovens on the other side of a serving counter.

"You like pizza?" asked Bellman.

Chandler nodded.

"This is the best. Try the complete with anchovies."

"Sounds good to me."

Bellman bellowed at the man near the cash register. "Hey, Louie. Two completes and a coupla beers, huh." He turned back to Chandler. "Take about fifteen minutes. We can talk now. When the pie comes," he said with a laugh, "I'll be too busy stuffing my face."

A waiter brought their beers, two frothy lagers in ice-cold mugs. Bellman took a good swallow of his beer and thumped the mug back on the table. "OK," he said, wiping his mouth with the back of his hand. "Downey said you were interested in this Greenfield murder."

"Yes; I knew him."

"He worked at your newspaper?"

"Yes. We had worked together on a story only recently. The thing that intrigues me is the fact that you won't confirm that his murder was the end result of an attempted burglary."

Bellman nodded, "That's right."

"Any particular reason?"

The cop turned evasive, his eyes wandering around the room. "The case is still under investigation. I don't want to jeopardize that investigation by releasing information to the press."

Chandler spread his hands, palms upward, on the table. "Look, I don't write hard news; I write a column. I'm not a news reporter, and I give you my word that whatever you tell me won't wind up in the paper."

"I've had reporters make promises to me before," said Bellman with a smile. He sipped his beer, then seemed to brighten. "You the guy who used to write about the Yanks and Mets?"

Chandler nodded. "I used to be a sportswriter."

Bellman whistled. "What a racket. I can't imagine getting paid to watch ball games."

It was a comment that Chandler had heard many times and he gave his usual stock response. "After awhile it gets to be a job just like any other."

Bellman seemed very doubtful. "In my job, people shoot at me."

Chandler raised his hands in mock surrender. "You got me there." The two were silent for a moment while Chandler thought about how to steer the conversation back on the intended track. "Can you tell me what it is that makes you think this case is something more than a simple burglary gone wrong?"

Bellman thought about it for a moment. "Off-the-record?"

"Off-the-record."

"Four things," said Bellman, displaying four pudgy fingers of his left hand. "One," he said, grasping the extended index finger with his right hand. "The murder took place on a Sunday afternoon. Burglars like to burgle empty apartments and Sunday is not a good day: Everybody's home. Statistically we get very few burglaries during the day on weekends. But if you want to find someone at home, Sunday is a good day."

Chandler, so far unimpressed with this logic, said nothing. "Two," said Bellman, moving to the middle finger. "Greenfield was killed with a silenced weapon. Burglars don't usually carry silencers with them. Too big, too bulky. You need a special holster to carry a pistol and attached silencer, unless you're going to carry the two pieces disassembled, and then it's no good to you at all in an emergency."

"Maybe the neighbors just didn't hear the shots."

Bellman shook his head. "Only one shot. We recovered the bullet—a special nine-millimeter projectile with a slow muzzle velocity."

Chandler looked puzzled and Bellman leaned forward to explain.

"When you fire a pistol, it makes noise in two ways. One is the explosion of the powder in the cartridge. That's what propels the bullet. You can fit most nonrevolver weapons with some kind of silencer that will absorb the sound of that explosion."

"How else does a gun make noise?"

"The second reason for noise," said Bellman smiling, happy to have such an attentive pupil, "is the bullet itself. Almost immediately after firing, a bullet attains the speed of sound. The sharp crack you hear is the bullet passing the sound barrier. Usually the sounds of the explosion and the bullet are so close together that it seems to be one bang, but the noise of the bullet passing the sound barrier takes place outside of the weapon itself." He paused to let that sink in. "So, no silencer can muffle that sound."

Now, Chandler was truly bewildered. "So how is it done?"

"It usually isn't. Most silencers muffle only the sound of the explosion. What's needed to really silence a weapon—in addition to a silencer—is specially manufactured, low-velocity ammunition."

"Low-velocity?"

"Right. The charge is such, that the bullets are propelled at just below the speed of sound. No speed, no sharp crack, no noise."

"Where the hell do you get something like that?"

Bellman smiled. "Government surplus," he said, and when Chandler's mouth opened in amazement, the cop laughed. "We're pretty sure that this particular weapon was a Smith and Wesson Model Thirty-nine pistol. The Model Thirty-nine and its special silencer were developed for the Navy SEAL teams during the Vietnam War. They called it the Hush Puppy. They used it to silence guard dogs," he added by way of explanation. "The pistol itself is commercially available. It's the silencer and special ammunition that are hard to get."

"How hard?"

Bellman shrugged. "If you've got the money, you can get most weapons overnight, right here in New York. This one," he said, "you might have to wait for, and it costs. It's not the kind of weapon that your typical street-punk carries."

Chandler pondered this, while Bellman drank his beer. He was beginning to believe that what Bellman was claiming might possibly be true, but he was not yet entirely convinced. "Go on," he said noncommitally.

"The third reason is the best one of all," said Bellman, his eyes twinkling like a novice poker player with a full house. "We know Greenfield wasn't killed during the progress of a robbery because the 'robber' wasn't even in the apartment when he killed him."

Chandler's raised eyebrows asked the question.

"Through the door," said Bellman. "We found the bullet entry hole in the door just below the peephole. The killer rang the bell, and when Greenfield looked through to see who it was, the killer zapped him." Bellman touched a finger to a point just below his left eye.

Chandler shuddered at the image and Bellman chuckled good-naturedly at the civilian's discomfort.

"You said you had four reasons," said Chandler.

"That's where you can help me," Bellman said. "You knew him."

Chandler nodded.

"How about drugs? Was he into dealing drugs?"

Chandler was stunned. "I don't know. It's possible, I suppose, but I really don't know." Could Allan Greenfield's ambition have driven him to such a thing? "What makes you think that?"

"Well, some people at the precinct don't agree with me on this, but I think that this was a drug-related hit. It has all the earmarks. Maybe he was holding out on somebody or maybe somebody just didn't trust him anymore. I think that whoever hit him was looking for something, probably cocaine or heroin. This guy Greenfield had something that somebody wanted and they killed him to get it."

"How can you tell that?"

Bellman seemed to be enjoying this chance to display his expertise. "By the way the apartment was searched. Whoever did it wanted us to think that this was a simple robbery but he made one mistake." He paused, waiting for Chandler to ask, "What?" but just as his listener was about to frame the question, he went on. "After killing Greenfield and searching the living room, he moved into the bedroom. Picture the bedroom," he said, moving the napkin holder, salt and pepper shakers, and his beer mug to indicate the objects in the room. "There's a closet, a dresser, and a night table on the left, a bed in the middle, and another dresser on the right."

Chandler watched in silent fascination, wondering where all this was leading.

Bellman continued. "The killer starts on the left and pulls everything out of the closets. Clothes, shoes, shoe boxes, everything." He pulled several napkins from the holder and left them crumpled on the table. "Then he goes to the dresser on the left side. He pulls out every drawer and dumps the contents on the floor." Bellman tipped over the salt shaker. "He does the same thing with the night table by the bed." He tipped over the pepper shaker, giving Chandler the smile of a master craftsman explaining his art to an apprentice. "Then he walks around the bed and goes to the dresser on the other side. He opens the top drawer but he doesn't dump the contents—he doesn't even open the three other drawers in the dresser. He doesn't touch anything else." Bellman raised his beer mug which had been the second dresser in his layout. He winked as he sipped the contents. "Why?"

"Maybe he heard someone coming?" said Chandler feebly, his mouth suddenly dry.

Bellman shook his head. "No one heard him. No one was in the hallway. No one went up those steps until Greenfield's girl friend did, and by that time the killer was already on his way down." He stared at Chandler. He had given his lecture; now it was time for the quiz. "So why didn't he open the other drawers?"

Chandler took a deep breath. He knew the answer, felt that in some way he had known the answer ever since he had read about the murder in the paper. "He found what he was looking for."

Bellman sat back, smiling proudly like a teacher who has taken a student, step-by-step, through a difficult problem. "Give the man a cigar," he said. "Hey, here comes the pizza."

Without really tasting it, Chandler chewed on his pizza. His taste buds had suddenly gone dead, and the pizza that Bellman raved over was like soggy cardboard to him. His only thought was that Julie Loonin had told him where Allan Greenfield had put a copy of the printout. Her words echoed in his brain. "In the top dresser drawer in his bedroom. I saw him put it there on Saturday. It's not there now."

Chapter 29

Lost in thought, Chandler walked south on Central Park West, his hands in his coat pockets, his eyes on the pavement. He was deeply disturbed by what he had heard about the death of Allan Greenfield, and, although he found it difficult to reconcile these facts with what he knew, it was possible that Allan had been killed because of the list that he, Chandler, had given him. Julie Loonin had said she saw Allan put the printout copy of the list in the top dresser drawer. Now the list was gone and his killer had stopped his search after looking through that one drawer.

It didn't make any sense!

First Romanello, then Carruthers had been killed because of the names on that list. Was it possible that Allan was killed for the same reason? But why? And who knew that Allan Greenfield had the list?

Petersen! Allan tells Petersen, then he gets himself killed. Was there any connection or was this merely a bizarre coincidence?

It was like one of those blank jigsaw puzzles—there were no guidelines or colors or patterns to help you put it together. The only possible approach was to connect the outer edges until you had a completed square or rectangle with nothing in the middle, and then slowly, gradually, painfully, work your way, piece by piece, into the interior of the puzzle. He had that now, he thought. He had the perimeter of the puzzle and a thousand loose pieces—faceless names and formless clues—that fit somewhere in this empty interior space. The trouble with blank jigsaws, he thought gloomily, is: What do you have when you put all the pieces together? Nothing. A blank rectangle.

Chandler entered the park at Ninety-sixth Street and walked east toward the reservoir. The day was crisp and clear and winter was in the air. He walked past the tennis courts, the neglected nets like battle-torn flags at half-mast. Then he came to the reservoir itself. This was one of his favorite spots in the entire city. Here, with the water stretched out before him, glinting sharply in the early afternoon sun, he could almost forget that he was in a city.

Chandler found a bench overlooking the water. It had lost its back supports to vandals, but he was able to rest against the concrete stanchions that anchored it to the ground. For a long time he sat, staring across the reservoir, mesmerized by the steady beat of the joggers who circled the water. He watched them pound their way around the path, some in bright-colored running suits, others in dull gray sweats, and wondered if this was where Shelley came to run. He could imagine her running, blond hair flowing in the breeze, red suit an appropriate blur. In his mind she loped past the other runners in long, graceful strides.

He did not direct his thoughts but let them carry themselves wherever they chose. Undirected, his thoughts went often to Shelley, and he had to struggle to clear his mind of her image or she would have overwhelmed everything else. He thought about Allan Greenfield and wondered if he had had time to be surprised at the moment of his death. Mostly Chandler felt disappointed in himself. Someone had been killed—apparently because of information that he himself possessed—and he didn't know why. He didn't even know what the information was. If it's important enough to kill for, he thought, why don't I know what the hell it is? All I have is a list of names.

He closed his eyes and saw the list. The names were burned indelibly in his brain, bright as neon signs. He could now add first names to complete six of the eight, but still it meant nothing. Greenfield had discovered a pattern in the deaths of three of the men named—Taylor, Watson, and Coleman. But the pattern did not hold for three others—Hughes, Arnold, or Jefferson. And he knew nothing—not even the first names of O'Brien and Harrison.

His mind blank, Chandler sat on the bench for a long time until his back ached from the pressure of the concrete. Finally, he had to get up to relieve the strain on his back, and when he did, the thought struck him that he had not had a cigarette in over an hour. He reached in his pocket and took one from the pack and put it to his lips. As he did, his eyes caught the motion of the joggers and in his mind he saw Shelley again, sneakered feet pounding the path around the reservoir. He dropped the cigarette to the ground and walked away, back in the direction from which he had come.

If Greenfield was killed because of what he knew, what was it that he knew? I know as much as he did, thought Chandler, and I know nothing. The inescapable conclusion was, that he, like Greenfield, possessed information that was of more importance than he realized.

Who could possibly have known that Greenfield knew anything? Unless he had bragged around the newsroom about his discovery, which Chandler doubted very much. How many people were aware of what Greenfield had? Two. His girl friend, Julie Loonin, and Andrew Petersen. The girl friend wouldn't tell anyone—she was too embarrassed that he had stolen the story from another reporter. That left Petersen. Why would he tell anyone? Reporters didn't usually share information.

It still didn't make sense. If you try, he thought, to find rhyme and reason for everything that happens in New York City, you're asking to be measured for a straitjacket and a padded cell.

By the time he reached Central Park West he was shaking his head and muttering to himself, "Coincidence. Nothing but coincidence. What else could it be?"

As he left the park at Ninety-sixth Street, a gust of wind hurtled across the street, blowing paper, dust, and debris at him from the gutter.

He called Shelley when he got back to his apartment but there was no answer. At the station he was told she was out on assignment, so he settled down in front of his typewriter to put together his column for the next day's paper. He wasn't having very much success. His concentration was shot and he found it almost impossible to generate any interest in what he was writing.

After about three hours of doing mostly nothing, he took the last page from the typewriter and read what he had written. It was so bad that he winced. He put the pages together and left them on his desk, then opened a lower desk drawer and extracted a manila folder where he kept his rainy day emergency columns that were reasonably timeless and could be used at almost any time without appearing dated. Occasionally, when time did not permit him to complete a column on deadline, he dropped in one from the emergency file. Sometimes when the columns came fast and furious, and he found himself getting a few columns ahead, he would write one for the emergency file against days, like today, when the words would not come. The fast and furious days happened only rarely and he tried never to deplete his small supply of emergency columns. With great reluctance, therefore, he selected one for use in tomorrow's paper. Sheehan, his editor, would know, he always knew. He would probably make some sarcastic remark about the column being aged like fine wine, but there was nothing else to do. Chandler could doctor the column he had done today and use it on Thursday.

His decision made, he fixed himself a cup of instant coffee and stood by the window, looking out as he drank it.

He wondered if Shelley had contacted Petersen yet. That thought made him vaguely anxious, but he managed to dismiss it as mere foolishness.

He wanted to call her again but decided not to make a pest of himself. She would get his message at work and if she had anything to tell him she would call back.

As he watched the traffic go by in the street, he wondered what was making him so uneasy.

When he heard Shelley's voice on the phone, it was as if he had willed it to happen. He had been thinking about her; the phone rang, and it was her.

"How are you?" he said, feeling silly that he was so happy to hear from her. He winced and told himself to stop acting like a lovestruck teenager. "Are you at work?" he asked, carefully modulating the enthusiasm in his voice.

"No, I'm home," she said. "I finished a piece for the Six O'Clock News and I don't have to be back for a few hours."

"Did you call Petersen?"

"We're in the clear," she said. "I called him and he said that Greenfield pestered him for a job but never offered him any story."

"You think he's telling the truth?"

"He's a skunk, but I believe him on this one."

Chandler was relieved that the story was safe, but somewhere in the remote corners of his mind a small voice still expressed doubts about Petersen. "Well," he said, "I guess I'll believe it if he doesn't print the story before we do. I talked with the police this afternoon and they seem to think that Allan Greenfield was murdered because he had something that somebody wanted."

"Like what?"

"I don't know. Drugs, perhaps. But I've had this sneaky little suspicion about Petersen."

"Petersen?" Her voice was incredulous.

"Allan went to see him about the list and then somebody shows up and kills him."

"You're starting to get paranoid, Chandler. The guy is a creep; but he has nothing to do with this."

Shelley had already discounted Petersen. "The reason I called," she said, "is to let you know how I've been doing on our list of names. I decided to do one at a time, so as not to raise any suspicions with the research people."

"Good," said Chandler. "Let's not involve anyone else."

"Anyway, I think I've found some interesting things. I decided to concentrate on Taylor, Watson, and Coleman, and each day go through the material on file on one of them. Today I did Watson."

"Find anything?"

"Well, as unlikely as it sounds, your friend Greenfield might have been right about someone killing these men for their money. Supposedly, Watson died of a heart attack while on a skiing vacation in Switzerland. However, his doctor back in Baltimore claimed that Watson had the heart of a twenty-year-old."

"Any autopsy?"

"That was my next question and I had to call our Baltimore affiliate to get more on the story. There was no autopsy. His wife, whom he had married five or six years before, after divorcing his first wife, had his body cremated in Switzerland. The rest of the family, according to the file, was stunned when she arrived home with only his ashes."

"I'll bet."

"The new Mrs. Watson was able to produce a letter, in her husband's handwriting, specifying that that was exactly what he wanted done."

"That should have calmed everyone down."

"Until they read the will. The new Mrs. Watson and the adopted son got practically everything. I mean this was a man with grown children and he practically cut them off. They contested the will, of course, and there were some settlements, but basically the original will stood up in court."

Thinking out loud, Chandler muttered, "Curiouser and curiouser."

"Wait," said Shelley. "It gets better. One of the stories mentions a woman who worked for the Watsons as a kind of housekeeper or nanny. It seems that she had helped raise his first family, and then, when they were grown, she was kept on as a housekeeper. When Watson and the new wife adopted their son this woman took care of him."

"What does all this have to do with anything?"

"Chandler," said Shelley, her voice triumphant. "The woman's name is O'Brien. She might be the one on the list."

Chandler's excitement grew. "Can we find her? Talk to her?"

"I'm trying to trace her now. So far no luck. But listen to

this: At the time of Watson's death she created a minor stir by claiming that there was something fishy about the whole thing. I don't think anybody paid much attention to her, though. She seemed a little on the odd side."

"Did she question the way Watson died?"

"No." Shelley paused, reluctant to go on.

"What then?"

"She thought there was something wrong with the son, the one who inherited all the money. She claimed it wasn't him."

"Wasn't him?"

"That's what she said. Of course it was easily verified that it was him. No one else ever doubted it."

Chandler thought about that for a minute and laughed. "Nothing about this seems to make much sense." He thought again about his blank jigsaw. "The more information we get, the less we know." He started to tell her about his conversation with the police about Allan Greenfield's death, when Shelley interrupted him.

"Wait a minute," she said, "someone's at the door."

Something clicked in Chandler's brain at that moment and a small piece of the puzzle fell into place. Greenfield had talked with Petersen and someone had visited Greenfield. Shelley had talked with Petersen and now . . . Before Chandler could respond, Shelley put down the receiver and started for the door. He heard her calling, "Just a minute; I'm coming," and suddenly Chandler had a vision—a vision where someone was waiting on the other side of the door with an automatic weapon and a long silencer. He saw Detective Bellman touch his finger to a point just below his left eye and Chandler was overwhelmed by a shuddering fear. He found himself screaming into the phone. "Don't open the door! Shelley; don't open the door!"

He stared helplessly into the phone, knowing that she could not hear him. He heard the sound of muffled voices and the latch clicking like a rifle bolt as she opened the door. He squeezed his eyes shut waiting for a sound he knew he would not hear.

Then, just as suddenly as she had left, she was back. "Hi," she said, her voice bright and cheerful and especially wonderful right now.

The tension drained from Chandler's body and he released his breath in one long, slow exhalation.

"It was the doorman, delivering a package," said Shelley. His eyes narrowed. "A package? What kind of package?"

"I'm not sure. It looks like—"

"Don't open it," he said sharply.

"What?"

"Don't open it."

"But, why not?"

"Just don't touch it. Put it in the bathroom and stay away from it. I'll be right over."

"Are you crazy, Chandler?"

"Just do it. I'll be there in ten minutes."

When Shelley opened the door, she gave him her most sarcastic stare. "Oh, it's you," she said. "I was expecting Kojak and the bomb squad."

"Where is it?" he asked, bursting past her into the room.

"Look, I know what it is."

He shot her a look through narrowed eyes. "You opened it?"

She shook her head. "I know how to follow orders, Captain. You said, don't open it, so I didn't open it. What's this all about?"

"The police think Allan Greenfield was killed because of something he had. I think it was our list."

"What?" she said in bewilderment. "How would anyone know?"

"He told Petersen. He's dead. You talk to Petersen and this package shows up."

"Brilliant deduction, Sherlock. This package is from the bookstore on Lexington Avenue."

Chandler stopped in his tracks.

"I told you," Shelley went on. "I went to find Jonathan's missing book. The owner said he'd send it to me. This must be it."

Embarrassed, but refusing to be so easily dissuaded from his heroic mission, Chandler said, "Let me open it first. Where is it?"

"You said put it in the bathroom—so I did." She smiled, enjoying his discomfort. "You're not going to flush it, are you?"

He ignored the humor and went to the bathroom. The package, a thin rectangle wrapped in brown paper and tied with string, sat on the vanity. Shelley's name and address were written in large red letters on one side. Chandler took a small penknife from his pocket and easily sliced through the string, inching it away from the package. He was aware that Shelley was watching him from the doorway. "Better stay back," he said. "Just in case."

She laughed and stayed where she was.

This was not going well, he thought. Somehow the heroic role had slipped away from him and he was beginning to feel very foolish. His impulse was to rip the wrapping from the package and be done with it, but instead he inched the knife into the wrapping paper and made one long slice along the edge of the package. He raised up the paper and looked inside. It was definitely a book. He could hear Shelley giggling behind him. He sliced along the bottom edge and lifted the wrapping away until the book, like a partially peeled fruit, lay revealed.

He turned to Shelley. "It's a book," he said, grinning sheepishly.

"Oh my. Isn't that remarkable!" she said.

He lifted the book out of the remnants of the wrapper and leafed through the pages. "No hidden surprises," he said and handed the book to Shelley.

She walked back into the living room with Chandler following. Shelley looked at the book. *"The Neuroscientific Significance of Chemical Imbalance in the Nature and Function of the Human Brain.* Sounds dangerous," she said. She put the book on the end table next to the couch, trying not to laugh at Chandler's embarrassment.

"I guess I've done it again," said Chandler. "I seem to be an expert in unnecessary rescues." He stuck his hands deep in his pockets and looked down at the floor. "It was stupid of me. I just thought . . ." His voice trailed away. He wasn't sure what he thought.

Shelley touched a hand to his cheek and Chandler caught his breath. "Thanks anyway," she said softly.

They were very close and Chandler felt frozen, immobilized.

Her hand went from his cheek to his shoulder as if she were reluctant to break contact. "I'm glad you were worried about me," she said. "It's nice to be worried about."

His arms went around her and pulled her to him, his mouth searching for hers. He felt the pressure of her body against his, her breasts flattening against his chest. Her arms went around him, holding him close, her lips, soft and gentle, opened for him.

Still holding her, Chandler drew back a little, looking into her face.

"What is it?" asked Shelley.

"Nothing," he said. "I just like looking at you."

"I noticed," she said with a sly smile.

"Was I that obvious?"

Shelley drew him to her and kissed him and Chandler pulled her down onto the couch. "I've got to get back to work," she murmured without conviction.

Chandler ignored her meek protest. He was nibbling on her ear, his eyes open. He wanted to take in every delicious sense that he could. As he gently pushed her down onto the couch his eyes fell across the book she had placed on the end table. At first he was unaware that his eyes had actually read anything, but his brain had registered something and sent up a small flare of alert. Disturbed at the interruption, he found his eyes wandering back to the book jacket. His mouth was on Shelley's ear and she was mumbling something barely intelligible about getting back to work when he stopped and sat up.

She looked up at him. "What is it?"

"Did you look at this book?"

She said nothing, surprised that he was talking about a book.

"Did you see the author's name?"

Shelley sat up. She read the name on the cover of the book. "Harrison. Dr. Reginald Harrison."

"That's the last name on the list," said Chandler. "That's why this book was missing from Carruthers's apartment."

Shelley ran her hand across her hair. She did not seem to share his enthusiasm for his discovery. She stood up, straightening her skirt. "Look, I've got to get back to work right now. Why don't you keep the book and let me know what you find?"

The tone of her voice pulled him back to the present. "The book can wait," he said, taking her hand.

"I really have to get going," said Shelley, pulling away. This time he realized that she meant what she said. "I'd better go fix my hair," she said and disappeared into the bathroom, closing the door with what Chandler thought was a rather resounding whack.

He contemplated the offending volume, picking it up and opening it to the title page. He read it, then turned his eyes to the bathroom door, behind which he could hear Shelley humming absentmindedly. Chandler shook his head and closed the book, wondering how he could have been so stupid. He thumped his forehead with the palm of his hand and muttered, "Dummy," to himself. He had wanted this woman for weeks, thought of hardly anything about her—and now when she was in his arms he had broken the mood by looking at a book. Sometimes he couldn't believe how dumb he was.

Shelley ran a brush through her hair while carefully inspecting her face in the mirror. She moved closer to the mirror to look at the small wrinkles at the outer corners of her eyes. "First time," she said quietly to her image in the mirror, "that I ever lost out to a book." She touched up her lipstick, pouting at herself in the mirror, then stepped back a little to inspect the overall effect. "Pretty damn good," she said defiantly.

When Shelley came back into the living room, Chandler was anxious to assuage her bruised feelings. "You were right about the importance of that missing book," he said.

"Was I?" she said tonelessly, not looking at him.

He winced, knowing he was facing an uphill battle. "That was pretty damned observant of you."

Shelley ignored his remarks. Instead she put on her coat and started for the door. Chandler, still carrying the book, followed her. "This book was published in London," he said. "Do you think maybe you could get one of your network people over there to check out this Harrison for us?"

"I can do that," said Shelley, her voice still flat. "No trouble."

Chandler stepped in front of her, blocking her path to the front door. "Sometimes, I do really stupid things," he said.

"I've noticed," said Shelley.

He held up the book. "This probably ranks as number one on my dumb list."

She was enjoying his discomfort. "You're probably right," she said.

"Should I call you later?" he asked.

Shelley looked at him for a moment before answering, and Chandler had the feeling that something important was being decided. "No," she said finally. "Don't call me. I'll get back to you if I find out anything about Harrison."

Chandler's face fell. "Oh," he said and then thought that perhaps he shouldn't say anything else right now.

Chapter 30

At 10:00 P.M. the phone rang. Before answering, Chandler put down his beer, removed his cat from his lap, and turned down the volume on the television set. He was surprised to hear Shelley's voice on the line. Chandler had expected that it would take some time before she forgave him for that afternoon's fiasco, but here she was already calling him. He felt good.

"I thought you were at work," he said cheerfully.

"I am. We go on in an hour. I'm working on a few details before airtime." She fell silent.

"What's up?" he asked, knowing instinctively that this was not a social call.

"Remember how I laughed at your theory about Allan Greenfield telling Petersen our story and then getting himself killed? . . ."

He could detect the strain in her voice. "Yes," he said.

"Someone just called me and said that my life was in danger."

"What! Did they say why?"

"No, nothing else. Just that I should be very careful because someone would try to kill me in the next few days."

"My God," muttered Chandler and then fell speechless.

"Chandler, I'm scared. What the hell is happening?"

"Look, maybe it was just a crank call," he said, trying to calm her. "You must get some of those."

"Not like this."

"Did the caller identify himself?"

"No, but . . ."

"But, what?"

"Well, the voice was muffled as if he was trying to disguise it, but I think it was Andrew Petersen."

"Petersen?"

"You're the one who said that he might be involved in some way."

"Yeah. I know, but—"

"But nothing. Greenfield talked with him and now Greenfield's dead. Petersen knows that I'm involved, and now I get death threats."

"Take it easy. It could be just a coincidence."

"You don't believe that. Everybody who knows anything about this story gets themselves killed. I'm scared and I don't even know what it is that I know. I'm afraid to walk out on the street."

"Do you want me to meet you after work? I can make sure you get home OK?"

"No. Someone from work can drop me off, but would you meet me at my apartment? I've got some information on your famous Dr. Harrison."

"I'll be there. What time will you get home?"

She thought for a moment. "By the time I get things wrapped up here and get home, it's usually a quarter past twelve. Is that too late?"

He smiled, knowing that she wanted someone to be there with her and glad that she wanted him. "No, it's not too late. I'll see you then."

"Thanks, Chandler," she said. "This thing has really got me scared."

Shelley opened the door to her apartment and, before stepping across the threshold, reached inside to switch on the lights. Everything seemed normal. She closed the door behind her, then looked at her watch. It wasn't even twelve o'clock yet. This was the earliest she had ever gotten home from work. Perhaps it was because she hadn't been in the mood for the usual postshow frivolity that ordinarily managed to release some of the tension of the production. Tonight she had been quiet and somewhat removed from all of that. A few coworkers had even commented that she didn't seem to be herself. She was nervous and distracted but had made it through the program without any problem. The only outward manifestation of her discomfort was that the usual between-stories-banter between Shelley and the other reporters had been a little tighter and less spontaneous than usual. Other than that, the show had gone quite well.

Shelley threw her coat over the couch and went to the kitchen. She put on the kettle for coffee, making sure there was enough water for both Chandler and her. As she walked back through the living room she checked her watch again. It was barely past midnight; Chandler wouldn't be here for fifteen minutes.

Feeling a sudden chill she wrapped her arms around herself and turned up the thermostat in the hallway connecting the small study and the bathroom with the living room. Wanting to abolish all pockets of darkness she turned on the lights in the hallway and in the study. As soon as she entered the study she knew something was wrong: Someone had been there. The drawers in the desk were partially open in a way she knew she had not left them. Her first reaction was to close the desk drawers and reshuffle the paperwork on the desk, but before she had taken two thoughtless steps forward, the thought struck her with shuddering conviction that whoever had been here might still be in the apartment.

As she began to back toward the door, her eyes darted around the room, noting the subtle manifestations of disarray. Someone had been looking for something. Her mind, like a panicked mouse, ran to every possible corner of concealment in the apartment. She had already been in the living room and kitchen, and was now in the study. That left only the bathroom, directly behind her.

Stopped in her tracks, her apprehension like a wall that prevented further progress, she was struck by a horribly indescribable fear that someone was standing behind her. Her knees grew weak and her heart pounded in her chest. She could not turn around, go forward, or back. She was paralyzed by the sudden certainty of this presence, immobilized by the sure knowledge of some faceless intruder.

Her brain exploded in a starburst of panic. Demanding motion, action, something, her brain sent a jumble of messages darting across her consciousness. *Move-turn-shout-scream-run*. Each short-circuited message resulted in a minor twitch in Shelley's body—nothing more. She was once again four years old and the bedroom was dark and the house was quiet. A dark shape that seemed to be a strange man was sitting in the chair next to the door. Shelley was too afraid to call for her daddy, too afraid to hide under the sheets, too afraid to move. Maybe if she just lay here quietly, without moving, the shape wouldn't know she was here.

For countless, interminable seconds she stood in the study, her back to the door, waiting for whatever was going to happen. But nothing did. Gradually her racing pulse diminished to near normal and the strength in her legs began to return. Just as she dared to think that it was all her foolish imagination and to seriously consider turning around to face the door, a hand was clamped over her mouth.

The hand was huge. It seemed to cover most of her face and for an instant she thought she might suffocate. Then a soft, deep voice close to her ear and with breath reeking of stale tobacco said, "No noise or I'll have to hurt you."

Shelley tried to nod her head but the pressure of the hand across her face made movement impossible.

"Understand?" said the voice.

Finally the hand gave her just enough room to move and Shelley nodded. He released her and Shelley turned to face her assailant. He was black and tall and lean and powerfully built. His face was devoid of expression—no anger, no fear, no hatred. He had a small scar under his right eye.

"Where is it?" he asked.

Shelley, unable to speak, could only shake her head in mystification.

"The list," he said. "You have a copy of the list."

She shook her head quickly.

The man struck her a sharp blow across the face with his open hand, the sound like the crack of a whip reverberating around the room, as Shelley went reeling to the floor. Sprawled in a corner of her study, Shelley held a palm across her mouth to prevent herself from screaming. Her cheek, where she had been struck, felt as if she had been branded with a hot iron.

The man reached into his pocket and removed something which he pried open, revealing a long, gleaming blade.

Shelley could feel her stomach spasm convulsively and the vomit rise to her throat. She fought to hold it back.

"I don't want to cut that pretty face," said the man in his curious expressionless way that told Shelley it was of little consequence to him whether he did or not. "So you'd better tell me."

Tears rolled down Shelley's cheeks, blinding her. "No more copies," she stammered, choking with fear.

"Who else knows about it?" he said as if repeating words he had learned by rote.

Shelley tried to think but her mind was a jumble of confusion. She hesitated, wondering if there was an answer which could save her life. The man moved toward her, knife poised. "No. No one else knows," she said, realizing as she said it that her answer would not prolong her life. Perhaps there was no answer that would.

The man smiled for the first time, showing rows of yellowed, uneven teeth. "Good," he said. He bent over and helped Shelley to her feet, his hand like a vise gripping her arm. "Let's get this over with."

He led her into the living room, the pressure of his grip so strong she felt her bones crack. The man held her so that her feet barely touched the ground. Shelley had never felt such power.

Shelley's eyes never left the knife in his left hand. Nothing, not even the excruciating pain of his grip, could have been more terrible than the gleaming, murderous efficiency of that blade. Her mind was flooded with horrifying images: stabbing, slashing, slicing, cutting. Her knees began to give way but the man continued to march her forward until she found herself standing in front of the sliding glass door to the terrace.

"Open it," he said, flashing the knife under her chin.

Shelley struggled to speak. "I'll do anything you want," she said finally. "Anything."

The man laughed quietly, his eyebrows going up with the thought. "I'll bet you would. And I bet it would be real nice, too," he said. "But you don't have the time. Open it."

Fingers trembling, refusing to collaborate in her own destruction, Shelley fumbled with the latch on the glass door until the man pushed her hand aside and with his knife-hand released the lock and slid the door open.

The sounds of the city welled up from below—night sounds, car and horn sounds, a constant murmur of activity. The city was still alive. Lights twinkled, flashing in a symmetrical collage of shifting patterns. The view had never been more intense or more awesome.

"Nice and easy now," said the man, moving her out onto the terrace. "Nothin' to it."

Shelley squeezed her eyes shut, blocking out the view of the city. Only the night sounds and the man's soft voice penetrated her consciousness.

Reassuring her in his soft, curiously gentle voice, the man maneuvered her toward the edge, when another sound intruded upon the sounds of the city.

Knocking! Someone was knocking at the front door. Shelley's head whipped around but the man's hand clamped across her mouth before she could respond. Chandler! She knew it was him. In her panic she had forgotten he was coming.

He knocked again as the man held her tightly, crushing her breath. Then she heard him call her name.

Please, she screamed silently. Save me from this.

Chandler rapped sharply on the door again. Again, no answer. He was puzzled. The doorman had told him that Shelley had arrived about ten minutes before he did and had left word that he was to go straight up. He was apprehensive about the mix-up but felt that perhaps he had too often exaggerated the danger in this situation. Maybe she had stopped off at a neighbor's before going to her apartment. He could wait by her door until she arrived.

Oh, my God, thought Shelley. He's gone. He's not knocking anymore. Chandler, for God's sake, don't leave me.

The man, hand still crushed over her mouth, waited a few more seconds, then began to move her again toward the edge of the terrace. Shelley dug in her heels. The possibility of rescue had snapped her out of her panic-stricken trance. If she could only make a noise, break something, so that Chandler would hear her. Adrenalin pumping, pulse pounding, she felt renewed strength surging through her body. She put her right foot up on the railing and pushed back on her attacker. In her mind she visualized him, caught off balance, stumbling back to smash through the glass doors.

He was immovable. Her strength was miniscule compared to his. Almost contemptuously, he lifted her off the ground and swung her feet out over the terrace. Shelley clamped both hands around the top railing. Hand still over her mouth he attempted to shake her loose, but she held on with a strength that surprised them both.

"I'm gonna have to cut you, bitch," the man said, his voice for the first time expressing emotion.

Just as he put the knife across the knuckles of her right hand, the kettle began to whistle. His head snapped around as if someone had set off a burglar alarm back in the living room.

In the hallway, Chandler heard the kettle scream. She *was* in there. He banged with his fist. "Shelley, are you there?"

But for the shriek of the kettle, there was no answer.

Without hesitating another second, Chandler slammed his full weight into the door, which, to his surprise, burst open. He saw Shelley struggling with a man on the terrace and ran toward her.

The man released her and stepped inside to meet him. He feinted with the knife and caught Chandler a blow to the side of the head with his other hand. Chandler fell back across the couch, and the man, calm and businesslike, kicked the end table aside as he pursued Chandler across the room.

Chandler wormed his way back toward the kitchen, away from the front door. "Get the hell out of here, Shelley," he yelled, but his pursuer backed up to block Shelley's avenue of escape.

Chandler stood up, the three of them forming an equilateral triangle. "What now?" said Chandler, strangely calm.

"I take you out," said the man. "Then I finish the little lady."

"Never happen," Chandler said. "You come after me, she gets away. You go after her and I'll have time to get the meat cleaver in the kitchen."

The man's eyes bored into Chandler's face, but through it all he remained emotionless. Finally he shrugged in resignation. "Maybe next time," he said to Shelley and headed for the door. He closed it behind him and Shelley and Chandler looked at each other in disbelief that the trauma was over so suddenly.

"Call the police," said Chandler, racing to the door. Cautiously he stepped out into the hall—it was deserted. He raced to the elevator—nothing. He went to the fire exit and opened the door. He listened but did not hear the expected sound of running feet. Either this was the most composed assailant in New York City or he had taken another route downstairs.

He went back to the apartment where Shelley sat on the couch staring at the floor. "Did you call the police?" he asked.

She looked up. "No."

"No! Why not?"

"What am I going to tell them?"

He was mystified. "That someone broke into your apartment and tried to kill you."

"Shall we tell them that the person who tried to kill me might also have killed Romanello, Carruthers, and Greenfield?"

"Yes. That's exactly what we'll tell them." He picked up the phone.

Her jaw set, Shelley shook her head. "I want this story. Until now I felt like it was your story and I've just been hanging on. But now"—her eyes looked toward the open terrace door—"I feel that I've earned my part of it. I don't intend to hand it over to every reporter in the country." She looked at him. "Do you realize how important this story must be? There are people who will kill to keep it secret."

"Shelley, there are people out there who will kill for bus fare."

She waved that aside. "This is what we do for a living. This may be the biggest story that either one of us will ever get a shot at."

"We're not even close. We're just whistling in the dark."

"We're getting closer," she said with conviction. Chandler was emphatically shaking his head. "Let's give it one more week," said Shelley. "Then if we don't have enough to break the story, we'll turn it over to the police."

"It's not worth your getting killed."

"I'll take that chance," she said defiantly.

Up until that moment he hadn't realized how tough she was. He had expected her to be broken by her experience but instead it had made her angry, made her want the story even more than he did. He put down the phone. "OK," he nodded. "But I'm not going to let you out of my sight until we break this thing."

"Chandler, do you think you could come over here and hold me?" Shelley said. "I don't think my knees will stop shaking long enough to let me stand up."

Very gently, he put his arms around her and she buried her face in his chest. They held each other for a long time, Chandler sensing that she only needed someone to comfort her. Finally Shelley spoke. "Lucky for me you came along."

"Lucky for me," he said without thinking. "I don't think I could live without you."

"I'm glad you said that," she laughed. "Now that you've broken down my door, I certainly can't stay here."

He drew back to look at her face.

"Help me pack a few things," she said. "I'll move in with you for a while."

While Shelley packed, Chandler was able to repair the splintered door frame so that from the outside it looked perfectly normal. One good hard push, however, would reveal the illusion. "I'll leave word," said Shelley, "for the super to fix it first thing in the morning."

And so with a small suitcase, a shoulder bag, and a garment bag that Shelley draped over Chandler, they made their way cautiously out of the building.

Chapter 31

It was almost 3:00 A.M. by the time they arrived at Chandler's apartment. Shelley put down her suitcase as they entered and looked around at the mess.

"Is this what they call Early Clutter?"

"I wasn't expecting company," he said, explaining the perpetual state of disarray.

"How long has it been since you had company?"

He laughed. "Not that long. It just needs a woman's touch."

"Don't look at me," said Shelley. "I have a woman come in and do my housework." From the small entryway she could look into the kitchen. "I'm going to make some coffee," she said. "You want some?" When Chandler nodded she went on. "I'm so tense that I'll never fall asleep anyway."

Chandler put the bags across a stuffed chair in the center of the living room. "I'll go put fresh sheets on the bed in the second bedroom."

Shelley smiled. "That would be nice," she said quietly.

The second bedroom had been his daughter's room and was the only room in the apartment that was uncluttered. Chandler's daughter was compulsively neat, and her room was still as she had left it. A few of the stuffed animals she had treasured as a younger child adorned the small night table by the bed. On the dresser was a large framed photograph, showing Chandler and his daughter, both wearing huge smiles, she displaying her missing front teeth, long dark hair, and large, luminous eyes. Behind the door, mounted with masking tape, hung a crayon construction-paper masterpiece from the second grade. It showed in intricate detail a house and flowers and a stick figure family—mother, father, daughter—and a larger-than-life brown cat. The drawing always made him sad. It represented a little girl's fantasy of a happy family that never was. He kept it because it reminded him of her.

He stripped the bed of its Raggedy Ann sheets and replaced them with a flowered print. As he worked, his eyes kept drifting to the photograph of his daughter, and when he finished the sheets he picked up the frame to inspect the photograph more closely. He wasn't aware, as he stood staring at the small, shining face, that Shelley was standing in the doorway.

"Coffee's ready," she said quietly as if realizing that one should never speak loudly in this room.

Chandler replaced the picture on the dresser.

"She's very beautiful," said Shelley.

Chandler nodded, fingers touching the frame. "That was about three years ago. She's even more beautiful now. She's nine. Be ten in April."

"Do you see her much?"

His eyes went around the room as though he saw her everywhere. "No," he said. "Not since her mother moved back to Pennsylvania. I fly her back here for holidays and things." He shrugged. "Coupla times a year, that's all."

"It must be rough on you," said Shelley, "and on her."

"The funny thing is," said Chandler dreamily, as if he were repeating an oft-told refrain, "Lisa, my wife, didn't want any kids. She had her career and all. She's a professional photographer. When things started going bad for us, she thought a child would keep us together." He shrugged. "Worked for a while, I guess, but we split up two—almost three—years ago. Six months after we separated, she moved back to Pennsylvania."

There was only silence for a moment, then Chandler spoke again. "I'm not blaming her, or anything. I was pretty rough to live with. I can be a . . ." His voice trailed off.

"A pain in the ass?" asked Shelley helpfully.

He laughed. "You've noticed."

"Come on," said Shelley gently. "Your coffee will be cold."

Shelley had placed the coffee on a tray on the table in front of the couch. Chandler's cat was lounging there lazily, awaiting their arrival, and as Shelley approached, he lifted his head so that she might scratch underneath his chin. After taking exception to all this late-night activity, Samson seemed to be quite smitten by his new houseguest.

"I see you've already made a friend," said Chandler as they sat down.

"Yes. What's his name?"

"Samson. He doesn't usually like strangers."

"Maybe he knows I'm not a stranger." She sipped her coffee, peeking at him over the rim of the cup.

Chandler could feel himself start to turn red. His mouth was dry and his heart was pounding. He desperately tried to think of something clever to say, but his mind was a complete blank. For some reason he kept wishing that he had put fresh sheets on his bed. He wasn't sure of the direction in which the conversation was drifting. There was—at least for him—an electricity in the air that had the distinct feel of the sexual sparring that went on as a preliminary to something more intense. But he wasn't sure. He felt rusty and out of shape at this sort of thing. She was here, living in his apartment—at least for tonight—but he was unsure about the arrangement. Nothing had been said. The worst thing now, he thought, would be to assume the best and make a damn fool of himself. They were too far apart in too many ways for him to hope that she could want him in the same way that he wanted her. She was younger than he and certainly more successful. She lived a completely different kind of life than he did. He imagined big network parties, evenings with celebrity friends at posh New York night spots, weekends in Vegas or Palm Springs. In addition to all that, she was one of the most beautiful women he had ever seen. What chance did he have that she would ever consider him as anything but a friend and colleague? Especially after he'd blown it last time. The silence stretched to what he thought were embarrassing proportions. Shelley, seemingly unperturbed, stroked Samson.

"You're really quite remarkable," Chandler blurted out suddenly.

Shelley smiled. "I'll let you count the ways."

"You know what I mean. A few hours ago someone tries to kill you, and here you sit, sipping coffee like nothing happened."

The smile slipped from her face. "Don't let this calm facade fool you. I'm still on the verge of screaming. You know what I thought when that bastard hoisted me over the railing?" She didn't wait for him to ask. "I said to myself: Now I know why Chandler doesn't like heights."

Chandler smiled. In some perverse way it pleased him that she had thought of him at such a moment.

"It will be a long time," she went on, "before I can make myself go out on that terrace again; that's for sure." She kicked off her shoes and tucked her legs beneath her, and Chandler thought she looked perfectly marvelous sitting on his couch in his living room.

"You know all about my depressing past," he said. "Tell me something about you."

She shrugged. "No marriage. No children."

It seemed a funny thing for her to say. With all the ways she could have summed up her life, he was surprised she had chosen that. "Why not?" he said, immediately feeling foolish.

Shelley made a face that suggested how unsure she was of the answer. "It's tough to find Mr. Right here in the big city. Most of them are already chosen." She looked down into her coffee cup, the smile fading. "Also," she said earnestly, "I think that I scare off some men."

"I'll bet you do," retorted Chandler a little too quickly.

She paused, looking at him steadily. "I don't scare you, do I?"

"Nothing scares me," he lied. "Except airplanes, tall buildings, small rodents, and women with hair on their legs."

She untucked one leg from beneath her and extended it toward him. "Look," she laughed, running her hand over her leg, "no hair."

Chandler swallowed hard. The temptation to touch her was overwhelming.

"Another thing," she went on, as if unaware of the effect she had on him. "I'm reasonably successful in my field and I'm very well paid. A lot of men have trouble dealing with that. They think they should bring home more money than the little woman or something." Chandler nodded and Shelley continued. "Some men think I'm unapproachable. I know they call me Ice Lady or something like that at the station, but I don't think I'm like that." She waited for Chandler to tell her she wasn't like that, but he didn't say anything. She sipped her coffee, but it was getting cold.

"Do you want to get married?" asked Chandler, who immediately felt he was rapidly becoming the master of the stupid question.

Shelley laughed. "This is really rather sudden, isn't it?"

"You know what I mean," he said.

"I guess so—yes," she admitted. "Of course, I do."

"Is there anyone now who . . ." Chandler struggled with the question.

"No," she said. "No one special."

"I thought that someone like you would have—"

She knew what he was going to say. "I'm available, if that's what you're asking."

He nodded.

"Did you mean what you said to me back in my apartment?"

"What?" He seemed puzzled.

"About not being able to live without me. Or is that just what you say to calm down hysterical ladies."

He took a deep breath. "I meant it. Every word."

She said nothing.

"I even gave up smoking," he said.

Shelley smiled and touched his hand. She looked around the room. "Usually I'd say your place or mine, sailor, but I guess we're past that point already."

Chandler, his heart thumping, his throat tight, squeezed her hand. "I guess I put the fresh sheets on the wrong bed," he said.

"I think you did," she said quietly.

He wanted to kiss her right then, was in fact desperate to kiss her. Their eyes locked and Shelley, as if in anticipation, touched the tip of her tongue to her lips. Their bodies moved almost imperceptibly toward each other and all at once they were in each other's arms. He crushed her to him, holding her more tightly than he had ever held anyone. If this was a dream he would not let go willingly. Her mouth opened and their tongues probed each other as his hands roamed down her back.

Then her mouth was at his ear. "It's about time," she whispered. "For a while I thought I was going to have to do a striptease in your living room."

He was kissing her again, wondering how he had gotten so lucky. Don't think, he told himself, just enjoy. But he couldn't help it. He knew that she was vulnerable. She had been terrified and he had arrived just in time to save her. She was grateful to him and felt more toward him than she had ever felt before, and perhaps more than she ever would again. This response, he thought as he ran his hand across the inside of her thigh, might be a momentary romantic impulse brought on by the trauma of what had happened to her and his involvement in her rescue. She wasn't thinking rationally and it wouldn't be fair of him to take advantage of that.

Too bad, he thought as he unbuttoned her blouse. He pulled it open and buried his face in her breasts. He kissed her mouth, then brought his lips back to her breasts, taking the nipples each in turn into his mouth until they were hard and erect.

Shelley was fumbling with the buttons on his shirt and he sat up, looking at her lying on the couch beneath him, her hair disheveled, her blouse open. She was devastating.

Finally she got his shirt open and ran her fingers across his chest. "I like a hairy chest," she said.

"Thanks," he said. "I got it in the Men's Shop at Barney's."

She laughed, a long, deep, incredibly sexy laugh. "You're crazy," she said, pulling him down on top of her and fumbling with his belt buckle.

Chandler moved off the couch and reached both arms under her to lift her up. Shelley drew back in protest. "I'm going to take you to the bedroom," he said.

She shook her head and pulled him back to her. "Right here," she said, her voice husky in his ear. "There's plenty of time for the bedroom. This time I want it right here."

They slipped quickly out of their clothes, each helping the other move toward nakedness, each touching the other's newly bared flesh as the garments fell away. When they were finally naked and he had banished Samson to the bathroom, Chandler came back to the couch and stood over Shelley, just watching her, drinking in her beauty.

"Do you want to turn off the lights?" she asked.

"You must be kidding," he said as he lay next to her, feeling the heat of her body on his.

His right arm behind her, he lightly traced the curve of her body with his left hand. He touched her gently, caressing her the way a musician would touch a fine instrument.

"That's nice," she whispered in his ear. Her hands ran down his belly, touching him. It was electric. Chandler felt as if he had never been touched before. Her strong fingers grasped him. "I think you're ready," she said, draping her leg over his.

"I've been ready since the first time I saw you," he said.

Then the two of them were all mixed up together—holding, touching, clutching, moving as one. Shelley whispered things, low, wonderful things, in his ear, and Chandler felt as if he were floating above the two figures on the couch. He was watching and feeling at the same time, somehow disengaged and detached but still sharing the ecstasy. He felt her warm breath in his ear and the heat of their bodies' contact, and he thought that this must be some kind of wonderful dream and hoped he would never wake up.

Chapter 32

When Chandler woke, the late morning sun was streaming through the bedroom window. Groggily he reached over to the other side of the bed but no one was there. For just an instant he imagined that he must have dreamed all of what had happened last night, but then he heard Shelley's voice on the telephone in the living room and he gave a long, satisfied sigh of relief.

Her voice, a low, soothing, unintelligible murmur, made him smile and remember. Chandler draped an arm across his face to shield his eyes from the glare as he listened to the tranquilizing sound of Shelley's voice. If, at that moment, another voice had told him he had died and gone to heaven he would not have protested. He was pleased with himself, so pleased in fact that his cheeks ached from smiling.

The bedroom door opened. "You awake yet?" asked Shelley and Chandler opened one eye to peer sleepily in her direction. She was wearing one of his flannel shirts as a robe, the sleeves hanging down beyond her fingertips. She sat on the bed next to him and gave him a quick kiss on the mouth. "How are you this morning?"

"Terrific," he said truthfully and wraped his arms around her.

"You want some coffee? I've got the pot on."

"Sounds good," he said, releasing her and sitting up a little. "Two eggs and toast would be great too."

"That *does* sound good," said Shelley with a sudden burst of laughter. "While you're fixing yours, make some for me." She stood up and began unbuttoning the shirt. "Meanwhile, I'm going to take a shower."

"One more button," said Chandler, "and you'll never make it to the door."

Shelley smiled and continued. She shrugged her shoulders and the shirt slipped to the floor. She stood there, not saying anything, and Chandler watched her, the sight of her naked in daylight taking his breath away. Finally he pulled back the sheet and she climbed in next to him.

"When do you have to be back at work?" he asked as Shelley nibbled on his ear.

"I just called my producer and told him I'm taking a week off."

"A *week!*" said Chandler in mock horror. "I don't know if I can keep this up for a week."

Shelley ran a hand down his stomach till she found him. "So far," she said, "you're doing just fine."

He shivered, feeling himself harden. "Can you just call in and take a week off?"

She shrugged. "I've got a week coming in December and another in February. I just told him I needed some time now. There are plenty of young and eager reporters ready, willing, and able to jump into my anchor position." As she spoke she was stroking him to readiness. "I'd like to give this thing a week and I want to give it my best shot." She rolled over on top of him, sitting up as she did, with her breasts over his face. "No more conversation," she said.

He smiled. "No more conversation."

* * *

They drank their coffee sitting on the two stools at the kitchen counter. Chandler wore blue jeans and a navy V-neck sweater over a white Oxford shirt, and Shelley wore brown slacks and a bulky fisherman knit sweater.

"I didn't run today," she said. "Tomorrow I've got to run in the park."

Chandler, the disbelief evident in his face, said, "Are you crazy? If somebody's looking for you, that's the worst thing you could do." He smiled lecherously. "Besides you can get all the exercise you need right here."

Shelley punched him playfully on the arm. "That's not quite the kind of exercise I had in mind," she said. "But I'm not worried. Anyone looking for me is going to have a tough time; we'll be out of the country soon."

Chandler was genuinely surprised. "Out of the country? What are you talking about?"

"I thought you'd want to talk with Dr. Harrison."

"Of course."

"Someone in our London bureau traced him for me. He lives in Thornwood, just outside London. He's a neurosurgeon and also teaches at St. Bartholomew's Medical College in London. I figured we'd go over there and have a chat with him. Find out if he knows anything about this."

Chandler nodded. "Good idea."

"Did you ever read that book of his?" said Shelley with some sarcasm.

"I looked through it. It's a little heavy for me. My taste runs to *The Boys of Summer* or *Great Moments in Red Sox History*."

Shelley smiled ruefully. "My luck. I would wind up with a jock—or worse, a sportswriter."

Chandler turned serious. "I wasn't always a sportswriter," he said, his voice taking on a misty quality. "I was once considered the top pitching prospect in the country. I was the number one draft pick by the Red Sox in 1963, the year I led Boston College to the college baseball championship. I was sixteen and scheduled to report to the Bristol triple-A club the next spring when I got my draft notice. My first day in Vietnam I dove on a grenade that was lobbed into my platoon. I saved everyone, but, of course, my pitching career was over." He smiled sadly as Shelley's eyes narrowed suspiciously. "I had no stomach for the game anymore."

"You really are a pain in the ass," said Shelley in mock anger. "You had me believing that story."

"Really! I should try it on women more often. What part was it that gave me away?"

"Never mind. What about Harrison's book? Any clue as to why it was so important that Jonathan needed two copies?"

"I told you it's too heavy for me. It's all about brain wave patterns, pituitary hormones, chemical imbalances, occipital lobes, and lots of other things I've never heard of. It's very dry stuff. It will never make the best-seller lists."

The phone rang, and Chandler started to rise. "Never mind," said Shelley. "It's probably for me." She got up from the stool, grinning impishly. "I'm expecting a few phone calls."

It was Nancy Kelley. "Shelley," she said, her voice dripping with delight, "I was told you're going to be at this number for the next few days."

"Right," said Shelley.

Nancy's voice dropped to an intimate whisper. "Shelley, isn't that Mark's number?"

"Right again, Nancy."

Nancy chuckled gleefully. "Didn't you tell me this was a strictly professional relationship?"

"It's still professional, but you know how these things are."

Nancy ignored her comment. "Here I had you figured for Robert Redford and you wind up with Walter Matthau."

Shelley cleared her throat noisily. "I don't think that's a very apt description, Nancy."

"Hey! I like Walter Matthau. He's very cuddly."

Shelley didn't comment.

"And you're taking a week off. Can't you guys get enough of each other?"

"We need the time to put this story together."

"Take all the time you want. They've asked me to fill in for you on the *Eleven O'Clock News* for the rest of the week."

"That's great, Nancy," said Shelley with as much sincerity as she could muster. Nancy Kelley was a friend, but she was attractive and competent, and in television one was always concerned with the competition.

"It's a big break for me," said Nancy. "It shows me that they at least think I've got potential."

Shelley grew weary of the conversation. "Nancy," she

said, her tone registering her change of subject, "did you get that information I asked for?"

"Yes. We traced her to Boston, and I contacted the Boston affiliate yesterday. Do you know how many Kitty O'Briens there are in the Boston area? Anyway, one of the reporters there, Chuck Wilson, remembered the story about the O'Brien who worked for the Watsons in Texas, so he was able to track her down for me."

"Do you have an address?"

"Yes, got a pencil?"

Shelley jotted down the address.

Nancy continued, "She lives with a sister. Wilson said she sounds like a cantankerous old coot. Kitty, not the sister."

"He talked with her?"

"To verify she was still living there." Nancy's tone changed. "What's this all about, Shell?"

"I just need some background, that's all." Shelley watched Chandler out of the corner of her eye. He was drinking his coffee, his back to her, apparently oblivious to her conversation. "Are you still working on the other one for me?"

"Jefferson?"

"Yes."

"We're just trying to set up an interview. He's saying he doesn't give interviews anymore."

"Tell him what I told you."

"That it's a matter of life and death?"

"Yes. Keep working on it. I'll call you from Boston." Shelley's tone changed again. "Do a good job with the show . . . but don't make it too good."

They both laughed and said good-bye. Shelley turned to Chandler. "Looks like I have to go to Boston."

He looked surprised. "I thought you took the week off?"

She picked up her coffee cup and sat next to him. "I did, but"—she looked down into her cup as if it held some secret message—"but we're finishing work on a story that needs some sourcing in Boston. I promised that I'd take care of the details." She looked at him and shrugged. "If you need a favor, you have to give a favor, right?"

Chandler didn't seem sure. "I guess so," he said reluctantly. "When do you leave? I'll go with you."

"No way," said Shelley firmly. "We have only one week and we can't waste time. You're going to London, and as soon as I'm finished in Boston, I'll join you there. You can set up the interview with Dr. Harrison and we'll do it together."

"I don't like it."

Shelley ignored his remark. "Is your passport up-to-date?"

He nodded. "I was in Europe last year. But I don't like this."

"Like what?" she said sharply. "You don't like what?"

"Leaving you alone. Have you forgotten that someone tried to kill you yesterday? I don't like you going off to Boston alone."

"If anyone is looking for me, they won't be looking in Boston. I'll keep a very low profile. You can see me off at the plane before you leave for England."

Chandler was still shaking his head. "Why can't they find somebody else to get this information in Boston?"

"Listen, Chandler," said Shelley, beginning to show her impatience, "when you tell your boss you're taking a week off and he says, 'Fine, but I want you to do me one favor first,' what do you say? 'Shove your favor buddy. I'm gone'?"

Chandler sighed. "OK, so you have to go to Boston. But why can't I—"

"Wait a minute," said Shelley softly. She went to him and put her arms around him and kissed him. "Let's not fight about this. I don't ever want to fight with you. Can't you just let me do this my way?" She was kissing him all over his face. "I want you to let me go to Boston. I want you to go to London and set up the interview. I also want you to get a nice hotel room with the biggest bed you can find." She drew back a little so that she could see his face. "OK?"

Chandler said nothing. Her face so close to his filled all his thoughts.

"If you really don't want me to go to Boston," said Shelley earnestly, "I'll call my producer right now and tell him that I just can't do it. I will."

Finally Chandler nodded. "Go to Boston," he said, grinning sheepishly. "I'll set things up in London."

Shelley kissed him hard on the mouth. "Thanks for trusting me," she said. Chandler pulled her closer, his hands reaching inside her sweater. "We'd better make some phone calls and arrange our flights," said Shelley. "Also we'll have to go back to my apartment so that I can get some things for the trip."

Chandler looked unhappy. "Do we have to do it right now?"

"What's the matter?" asked Shelley, touching his face.

"I'm going to have to sleep alone tonight."

Shelley smiled. "Don't worry. We'll make up for it in England."

Chandler pulled her closer. "Do you think I might have a small deposit in advance, a sort of a layaway plan?"

Shelley kissed him. "I think that just might be arranged." She took his hand and pulled him from his seat. "Why don't you come with me to the bedroom and we'll see if we can't take care of this evening's installment?"

The temperature in Boston was in the upper forties with a stiff breeze that made it feel at least ten degrees cooler. Shelley wore a long, quilted coat and a striped wool scarf around her neck. With one hand she held the neck of her coat closed, while with the other she held the small carryon bag that she had brought with her.

Outside, near a line of waiting taxis, she found a public phone and dialed Kitty O'Brien's number.

The woman's sister answered. "I called earlier," Shelley said, "before leaving New York. I'm here now and I wondered if it would be convenient for you if I came over directly from the airport."

Kitty's sister, Agnes, agreed that it would be fine and Shelley went to the first taxi in line.

The sisters lived in an older neighborhood in Boston's North End. The homes were closely spaced and neatly maintained, two- and three-family dwellings. The O'Brien residence was the right half of a white clapboard duplex with a freshly painted white fence surrounding the property and a single path that dissected a small lawn. It led to a porch that sheltered visitors to the front doors of either half of the duplex.

Shelley pushed the button beneath the O'Brien nameplate and heard the muffled reverberation of the buzzer. Almost immediately the door was opened by a slight, grayhaired woman who must have been close to seventy. "I'm Agnes Moore," said the woman, extending her hand after wiping it carefully on her apron. "I'm Kitty's sister—her youngest sister," she added proudly. "There were seven of us—four girls and three boys—but Kitty and I and a brother who went back to Ireland forty years ago, are all that's left." She led Shelley across the threshold and into a small, dark foyer.

"It was good of you, and her, to see me on such short

notice," Shelley said. "I really am on a very tight schedule and I hope to get back to New York sometime tonight."

"Well, that nice Mr. Wilson from Channel Four called us himself." Agnes giggled shyly. "We watch him every evening on the news. We couldn't believe he was calling." Her eyes sparkled, and Shelley could see how beautiful she must have been when she was young. "He's so"—she thought about it for a moment, then finished—"young."

Shelley nodded. "That he is," she said.

"Come with me," said Agnes, starting toward the stairs. "I'll take you up to Kitty's room. She doesn't get down these stairs very much anymore."

Kitty O'Brien sat in a chair by the window watching the activity on the street below. She turned her head as they entered the room. She was a small, frail woman in her seventies, but with a jutting jaw and a cool-eyed look that suggested fortitude. She eyed the newcomer suspiciously.

"Kitty," said her sister, "this is the famous lady from New York. She's on television."

Kitty's eyes narrowed. "Don't look famous to me. I never saw her before."

Shelley smiled amiably and moved toward the old woman, who had turned her attention back to the window and the street.

"I'll just leave you two alone then," said Agnes, backing toward the door.

"What about my tea?" said Kitty sharply. "When do I get my tea?"

"I'll bring it soon, Kitty. The water's on now." Agnes smiled patiently in Shelley's direction. "Would you like some too, Miss James?"

Shelley nodded, wondering why the sister put up with such surliness.

Kitty saw the question in Shelley's eyes. "She thinks that she'll own this house when I die. Got news for her. I'm goin' to outlast all of 'em."

"This is a very nice room," said Shelley, hoping to begin her interview on a pleasant note, but Kitty merely grumbled something and turned back to the window. Kitty's room was small and frugally furnished with a dark dresser against one wall, a table against another, and a double bed with a heavy wooden headboard taking up much of the space. In a corner, visible from the window seat, was a black-and-white portable television set which was on but emitted no sound.

Shelley, uninvited, sat in a chair across from Kitty.

"Why do you want to see me?" said the old woman sharply. "I've got nothing anybody wants."

"I wanted to ask you about when you worked for the Watsons."

"Don't know nothin' about the Watsons."

"I was hoping that you could help me with a piece I'm doing on the Watson family. I was told that you know more about them than anyone."

Kitty's face contorted into a wrinkled mask. "I worked for them since I was seventeen. Raised the whole damn family. I was with that family for almost fifty years."

"How about the newest son?"

Kitty fell silent.

"Justin," said Shelley.

Kitty slowly raised her eyes to look steadily at Shelley. "You want to laugh at me, too."

"No, Kitty. I don't want to laugh at you. I want to listen to you. I want you to tell me what happened."

"They all said I was crazy."

Shelley smiled encouragingly. "You don't seem crazy to me."

Kitty laughed, a cackle that rocked the room. "Not by a long shot."

"Tell me about Justin," Shelley insisted.

A wistful look came over Kitty's face. "He was my angel. The sweetest and most beautiful of all the Watson children I raised. They're grown now—two boys and a girl. The first Mrs. Watson was a darling woman . . ."

"The new one?"

Kitty's face darkened. "A witch—a real witch." Her eyes narrowed. "I was the real mother to that boy—and father too. Mr. Watson never paid any attention to him. Treated him as if he weren't even there."

"Why?"

Kitty shrugged. "He already had his family. The new wife wanted a child"—her eyes turned sly—"but only to turn Mr. Watson against his other children. She didn't want the boy, either. He wasn't hers; they adopted him you know. Poor harmless angel." Her eyes clouded with tears. "But I loved that boy, and he loved me." She smiled. "He called me Nanna-Kitty. I was all he had."

Shelley waited while the old woman stared blankly at the floor. "What happened, Kitty?" she prompted.

Kitty squinted as if focusing a picture of what had happened. "Mr. Watson and his new wife went off skiing in Switzerland. They took the boy with them. It was the first time they had ever taken him anywhere. Why they wanted to take a five-year-old skiing, I'll never know. Anyway, that's where Mr. Watson had his heart attack and died. He was at one of those health spas where the rich go to stay young." She chuckled with the irony of the situation. "He'd been going there for years. This time he keeled over and died."

"What about the boy?"

Kitty's face saddened. A cloud passed over her eyes. "My Justin? They took him away from me."

Shelley watched the old woman. Although her eyes were damp with tears she seemed perfectly lucid. "How?" asked Shelley. "How did they take him away from you?"

Kitty's head nodded rapidly. "As soon as Mrs. Watson came back from Switzerland she let me go. Said she didn't need me anymore." Kitty's eyes burned fire now. "I was dumbstruck, couldn't believe it. I'd worked in that house for almost my whole life and this . . . this . . . woman threw me out." She straightened her back in the chair. "Well, I've got my pride. I just packed my things and moved out that day. She didn't want me to see Justin, but I couldn't leave without telling him that if he ever needed me I'd be there. So I sneaked into his room, and when he saw me he looked at me as if he didn't know me. Me! His Nanna-Kitty. I went to him and put my arms around him and he pushed me away." Tears came to her eyes. "He pushed me away. He looked at me like I was some creature from the gutter. Then he said to me in a very cold voice—not at all like my Justin's—'Miss O'Brien, I think you'd better leave now.' Miss O'Brien. Imagine. My angel calls me Miss O'Brien like he hardly knows me." She shook her head back and forth. "I don't know what they did to that boy, but I tell you it wasn't my Justin. It was someone else."

"But everyone in the family knew it was him."

Kitty shrugged. "They didn't know him like I did."

They sat silent for a moment, then Kitty, in a voice loud enough to break windows, bellowed, "Agnes, where's my tea?" She turned to Shelley. "If I didn't make a fuss around here, I'd never get anything."

Chapter 33

Chandler was met at London's Heathrow Airport by a tall, distinguished man in his early fifties, whom Chandler recognized immediately as Kyle Warner, NBC's London-based correspondent.

"Chandler?" asked Warner as he approached.

"Yes," said Chandler, surprised to be greeted by anyone.

"Shelley asked me to meet you and see that you got settled in all right," said Warner by way of explanation. Warner wore a tan trenchcoat over a dark suit. He had the kind of rough-hewn, pleasant good looks that most people found comforting. On camera his casual smile was reassuring. He was, as they called it in the business, a credible face.

Looking at his watch, Chandler said, "It's after midnight. I really didn't expect anyone to be here."

Warner laughed. "It's not even eight o'clock in New York. A little less than an hour ago I was on live back in the States giving the latest dope on the North Sea oil glut. I'm very used to odd hours."

Chandler shook his head. "It must be tough living in one time zone while working in another."

"It has its moments," said Warner simply as he picked up one of Chandler's bags. "If you're all checked through customs, let's get you to your hotel. I've picked out a nice, convenient location for you. Shelley knows it rather well." He looked at Chandler as if inspecting him carefully. "By the way, are you the new man in her life?"

Chandler shrugged. "I'm working on it."

Warner turned away. "Lucky bastard," he said without malice and headed toward his car.

On the way to the hotel Warner explained some of the groundwork that had been laid. "I've talked with this Dr. Harrison. He's expecting you this afternoon around two. I'll give you a map that shows you how to get to his place. He's about forty minutes outside London in Thornwood. I told him only that American TV was interested in interviewing him. He seemed pleased about that. I couldn't really tell him much more, since I don't know more." He waited, giving Chandler an opportunity to fill him in on the details, but Chandler stayed engrossed in the view of the darkness rushing past the car.

After a few moments of silence, during which Warner kept his eyes glued to the road and the car moving down the M4 at a steady pace, he turned to his passenger. "Shelley said you were working on a story together."

"Yes, she's supposed to be here so that we can do the interview tomorrow."

Warner shrugged. "You'll have to check with her on that. She asked me to make the arrangements and that's what I've done. She said she'd call you when you get in."

Chandler seemed cheered by the prospect. "How long before we get there?"

"We're approaching the city now. Another fifteen minutes, maybe. Shelley also said that one room would be enough for the two of you." Warner made a clucking noise with his tongue. "Lucky bastard," he said again good-naturedly.

Chandler thought about Shelley, wondering what she was doing at that moment. A smile creased his face. "Yes, I am," he said aloud. "I am a lucky bastard."

At that moment the object of all this attention was preparing to fasten her seat belt as Pan Am flight 869 began its descent into Dulles International Airport outside Washington, D.C.

After her interview with Kitty O'Brien, Shelley had called Nancy Kelley at the studio in New York.

"How are we doing on the Jefferson interview?"

"It's a go," said Nancy. "He's agreed to talk with you as soon as you can get there."

"How did he sound?"

"Not too thrilled, but I told him it was a matter of life and death." Her voice sounded doubtful. "That is what you wanted me to tell him, wasn't it?"

"Exactly."

"I felt kind of dumb saying that and not being able to tell him why."

Shelley smiled. "Don't worry, Nancy; you'll know all about it soon enough. Look, I've got to get going. I'll call Jefferson and arrange a time; then I'll get a direct flight out of here as soon as possible."

Lawrence Jefferson sat in a wicker chair in the sun room of his Virginia home. Although it was many hours past sunset, the brick walls and floor still radiated the accumulated heat of the departed sun. The sun room was the most recent of the several changes that the new Mrs. Jefferson had made in the family home. He couldn't say that he liked most of these alterations, but he did enjoy this glass-walled greenhouse that had been added to the southern wing.

He also enjoyed the greenery that his wife nurtured and protected in this sunny environment. But more than the greenery he enjoyed the luxurious warmth. Outside, the trees were bare and his beloved rolling hills had lost their deep, luxuriant color. But here in the sun room the green was still lush and vibrant; it was possible to think that winter was only a figment of the imagination. Here spring had conquered winter.

Jefferson smiled wryly. If it were only true, he thought.

A tall, black man appeared quietly, almost magically, by his side. "Would you like another drink, Mr. Jefferson?"

"No, thank you, George," Jefferson said without turning his head toward his questioner. "That will be just fine. You can take the glass if you like."

George put the empty glass, ice-cubes clinking softly, on a small round tray and turned to leave.

"I take it," said Jefferson, "that this Miss James hasn't arrived yet."

"Not yet, Mr. Jefferson. I'll bring her out here the moment she does."

Jefferson nodded, then reconsidered. "On second thought, I'll meet with her in my study. You can take her in there. Make sure there's a pot of coffee available, will you, George?"

"Anything you say, Mr. Jefferson."

Jefferson watched his servant turn and leave as softly as he had come. The man's quiet dignity had always amazed Jefferson and he often wondered how, if their roles had been reversed, he would have reacted to his lot in life.

He shook his head sadly. Faithful George, he thought. He is probably the only person in this world who will really miss me.

* * *

It was almost two o'clock in the morning in London when Chandler's hotel room phone rang.

"Hi; it's me," said Shelley. "I know it's late, but I just called to make sure you got in OK."

"It may be late here," said Chandler, "but to me it's only nine o'clock. Thanks for sending Kyle Warner to greet me. He was very helpful."

"Kyle's an old friend. You can trust him."

"When are you getting here?"

She hesitated. "Well . . . I'll be there sometime to-morrow—but it won't be until pretty late."

"Are you still in Boston?"

She swallowed once. "Yes. I got hung up here a little bit, but I should be able to clear things up by early tomorrow and be on my way."

"I'm supposed to talk to this Harrison at two tomorrow. You're not going to be here?"

"No way," said Shelley. "You go ahead and do it alone."

"Look, if you're not going to be there for the interview, why bother coming? I'll do the interview and take the next plane home."

"Is the bed in that room comfortable?"

"Sure it is."

"Good. I'll be there sometime tomorrow."

Chandler couldn't help the smile that spread across his face. "Sounds good to me."

"Try to get some sleep tonight. If you have an interview at two, I want you to be sharp."

"Don't worry. I'll be sharp."

"Don't forget anything. Take notes. I don't want you holding out on me."

He laughed. "I wouldn't do that to you. We're in this together, right?"

"Right."

They said their good-byes and Shelley hung up the phone. For a long time she sat in the booth, watching the other passengers scurry about the terminal. We're in this together, she thought, then shrugged her shoulders before heading to the car rental counter at the lower level of the terminal.

There was a soft knock on the door to the study and then the door opened and George put his head inside. "Car pulling into the driveway, Mr. Jefferson. That must be the lady now."

"Thanks, George. Show her right in."

A few moments later Shelley James was led into Lawrence Jefferson's study. She looked around, noting the quiet luxury of the room and the distinguished presence of the man himself.

Jefferson motioned toward a chair across from his own. "Have a seat, Miss James." Shelley sat and Jefferson went on cordially, "I was having my evening coffee. Perhaps you'd care for a cup." Before Shelley could frame an answer he poured the coffee. "Cream?"

"Please, but no sugar."

Jefferson smiled and passed the cup and saucer to Shelley. "I must confess," he said, still smiling, "I wasn't expecting someone quite so beautiful."

"Thank you," said Shelley. She was anxious to begin. "It was good of you to see me."

The smile faded slightly from Jefferson's face as he remembered the reason for her visit. "I *am* a very busy man, Miss James, and I really don't have the time to grant interviews. Perhaps you'd be good enough to come to the point and tell me what this is all about. Your secretary—I think it was your secretary—told me that this was a matter of considerable importance."

Shelley placed her cup on a small table next to her chair. "Yes, Mr. Jefferson. I think it's a matter of life and death."

Jefferson seemed unimpressed. He looked at his watch. "Can you tell me all about it in ten minutes?"

Shelley leaned forward. "I'm investigating a series of very unusual deaths. Unusual in the fact that all of them involve very wealthy men. Most have involved men who have remarried and adopted a son."

Jefferson's eyebrows went up slightly, but he said nothing.

Shelley went on. "You seem to fit into that category, Mr. Jefferson."

He shrugged. "I'm sure lots of men do, Miss James."

"These men died rather suddenly—mostly from heart attacks—"

"I'm afraid," he interrupted, "that death from a heart attack can hardly be described as unusual—especially among men of means." He smiled. "There are certain stresses that go along with acquiring and maintaining large sums of money."

"Most of these men died when the adopted son was between his fifth and sixth birthday." She paused. "How old is your son, Mr. Jefferson?"

His face hardened and he swallowed several times before he answered. "He is five."

Shelley, assuming the facts would speak for themselves, made no comment.

"I'm not sure I understand," said Jefferson. "What is it that you're trying to suggest?"

"I think that someone killed the others; someone may be trying to kill you. Your name was on a list that came into my possession. The others were already dead; yours was the last name on the list."

Jefferson stretched out his hands as if appealing to her reason. "Why would anyone want to kill me?"

"You are a very wealthy man."

"But what is accomplished by killing me? I have a will. I will leave everything to my family."

"What about your older children?"

Jefferson seemed uncomfortable. "They will be adequately provided for."

"But most of the inheritance will go to your new wife and your adopted son?"

Jefferson was silent.

"That's the pattern in the other deaths. They all left their money to an adopted son, not the natural children. Somehow, someone made these men disinherit their families and leave almost everything to an adopted child."

"No one has coerced me into making any changes in my will. I have decided, on my own, how my estate is to be divided, and I don't think it is of concern to anyone else." His eyes bored into Shelley.

"I know you think I'm prying, Mr. Jefferson, but I think your life is in danger."

He was silent.

"I'm trying to save you," said Shelley.

Jefferson smiled weakly. "And get a rather sensational story at the same time."

"That too."

"I want no part of that," he said. His eyes lit up. "I can see it now in the headlines: 'Millionaire saved by daring young reporter.'" He shook his head sadly. "Perhaps if I told you a little secret, Miss James, you might not be quite so concerned about my health."

Shelley frowned.

"To put it quite simply," said Jefferson, "I'm dying. Cancer. Incurable, inoperable cancer. Anyone who wants to kill me had better do it in a hurry."

Shelley's face fell. "I'm terribly sorry."

Jefferson merely shrugged nonchalantly.

"There's nothing that can be done?"

"I'm afraid not. I've rejected some of the more radical proposals. I'm undergoing treatment but . . ." His voice trailed away then he smiled softly. "When you discover that I am among the departed I hope you will not find it necessary to embarrass my family with some ridiculous story about someone wanting me dead for my money."

Shelley stood up. "I'm sorry that I bothered you, Mr. Jefferson. Obviously there's been some mistake. I hope you'll accept my apologies, and my sympathy."

Jefferson made a small motion with his hand, waving away her words. "Not necessary," he mumbled.

Shelley shook his hand. "I've taken enough of your time; I'll just let myself out."

As soon as Shelley had left the room and closed the door behind her, Jefferson picked up the phone. He dialed a number and waited impatiently as the phone rang. "A woman reporter was just here," he said when the phone was answered. "She knows about the others, and she knows that I'm next." He listened. "Her name is Shelley James; she works in New York. . . . She just left. . . . I don't know where she is staying—that's not my concern. You'd better do something quick. I don't have much time." He listened to the voice on the other end. "No, I don't want to wait," said Jefferson, a small note of hysteria creeping into his voice. "I want to leave for Switzerland immediately. Tell Dr. Bauer I want this done now."

On the other side of the door Shelley listened intently until she heard Jefferson hang up the phone. Then quietly and quickly she made her way to the front door and down the steps to her car in the driveway.

Her mind was a jumble as she drove back to the highway. He knew! He knew that he was next. The thought stunned her, paralyzed her ability to reason. What sort of madness was this? Shelley struggled to clear her mind of all disjointed images as she tried to formulate some logical explanation for what was happening. The only possibility was that these men who had died suddenly were all suffering from some incurable disease. Rather than suffer the pain and indignity of a long, hopeless struggle against certain death, they had somehow found someone who, for an appropriately large sum, would arrange a quick and painless early death.

Was that it? Were the others dying also, before they too were relieved of their misery? Was this some sort of euthanasia for the wealthy?

Immediately she thought of ten reasons why this could not be so. Why wouldn't they just overdose on barbiturates? Why did no doctor verify any terminal illness with any of the others? Why the unusual pattern of new wife and adopted son? She could have gone on and on, but her mind rejected further reason. Everything about this was unreasonable.

Chapter 34

The afternoon sun struggled vainly to break through the overcast skies as Chandler's rented car made its way down a narrow road. The threat of rain had been in the air when Chandler had taken the M11 out of London, and now a heavy, constant drizzle drenched the countryside, forcing him to peer intently between the strokes of the wiper blades. For twenty-five miles or so it had been smooth sailing on the modern roadway, but then he had turned off the highway and soon found himself on this two-lane country road, bordered on both sides by a fieldstone wall.

Finally a sign said Thornwood, and Chandler breathed a sigh of relief. At least he was still on the right road. He passed an old church with a small cemetery on the left, and took the next right at the intersection. Two miles down the road he turned into an even narrower roadway—a sign declared Private Lane, No Trespassing—and knew he was almost there.

Large homes were spaced on both sides of the lane and Chandler knew instinctively that the people who lived here were not true residents of the community. These were the homes of merchants and bankers and doctors and solicitors, people who fought the crowds in London and had opted for the quiet life of a country town in the few hours that their jobs and commuting did not demand.

Chandler slowed his car and pulled into a gravel driveway that led to a closed gate. He got out and crunched his way up the driveway as he approached the house.

Dr. Reginald Harrison's country home was very impressive. Red brick, ivy-covered walls shielded the house from the road and a wrought iron gate opened into a path that led up to the house itself. The house was a three-story red brick affair with a multitude of chimneys projecting from the steeply sloped slate roof.

Chandler rang the doorbell at the front door and fully expected a tuxedoed butler to answer, but instead a pleasant-looking, middle-aged man wearing a heather-green crew-neck sweater and brown tweed slacks opened the door and smiled cheerfully.

"Mr. Chandler?" he asked, extending his hand. "I'm Reginald Harrison."

"Yes," said Chandler, allowing himself to be drawn into the foyer. There were open doors on both sides and a stairway leading to the upper floors. "I do appreciate your finding the time to see me, Doctor." Chandler found himself falling into a clipped British politeness in his speech, a refreshing change from the brusqueness of New York.

"No trouble, really. I was rather curious as to why American television would want to interview me. Let me take your coat and we can step into my study. My wife is off shopping right now. Perhaps she will join us later." He laughed crisply. "But one never knows."

Harrison's study was a large room with an arched window overlooking the front lawn. There was a large desk and a comfortable-looking chair in front of the window. Three walls, including the walls containing the window and door, were covered with books. This was obviously the library. On the fourth was an oversized fireplace from which a fire crackled warmly. Chandler could feel the heat radiating from the fireplace and immediately moved in that direction. Around the fire was a grouping of small couches.

"Why don't you sit by the fire and I'll pour us a brandy," said Harrison. "Not too early for you, is it?"

"I'd love a brandy," said Chandler, getting close to the fire. "It's a little brisk out there."

Harrison went to a small table behind one of the couches. On a silver tray sat several glasses and a single decanter of a gleaming brown liquid. "I don't know what has happened to our English winters," he said as he filled a glass. "They seem to start sooner, last longer, and are much more severe than they ever were." He shook his head as he poured the second glass. "When I was younger, winter seemed so much milder."

Chandler grinned and Harrison picked up on his thought. "Oh, I know what you're thinking. Everything seems different to a child. You don't have to dig your car out of the snow. You just have to build snowmen and go sleigh-riding."

"You got me, Doctor," said Chandler. "That's exactly what I was thinking."

Harrison gave Chandler his brandy. "I know what you mean," he said. "But somehow the winters have taken a nasty turn for the worst over here." He poked a thumb toward the ceiling. "Seems that the man upstairs no longer looks upon the British as among his favorites." He sat down across from Chandler. "Strangely enough, the nicest weather that I can remember was during the war. Lovely summers, mild winters." He looked at Chandler, who said nothing. He went on. "World War Two, I'm talking about, of course. You're probably too young to remember much of that."

"I was about five when the war ended. I remember very little."

"I was fourteen in 1945," said Harrison. "I know it sounds rather perverse, but it was an exciting time to be alive. I can remember being evacuated—waiting for the bloody Germans to arrive. Damned exciting!" He sipped his brandy and stared into space, seeing, thought Chandler, a host of invading Germans landing amid the sunbathers during an unusually warm English summer.

Harrison raised his glass. "Those were the days."

Chandler, unsure that those were in fact the days, sipped his brandy with slightly less enthusiasm. "Doctor," he said carefully, "I wonder if we might begin our interview."

"Of course, old man," said Harrison good-naturedly.

"You've come a long way to see me and I've bored you with stories about the weather and England with her back to the wall. But when you American TV chaps get after someone, there's nothing to do but capitulate, I always say."

"I'm actually a newspaperman," said Chandler defensively.

Harrison frowned. "Oh. I thought this had something to do with TV." He seemed disappointed.

"Well," said Chandler. "This is sort of a joint venture. I'm doing the story in conjunction with the TV people. I do the story for the newspaper. They do it for television."

Harrison beamed happily. "I see."

Goddamned television, thought Chandler. It'll ruin everything someday. "If things work out well," he lied cheerfully, "a TV crew will arrange to put you in front of the camera."

Harrison's smile widened. "Jolly good fun," he said. "Now what is this all about? For the life of me I can't imagine why American TV would want to interview me. The chap on the telephone said you'd let me know all about it."

Chandler stood up. "If I might get something, we can begin." He retreated to the hallway and retrieved his notebook and the copy of Dr. Harrison's book.

"I say," said Harrison as Chandler returned to the couch. "What's that you've got there?"

Smiling broadly, Chandler displayed the book so that the doctor could read the title. "Your book," he said.

Harrison's eyes widened. "My book? That's not my book. I'm afraid you've got the wrong man."

Chandler was stunned. He looked again at the title. "It says by Dr. Reginald Harrison," he said weakly.

"Yes, it does," said Harrison. "But I didn't write it. My father wrote that book over twenty years ago." He seemed amused by all of this.

Chandler's face fell. "Where is your father now?"

"You'll find him at Greenvale Cemetery in Somerset."

"Dead?" asked Chandler without any real hope.

"Quite," said Harrison.

Chandler sat back in his seat, sinking into the soft cushions like a deflating balloon.

"Perhaps," said Harrison, "you'd like another brandy. It seems you've made a long trip for nothing."

Chandler downed his drink and gave the glass to Harrison, who proceeded to pour them both a refill.

"I assume that you are interested in my father's research."

"Yes," said Chandler, trying to recover from the disappointment.

Harrison smiled. "It's about time someone reevaluated his work. I don't think he's ever been given credit for his accomplishments."

"Perhaps," said Chandler, "you could tell me about his work. About this book."

Harrison returned with the drinks. "I don't know how much help I can be. I really don't know very much about my father or his work. Quite frankly I'd prefer not to dredge up some of the old memories."

Chandler seemed puzzled and Harrison explained. "My mother divorced my father shortly after the war, and I saw him only rarely after that. My father was not a well man. I think the war affected him deeply. He worked for the government before and during the war on all sorts of hush-hush crackpot projects. I don't think any of them ever amounted to much. We didn't see him very much during the war, and afterward he seemed quite changed. At least that's what my mother used to tell me. As far as I know he might have been mad all his life."

"Mad?"

"Mad as a March hare, Mr. Chandler. My father was quite insane."

"But this book—"

"No one in the scientific community ever took him or his work seriously. It's quite embarrassing, really. I still suffer from a kind of prejudice. You know, a bit of 'There goes crazy Harrison's boy.' 'Do you think he's crazy too?' "

"I'm sorry. I didn't mean to bring up unpleasant memories."

Harrison gave a tired smile. "I suppose I'm used to it by now." He glanced around the room. "I've been quite successful—as you, perhaps, have noticed." His smile grew. "That has taken some of the sting out of my earlier feelings of rejection."

Harrison left his seat and went to the bookshelves near the window. He removed a book and brought it back to Chandler. "I, too, have a copy of his book," he said, opening it to the first inside page and allowing Chandler to read the inscription:

To Reginald: Someday I hope you will understand.
Love, Father.

He snapped the book closed. "I'm afraid I never did."

Chandler shook his head slowly as if unwilling to accept what had happened. "I can't believe I came all this way to speak with the wrong man."

Harrison chuckled. "But you're not the first person to come all the way from America to speak to me about my father. I'm beginning to think that there *is* some revival of interest in his work."

Chandler's eyes narrowed. "Someone else was here?"

"Yes, about five months ago. He was also a reporter. He was very interested in my father's work."

Chandler perked up immediately. "Do you remember his name?"

Harrison thought for a moment, then shook his head. "Afraid not. Rather sleazy-looking chap. I remember thinking that he couldn't be on television. Italian, I think he was."

"Romanello?"

"Yes. That's him. Do you know him? I found him to be a rather unpleasant sort of fellow—not at all like you. I rather like Americans, actually."

"Romanello's dead."

Harrison's eyebrows went up. "Terribly sorry."

"What did he want?"

"Same thing you wanted. He wanted information about my father and his book, although I must say that he had a great deal more information than you did."

Chandler leaned forward, his elbows on his knees, his hands clasped together. "Dr. Harrison, it would be of great help to me if you could tell me whatever you can remember about your meeting with Romanello. What did he want to know? And, also if you could tell me anything about your father and his work."

Harrison's face hardened a little. "Perhaps you could tell me why. What is this all about?"

"I'm not really sure," said Chandler, spreading his arms apart, "but it is quite possible that people, including Romanello, are being murdered because of something your father wrote about."

Harrison looked away as if he had been slapped. A terrible sadness came rushing across his features. "During the war," he began slowly, "my father worked for British Scientific Intelligence. Before that, he and a colleague had made some rather startling discoveries about chemical properties of the brain as related to intelligence, function, and memory. My father was one of the first men to understand that many of the brain's functions are a result of chemical reactions. Most of my father's, and his colleague's, work had to do with the improvement of memory. They found that by introducing certain chemicals into the body, memory could be dramatically enhanced. Up to that point, my father's work was really quite remarkable—and visionary. He was able to extract and refine, in very minute quantities, the desired chemical."

Chandler interrupted him. "Why was the government so interested in this work?"

Harrison smiled. "The machinery of war was becoming ever more complicated, Mr. Chandler. The new weaponry—airplanes, tanks, artillery, detection devices—was incomprehensibly more complicated than previous equipment. Did you know that in the early part of the war ten percent of the aircraft losses in the RAF were due to the fact that the pilots forgot to change pitch in their propellers during takeoff. It was something new, and the pilots simply forgot."

"And your father's chemical would help them remember?"

"Precisely. Remember that and a host of other more complicated problems. It was hoped at the time, although for very good reason it was never publicly acknowledged, that the typical British soldier, who was found to be poorly educated and in some cases practically illiterate, could be taught even the most complicated tasks through memory enhancement."

Chandler nodded. "Sounds like a good idea."

"It was, except for one thing. They were never able to synthesize the required chemical. They were able to extract only miniscule quantities from living donors, and the chemical from the brains of cadavers proved to be useless."

"You mean they got this chemical from the brain?"

Harrison nodded. "I don't know if you are aware of the fact that today there are synthetics which, although experimental, accomplish the same thing." Chandler shook his head and Harrison went on. "Vasopressin, for instance, is a pituitary hormone which was first synthesized over fifteen years ago. It has been used to help amnesia victims recover their memories and has been shown to enhance learning ability." He shrugged. "Back in the thirties, of course, no such chemical had been synthesized. I like to think that my father's work paved the way for some of the latest developments in this field."

"But nothing ever came of your father's research?"

"Some things did," said Harrison with a small smile. "They were able to train guard dogs more efficiently by injecting the brain fluid from a dog who had already been trained." He waved his hands as he explained. "A trained dog gets old and is no longer useful. The brain fluid is extracted, refined, and injected into several other untrained dogs who can now be trained in a fraction of the time it would normally take. I believe your navy has done similar experiments with dolphins."

"But the human research, what happened?"

"Without being able to manufacture the synthetic chemical, the research came to a halt. The British government would never allow extraction of fluid on the scale required to accomplish anything useful." He smiled. "We're much too civilized for that. We don't regard old soldiers as if they were old guard dogs. The initial experiments also turned up some odd side effects."

Chandler's eyebrows went up in question.

"The recipients of even the most minute quantities of the chemical found that their memories were indeed enhanced. Unfortunately some of the memories weren't theirs."

"I'm not sure that I follow you," said Chandler.

"It was found that the recipients had flashes of memory—brief momentary visions—that belonged exclusively to the donors."

"You mean they remembered things that had never happened to them but had happened to the donors?"

"Precisely. But not in any true sense of usable memory. It was merely a kind of jumbled flashback, something akin to déjà vu—brief, momentary, often incomprehensible visions that proved distracting and often confusing to the recipients. The modern synthetics, of course, have none of these disturbing side effects."

"The research was terminated?"

"Oh, yes, several years before the war. My father worked on other scientific projects. His colleague refused to give up the research, and I'm sure my father continued off and on with it even after the war. I'm convinced that he was using himself as a guinea pig and that that contributed to his later insanity."

"You said his colleague refused to give up his research. What did he do?"

Harrison sipped his brandy and sighed. "He went where the government would allow him to continue his experiments with human beings."

"Where?"

"Where else? In 1939, only months before the outbreak of the war, my father's colleague, Dr. Richard Stokes, accepted a teaching-research position at the Kaiser Wilhelm Institute in Berlin. It is believed that during the war he was never lacking in donors—if an unwilling subject can be called a donor." Harrison went to the fireplace and prodded the logs with a long poker. "Records show that he was allowed to experiment with human subjects in several different concentration camps. He even set up a permanent facility at Treblinka, where most of the experiments took place." He carefully added another log to the fire. "Many of the so-called donors were left as vegetables, with literally no mind of their own. Most of the recipients went mad." He paused, weighing his words carefully. "So, once again, nothing of any value came of the research, only unbelievable suffering. I was glad that my father was not involved in such sorrow."

"What happened to Stokes?"

"He was declared a war criminal by the Allied tribunal in Berlin in 1946 and was sought for prosecution. He died in 1947, however, before he could be brought to trial." He shrugged, his story at an end.

Chandler seemed dazed. He didn't know what any of this had to do with his search, but something, some nagging voice in his brain, told him that it was important. He could think of nothing to ask that might possibly relate Harrison's story to his investigation. He thought carefully. Nothing. "Is there anything else?"

"About my father?"

Chandler nodded.

Harrison downed his brandy. "The rest," he said reluctantly, "is rather sad, I'm afraid. My father's mental decline began at around that point. He would accuse my mother of things she had never done, talk about places he had never been to. It was quite dreadful. His behavior became more and more peculiar."

"That's what convinced you he was continuing his experiments?"

"I didn't think so then, but I am convinced of that fact now. My mother divorced him shortly after that, but his behavior continued to deteriorate until he was the laughing-stock of the scientific community." Harrison shook his head sadly. "Finally, a year or two before his death, he became involved in what must have been his most bizarre incident." He looked to the window as if he wished he could be someplace else. "A Swiss medical researcher announced that he had perfected a synthetic hormone—a substitute for the memory enhancer that my father had sought for decades. I think the realization that someone else had found what he was looking for jolted his mind irreparably from sanity."

He paused and Chandler prodded, "What happened?"

Harrison seemed embarrassed and reluctant to continue. "He claimed that the doctor who had synthesized the chemical was his old colleague, Stokes. Insisted it had to be him because no one else had the knowledge to make such a discovery. When he was reminded that Stokes had been dead for over twenty years he refused to acknowledge that fact. When others in the medical profession pointed out to him that the Swiss doctor was less than thirty years old and that Stokes, if alive, would have been close to seventy, he ignored their logic. He ranted and raved until finally he was a pariah in the medical and scientific community. Those few people who had still considered him to be a brilliant research physician finally turned their backs on him. He was poison."

Harrison got up from his seat and went to the fire, where he warmed himself from the chill of his story. "He killed himself about a year later," he said matter-of-factly. "No doubt driven over the edge of insanity by his ludicrous experiments."

Chandler said nothing for a moment while Harrison, his back to his guest, continued to warm himself at the fire. "Did you tell all of this to Romanello?" asked Chandler.

"Yes," said Harrison turning around. "He seemed quite keen on the whole story. I think he even went to visit Dr. Bauer in Switzerland."

"Dr. Bauer?"

"He's the young doctor who had to suffer through my father's insane accusations. My understanding is that he now owns and operates a rather exclusive health spa in the Swiss Alps, near Bern, I believe. It's one of those places where the very rich go to be pampered and exercised and made to feel young and fit again."

Without knowing why, Chandler found himself becoming very restless. Something in the conversation was making him uncomfortable. He formulated a few more questions but none seemed terribly important and so, with little else to say, he thanked Harrison for his hospitality and cooperation and rose to leave.

The doctor saw him to the door. He said quietly, "I do hope you're not going to make this one of those sensational stories about insane doctors and their lunatic experiments."

Chandler stopped. "No, Doctor, I have no desire to further embarrass you or your family."

They walked to the front door, where Chandler shook hands with his host. "If I might ask one more question?"

"Of course," said Harrison pleasantly.

"You refer to your father's experiments as ludicrous. Do you think they were ludicrous?"

Harrison laughed, but it was a low, cheerless laugh. "Mr. Chandler, my father was not well. In his last days he"—he paused and looked down at the floor—"well, he said all sorts of foolish things, but the idea that consumed him near the end of his life was that he thought it was possible to live forever."

A wild thought raced across Chandler's mind, but he dismissed it as absurd before it could even register in his consciousness, and he was only aware that something had momentarily agitated him.

There was nothing else to say, and Chandler, feeling an intense burning sensation in his chest, turned and walked away.

Chapter 35

At 10:30 A.M. Shelley's plane from Washington arrived in New York. She took a taxi to the Pan Am terminal, checked her bags there, and took the same cab back to the studio in Manhattan.

Once in her office she placed a call to Chandler's hotel in London, but he was out. She left her number and a message for him to call if he returned within the next few hours. Then she settled in to study the information she had gathered. She prepared a chart with all the names, dates of marriage, age at time of death, and ages of children, noting that although Jefferson was apparently dying of natural causes, everything on his chart matched up with the others who had died before him.

After staring at her chart for some time, she added two new categories: Cause of Death, and Place of Death.

She listed:

Hughes—kidney failure—Houston (in transit). Taylor—stroke—Houston. Watson—heart attack—Switzerland. Coleman—heart attack—Switzerland.

The information on Taylor showed that he had been in a deep coma for more than two weeks before he died. Shelley's eyes narrowed as a question crossed her mind, and she leafed through the folders on her desk before extracting one labeled Clinton Taylor. She read the biographical material on the man, racing through much of it until she came to the final few paragraphs. There it was! The word she was looking for jumped into focus. Switzerland. Although Clinton Taylor had died in Houston, he had suffered his debilitating stroke while on a vacation in Switzerland.

Lawrence Jefferson's words boomed in her ear: "Tell Dr. Bauer I want to leave for Switzerland immediately."

About an hour later, when her chart was crisscrossed with red lines and question marks and she was well on her way to a tremendous headache, the phone rang. It was Chandler. "Where the hell are you?" he asked.

"You're talking to me on my office phone," she said, "so I guess I must be in my office."

"You know what I mean. Are you coming over, or what?"

"I'm taking one of the Pan Am flights tonight. I'll call you later and tell you which one."

"Great. I'll pick you up."

"If it's any problem, I'll take a taxi."

"No problem. I can't wait to see you. How are you?"

"Fine."

"How did it go in Boston?"

She closed her eyes. "Just fine. Everything's taken care of."

"I met with Harrison," he said. "I've got lots of interesting things to tell you when you get here. I'm not sure what they mean, but they're certainly interesting."

"I'm looking forward to it."

"Your friend Kyle Warner has invited me to dinner tonight. He seems like a nice guy."

"Yes, he is," said Shelley.

"What've you been up to?"

"I've been calling Petersen all day," Shelley said. "He won't answer my phone calls."

"That bastard knows something. He may be ready to go to press with his story, and we'll be out in the cold. I think we're running out of time on this one. One way or the other, we're running out of time."

"One more thing," she said hesitantly. "Do you know anything about a Dr. Bauer?"

Chandler was silent for a moment. "Yes," he said tentatively. Her question had surprised him. "Heard about him for the first time today. How did you hear about him?"

"I overheard Lawrence Jefferson use the name; that's all."

"Jefferson?"

Shelley bit her lip. "I went to see him last night."

"Last . . . I thought you were in Boston?"

"I was, but the chance came up to talk with Jefferson, so I grabbed it."

His voice was a little edgy. "You didn't tell me anything about interviewing Jefferson."

"There's not much to tell. He's dying."

"Dying?"

"Yes. Cancer. I'm beginning to think that what we've got here is a story about euthanasia."

"Mercy killing?"

"Yes. Rich men who don't want to go through the agony of a long, protracted illness. I think they've found someone to make things easier for them. This Dr. Bauer might be involved."

Chandler was speechless. "I can't imagine . . ."

Shelley interrupted. "Who is this Bauer?"

"According to Harrison, Bauer runs a health clinic in Switzerland. Near Bern, he said."

"Perfect," said Shelley.

"Perfect?"

"What could be better? A health clinic that kills people for profit. I'll see if I can find out a little more about this Dr. Bauer. I'll fill you in on everything when I get there tomorrow."

They said good-bye, Shelley promising to get back to him as soon as possible with her flight time. The minute Chandler hung up, Shelley dialed an inside number. "Hello, research department. This is Shelley James. I'd like to know what we've got on a Dr. Bauer, no first name, who runs a health spa in Switzerland. . . . Yes, you can reach me at extension six-three-seven or have someone bring what you find to my office. This is a rush. I'm leaving town today and I need whatever you've got as fast as I can get it."

Less than fifteen minutes later the phone in Shelley's office rang. She answered before the first ring ended.

"Shelley, this is research. I think we might have something on your man Bauer."

"Who is he?"

"Runs some kind of health spa in a place called Murren, in Switzerland. It's called the Renaissance Clinic."

"Anything else?"

"Must be a pretty swanky joint. Seems that most of the clientele belong to what we used to call the idle rich. This info comes from a segment on *NBC Reports* we ran a few years ago."

Shelley thought for a moment. "Any chance that there's a list of clients?"

The voice paused, and Shelley could imagine the man in research scanning the material. "As a matter-of-fact, there is."

"Howard Hughes on there?"

"No. Some movie stars, though."

"How about Clinton Taylor?"

"Never heard of him."

"Is he on the list?" Shelley insisted.

There was another pause, and Shelley could hear pages being turned. "Yes; he's here."

"How about Forbes Coleman?"

"He's here too."

"Winthrop Watson?"

"Right again."

"Lawrence Jefferson?"

"You got it."

"OK, research. Send everything you've got up to my office. And I'll need duplicates because I'll want to take the stuff with me."

Shelley hung up and sat back in her chair. She could feel her heart pounding in her chest. This was it! This was the link that tied the men together, but once again Hughes was the odd man out. This was the key that would open the door. She could feel it. The answer would be found at this clinic in Switzerland.

Chandler met Kyle Warner for dinner at the Connaught Hotel in Mayfair. Warner was waiting for him in one of the small paneled rooms that constituted the bar, and Chandler found his host sitting by a small fireplace, sipping a whiskey.

"Nice place," said Chandler, impressed by the opulence of the room. "A little rich for my blood."

Warner laughed and beckoned a waiter. "Expense accounts are the most wonderful invention," he said to Chandler as they ordered drinks. "They let you live the life you wish you could afford."

The waiter returned with menus and informed them that their table in the dining room would be ready shortly.

Chandler eyed the menu, his eyes popping at the prices.

"Prime rib is superb," said Warner. "But just about anything on the menu is excellent."

"Prime rib will be fine," said Chandler.

They were both somewhat self-conscious, two men who didn't know each other well enough to fall into easy conversation.

"So how was your interview with Dr. Harrison?" Warner asked.

Chandler smiled. "Turned out to be the wrong guy."

"You're kidding!"

"No. It seems that it was this Dr. Harrison's father we were after."

"I'm sorry," said Warner. "He was the only Dr. Reginald Harrison listed."

"It's not your fault. The father is dead. Shelley and I should have anticipated something like this."

Warner was still filled with remorse. "I feel terrible anyway. It's a long way to come to see the wrong person."

Chandler shrugged. "I had a nice talk with Dr. Harrison. He was quite helpful."

The waiter came to tell them that their table was ready any time they wished, and they finished their drinks and made their way into the dining room.

The room was luxurious without any hint of ostentation. The walls were a soft, relaxing cream color, the carpet thick, and the chairs at their table were soft, padded wingbacks, more commonly found in a living room than around a dining table.

During dinner the talk turned to other things, and Warner, obviously homesick for America, pumped Chandler for details of just about every facet of what was happening there.

"I do this with every American I meet," he said. "Make a proper nuisance of myself. I miss American sports most of all. I can't get into soccer, and cricket"—he made a face—"is incredibly boring. Give me a good old-fashioned baseball game anyday."

Chandler's ears picked up. "Baseball? Who do you root for?"

"Cubs," said Warner, smiling guiltily as though some apology were required.

"Red Sox," said Chandler, and both shook their heads wearily in recognition of their plight. "Rooting for the Sox is no picnic," said Chandler. "But the Cubs! You must be a real masochist."

Warner nodded. "It's a chronic illness," he said. "Helps me forget my other problems."

Throughout dinner the talk was about baseball, and afterward they adjourned to a corner table in the bar. Over a few whiskey and sodas the talk continued. Williams and Yaz; Williams and Banks; Fenway and Wrigley. The bad seasons; the few and far between good seasons. The almost-years of the Durocher-led Cubs; the historic collapse of 1978, when the front-running Sox, fifteen games ahead in July, lost to the anti-Christ Yankees.

Warner and Chandler were now comrades in arms, companions in misery, partners in futility. Nothing creates a bond more quickly than being part of a losing cause, and baseball creates more bonds than anything else.

Finally, after they had exhausted their capacity to further punish themselves and each other with tales of hopeless causes, they sat quietly, their demons apparently exorcised.

Warner leaned across the table. "I know it's none of my business, but I wonder if you could answer just one question?"

Chandler nodded, somehow certain that Warner would ask him how Shelley was in bed. He was already fighting to keep the stupid leer from his face when Warner asked, "What's this story that you and Shelley are working on?"

Surprised, Chandler laughed drunkenly. The question had caught him off guard, and he struggled to tell a little without telling too much. "Well," he said, stalling for time, "we're working on a story about very wealthy men who die and leave their fortunes to their new wives."

Warner stared at him for a second. "That doesn't sound so out of the ordinary. Things like that happen all the time, I imagine."

"Maybe," Chandler mumbled into his drink.

"Wealthy men are always coming up with new wives to leave their money to. I interviewed one myself a year or two ago. An American woman had married a very wealthy Englishman. Four or five years later he pops off and leaves her a bloody fortune. Now she lives in a mansion." He paused, looking into Chandler's eyes. "Things like that happen all the time."

"But," said Chandler, angry at Warner's smugness, "did they have an adopted son, about five years old who—"

"As a matter-of-fact they did," Warner said, his face registering surprise.

"They did?" Chandler was suddenly sober.

"Yes. How did you know that? It caused quite a stir over here when it happened. Most of the money was left in trust for the child."

"Who was this?" said an alert Chandler.

"Man's name was Charles Collins. He was the Earl of Something-or-other. Made a fortune in shipping just after the war. He had the kind of money you don't find in England anymore."

"And you interviewed the wife?"

"Yes. Interesting woman. Had been a finalist in the Miss World contest. She married Collins when she was in her late thirties. He was sixty. They adopted a son and a few years later Collins died. I interviewed her about a year after he had passed away. She seemed numb, still in shock. I felt sorry for her." He smiled, thinking that was foolish. "She seemed lost sitting in that big house, in all that luxury."

"I want to see her," said Chandler.

Warner's eyes popped open. "What?"

"I want to talk with her. Can you arrange it for me?"

"When?"

"Today. Tonight. As soon as possible."

Warner sputtered. "I suppose so. What should I tell her?"

"Just say that someone from American TV wants to do an interview with an American who is now living as an English lady. Y'know, what it's like? The contrasts between her former life and the life she lives now."

Warner looked at him skeptically. "That's the interview I did."

"Then tell her I'm from *Time* magazine or *People* or *Reader's Digest*. What the hell's the difference? Tell her anything."

Warner shrugged. "OK. I'll have a go at it."

That settled, Warner tried to rekindle the spark of their earlier discussion, but Chandler's mind was elsewhere. After another round of drinks, Chandler barely touching his, Warner said, "When do you want me to contact her?"

Chandler smiled. "Now would be fine."

Reluctantly, Warner got up. "I'll see if I can get through." He wandered off to the telephone and was gone for what seemed to be a long time. Finally he was back. He was not smiling. "You're in luck," he said. "Mrs. Collins, otherwise known as Lady Chatham, is staying at her London residence."

"Will she see me?"

Warner nodded. "She'll see you tomorrow afternoon at four. You must promise not to take photographs. If photos are required, she will provide them."

"Did you have to twist her arm?"

"No," said Warner, seeming a little surprised. "She was quite willing to be interviewed." He smiled. "Actually she wanted me to come with you. She remembered me from our last meeting. Seemed disappointed when I told her I wasn't coming along." He waited, giving Chandler the opportunity to rectify the situation.

Chandler said nothing.

Warner pouted slightly. "I told her, of course, that I was unable to be there." He waited, but again Chandler was silent. "I did, however, vouch for your credentials as a journalist." He eyed Chandler seriously. "I hope I wasn't mistaken."

Chandler nodded absentmindedly. "Just tell me how to get there."

Warner sighed and produced a notebook from his jacket pocket. In a small show of displeasure he ripped out a page and proceeded to write the address and directions.

Chandler was making himself a drink in his room when the phone rang.

"I'm all set," said Shelley. "I'm leaving at eight forty-five. Be there around nine A.M., your time. I could have taken the seven P.M. from here but that would get me in at seven in the morning. I didn't want you to have to get up so early."

Chandler beamed. "I wouldn't mind. The earlier the better."

"Sure," said Shelley laughing. "I'm probably going to be a basket case. It may be nine A.M. over there when I arrive, but my body will know it's really four in the morning."

"What are we doing tomorrow?" she asked.

"I've found a woman here in London who seems to be in a similar situation as our wealthy widows."

"Oh?"

"Yes. Rich husband, young son. The whole bit. I'm interviewing her tomorrow. You can come along with me."

"All right."

"Listen, did you find anything on that Dr. Bauer?" Chandler asked her.

Shelley looked down at the folder on her desk. On the raised index someone had printed in neat, block lettering,

Dr. Anton Bauer—Switzerland.

Shading her eyes with her free hand, Shelley said, "No. Not yet. So far nothing."

They talked for a little while longer, but Shelley was anxious to disengage herself from the conversation. "I've got to get going," she said. "I've got a few things to do before I catch my plane."

"OK. I'll meet you . . . I love you," he said.

As if by rote, Shelley repeated his words. "I love you, too." After hanging up, she opened the folder and looked again at the top page. For the first time since the investigation had begun she felt she knew more than Chandler. It disturbed her a little that she had been withholding information from him, but that's the way it goes in the news business, she said softly to herself, as if she could convince herself of this uncertain truth.

It was not, she told herself, that she wanted to cut Chandler out of the story; only that she wanted to be able to share something with him, to be able to say, "Here, this is what I found." It was important to her that she know and Chandler know, even if no one else did, that she had been an equal partner in this investigation.

She picked up the phone again. "Get me the Renaissance Clinic in"—she looked at the sheet in front of her—"in Murren, Switzerland. I'd like to speak to Dr. Anton Bauer. Make sure you say this is long-distance from New York."

In just a few minutes she heard a deep, almost accentless voice say, "This is Dr. Bauer. How may I help you?"

"Dr. Bauer, my name is Shelley James, and I am with NBC television here in New York."

There was no response.

"I was wondering," continued Shelley, "if I might come to your clinic to interview you for a feature I'm doing on health spas?"

Bauer let loose an explosive sigh. "I'm very sorry, Miss . . . James?, but I'm afraid I am much too busy right now to grant your request. I will be in New York in a month or so. Why don't you call my office there and perhaps something might be arranged?"

Shelley thought quickly. "I really think that now might be an advantageous time for both of us, Doctor."

Bauer's voice was flat. "In what way?"

"It has come to my attention, through what you might call the journalistic grapevine, that a prominent American newspaper columnist is planning a series of columns blasting the health spa industry, and I understand that you and your clinic are prominently mentioned. I thought you might want equal time."

"I am not concerned with what is said in newspapers, Miss James."

"This happens to be a very influential columnist, Dr. Bauer. What he says means a lot to a great many people."

"Who is this person?"

"I'd rather not say."

"Then," said Bauer in a voice that suggested a shrug, "I'd rather not continue this conversation. Good-bye."

"Wait. Wait," said Shelley. "His name is Andrew Petersen, and he's a syndicated columnist in Washington."

There was a brief silence. "I've never heard of him," said Bauer.

"Very powerful man here in the States."

"You are a very persistent woman, Miss James."

"Yes, I am," said Shelley, smiling.

"I would like to consider your request for a short time before I give my answer."

"Fair enough," said Shelley. "How short a time?"

"A few hours perhaps. I must go over the schedule here at the clinic and make certain that I have the time for such an intrusion. Let me have a number where you can be reached."

Less than an hour later the phone rang in Shelley's office. Bauer's deep voice boomed in Shelley's ear. "Miss James, I have decided to honor your request for a visit to my spa, but I could not possibly allow television cameras to disrupt the routine here at the clinic. My guests demand absolute privacy."

"I'd come alone—no cameras—no crew—just me."

"You understand that I am not interested in defending myself against any absurd charges that this columnist, or anyone else, might make."

"Absolutely."

"Then you are welcome to visit my clinic."

"When?" asked Shelley.

"I will be at your service whenever you arrive."

At 5:00 A.M., midnight New York time, Shelley sat in the darkened cabin of the jet liner on her way to Switzerland. Some of the passengers tried to sleep, but most, too excited by the prospect of foreign travel, were content to sit in the darkened cabin and converse quietly with traveling companions.

Under the glare of the overhead light, Shelley studied the research material she had been able to compile. She now had a separate sheet on each of the men who had died and on Lawrence Jefferson. In addition to the printed material, she had a photograph of each of the five principals on the list. From the original group she had eliminated Arnold, O'Brien, and Harrison because they obviously did not fit the character-

istics of the others, and had been included only for some
peripheral involvement.

Of the remaining five, Hughes was the standout. He
was, of course, wealthy, but he was older than the others at
the time of his death and was unmarried without children,
adopted or otherwise.

The lives and deaths of the rest were strikingly similar.
All had been incredibly wealthy; these men were the vestigial
traces of a vanishing capitalist breed. They were the last of
the robber barons, the heirs to the tradition of the Vanderbilts
and Rockefellers. All had remarried late in life after being
widowed, and even the new wives were cut from the same
mold. The new wives were in their late thirties when married; one had been a model, two had been movie starlets, and
the fourth had been a runner-up in the Miss America pag-
eant. Although three of the women had been married before,
none had any children, nor did they have any after their
lastest marriage. Shortly after marriage, all had adopted sons,
and between the children's fifth and sixth birthdays the fathers
had died. Most of the inheritance had gone to the new sons
and the wills had been hotly contested by the other family
members, to no avail.

Shelley closed that file folder and opened another, which
contained information about Dr. Anton Bauer; four pages of
biographical material, one photograph, and the transcript of
the program on which the story about Dr. Bauer had appeared.
She looked first at the photograph. It showed him to be in his
early forties, with dark hair and a full beard. He was handsome, and his eyes had a clear, confident look of authority,
his lips a slightly cynical sneer. As she read the rest of the
file, Shelley found her eyes drawn back, again and again, to
the photograph.

The information on Bauer seemed reasonably complete
and Shelley read through it quickly, pausing only where she
considered the information pertinent or unusual. Bauer had
been born in Germany in 1939. He and his family—mother,
father, and older sister—had been detained in concentration
camps throughout most of the war. The family had miraculously survived the war intact, and in 1945 had settled in
Switzerland. Ironically, after the horrors of the camps, the
family seemed dogged by tragedy. The sister, two years older
than Anton, had drowned in a boating accident when she was
ten; the mother and father had died in a fire when the boy

was thirteen; the only surviving relative was an uncle who now lived in New York City.

At an early age Anton had displayed his scholarly brilliance and entered the University of Bern at the age of sixteen. At nineteen he had entered medical school in Geneva. By the time he was in his late twenties he was already a respected medical researcher in the field of gerontology. In the sixties he had discovered a synthetic memory hormone which had further enhanced his reputation. In 1970 he had established his Clinique La Renaissance in Murren and soon was treating the problems of aging among his wealthy clients. Over the years, his clinic had become a luxury health spa with prices that excluded all but the very wealthy.

Those who frequented La Renaissance apparently signed on for an extensive and expensive course of treatments. Bauer operated health spas in Palm Springs, New York, Fort Lauderdale, and Houston, as well as in London, Paris, and Rome. Clients in these cities visited the local spas on a fairly regular basis and once each year made the pilgrimage to the spa in Switzerland.

The client list was impressive: royalty, film stars, wealthy industrialists. Anyone familiar with the names of the richest families in America would have little difficulty identifying the latter. Prominently listed among the names of present clients was Lawrence Jefferson of Virginia.

Chapter 36

Chandler was up early, whistling happily and winking at himself in the mirror as he shaved. When he was dressed, he pulled back the curtains and looked from his window to Hyde Park across the street, noticing that it had rained last night. Everything had that peculiar early morning misty glow. The colors were vivid, the greens lush and vibrant, the trees and paths freshly washed as if some mysterious night crew had spent the evening preparing the scenery for the new day.

He felt good. Shelley would be here in two hours.

Still whistling, Chandler went downtairs, planning what would be, for him, a huge breakfast. As he crossed the lobby, the young man behind the desk smiled and beckoned him. "Mr. Chandler?"

Chandler nodded. "Yes?"

"I have a telegram for you, from New York."

Chandler took the offered envelope and opened it cautiously. His eyes widened in disbelief as he read.

SORRY. CAN'T ARRIVE TODAY. IMPORTANT ASSIGNMENT. WILL CALL. SENDING NEW MATERIAL BY EXPRESS MAIL. LOVE SHELLEY.

Chandler crushed the telegram into a ball and threw it across the hotel lobby. The clerk eyed him suspiciously, but Chandler was oblivious to the other man's stare.

"When did this get here?" asked Chandler.

"It arrived during the night," said the clerk. "But the instructions were that it was not to be delivered while you were asleep, but given to you before you left the hotel this morning."

Chandler sighed. He felt like going to the airport and taking the first plane home. If he had not had an interview arranged for that afternoon, he told himself, that is exactly what he would have done.

He glared at the clerk as if the man himself were responsible for Chandler's disappointment, then stomped off to the dining room for breakfast.

After a change of planes in Zurich, Shelley flew on to Bern. There she rented a car and drove to Lauterbrunnen, where by early afternoon she found herself at the base of the Schilthorn looking up at the resort village of Murren.

The village, at an altitude of over five thousand feet, was the second station for the Schilthorn cable car, which continued up to the summit of the Schilthorn in two more stages to a height of almost ten thousand feet. Murren itself was perched on a shelf overlooking the Lauterbrunnen Valley and was completely inaccessible to vehicular traffic.

Shelley boarded the cable car and was whisked silently

upward over some of the most magnificent scenery she had ever seen. At the journey's end, she boarded a horse-drawn sleigh for the short trip to the Hotel Adler. She rode through the picturesque village, the clip-clop of the horse's hooves on the hard-packed snow and the rhythmic jingling of the sleigh bells conjuring up images of storybook Christmases in other, simpler times.

There was one main road through the town and a scattering of homes spread around in no discernible pattern. On the street was a church, post office, two small hotels, numerous guest houses, several stores, and a few restaurants. Such was the sense of unreality that the buildings, all of the same basic architectural style—two-story, wood frame, with high, sloping roofs—looked as if they might have been transplanted en masse from a Hollywood back lot.

A short winding road led up to the modern Hotel Adler, which sat above the village and was in many ways detached from the rest of the community. The Adler was the only modern structure of any consequence in Murren and had been built in response to the tremendous influx of skiing enthusiasts who had flocked to the wide variety of runs available at the resort. It was perched on the edge of a deep cleft that ran like a ragged scar across the face of the mountain. To accommodate its guests and provide access to the magnificent trails on the other side of this ravine, the hotel management had built a cable car system, which in a matter of minutes transported skiers to the other side. Before the advent of the cable car, helicopters had been required to take the more adventurous skiers across.

In addition to the chair lifts and gondolas on the other side, the hotel had also built a restaurant with a breathtaking view of the entire valley and of the full range of the Bernese Oberland in the distance. From the terrace of the restaurant it was possible to see the three giants of the Bernese Alps: the Jungfrau, the Eiger, and the Mönch.

Just above and behind the restaurant, roosting on a rocky finger of granite, was the Château du Lac. With its turrets and battlements, the château dominated the valley like a medieval castle looming above its feudal subjects. It housed the Clinique La Renaissance of Dr. Anton Bauer.

At the hotel, Shelley asked the desk clerk about the procedures for visiting the clinic.

The young man looked at her as if she had asked, "Does it snow in the Alps?"

"No one 'visits' the Clinique La Renaissance," he said, the bemused expression still on his face. "Only clients of the clinic are allowed inside. It is very protective of the privacy of its guests." He smiled proudly. "Several of the guests stay here with us and visit the clinic on a daily basis."

"Why," asked Shelley, "don't they stay there?"

"If they come alone—as many do—they stay at the clinic. But some of the guests come with their families. Family groups usually stay with us. They go over each day with our skiing guests on the hotel's cable car system."

Shelley looked puzzled. "Cable car?"

"Not the Schilthorn cable car," said the clerk. "We have our own cable system for the exclusive use of our guests. It begins service each morning at six A.M. and the last run, bringing mostly restaurant staff, returns to the hotel at eleven at night."

Shelley thanked him for the information and went to her room to unpack. The room was bright and cheerful with a large window overlooking the ravine between the hotel and the château. From her vantage point she could clearly see the cable car that ran between the two.

She thought about calling Chandler and telling him where she was, but instead she picked up the phone and asked the hotel operator to connect her with the Clinique La Renaissance.

A pleasant voice answered, and when Shelley explained her purpose, she was connected with a Dr. Voss. He was cooperative but cool.

"Yes, Miss James," he said in a slight accent of indeterminate origin, "we have been expecting your call. Dr. Bauer has asked me to personally conduct you on a tour of our facility and to invite you to dinner here at the château."

"That's very nice of you, and of Dr. Bauer."

"Would this evening be convenient? About eight?"

"That would be fine."

"Good. I'll show you around the clinic, and then you can have dinner with Dr. Bauer.

Shelley thanked Dr. Voss and, hanging up the phone, found herself wondering again about Chandler. She knew she should call him. If something big happened—if she got to the bottom of the story—he would never forgive her. But, then again, she knew that if she could break the story right now and didn't, she would never forgive herself.

After only a brief moment of reflection, she decided to go with her instincts. "Chandler will understand," she said, not really believing herself. "In my place, he'd do the same thing."

Chapter 37

The town residence of the widow of the Earl of Chatham stood on the northern corner of a large parklike square. Other large homes surrounded the square, almost all flying the flags or bearing the markings of foreign nations. Most of these homes, too large to maintain, had been sold to foreign governments and were now used as embassies. Although not the largest, the private residence of Lady Chatham was by no means less grand than the others.

The residence itself was a two-story granite structure that to Chandler's untrained eye looked more like a university library than the living quarters of a private citizen. The front of the house—if indeed "house" was the right word—was dominated by a classical portico, six granite columns supporting a triangular roof that sheltered visitors from the weather. The front door was a dark mahogany, in sharp contrast to the bright, polished doorknocker prominently displayed in the center.

Chandler grasped the knocker, a large, brass circle held in the teeth of a formidable-looking lion's head, and gave it one sharp rap. The booming sound shattered the tranquillity of the afternoon, and Chandler guiltily looked up and down the street, half expecting angry faces to appear from windows and doors to investigate the source of this unseemly clatter. There was only silence.

The door was opened by an elderly man in formal attire, who seemed as venerable as the homes on the street. With considerable effort he held himself erect and examined Chandler, who although several inches taller than the old man, had the distinct impression that he was being looked down upon.

After this brief inspection the old man said, "Lady Chatham will see you in her private study," and stepped back to allow Chandler entry into the large foyer. He closed the door and helped the visitor remove his coat. "Please follow me," he said, then pivoted and led Chandler past a winding staircase on his way to a doorway at the back.

As they passed the staircase, Chandler noticed a boy of about ten or eleven sitting on the stairs watching him through the railing. Chandler smiled a silent greeting, but the boy, face expressionless, eyes fixed on the interloper, made no response.

As Chandler followed the old man toward the study, he could feel the boy's eyes still on him, and just before entering he turned quickly to look back in the boy's direction. The boy still stared, eyes burning brightly, but strangely, without emotion. Chandler watched him for a moment before going into the room, but the boy's eyes never wavered.

The room, dimly lit from a single lamp on a table near a stained-glass window, was large and tastefully decorated with small groupings of antique furniture. It had the distinct feeling of a Victorian drawing room: high ceiling, Oriental rugs over parquet floors, and wing chairs with small Queen Anne footstools. At the window end of the room stood a baby grand piano and at the far end an oversize, leather-topped writing desk, with an ink bottle and quill pen, looking for all the world as if Dickens had just stepped out for a moment.

"Mr. Chandler," said a voice peremptorily. "I am Beverly Collins. Lady Chatham to those who care about such things." She swept into the room like a wave, overflowing everything with the magnitude of her presence. She was tall, patrician in bearing, and, to Chandler's surprise, beautiful.

Chandler stumbled over a greeting. "Uh . . . How do you do?"

"Call me Beverly, please," she interjected.

"Beverly," he said. "I'm Mark, but everyone just calls me Chandler."

She ignored his comment. "I like Mark," she said brightly. "Can I get you a drink, Mark?"

He nodded. "Whiskey and soda, please."

"Sit down and I'll fix us both something. Then I'll tell you all about how a poor little American girl became the very wealthy Lady Chatham."

Chandler sat on the couch and Beverly Collins went to a small table where the liquor was stored. "Are you married, Mark?" she asked casually.

"No, not anymore."

She pouted. "Oh, poor boy. No little woman at home waiting for you?"

It was clearly not the moment to mention Shelley, so instead he merely smiled and shook his head. As she poured the drinks, he took a careful look at her.

Beverly Collins was in her late forties, but she had kept her figure, which now seemed somewhat restrained by the tight-fitting silk blouse and wool slacks she wore. Her dark hair was up, accenting her high cheekbones and large, sparkling eyes. Her lips seemed framed in a perpetual pout, and Chandler found her immensely attractive. If age had caused any diminution of her beauty, Chandler was unable in the dim light to notice it.

She handed him his drink and sat on the couch with him, curling her legs up beneath her. His scrutiny had not escaped her notice. "I think you were expecting someone else, Mark." She laughed. "Perhaps someone who walks with the aid of a cane?"

He smiled. "I knew you weren't old, but I wasn't expecting someone quite so . . ."

"Say it," she demanded. "I haven't had a man tell me I'm beautiful in . . ." She squeezed her eyes shut as though she were thinking hard. "It must be days," she said, laughing boisterously, and Chandler, unable to resist her laughter, joined in.

"Kyle Warner said you're doing a magazine piece. Which magazine?"

"Well, I work for a newspaper in New York," Chandler said, tempering his lie with some truth, "but I do free-lance magazine work. I thought your story would be perfect for the women's magazines: *Ladies' Home Journal, Better Homes,* you know?"

She nodded, and for the first time he saw a hint of seriousness in her eyes. "Every woman's fantasy, right? Marry a rich man and become an English lady."

"You must admit," said Chandler, "it is rather fantastic."

Beverly finished her drink in one gulp. "Yes, I must admit." She looked at her empty glass, and Chandler had the feeling that it was not her first empty glass of the day. "You ready for another?" she asked.

"I'm fine, thanks," said Chandler, watching her as she went back to the bar. "How long were you married before your husband died?"

"Which one?" She laughed, the gaiety back in her voice. "Only kidding. I've been married three times, but only the last one left me the hard way. The others departed the marriage bed in a more conventional fashion." She thought for a moment. "I was married to Charles Collins for almost seven years before he died and that was almost five years ago."

"How did he die, if you don't mind my asking."

"I put arsenic in his poached eggs." She laughed again, a loud, deep, belly laugh that seemed odd coming from this woman.

Chandler chuckled politely, and she went on less frivolously, "Heart attack. We were on a skiing vacation in Switzerland when his heart just decided it didn't want to go on anymore. He was sixty-seven." She shrugged and made a face. "Dropped dead right on the slopes." She came back with her drink.

"Were you with him when he died?"

She sat down, and Chandler immediately noticed that her blouse was more open than before. "With him?" said Beverly, in a tone indicating how absurd such a question was. "He was out there doing some early skiing. They found him lying in the snow at about seven in the morning." She sipped her drink, staring directly into his eyes. "I rarely get out of bed before noon. I usually save all my exercise for nighttime."

Chandler wasn't sure where this was leading but decided to keep the conversation rolling. "You seem to be in . . . excellent physical shape."

Beverly smiled, expanding her chest, forcing the opening in her blouse further apart, and Chandler's eyes, like missiles directed of their own volition, homed in on her breasts. "I do manage to exercise regularly," she said triumphantly.

Chandler forced his eyes up. He gulped his drink and looked at her face. In an absurd parody of bashfulness, Beverly Collins lowered her eyes.

"You have a son, don't you?" he said.

Her eyes came up warily. "Yes," she said simply.

"Was that who I saw when I came in?"

"Probably. When he's not away at school with the other little monsters, he's always lurking around."

"I read somewhere that he's adopted."

"Yes. That's right." She seemed cautious now and unwilling to say anything more than necessary.

Chandler said nothing.

"Was that a question of some kind?" she asked.

He shrugged. "No."

She drained her glass. "Drink up," she said, and Chandler took a good swallow. "My husband needed an heir. Earls always need heirs," she added sarcastically. "His first wife had never given him any children. Then he married me and still couldn't have any children. It turned out to be his fault, of course. All my parts are in good working order. So we adopted little Roger." Her voice grew loud as though she were speaking to another person in the room. "Darling little Roger. He's almost eleven now."

Chandler raised his glass to his mouth, and Beverly reached out and held the glass to his lips until he had finished. He coughed a little, clearing his throat. The drink was too strong, too much whiskey, not enough soda.

She took his glass. "Let's have one more," she said, and before he could protest, she was off again to the bar. She returned quickly. "Let's drink to the new earl," she said, sitting close to Chandler, her leg touching his knee. He moved slightly and Beverly moved her leg closer.

"Did you know that I was a finalist in the Miss World contest?"

"No, I didn't," said Chandler, as he looked more closely at her face. The heavy makeup and the dim light could not conceal the lines around her mouth and eyes. The eyes seemed incredibly sad.

"Yes. I won the bathing suit competition that year." She did not say what year. "I even appeared in a couple of movies." She moved closer. "I was going to be a centerfold in *Playboy*, but at the last minute my agent wouldn't let them use the pictures."

The room was getting warm, and Chandler found himself beginning to sweat a little. With nothing to say, he nodded agreeably as Beverly Collins droned on about herself.

"I still have the pictures," she said. "Would you like to see them?"

Chandler said noncommittally, "I'd love to see them sometime."

Beverly moved as if to rise, then slumped back down. "They're upstairs. Take me too long to get them." Her hand moved to the buttons on her blouse. "Perhaps you'd like to see the live version."

"Didn't you say your son was lurking about?"

"I'll lock the door," she said, moving close to him and kissing him hard on the mouth. She took his hand and directed it inside her blouse. "Don't be shy," she said. "It's all yours."

Chandler considered his avenues of escape. His eyes went to the door and Beverly misunderstood. She smiled and stood up. "Don't worry. I'll lock it right now."

She went to the door, turned a key in the lock, and as she returned she removed her blouse, then unhooked her bra, and dropped it to the floor. Naked to the waist, she stood in front of the still-seated Chandler. "What do you think?" she asked. "Do you like them?"

Her breasts were large and pendulous, hanging almost to her waist. Even in the half-light the stretch marks were obvious. "They're beautiful," said Chandler, not knowing what else to say.

"You should've seen them ten years ago," she said, pointing both index fingers at him. "They stood out straight as arrows." She shrugged sadly and her breasts jiggled. "Now they're starting to sag a little."

Chandler couldn't think of an appropriate response, so he said nothing.

Beverly Collins knelt in front of him and began to unbuckle his belt. She unzipped his fly, and Chandler raised his hips as she pulled down his trousers and underwear to his ankles. Reaching back, she removed the pins from her hair, then shook her head letting the hair fall loose.

In a loud voice that was almost a song she said, "It's so nice to have a man around the house," and once again Chandler had the distinct impression that she was actually speaking to someone else. It was as if she were aware that someone was listening at the door, and she was responding to that knowledge. She threw her head back and laughed. Suddenly she was silent for a moment, her tongue circling her lips, and then she moved forward, her mouth enveloping him.

Chandler lay back, feeling the heat radiate to every part of his body. His hands went to Beverly's head, holding her as her hair tumbled down into his lap. From beneath her hair she made loud, gutteral, animal noises.

Then she was naked, pulling him from the couch onto the floor. He rolled onto her, and she let loose a burst of obscenities that startled him. As her passion grew, her cries grew louder, and Chandler felt that he was a performer in some perverse game.

"Do you like that?" she yelled. "Can you hear that??" As she reached the peak of her passion she screamed, "You bastard!" then fell into a guilty silence.

They dressed, she chatting quietly as if nothing had happened, Chandler silently brooding. Beverly went to the bar.

"Want another drink?" she asked.

He didn't look at her. "No, thanks. I've had enough."

"Don't let all the yelling bother you," she said. "That's the way I am. It's nothing personal."

"Didn't bother me," he said sullenly.

She took a good swallow of her drink and placed the glass on the table. "You hate me, don't you? You think I'm horrible."

"No, of course not," he said.

Beverly's arms hung listlessly at her sides, her shoulders dropped. "You would have liked me ten years ago. I was beautiful then."

Finally, Chandler looked at her. She seemed suddenly younger, more vulnerable. "You're beautiful now," he said.

She slumped down into the chair nearest the couch. "Don't pretend with me. I'm ugly. I feel ugly. I'm just a shell. There's nothing inside." Her smile was sad. "I used to be beautiful—on the inside too"—her eyes had a faraway look—"but that was a long time ago."

"What happened?"

Her eyes went to the door and she silenced him with a finger to her lips. She listened carefully for a moment, then, satisfied that no one was at the door, she turned to him as if to speak but the words seemed caught in her throat. Chandler, certain that she was about to tell him something important, leaned forward encouragingly, but the moment had passed. "Nothing happened," she said. "I just got old."

"You're not old."

She laughed. "I'm forty-nine. For a woman that's old. I'm sagging, wrinkling, coming apart."

"Me too," said Chandler, trying to inject a small note of levity into what had become a somber conversation.

Beverly looked coldly at him, her eyes piercing him with their chill. "Do you know what it's like to be one of the most beautiful people in the world? To have men falling at your feet from the time you were fifteen years old?"

Chandler said nothing.

She laughed derisively at his silence. "Then you sit back and watch it all slip away. The same men who once worshipped you now look at younger women."

"Nothing lasts forever," said Chandler.

Beverly's eyes burned with a fierce manic glow. "You would give anything to have that back again, wouldn't you? Anything to recapture that blush of youth?"

"But why concern yourself with the impossible?" Chandler said.

She laughed as though he were incredibly funny. "You're so right. But look at my husband," she said in her loud booming voice, intended, Chandler was certain, for the entire household. "He wanted to stay young. He visited his health spa every year for his youth injections: vitamins, hormones, animal placenta, and God knows what else."

"Did it work?"

This time her laughter was near hysteria. "The last time he was there he dropped dead."

"I thought you said he had been skiing?"

Her eyes narrowed, and her voice became more subdued. "That's right. He was skiing. His spa was in the Swiss Alps."

"This was Dr. Bauer's spa—in Switzerland?" The question had leaped to Chandler's tongue on its own. He had no foreknowledge of how it had been formed in his brain.

Her eyes opened slightly as if several minor explosions had gone off behind them. "Did I say that?" she asked. "I must have been drinking too much. I don't remember mentioning that."

Remembering Shelley's euthanasia theory, Chandler asked, "Was your husband ill before he died?"

"Ill?"

"Yes. Any serious illnesses? Heart trouble? Cancer?"

Beverly Collins chuckled without a trace of humor. "No. He was healthy as an ox until the day he died."

She stood up quickly, wavering for just a second before she gained her balance. She tucked her blouse carelessly into her slacks. "I think we'd better complete this interview at some other time." She smiled, some of the earlier lust returning to her eyes. "Perhaps you could come back tomorrow? I don't make quite so much noise when I'm sober."

She escorted Chandler to the door, and they both stepped out into the hallway. On the stairs sat the boy whom Chandler had noticed when he entered. His face was just as expressionless now as it had been then, and Chandler wondered if the boy had been sitting outside the door all this time.

"Little Roger," said Beverly in a tone that Chandler found strangely sarcastic, "have you met the nice man? This is Mr. Chandler."

The boy did not acknowledge Chandler's presence. His eyes never left his mother's face. Large and luminous, they burned with what Chandler could only describe as hatred. "Have you been drinking again, Beverly?" the boy said. "Embarrassing yourself?"

Beverly laughed drunkenly, steadying herself on Chandler's arm. "Wouldn't you just love to know what Mommy's been up to, my little darling."

The boy turned his gaze on Chandler, and the man felt assaulted by the intensity of the stare. There was such animosity that it hit him like a battering ram, driving him back a step.

"I'm sure Mr. Chandler got everything he came for, Beverly," said Roger, venom dripping from each word.

Beverly Collins laughed. She turned to Chandler. "He's such a sweet little thing; don't you think?"

Mumbling ambiguously, Chandler edged cautiously to the exit, anxious to avoid this spiteful family squabble. Beverly gave him his coat and he went quickly to the door. As he bounded down the steps, thankful to be free, he heard the boy shout something in his high-pitched prepubescent whine. Beverly Collins's maniacal laughter filled the air.

Chapter 38

With time to kill before her visit to the clinic, Shelley decided that she should find something to wear that was more appropriate than the clothes she brought with her. She walked down into the village and tried to occupy herself with browsing, but her thoughts kept returning to the clinic and what she would find there.

She couldn't wait, she decided. It was impossible to relax. She had to go over to the clinic now and see what, if anything, was going on. Even if she just got a look at the place, it was better than doing nothing until this evening.

Her decision made, she quickly selected a down parka, a pair of heavy wool slacks, and some lined boots and then started back toward the hotel. On the way she saw a display of binoculars in a store window, and with the thought that she might be able to get a closer look at what she was getting herself into, she went inside and purchased a pair.

Back at the hotel, Shelley changed into her new clothes and, with her binoculars hanging around her neck, made her way to the cable car.

The cable car was very much like a small trolley with large windows all around. Inside, instead of seats there were handrails and floor-to-ceiling posts for passengers to hold onto. The car hung by a suspension arm from a thick steel cable that ran from a tall, narrow building attached to the rear of the hotel, to a similar building on the other side. There were doors at both ends of the car—one in back for entry and exit at the lower station, and one in front for entry and exit at the upper.

Shelley walked to the entry platform, shuffling forward with the other passengers, most of whom carried skis, until she stepped through the rear door into the car.

As each passenger stepped on board, the car swung slightly on the cable. Shelley found a spot on the handrail near the front door, and when the car was full, the door was slammed shut from the outside and securely locked.

Then the car lurched into motion. As it cleared the platform of the lower station it swung back, and Shelley felt her stomach drop to her toes. Twenty yards out from the lower station the car steadied itself and proceeded with only the gentlest suggestion of a rocking motion.

"We're lucky today," said a passenger standing next to Shelley. "When the wind is strong, the car swings like a pendulum."

"Thanks," said Shelley. "Now I've got something to look forward to."

The ground fell away beneath them, and as the hotel receded in the distance it was difficult to judge the distance to the snow-covered ground below. They were surrounded by whiteness—gleaming white mountains wearing halos of frosty clouds, glistening glacial ice that sparkled in the sharp sunlight. Everywhere—above, below, all around—the vast whiteness of the ever-present snow.

Five minutes after leaving the lower station the car slowed and coasted into the upper one. The passengers disembarked through the front door and walked along a path that led to the chair lifts that would take the skiers higher up the mountain. To the right of the chair lifts was a modern A-frame restaurant with umbrella tables and chairs on a large terrace overlooking the ski slopes.

Sitting above and behind the restaurant was the château that served as the home of the Clinique La Renaissance. A single path curved up the slope, cut behind the restaurant, and snaked its way for about seventy-five yards to the château.

Shelley paused for a moment before continuing. The château sat, dark and forbidding, with no sign of life from any quarter. For one brief moment, Shelley's thoughts were filled with misgivings and she allowed herself to wish that Chandler was with her or that, at least, he knew where she was. Then she quickly pushed that thought to the back of her mind and moved forward.

Most of the cable car passengers had headed for the chair lifts. A few went to the restaurant. No one approached the path to the spa.

Shelley trudged to the restaurant and selected a table on the terrace where she could watch the château and the path leading to it.

A waiter approached and Shelley ordered a mug of hot chocolate. As she waited, she surveyed the scenery through binoculars, occasionally sweeping them in the direction of the building which loomed above her.

There was someone standing by the gate of the château. The man was young. He wore a bright red ski parka and a blue knit cap. Apparently he was satisfied to stand at the gate, smoking a cigarette.

Might be a guard, thought Shelley.

She watched him for a few minutes, but the man remained at his post. Then she lowered the binoculars and looked back toward the cable station. Another car was coming across.

Once again most of the passengers headed for the slopes and a few came toward the restaurant. No one went near the clinic.

Shelley sat drinking her hot chocolate, observing the ski slopes and the mountains, and every few minutes training the binoculars on the château. Other than the man at the gate, there was no sign of life.

Another car arrived from below.

Again the passengers disembarked and broke into the usual groups for the chair lifts and restaurant, but this time as the smaller group approached the restaurant, three of them disengaged themselves and turned toward the path leading to the château.

"Here we go," Shelley said to herself, taking the binoculars from the table. "Now we can see what happens when they get to our friend at the gate."

She watched as the three men began the trek up the slope. As she watched, the last man, obviously not as strong as the others, fell farther and farther behind. One of the others stopped and turned and said something to the man who brought up the rear, and Shelley watched the pantomime. If only she could lip-read.

She trained the binoculars on the last man. He was obviously older than the others and had stopped to rest. He was breathing heavily, the vapor of his breath clouding around him. The man was leaning forward, hands on his knees, and then, as if to judge how far he had come, he turned to look back down the slope. As he did, he looked almost directly into Shelley's binoculars.

Her mouth fell open. It was Lawrence Jefferson.

*   *   *

Shelley turned away, looking across the ravine toward the hotel as if fearful that Jefferson, even at this distance, might recognize her. After a brief wait she turned back and continued to watch as the men kept moving up the slope. At the gate they waited for Jefferson to catch up, then spoke briefly with the man stationed at the entrance, and passed out of view.

Definitely a guard, thought Shelley, noting that the three men had stopped and said something before he had let them through.

Shelley lowered the binoculars. Jefferson was here! She was more certain now than ever that her intuition had been right. Here was the answer to all her questions. She looked up toward the château, which seemed to look back with stony malevolence.

Shelley sipped her chocolate, but it had turned cold.

Over on the corner of the terrace, sitting near the railing was a small boy of around five. Shelley spotted him, and when the boy's eyes met hers he burst into a radiant smile. She returned the smile and the boy gave a small wave with his fingertips.

As Shelley continued to watch the child, a woman appeared at his table with two cups of hot chocolate. The woman, apparently the boy's mother, placed the cups on the table and sat next to him. She was strikingly attractive, tall, and slender, and although it was difficult to ascertain her age, Shelley guessed her to be in her early to middle forties.

The child sipped his hot chocolate, occasionally giving shy glances in Shelley's direction.

Shelley sat on the terrace for another hour as daylight gradually faded. During this time the boy and the woman left, the boy looking back over his shoulder at Shelley as his mother led him away, and the cable car made regular trips from the hotel. But no one else went up the slope to the clinic.

With a quick glance at her watch, Shelley decided that it was time to return to the hotel to get ready for her trip to the clinic. She took a final look through the binoculars at the château and then walked down the path toward the platform of the upper station to await the arrival of the cable car.

Chapter 39

Shelley dressed carefully for her dinner engagement with Dr. Bauer. She had a very slinky black evening dress that she had brought with her for romantic evenings in London, but realized how foolish she would look crunching her way through the snow in heels and evening wear here in Switzerland. Reluctantly she put the dress back in the closet and selected a pair of wool slacks and a cable-knit sweater that fit, she thought, rather nicely.

As she applied a slight touch of blush to her cheeks she thought that looking good never hurt any interview. There were some who claimed that beautiful women were not good interviewers because they distracted the subject from the interview itself, but Shelley knew that in her experience men were often disarmed by her looks and were more open with her. Many times her subjects was too interested in her looks to be evasive about their answers.

As a gesture to formality, she wore her hair up, allowing several curled strands to dangle loosely from her temples, and then stood back to admire the overall effect in the mirror.

"It'll do," she said aloud as she slipped into her ski parka.

On her way through the hotel lobby, Shelley saw the boy she had seen that afternoon on the terrace. He was sitting alone in a chair near the exit, and when he saw her he smiled. He had put on a Baltimore Orioles baseball cap.

Shelley found it impossible to pass the boy without some friendly comment. "Hello," she said, stopping in front of him.

"Hi," said the boy shyly.

Shelley grinned. "I saw you this morning up on the mountain. Was that your mom with you?"

"Yes," said the child. "Are you an American?"

"Yes."

The boy beamed. "Me too."

Shelley winked. "We Yanks have got to stick together."

The boy frowned. "But I'm an Oriole fan," he said seriously.

"OK," said Shelley, laughing, "we Oriole fans have got to stick together. What's your name?"

"David. I'm five."

"I'm Shelley. Do you like baseball, David?"

David nodded, a wide smile spreading across his features. "Doug De Cinces is my favorite player."

"That's a good choice," said Shelley. "Does your dad take you to baseball games?"

The small mouth sagged a little but quickly rebounded in a smile. "No, but I watch the Orioles on TV a lot." He yawned, rubbing his fingers into his eyes.

"You look tired," said Shelley.

He nodded. "I was up late last night. Later than I've ever been up in my whole life," he added proudly. "I saw the sun come up this morning."

"Boy," said Shelley. "That is late. Where is your mother now?"

"She went to pick up my dad. He's not feeling well."

"That's too bad," said Shelley.

David nodded. "I want to go skiing with him, but he's too tired."

"Do you like skiing?"

"I don't know," he said. "I've never tried it before."

"I haven't either," said Shelley. "Maybe we could start together."

David's eyes widened. "Would you take me?" he said in disbelief.

"Sure, if it's OK with your mom and dad."

The child was ecstatic and Shelley warmed to him even more. "Did you see those mountains?" he said, his eyes wide with the amazement of the recollection. "We took this kind of bus that went on . . . cables, my dad called them. We went right up to the mountain. Last night my dad took me over to that castle on the other side. It was really something."

Shelley's eyes narrowed a little and the smile slipped from her face. "What did you do over there?" she asked.

"That's none of your business, Miss James," said a voice and Shelley, startled, turned to see Lawrence Jefferson and his wife standing in front of her.

"Daddy," said David enthusiastically, "this nice lady is going to take me skiing."

Jefferson ignored his son. His face was tired, a kind of deep gray color that went beyond mere physical fatigue. He spoke only to Shelley. "I want you to know, Miss James, that I resent your following me here, prying into my personal affairs."

Shelley stood up. "I did not follow you here, Mr. Jefferson. I'm on an assignment. Your being here has nothing to do with it." She looked from him to his wife, who stood somewhat nervously a few paces behind her husband. Mrs. Jefferson was much younger than her husband and even more attractive close up than she had seemed on the terrace that afternoon. In her ski outfit she might have been modeling sportswear for Bloomingdale's.

Jefferson took his son by the hand and pulled him to his feet.

Shelley's face registered her protest at this rough treatment. She was about to say something, but Jefferson turned on her with a snarl. "Mind your own business," he snapped and then, his eyes narrowing into a dangerous glare, he growled, "and stay away from my son."

Shelley said nothing, and Jefferson turned and pulled the bewildered boy away, dragging him through the hotel lobby. Mrs. Jefferson stayed, not saying a word until her husband had gone, and Shelley knew that the woman was waiting to tell her something.

Finally she spoke. "I'm Karen Jefferson. Don't judge my husband too harshly," she said. "He has been under a great deal of stress lately. He told me that you had been to see him, and that he told you about his . . . illness." Her voice broke a little. "He's very upset. He's not usually like this."

"I'm sure he's not," Shelley said simply. "I meant no harm. I didn't even know who the boy was. He's such a beautiful child. I only meant to be friendly."

Mrs. Jefferson's eyes filled with tears. "Yes," she said

with difficulty, "he is beautiful." Her voice choked and she could not continue. She waved her arms as if pleading for help, then spun around and quickly made her way out of the lobby.

Chapter 40

At 7:45 Shelley took the cable car back across the ravine. Someone new was waiting at the gate. The man, short and bullish, smiled pleasantly and asked, "Miss James?"

"Yes," said Shelley.

He opened the gate and allowed her to enter. "Just walk straight ahead," he said. "That's the front door with the lights shining. I'll call ahead and say you're on your way."

Shelley walked through a courtyard enclosed by the high masonry wall around the château. Just as she walked up the steps the front door was opened by a tall, slender reed of a man, who appeared to be in his mid-fifties.

"Miss James," he said, shaking Shelley's hand enthusiastically. "I'm Dr. Voss. Please come with me," he said, leading her inside.

The entry hallway was two stories high with a double staircase against the opposite wall. A single stairway went up for five or six steps to a large landing and then branched into two staircases going left and right leaving a V-shaped wall on which was displayed a huge tapestry of what was apparently St. George, or someone, slaying a dragon. Beneath the tapestry on an antique table was a huge hourglass. The hourglass stood at least two feet high and was enclosed in intricately carved hardwood. The legs were four serpents coiled around slender tree trunks, and each reptile seemed to be watching the sand race from the top section of the glass to the bottom. It was the largest hourglass that Shelley had ever seen, and she could only guess at how old it was or how long it would take for the sand to run out.

Voss saw Shelley eye the hourglass. He smiled and walked toward it. "This is the symbol of our work," he said, placing a hand on the hourglass. He waved his arms to encompass the entire château. "Here we delay the ravages of time. Here we postpone the inevitable." He grasped the hourglass firmly in both hands and flipped it over, reversing the flow of sand. "Here we help defeat our oldest adversary . . . time."

He gave the glass a reassuring pat and then continued up the stairs. "I hope you will forgive the lateness of this little tour, but it is absolutely essential that we not disrupt the work of the clinic or disturb our patients."

"You call your clients 'patients'?" asked Shelley.

Voss smiled. "This is a true medical facility, not one of those hot-tub carnivals so common to your part of the world. We like to think of the Clinique La Renaissance as a combination health spa and medical clinic. In addition to our health rooms we have two fully equipped operating rooms."

"Operating rooms? You do surgery here?"

Voss had started up the stairs. He turned to face Shelley, looking upon his visitor with what was almost disdain. "Yes, surgery. We do every kind of cosmetic surgery here: noses, ears, chins, breasts, stomachs, thighs, buttocks."

"Oh," said Shelley. "Cosmetic surgery."

"Yes, but we also have done intestinal bypass and even heart surgery here."

The upper floor was divided in two by a wide corridor, and on each side were several doors.

Shelley's eyes narrowed as she trailed behind Voss, walking down the thickly carpeted hallway. Voss stopped in front of a door and opened it. "This," he said, "is our exercise room." In contrast to the antique look of the château itself, this was a sparkling, modern exercise facility. Flashing chrome weight machines, padded slant boards, chinning bars, and exercise bicycles were everywhere in the spacious room. "From seven A.M. this room is staffed by three attendants and a medically trained supervisor. There are never more than five patients in here at one time, and all are on a strictly regimented and supervised exercise program."

Against a far wall was a row of five treadmill machines with chrome hand supports, and behind each treadmill a digital readout where heart rate could be monitored. Each of the five stationary bicycles also had a digital readout.

"As you can see," said Voss, his mouth frozen in a

cardboard smile, "we are not lacking in the most modern equipment."

Shelley pretended to be impressed. "It all seems so brand-new and shiny. The whole place has a very up-to-date look."

"What about cell revitalization treatments?" asked Shelley, remembering a question from her research material.

Voss's eyebrows went up. "You've been doing your homework Miss James." Shelley said nothing. "Yes, we do use the revitalization theories here," Voss continued. "It is our belief that worn-out organs can be rejuvenated with injections of living cells from an unborn animal. We do, however, use freeze-dried cells, as we've found that there is less chance of an allergic reaction. We have had miraculous results with these treatments. Many of our patients swear by them."

"What about the so-called youth pill we hear so much about?"

"If you are referring to Gerovital H_3, we do not, as a general rule, recommend its usage. We feel that our other treatments are much more beneficial. For certain patients—older, more sedentary individuals—it does have some positive effect."

Dr. Voss smiled, satisfied that he had adequately answered the questions. "Now," he said, "if you will follow me, I will show you our X-ray equipment."

The rest of the tour led them through a steam room, a sauna, a blue-lighted relaxation room, a greenhouse-style solarium, a massage room, an ultraviolet tanning room, and finally at the other end of the hall to a room labeled: Doctor.

"This," said Voss, "is the examination room and perhaps I should have brought you here first, because it is the first stop for all our patients. Even our regular patients must go to the examining room each time they visit us. It is here that we formulate the individual diet and exercise program for each of our clients."

The room was about the size of a good-sized bedroom. In it were an examination table, two wooden chairs, low cabinets around the room, a glass cabinet with various examination devices, a treadmill with the ever-present digital readout, and sitting against the back wall, a computer with a TV screen and typewriter keyboard.

"Each guest undergoes a complete physical at the time of his arrival . . ."

"What's the computer for?" Shelley interrupted.

Voss seemed slightly annoyed. "I was coming to that. The computer allows us to keep a complete dossier on the medical history of all of our patients; he has a much better memory than any human doctor. All the information is fed into the computer and he retains, ready for instant recall, any information required by the examining physician."

"Pretty handy," said Shelley.

Voss smiled. "But that's not his most important function. Dr. Bauer has modified and programmed this particular computer to make individual nutritional diagnosis for each patient."

"I'm not sure I follow you," said Shelley.

Voss turned back to her. "Here," he said kindly, as if explaining an intricate process to a rather stupid but delightful child, "we do a complete blood count. We do all the usual examinations: thyroid, cholesterol, hemoglobin, et cetera, et cetera. But Dr. Bauer has programmed this computer to identify and isolate traces of disease which otherwise might go unattended. As important as this function is, we feel that the most crucial role of the computer is to provide a total diagnosis of individual, nutritional requirements of our patients through an analysis of a blood sample."

"Very impressive," Shelley said and Voss nodded in agreement.

They went back into the hallway and Shelley looked toward the stairway leading to a third floor. Voss saw her gaze and quickly said, "Upstairs are the private rooms of the patients, where we have a game room, a small movie theater, a library, and a conference room. Visitors are never allowed on that floor," he said as an afterthought. "The operating rooms are also there."

"How many private rooms do you have?" asked Shelley.

"Fifteen. At present all are occupied. Many of our patients stay at the Hotel Adler below and visit us each day for treatments. Some bring their families with them; they are required to stay at the hotel because we have no facilities for family members."

"Could you tell me how much all this costs?" Shelley asked.

Voss made a soft clucking noise as if some internal machine was computing the answer to Shelley's question. "It's quite expensive—as you might imagine."

"That's obvious," said Shelley. "But in round figures, how much would it cost to come here?"

"Perhaps Dr. Bauer would prefer to discuss that with you," said Voss, nodding and smiling. "That's really his area of responsibility." He looked at his watch. "Now we can go to the ground floor. The staff lives there, and Dr. Bauer has his private wing at the rear of the château."

They went downstairs and Voss led her to an arched opening and another hallway. "These are Dr. Bauer's private quarters. He stays pretty much to himself," he said as he marched down the hall. Voss opened a door and they entered a comfortable dining room with a fireplace at one end, and a couch and several chairs grouped around the fire.

"Dr. Bauer will be with you in a short time," said Dr. Voss. "If you will make yourself comfortable, I will tell him that we are ready." He paused. "I hoped you enjoyed my brief tour and that I have been of some help to you. If you have any further questions, I am sure that Dr. Bauer himself will be glad to answer them for you." With that he turned and was gone.

Shelley looked around the room. In spite of the warmth of the fire the room seemed cold.

It gives me the creeps, she thought.

At that, the door opened and in strode Dr. Anton Bauer. Bauer was in his early forties, tall, powerfully built, and, thought Shelley, surprisingly young looking. His dark hair and beard had no hint of gray and his eyes were like black marbles.

Before saying anything, Dr. Bauer fixed Shelley in a steely glare and she felt her stomach churn as he approached. "Miss James," he said, kissing her hand, "I had no idea you would be so distressingly beautiful." His eyes devoured her, and Shelley had the distinct feeling that Dr. Bauer knew why she was there. "I must say that I often envy the life of a reporter," he said. "It must be wonderful to travel the world in search of stories. I often feel confined by my research and my patients."

"But your work seems so fascinating," said Shelley.

Bauer was still holding Shelley's hand. "Come, let us sit at the table. I'm afraid I've kept you waiting. I hope you'll enjoy our simple meal."

Bauer sat at the head of the table and a servant, as if on cue, appeared with a tray on which sat a large soup tureen.

He placed the tureen on the table, ladeled a portion into each diner's soup plate, and then stepped back. Bauer, without speaking, pointed to the wine on the table, and the man sprang forward to fill the glasses.

"A toast," said Bauer. He raised his glass and looked directly at Shelley. "To beauty. May it always be with us."

Shelley nodded uneasily, acknowledging the compliment. Bauer downed his glass in one gulp and then attacked his soup as if ravenously hungry.

"There is more," said Bauer. "The vegetables are all fresh and my chef prepares the stock himself. It is very good for you. We eat a lot of vegetables here at the château."

They were well into the meal before Shelley was able to shift the conversation to the reason for her visit. "Dr. Bauer," she said, "can you tell me something about the kind of people who come to your spa?"

Bauer dragged his eyes away from Shelley and looked around the room, seeming to see the faces of his clients. "They are very wealthy," he said, as if that explained everything.

"But how old? Where do they come from?"

Bauer trained his black eyes on Shelley, and she felt herself inwardly shiver. "They're mostly from Europe and America, but lately many come from the Middle East," Bauer said. "If you're looking for a profile of our typical patient, I would say that it's someone who begins to be concerned about his or her declining physical condition and decides to do something about it." He sipped his wine, never taking his eyes from Shelley's. "We don't have to give in to Father Time, Miss James. He is a patient old fellow. He will wait for us."

"And you help people postpone the inevitable?"

"That's one way of putting it, yes."

"How?" asked Shelley bluntly.

Bauer smiled at her directness. "We teach people to be physically active, to eat healthy foods, to avoid stressful situations—"

"I'm sure they don't have to come here, Doctor, to learn that. Everybody knows that."

Bauer went on as if Shelley had not interrupted him. "Ours is a lifelong program. Our patients return to us year after year. During these annual visits, we monitor the progress they have made and make necessary adjustments in the program. We may recommend that someone visit us again in six months to adequately benefit from our advice."

"How much does all this cost?"

Bauer shook his head. "You Americans are so direct." He smiled at Shelley. "You're always concerned about money. Our services go beyond any measurable cost. We keep our patients young. How can you put a price on that?"

"Can we just say that it's very expensive?" asked Shelley.

Bauer said, "Yes, you may."

After dinner they retired to Dr. Bauer's private study where he poured two glasses of brandy.

Shelley asked, "What else do you do for your patients, Doctor, besides the exercise, the food, the vitamins, and the cell injections?"

Reluctantly, as if he would rather discuss other subjects, Bauer responded. "I'm sure you saw all our facilities. We provide, in addition to our physical conditioning, complete cosmetic surgery."

"Aren't you the Dr. Bauer who discovered the memory hormone about fifteen years ago?" Shelley broke in suddenly.

Bauer's eyes widened.

"Do you ever use that on your patients?"

"You've surprised me, Miss James. You obviously know more about me than I thought you did."

Shelley shrugged.

"In answer to your question about the hormone—which I call Mnemosyne, by the way—yes, we do use it here on occasion. Unfortunately one of the first signs of physical deterioration is a slippage of memory. We are able to considerably alleviate the condition through the use of this compound which I was fortunate enough to be able to discover some years ago. Of course, if our patients come to us early enough, they won't need Mnemosyne until they are in their eighties."

"I think it's marvelous," said Shelley. "I wish I could afford to be a patient here myself."

"I would consider it a privilege if you would allow us to prepare a physical and nutritional program for you. If you'd care to come back tomorrow, we'll have lunch and I'll see to it personally." Shelley felt a sudden chill as Bauer's eyes ran over her body. "You are obviously in beautiful physical condition," he said. "It would be a shame to squander such beauty any earlier than absolutely necessary. With our program you will look thirty when you are forty and forty when you are fifty."

"Sounds good to me," said Shelley.

Bauer smiled. "It is always so sad to see beauty wither."

"Do you have many women clients?" Shelley asked.

"Yes. In a way women are more fortunate. Because they generally mature more quickly, their youthful looks begin to deteriorate at an earlier date than do those of men. Consequently women tend to come to us earlier than men; usually in their thirties. Men very often wait until their physical strength begins to wane. They delude themselves into thinking that wrinkles are character lines and gray hair makes them distinguished. Wrinkles and gray hair are signs that the body is aging, nothing more, nothing less. Women instinctively understand this. Beauty is a blessing. It should be preserved at all costs."

He looked at Shelley, his eyes drinking in her beauty. His stare was hypnotic. There was a long silence and then Dr. Bauer said, "I do hope you *will* come back tomorrow. I promise you that I can extend your youthful years by ten years, perhaps even longer."

"How can I refuse?" said Shelley. "It isn't every man who can promise to keep me young."

It was almost ten-thirty when Dr. Voss reappeared. He came to the table and whispered something in Dr. Bauer's ear. Bauer nodded and smiled. "There is no rest, I'm afraid, for the wicked."

"I should be going anyway," said Shelley. "The cable car stops running at eleven."

"Don't worry," said Bauer. "We can control the car from this side. We pick up and drop off patients at any time during the night. Let the restaurant crowd leave; then you can take a nice leisurely ride home."

"Why," Shelley asked, "would you bring patients here in the middle of the night?"

Bauer paused a moment as if he were pondering his answer. "Sometimes our patients require medication or injections every four hours," he said, then quickly rose and took Shelley's hand. "You promise you will come back tomorrow?"

After a moment's hesitation, Shelley said, "I promise. I wouldn't miss it for the world."

Bauer's face was lit by an odd smile. "One of my men

will accompany you over," he said, "and the other will operate the cable."

"The escort's not really necessary," said Shelley.

"It's no trouble at all, Miss James," Bauer said firmly. "We want to make sure that no one comes back by mistake."

Chapter 41

It was a bright, clear moonlit night as Shelley and her two escorts made their way down to the cable car station. During the walk, Shelley made some vague attempts at conversation. She commented that the clinic was marvelous, and that Dr. Bauer and his staff seemed eminently qualified.

Neither of the men said anything.

At the cable car one of the two opened the door to the small, narrow building near the platform. He stepped inside and in seconds a motor sprang to life. The second man opened the rear door of the car and allowed Shelley to step on board before following her.

Shelley moved to the front of the car as it lurched forward. She rode in silence while Bauer's man stood near the door at the rear of the cable car. The man was short and bull-necked. Even beneath his bulky clothing his powerful frame was evident.

His eyes devoured her and, feeling distinctly uncomfortable, Shelley turned away as if to admire the moonlit view around her.

The man stood rigidly, holding himself in the parade rest position, hands behind his back, feet apart. His face was totally without expression, but his eyes never left Shelley. In the reflection of the glass she saw him watching her. She felt his eyes touching her, disrobing her.

Shelley turned to face him. There was something supremely arrogant in his stance and demeanor. She felt a kind of violation under his scrutiny.

Finally he spoke. "Are you here alone?"

Shelley was surprised that he spoke English. "Forget it, pal. I'm not that alone," she said and turned away.

They rode the rest of the way in silence and when the car pulled into the lower station, Shelley yanked on the handle of the front door so that she could leave quickly. The door wouldn't open.

"Damn this door," she mumbled, struggling with the handle.

The man approached. He took the door handle, managing to brush against Shelley in the process, and said, "You must turn it all the way, like this." He twisted the handle a full one hundred and eighty degrees. "That releases the lock."

Shelley was not listening. She pushed open the door and stomped angrily across the platform.

The man, grinning obscenely, watched her leave.

As Shelley walked into the lobby she saw Lawrence Jefferson, looking tired and old, slumped in a chair. To get to the elevator, Shelley would have had to walk past him, and she did not feel up to another confrontation.

Jefferson had not yet seen her, so Shelley did a quick about-face and ducked into the restaurant-bar at the opposite end of the lobby. As she did, the elevator door opened and out stepped Mrs. Jefferson and David. Jefferson struggled to his feet and moved to meet them.

From her vantage point, Shelley watched them cross the floor. Lawrence Jefferson's face was drawn and had a sickly gray pallor. He seemed incredibly weary. The boy, eyes bleary as if he had just been awakened, clutched a stuffed bear with his right arm, while with his free hand he rubbed his eyes. Mrs. Jefferson's eyes were red, and she seemed on the verge of tears.

The three, holding each other up, passed Shelley on their way to the door which led to the cable car. At the door, Mrs. Jefferson hugged her son and then, tears streaming down her face, turned and, without looking back, walked quickly to the elevator.

Shelley waited until Jefferson and his son had disappeared, and Mrs. Jefferson had gone into the elevator before coming back into the lobby. Curious, she went to the desk clerk. "Excuse me," she said. "The man and the boy—did they just go to the cable car?"

"Yes," said the clerk, smiling pleasantly.

Shelley frowned. "I thought this cable car stopped running at eleven."

The clerk nodded. "That's right, but each evening after the eleven o'clock crossing, the car returns to the upper station. It can be operated from that side and quite frequently guests at the health clinic will return to the hotel after eleven."

Shelley looked at her watch. "What do they do over there at this time of night?"

The clerk was amiable. "There are all sorts of scheduled treatments. I suppose some of the timing seems rather odd."

"Yes," said Shelley. "I suppose it does."

Still unable to adjust to the time change, Chandler spent a fitful night in his hotel room. Most of the night he sat up in a chair by the window staring into the darkness. His room looked across Park Lane into Hyde Park, and occasionally a car or double-decker bus would roll by quietly. Gradually the traffic decreased until an hour might pass between vehicles.

On his lap was the material Shelley had promised in her telegram, and on the night table next to him sat a bottle of Scotch and a glass. He had already put a good dent in the bottle.

Why didn't she call? he asked himself for the hundredth time. She had said she would. He'd spent much of the evening trying to contact Shelley in New York, but no one seemed to know where she was. Even Nancy Kelly had been unable to tell him anything about the important assignment that had kept her from meeting him in London.

He turned his attention back to the material in the package that had been waiting for him when he'd returned to his hotel that evening. There were some new facts on the men from Romanello's list, and the information on this Dr. Bauer was very interesting. But what, if anything, did it mean?

He wondered how close Romanello and Carruthers might have been to unraveling the mystery that had killed them. Now he knew that his list was only a partial accounting of similar episodes. He had found another right here in London. Who knew how many more there were to be discovered? How many rich men had died, leaving their fortunes to adopted children? And what was the secret that was worth killing for? He studied the photograph of Dr. Bauer. Who was this Dr. Bauer and what did he have to do with any of this?

Beverly Collins was a former beauty contestant and one of the other men, Forbes Coleman, had been married to a former Miss America contestant. Shelley's new material showed that the other wives had been involved in similar activities. Was this another pattern to the bizarre story, or just a strange coincidence? Chandler made a mental note to check the backgrounds of the wives of the other men.

Sometime after 3:00 A.M. he lay fully clothed on the bed and slipped off into a restless sleep in which he envisioned old men calling him from the grave. In his dream he was at a wake and was being drawn relentlessly toward an open coffin. He tried to step out of line but it was impossible; he was pushed and shoved from behind until he stood in front of the casket. Fearfully, he looked inside, but to his surprise it was empty.

Standing near the coffin, dressed in black, her face behind a black veil, Beverly Collins stuck out her tongue and leered suggestively. Next to her stood her son, yet in the dream it wasn't the boy whom Chandler had seen at the house. This boy was older—much older—but his eyes captured Chandler in their hateful stare. The earl himself—or what Chandler in his dream imagined the earl would look like—sat in a chair next to his son. His face was ghastly pale, his features waxlike. His eyes were closed and his arms folded across his chest. Chandler tried to tiptoe past this apparition, but as he did, the earl opened his eyes. Chandler backed away as the earl rose from his chair to greet him. The same hands that had propelled Chandler to the casket now prevented his retreat, and the earl, arms outstretched, lurched forward to embrace his new friend.

Beverly Collins laughed hysterically at Chandler's panic: the boy began to laugh; then the other mourners, until the dream was filled with raucous laughter.

Chandler awoke in a sweat at 5:00 in the morning.

Chapter 42

The two men in the gray sedan sat without speaking to each other outside Mario's Restaurant in Georgetown. One of them read the sports pages of the *Washington Post* by the dim glow of a small penlight, while the other kept a constant watch on the front door of Mario's. The man reading the paper was large and burly; the watcher was short and ferretlike. They were a team.

During their vigil, they had seen several of Washington's most prominent citizens arrive and leave through Mario's front door. The restaurant was a very popular Washington institution. Started in 1947 by an Italian prisoner of war who had married an American girl to avoid repatriation, Mario's had grown from a low-cost spaghetti place, to an exclusive restaurant serving fine Italian food. There were some who whispered that Mario's association with certain Mafia figures had as much to do with his rise to prominence in Washington, as did the excellence of his fare.

Neither of the men in the gray sedan had ever been inside.

"There he is," said the ferret, whose name was Rinaldi, as he spotted their quarry. The other, known as Murphy, put aside his paper and penlight, and the two watched Andrew Petersen wave aside the valet parking attendant and walk to his car in the parking lot.

Both pairs of eyes watched anxiously as Petersen disappeared into the darkness of the lot. "Navy-blue Seville," said the ferret, chewing anxiously on some gum.

"You told me ten times already," said Murphy calmly. "You fix the seat belts?"

"Yep. Once he buckles in, they won't release."

"If he buckles in," said Murphy.

The ferret shrugged. "Information says the man is a

318

creature of habit. He eats in the same place almost every night; he drives home by the same route every night; and he always uses his seatbelts. He's a very safety-minded individual."

They both laughed. "Habits can be very bad for you," said Murphy, chuckling at his own joke.

Petersen nosed his Cadillac out into the street, looking both left and right before inching into the traffic flow. He had not enjoyed his dinner tonight, and even Mario himself had come to his table to ask if anything was wrong. The food, as usual, was excellent, but he had other things on his mind. It would be a shame if Shelley James were eliminated in one of those nasty accidents that these people were able to manufacture. He had entertained daydreams and fantasies about this woman for a long time and such was his ego that he actually believed that someday, given the right circumstance and opportunity, he might actually be able to bring one of his dreams to fruition. He smiled momentarily, thinking about one of his favorite scenarios where Shelley desperately needed his help to complete a big story. "I'll do anything if you'll help me, Andrew," she would say, and he would smile wickedly.

The irony was that now she did desperately need his help, but there was nothing he could do to save her. He had suggested that she might be useful to them, just as he himself had been advanced and promoted to further their cause. He had even called her anonymously to alert her, and if she were allowed to live he would, of course, remind her how much she owed him. But, until that decision was made, there was nothing else he could do.

He shook his head sadly, thinking what a waste of a magnificent creature it would be. If he could possess that body just once, then he wouldn't mind what they did with her. He pulled his car onto the Rockville Pike, heading north.

It never occurred to Petersen that he was being followed.

"Make sure," said Murphy, "that you give me plenty of warning before we come to the first spot."

"Don't worry; don't worry, I'll let you know. And just remember it's a go only if the road is quiet. It has to look like an accident. I've got three other spots picked out just in case."

"What if none of 'em are quiet? This road can get pretty busy at night."

"Don't worry about it, Murph. Just drive."

Skillfully, Murphy followed Petersen's Cadillac at a discreet distance, close enough not to lose him and far enough not to be noticed. Once, Murphy switched off the headlights so that if by any chance Petersen were suspicious, he would think the car behind him had turned off the road.

The road was quiet.

"OK," said Rinaldi, pointing to an exit sign looming in the darkness. "We're coming up to our first spot now. It's six tenths of a mile past this overpass and you'll have nine tenths of a mile to get the job done. That'll only give you about three minutes to get him off the road."

Murphy waited, his eyes flicking occasionally to the odometer. At the five-tenths mark he began to accelerate steadily, closing in on the car ahead. With the gray sedan in the passing lane, Murphy drew alongside Petersen's car until his front bumper was even with the rear door of the Cadillac.

From the passenger seat, Rinaldi could see the fat man, blissfully unaware of his predicament, whistling in accompaniment to the car radio. The ferret's eyes scanned the roadside for the exact spot he had selected. "Here it comes," he said. "When I say the word, you can give it to him." He paused, holding his breath for just a moment as they passed his marker. He wanted no mistakes.

"Shit," said Murphy.

"What?"

"Another car. Just saw it in the mirror."

"Shit," echoed Rinaldi. He turned and saw through the rear window the car that Murphy had spotted. The car was still a good distance behind them but gaining rapidly. He pointed to Petersen's Cadillac. "Pass him," he said, "and get off at the next exit."

"Huh?"

"Pass him and get off. We'll get right back on and fall in behind him again."

Murphy accelerated past Petersen, watching the headlights in his rearview mirror. "Doing a steady fifty-five," he said. "Must have cruise control in that Caddy."

"Fifty-five saves lives," said the ferret without humor.

Murphy laughed anyway.

They left the highway, went down a long, curving exit

ramp, and came to a two-lane road. Across the road was the entrance to the highway they had just left.

"Perfect," said Murphy in obvious satisfaction with his partner's expert reconnoitering. He waited for a few minutes, then crossed the road and reentered the highway. "Think he's passed us yet?" he asked.

"Must have."

Murphy accelerated and soon the car was traveling at close to eighty miles per hour, the engine purring in quiet precision.

"That's him," said Rinaldi, pointing to the taillights ahead, and Murphy allowed the car to decelerate as they fell into place well behind Petersen's Cadillac.

Rinaldi borrowed Murphy's penlight and consulted the map he had opened across his knee. "Next spot's coming up in just a few minutes." He waited until they had passed under an overpass and said, "Get ready." He looked behind. All was clear.

Murphy maneuvered the car into position behind Petersen, then swung out as if to pass. Instead, he pulled alongside and waited for the word from his partner.

"Now," yelled Rinaldi and Murphy pulled the car slightly ahead of Petersen's Cadillac and swerved violently to the right. The cars crunched together, metal grinding, sparks flying. Murphy kept his steering wheel hard right.

Petersen screamed, his voice a mixture of fright and surprise, as his car was forced to the edge of the highway. He fought the wheel to keep the car on the road, but the other car, locked onto his, relentlessly forced him to the right. The Cadillac left the highway, smashed through the steel cable and post fence that bordered the roadway, and plunged down a deep embankment through heavy brush. Like a giant scythe, the Cadillac cut a swath through the foliage, snapping saplings and uprooting bushes. With a shuddering jolt the car slammed into a large tree and stopped dead in its tracks.

There was only the high-pitched hiss of a disconnected radiator hose and the soft tone of the FM radio as Petersen, groggy from the impact, touched a hand to his forehead. The hand came away sticky and damp. Instinctively he turned off the ignition key, then pressed the release on his safety belt. It would not release.

He opened the door, illuminating the interior of the car

with the overhead light, then looked at himself in the mirror. Blood was oozing from a gash just below his hairline, the hair matted on his forehead.

He tried the seat belt again. Still it would not release. "Son of a bitch," he muttered.

Behind him he heard a noise of something coming through the brush. He twisted around in his seat but it was too dark to see anything. "Over here," he yelled. "I'm over here."

In a moment a man approached the car. "Jesus Christ," he said, breathless from his trip down the embankment, "I saw that car force you off the road. You all right?"

"I think so. Got a cut on my forehead. Bleeding a bit. I think my seat belt is jammed. I can't seem to release it."

"Lucky you were wearing that belt. You could've been hurt bad."

Petersen nodded wearily. "Yes," he said. Then he heard something from the rear of the car. "What's that?" he asked, straining to look behind him.

"That's just my friend," said the man. "He's opening your gas tank."

"What?" Petersen stared blankly at the man without comprehension. "What's he doing that for?"

The man said nothing; he was watching the man at the rear of the car. Petersen squirmed around, fighting the seat belt, to see what was happening. The second man held a large can in his hand and was sprinkling a liquid over the rear of the Cadillac. Petersen heard it gurgle and splash and the drumlike sound as the can expanded and contracted. He could smell gasoline.

"What's he doing with that gas?" he asked, his voice cracking.

"Got a light?" asked Rinaldi as Murphy came forward, splashing gasoline inside the passenger compartment.

His eyes wide, Petersen looked down. His clothing reeked of gasoline. "What are you doing?" he shrieked, his voice beyond hysteria.

"You don't smoke; do you?" asked Rinaldi casually, his voice and expression devoid of emotion.

Petersen scrambled frantically against the confinement of the seat belts. He slipped off the shoulder harness and turned on his side, trying to squeeze himself out of the lap belts, but there was insufficient slack. He struggled furiously against the restraints, turning himself left, then right, contorting his body in an effort to escape.

Rinaldi went on as if none of this were taking place. "Never mind," he said. "I think I've got matches here someplace." He reached in his coat pocket and produced a pack of matches.

Petersen struggled even more violently and the car rocked with the intensity of his exertion.

Rinaldi struck a match against the box. It burst brightly into flame, and Petersen, mesmerized by the flame and by what he knew was coming, ceased his struggle against the implacable belt. His staring eyes focused only on the tiny flame. Petersen watched the match burn down. Rinaldi tantalized him by letting the flame almost go out and then, just as the match neared the end, he dropped it next to the car and stepped back.

Petersen saw the flame ignite a small pool of gasoline just below the open car door. He clutched the wheel of his car as if wanting to be transported to another time and another place and screamed a long, shuddering "No-o-o" that reached far out into the night before the car, with a soft whoosh like air rushing through an open door, burst into flame and silenced his screech.

Rinaldi and Murphy, standing back from the intensity of the heat, watched until the Cadillac was completely enveloped in flame before they started the hike back up the hill to the highway.

Chapter 43

Shelley was just beginning her second cup of morning coffee in the hotel restaurant when she noticed a minor commotion out by the cable car. A small crowd had gathered near the platform as the car approached. She saw a waiter standing by one of the windows watching the car and waved to get his attention.

"What's going on out there?" she asked. "Do you know?"

The man shrugged. "I heard someone say earlier that they had found someone dead in the snow over on the trails." He jerked his head toward the mountain. "They're bringing the body over now on the cable car."

"Anyone know what happened?"

"I don't know. I heard the man had gone over on the first car for some early morning skiing. He was alone on the slopes when he suffered a heart attack."

Shelley sat straight up in her chair. The story was too familiar. "Do you know who it was?"

"I don't," said the waiter. "But I believe he was a guest here in the hotel."

Shelley hurriedly paid her bill and went downstairs to the platform. She waited with the crowd as the car came in and watched the doors open. Several white-clad attendants emerged with a stretcher onto which was strapped a blanket-covered body. The stretcher was placed on the ground and a path formed in the crowd to permit someone to come forward. Shelley watched as Karen Jefferson passed through the gauntlet of curious faces. A short man in a gray suit beckoned the woman to approach, and as she did, he pulled back the top of the blanket.

Shelley did not see the face of the dead man, but she did see Karen Jefferson nod, then, shoulders slumped, turn and walk back up the steps to the hotel. Shelley watched the attendants pick up the stretcher and place the body in the back of a horse-drawn wagon to drive off to the village before she followed Mrs. Jefferson and the small crowd behind her.

Karen Jefferson had already disappeared into the elevator when Shelley reached the lobby, but many in the crowd remained. The talk was subdued after the reminder of mortality. Soon, however, the thought of death was pushed aside in favor of the holiday atmosphere.

At the main desk the clerk was already preoccupied with the business of the day.

"Excuse me," said Shelley, and the young man looked up. "Did anyone see Mr. Jefferson—the man who died—go over on the first cable car this morning?"

The young man smiled. "Those cars are usually jammed with passengers. Everybody wants to get to the trails early." He shook his head. "I doubt if anyone would remember which car he took."

Yes, thought Shelley, an old man who was having trouble walking wouldn't attract any attention if he went skiing at six o'clock in the morning.

Instead she asked, "Does this sort of thing happen often?"

The desk clerk thought for a moment. "I suppose it happens occasionally—once, perhaps twice, a year." He sighed. "An older man forgets his limitations; he is out of condition and overexerts himself on the slopes. Skiing is rather strenuous exercise."

Shelley turned away, saying to herself, "A perfect way to go, if you really want to go."

On her way back to her room, Shelley was filled with a grim satisfaction in knowing that she had been right about this clinic. Things were falling into place now—the story was coming together. Lawrence Jefferson's death was the piece of the puzzle that had eluded her. He had been dying and now he had found a way out of his misery. That's what this was all about. She had guessed it after speaking to Jefferson in Virginia; now his death proved that she was right.

With the thought that the story was almost over, her mind turned to Chandler and she felt an immediate sense of guilt. She knew that, quite deliberately, she had cut him out of her investigation, and now she was on the verge of closing him out of the story, too. She had never intended to break it by herself, only to be sure she had a part.

Shelley winced when she thought of how Chandler would react to what she had done. With that thought came the realization of how much she cared for him.

She could only hope it was not too late to set things straight between them.

When the phone rang Chandler pounced on it like a predatory animal. "Yes?" he barked.

"It's me," said Shelley. "Sounds like you're having a wonderful time without me."

"Where are you? I've been going crazy trying to track you down. I would have gone home, but I was afraid you'd be on your way here and we'd cross paths in flight."

"I've been working—on our story," said Shelley cautiously.

"Where are you now?" persisted Chandler.

"I'm in Switzerland. At the Hotel Adler in Murren."

"Switzerland?" he exploded. "What the hell are you doing in Switzerland?"

"I thought you'd be glad to hear from me."

"Of course I'm glad. I just want to know what the hell is going on."

"I interviewed Dr. Bauer last night."

Chandler's eyes narrowed. "What? You've got me stuck over here in London while you're doing the story. First Jefferson, now Bauer!"

"I was going to tell you."

"Tell me what? That you've been holding out on me?"

"I sent you the information, didn't I? I'm calling you now, aren't I? I want this story to be ours. Not yours, not mine, ours. So far everything about this story has been yours. I want it to be my story too."

Chandler was surprised. "But it is your story—our story."

"I just felt that I wasn't contributing enough. I had to do this alone."

Chandler was silent. "OK," he said finally. "I'm sorry, but I've been worried about you. I want you with me, not out there running around by yourself. How did you get the interview anyway?"

Shelley laughed. "I told Bauer that Petersen was going to write an exposé on his clinic and that I wanted to give him equal time."

Chandler frowned. "I'm not so sure that was wise, Shelley. I think it would be better if you just got over here as soon as possible."

"I'll be in London tonight. I promise. I just have to talk with Bauer one more time. I think I can crack this thing today."

"Why? What's happened?"

"That's the reason I called you. I wanted to tell you that Jefferson is dead."

Chandler was stunned into silence.

"They found him out in the snow this morning. Supposedly a heart attack. Sound familiar?"

"Very. Listen, Shelley. I want you to get out of there right now."

"Wait a minute. That's not all. Last night around midnight I saw Jefferson and his son go over to Bauer's clinic. I don't think they ever returned to the hotel. The boy may still be there."

"Shelley, you have to get out of there immediately."

"I need one more visit to the clinic and . . ."

"I want you to promise me that you won't go near the place."

"I'll be all right. I just have to find out what happened to the boy."

"Shelley, I mean it."

"I'll see you tonight," she said cheerfully and hung up.

When Shelley arrived at the château it was after eleven o'clock and Dr. Bauer himself was waiting for her.

"I'm so glad you came," he said.

There was fire in his dark eyes. Shelley found him attractive and at the same time repulsive. There was something about him that frightened her. He was too confident, too sure of himself. Perhaps, she thought as he escorted her inside, he was too sure of her.

Bauer walked her up the staircase to the second floor. "One of my assistants will handle your physical," he said. "I have some work to do. We can meet downstairs and have a late lunch together."

Shelley nodded as Bauer took her arm. "That would be nice," she said.

Bauer pointed to a door at the end of the hall. "If you'll wait in there, Dr. Meleck will be with you shortly."

On the way down the hall Shelley walked past the stairway to the third floor. She paused to look up, but apart from another hallway at the top, she could see nothing.

She continued to the examination room, went inside, and waited.

Shelley was somewhat relieved to find that Dr. Meleck was a woman. "Good morning," said the doctor, smiling as she entered. "Or should I say good afternoon? I'm losing track of the time. We are so busy today." She shook Shelley's hand. "I've been assigned to do your preliminary work-up."

"I hope it's nothing too exotic," said Shelley. "This is just a kind of informational checkup."

Meleck laughed. "I understand. We'll do a brief physical exam and a complete blood work-up. Then we'll let the computer analyze you. That's really where we get most of our information."

Shelley smiled. "I'm all yours," she said.

* * *

It was raining hard when Chandler jumped from his taxi and ran into the small, red brick pub near Piccadilly Circus. He spotted Kyle Warner, who waved from a table near the back corner of the dimly lit establishment.

Chandler made his way toward him weaving around lunching businessmen. The room was dark and smoky, and with its wood-beamed ceilings and trophy-covered walls, had the feel of a genuine pub, the kind that Chandler had seen only in movies.

Warner saw his eyes take in the decor. "I thought you might enjoy a little bit of authentic London," he said when Chandler sat beside him. "This place has been here for about a hundred and fifty years. It was bombed out during the Blitz and rebuilt just after the war."

Chandler took off his coat. "Looks like the real thing to me."

"I was beginning to think you weren't going to make it," said Warner.

"Shelley called, finally," Chandler said. "She's in Switzerland."

"Switzerland," said Warner, laughing. "I thought she was meeting you here in London."

Chandler shrugged. "She'll be here tonight. At least that's what she says."

A waitress appeared and they ordered sandwiches and beer.

"I feel better," said Chandler, "knowing where she is. But I wish she would get here."

"So what is she doing in Switzerland?" Warner asked.

"She's interviewing a Dr. Bauer at some health clinic there, while I sit around here waiting."

"Are you working, or just waiting?"

Chandler took a bite of his sandwich. "I did a column yesterday afternoon and sent it back to New York." He shook his head. "Some drivel about the trade unions' domination of the Labor party." He chewed his sandwich and then gulped half his beer. "A columnist has to keep pumping out columns, no matter what."

"Speaking of columnists, did you hear about Andrew Petersen?"

Chandler stopped in midbite. "No. What?"

"Dead."

Very calmly, Chandler put his sandwich back on his

plate. A sudden wave of nausea swept over him, and he felt the blood drain from his face. "What happened?" he asked. "Don't leave anything out."

Warner told him what he had gleaned from the news reports from the United States and concluded, "The police seem to suspect foul play of some kind. Wouldn't surprise me one bit. Probably somebody that Petersen skewered, decided to get back at him."

"You mean they think he was murdered?"

"Precisely."

Chandler stood up. His breath came in short gasps; he could feel his pulse racing.

Warner, puzzled, stared at him. "Don't tell me he was a friend of yours?"

Distractedly, Chandler shook his head. "I've got to go, Kyle. Sorry. I'll be in touch."

Shaking his head in bewilderment, Kyle Warner watched as Chandler stumbled toward the door and out into the pouring rain.

Chapter 44

"I understand you're having lunch with Dr. Bauer," said Dr. Meleck as she placed the blood sample in the centrifuge.

"That's right," Shelley said. "Are we finished here?"

"Yes. I'll run the samples through the analyzer and the computer will give us a complete rundown of all your nutritional needs. I'll have the information for you in a very short time if you'd care to wait."

"Why don't I just stay downstairs in Dr. Bauer's study? He told me to wait for him there when I was finished."

Dr. Meleck smiled. "Fine. I'll have someone take you there."

"Don't bother," said Shelley. "I can find my own way—if it's all right?"

Dr. Meleck's eyes twitched once or twice. "I suppose so," she said. "Most of the patients will be downstairs in the dining room. As long as you know how to get there, I suppose it's all right."

Shelley left the examining room, closing the door quietly behind her. She walked calmly down the hall, and when she got to the third-floor stairway, looked carefully over her shoulder to make sure no one was watching her. The hallway was deserted and Shelley moved quickly. Taking the stairs two at a time she moved quickly to the top and onto a long narrow corridor with doors spaced evenly apart on either side. Shelley went to the first door on the right, listened, heard nothing, then opened the door quietly and cautiously stuck her head in.

The room was empty.

The second room was also empty. Everyone must be at lunch, she thought. In the next room an old man was asleep, mouth open, snoring softly. The next two rooms were also empty, but in the last room on that side of the corridor Shelley found what she was looking for.

David was apparently asleep in bed, his head bandaged. Slipping quietly into the room and closing the door behind her, Shelley went to his bedside.

"David," she said softly.

He stirred a little and Shelley touched him lightly on the arm.

"David," she whispered, and his eyes fluttered open. "It's me, Shelley. Are you all right?"

The boy, his eyes blinking, looked at her without comprehension; then there was a spark of recognition and his face broke into a smile.

Feeling a flush of relief, Shelley started to speak, but suddenly a cloud passed across David's eyes and his face darkened. His mouth twisted into a vicious snarl and he struggled to sit up.

Jolted by his transformation, Shelley fell back, away from him. David, his eyes burning hatred, glared at her from his position on the bed and she was driven back across the room until she felt the door behind her.

As quickly as it had come, the hateful stare slipped from his eyes, and David slumped back onto the pillow with a small sigh.

Cautiously, Shelley approached him again. "David? David? Are you all right?"

The boy smiled and Shelley took his hand. He struggled to speak, his voice like a bird trying to escape a cage. "I'm glad you came . . ." he began painfully, his eyelids fluttering. Then his face twitched convulsively and his eyes rolled up into his head. "I told you," croaked the boy, in a voice that was like no child's she had ever heard, "to stay away from my son."

Shelley stifled a gasp. She scrambled to open the door, struggling frantically with the knob. She dashed down the hall, the sound of David's croaking voice echoing behind her. Only when she'd reached the second floor did she force herself into a walk.

Stay calm; stay calm, she repeated over and over, but the boy's horrible voice followed her down the stairs, enveloping her in its dreadful reverberation. As quickly as she could, she made her way to the stairway leading to the ground floor.

As she was descending, her eyes fixed firmly on the front door, she heard a voice calling to her, from below.

"So there you are," said Dr. Bauer. "I thought you'd gotten lost." His eyes were dark, piercing, burning into her.

She forced a weak smile. "I thought I'd take another look at your exercise facilities. They are certainly the most complete I've ever seen."

Bauer's smile was frozen, a terrible mask, on his face. "The exercise rooms are always locked when they are not in use."

Shelley said nothing.

Bauer waited at the foot of the stairs. "Our lunch is almost ready," he said as if nothing had happened. "I thought we'd wait until the patients were finished. Perhaps you'd like a drink first?"

Shelley reached the bottom step. "I'm afraid I'm going to have to skip lunch today. I just remembered that there are some people I have to see back at the hotel." Shelley moved toward the door.

Bauer's eyes narrowed and he moved between Shelley and the exit. "I was looking forward to our lunch," he said quietly.

"Hold it," said a voice, and both Shelley and Dr. Bauer looked up to see Dr. Meleck leaning over the second-floor railing. "She's been up on the third floor. She's been in the child's room."

Bauer's face turned red. Shelley started to reach for the door, but he clamped a hand around her arm. "Perhaps," said Bauer, "we'd better have that lunch after all."

"Let go of my arm please," said Shelley calmly. "I'm leaving now." She tried to extricate herself from Bauer's grasp, but he would not let go.

"Listen to me," he began, but Shelley cut him off with her best on-the-air voice.

"You'd better let me go, right now. People know where I am. People expect me back very soon."

"I think you'd better listen to the doctor, Shelley," said a familiar voice from the second-floor railing, and Shelley spun around.

"Mrs. Gresham," she said startled, "what are you doing here?"

Sylvia Gresham began to descend the stairs. "I was upstairs receiving treatments when I heard all the commotion."

Openmouthed, Shelley could only watch as Mrs. Gresham approached.

"I've been coming here to La Renaissance for quite a few years, my dear." Mrs. Gresham laughed. "Why do you think I look so marvelous for my age?" She detached Bauer's hand from Shelley's arm. "That won't be necessary," she said. "Let's go have that lunch, shall we? I'm sure Dr. Bauer won't mind if I join the two of you."

With that, she led a bewildered Shelley toward Dr. Bauer's private quarters; he followed quietly, a few paces behind the two women.

Back at his hotel, Chandler immediately placed a call to the Hotel Adler in Murren. He let the phone in Shelley's room ring for several minutes before he gave up. Ten minutes later he called again. This time he got the desk in the lobby where he was told that Miss James was not in the hotel.

"Is she still registered?"

"Oh yes," said the man at the desk. "She is still a guest here. Is there any message?"

"Yes, tell her that Mr. Chandler says she is not to go anywhere or do anything until I arrive."

The clerk cleared his throat to disguise the chuckle in his

voice. "Very well, sir. I will see that she gets your message as soon as she returns to the hotel."

Chandler hung up and started dumping his clothes into the open suitcase on the bed.

"I can't believe it," said Shelley. "It's just too crazy to be true. It's not possible."

"Oh, it's possible all right, my dear," said Mrs. Gresham. "It's been done many times. I don't pretend to understand the principle behind it, but I can assure you that it does work."

They were sitting at the dining room table in Dr. Bauer's quarters. Shelley's food sat untouched before her, while Bauer and Mrs. Gresham had both eaten hearty portions. The doctor had said very little since Mrs. Gresham had arrived on-the-scene. Instinctively, he seemed to know that her power over Shelley was far greater than his own.

"Thanks to Dr. Bauer," said Mrs. Gresham, "those of us who have so much to give to society are able to keep on giving."

"It's too bizarre," said Shelley. "I just can't believe it."

"Jonathan Carruthers didn't believe it at first either. He was my favorite, you know. He would have gone straight to the top. But he found out about us." She shook her head sadly. "We tried to reason with him, but his ego was too big. We tried to convince him that if the world knew our secret there would be chaos. We even offered to let him join us—he *was* my favorite—but he thought he could have it all. Something had to be done." She seemed genuinely sad.

Shelley looked at her in amazement. She started to speak. "You—"

Mrs. Gresham interrupted her. "Have you ever met my children?"

"No."

"Not many people have. Very few are even aware that Mr. Gresham and I even had any children. The children are both very bright and very beautiful." She nodded to Dr. Bauer. "The doctor was good enough to find them for us. We adopted rather late in life." She smiled grotesquely, her voice breaking into a horrid facsimile of song. "A boy for you, a girl for me."

Shelley struggled to maintain her calm. She was living through some terrible nightmare. This could not be happening.

Her little joke over, Mrs. Gresham continued her story. "I have a son, Todd, almost twelve. He goes to a private school in New York with a group of other boys just like him. I see him rather infrequently. My husband, who owned all the stock I now control, died when our son was about six."

Shelley shook her head in disbelief. "Don't tell me anymore," she said. "I don't want to hear it."

Mrs. Gresham went on as if Shelley hadn't spoken. "I have a daughter, too. Darling little thing. She's five years old now. I think that maybe next year I'll bring her along with me on my trip to Switzerland . . . I have struggled for years—rather successfully, I think—to battle the ravages of time, but one can only struggle so long before the battle is ultimately lost." Mrs. Gresham laughed and took another forkful of salad. "It is at that point that new tactics are required."

Shelley looked down at the tablecloth. She could not make herself look at the other two.

"And now," said Mrs. Gresham to Dr. Bauer, "what do we do about our little inquiring reporter?"

"I'm not alone," said Shelley. "I'll be missed if I'm not back soon."

Mrs. Gresham shrugged disinterestedly. "We know all about your friend Chandler. He can't be of any help to you now."

Bauer turned to Mrs. Gresham. "If he does show up, I have people who are very efficient in such matters."

"Probably," said Mrs. Gresham, "but I had such high hopes for you, Shelley. I really thought that you had everything going for you. When Dr. Bauer called and told me that one of my people was trying to get an interview, I was surprised to find out it was you. I told him to let you come and I flew over as quickly as I could." She paused. "I was hoping that at some point you might be persuaded to join us."

Bauer chimed in eagerly. "Yes. Beauty and talent such as yours should not be wasted on a few short years."

Shelley's jaw dropped. "Are you suggesting? . . ."

Bauer and Gresham both shrugged. "Perhaps," said Mrs. Gresham. "You have many years of youthful vitality left, but believe me, it passes in what seems like an instant. You could be of great value to us in a position of responsibility in your field." Her face cracked into a devilish grin. "I, of course, could take care of that."

Shelley's mind was racing. Her eyes went from one to the other as she carefully considered her options. No one said anything until Shelley picked up her wine glass and smiled. "Why don't we talk about this?" she said.

Chapter 45

Chandler reached Murren, Switzerland, by taking the late afternon Dan Air flight from Gatwick to Bern, then renting a car at the airport and driving through Interlaken and on to Lauterbrunnen. Less than two hours after leaving London he found himself on the Schilthorn cable car, being whisked up the five thousand feet to the small village of Murren.

Most of the passengers had hurried to secure vantage points at the handrails by the windows. Not Chandler. His suitcase at his feet, Chandler clung desperately to one of the vertical posts in the interior of the car. While the other passengers oohed and aahed at the spectacular mountain vistas outside their windows, Chandler kept his eyes fixed firmly on the floor. The only thought that sustained him was that this contraption was bringing him closer to Shelley. He hoped that she had heeded his warning and was waiting for him at the hotel.

At one point the car lurched and swung in a wide arc as it passed a support pylon, and Chandler involuntarily looked up. At the sight of the looming distance between the car and the valley, Chandler immediately went back to his floor inspection.

Finally the ordeal was over, and he and his suitcase boarded a horse-drawn sleigh for the brief ride to the Hotel Adler.

At the hotel Chandler inquired immediately about Shelley, only to be told that she was not in. The message he had given from London still waited in the slot with her room key.

"And you're sure she hasn't returned this afternoon?" Chandler asked the desk clerk.

"I've been on duty since noon," replied the young man, "and I haven't seen her."

"Where is the Renaissance Clinic?" Chandler asked. "I think she might be there."

"On the other side of the ravine. You can see it from the restaurant-bar," said the clerk, pointing to a doorway in the lobby.

Chandler ordered a drink in the bar and then stood by the window looking across the ravine to the château, which, despite the symmetry of its spires, seemed squat and ugly in the fading light.

She's over there, he told himself. I can feel it.

From a phone at the back, he placed a call to the clinic. Chandler looked around. The bar was almost empty. "I'd like to speak with Miss Shelley James, please," he told the woman who answered.

After a brief pause the woman replied, "I'm sorry, sir. We have no patient here by that name."

"She's not a patient. She's a reporter. She was supposed to interview Dr. Bauer today."

"Hang on, please," said the voice, and Chandler was put on hold.

A minute or two later a man's voice came on the line. "May I help you?"

"Is this Dr. Bauer?"

"No. Dr. Bauer is busy at the moment. I am Dr. Voss, his assistant. How may I help you?"

"My name is Mark Chandler. I'm trying to locate Shelley James, the reporter who interviewed Dr. Bauer earlier today. I was wondering if she was still at the clinic."

"I'm afraid not," said Voss. "Miss James left the clinic several hours ago."

Chandler returned to his table, frustration etched in every line on his face. He sat for a while nursing his drink in agonizing uncertainty. If she's not at the clinic, he thought, where is she? A crowd of tourists wandered into the bar boisterously, and Chandler, disturbed by their levity, hurried away without knowing where to go or what to do next.

When he walked into the hotel lobby, the clerk waved him over to the desk.

"Miss James has checked out," said the clerk.

Chandler was incredulous. "What! Did she get my message?"

The clerk seemed embarrassed. "She sent someone to pay her bill and pick up her things. A young man," he said apologetically. "I gave him the note, and he said he would give it to her."

"When does that cable car stop running? The one across to the clinic?"

"The last car is at eleven o'clock," said the clerk. "The next is not until six A.M."

Bewildered, Chandler walked across the lobby and went into the restaurant. He stood by the window gathering his thoughts. On the far side, the restaurant and the château, lights blazing, were both visible in the darkness. The cable car, a spot of light against a mass of blackness, was in transit between the two stations.

"She's still there," he said to himself. "I know she is."

"I know it's not an easy idea to come to grips with," said Dr. Bauer. "But once you accept the concept you will realize the fantastic possibilities in my work."

Shelley sat on the couch in Dr. Bauer's study in front of a blazing fire. She had a brandy glass in her hand and the combination of the drink and the heat of the fire had her feeling feverish. She put her hand to her brow to check her temperature, and Bauer misunderstood her gesture. "Don't worry," he said. "Once you understand our process, your worries will be over. It will be the beginning of a whole new world of experience for you." His eyes never left her face and Shelley was sure that he was testing her.

Bauer sat next to her and placed his hand on her knee. "Imagine, to be able to shed an old and misused body for a new one as easily as you might change overcoats in the spring."

Shelley, afraid of Bauer's eyes, looked into her glass. "But, would it still be me?"

His laugh was cold. "Of course. What is it that makes us what we are?" He tapped a finger to his temple as Shelley looked up. "Memory," he said softly. "What we are is merely an accumulation of recollections: remembered incidents, acquired knowledge, various assortments of gathered data. Our brain collects and stores this information for us, ready to be recalled at any moment. In our process, we simply transfer that information to a newer receptacle."

Shelley allowed her eyes to drift up to the ceiling as if she might see up to the third floor. "What about David?" she asked. "What happens to him?"

Bauer shrugged. "In another three days there will be no more David. Daily treatments will gradually overcome his own residual memory patterns. Right now he is more son than father, but soon that will change permanently."

Shelley struggled to keep her face expressionless. "I don't know," she said doubtfully.

Bauer smiled knowingly. "If you were old and tired and sick, and the new you was young and strong and healthy, you would feel wonderful."

Shelley nodded. "I suppose in that case I would."

"You see," said Bauer triumphantly. "That's what this is all about." He stopped and eyed Shelley admiringly. "Of course, you don't have to worry about all of this for another twenty or thirty years, or even longer, if you prefer."

Shelley looked relieved, and Bauer went on. "During that time you will have the tremendous advantage of knowing that you need not fear growing old. Also, with Mrs. Gresham's help and influence, you will rise to the top of your profession. You will wield incredible influence. Who knows? Later you may be drawn into politics, where you could have an even greater effect on world events." He smiled. "We are not without influence in the political arena."

Shelley's eyes widened. "Who?"

Bauer shook his head as if this were not important. "At present we concentrate on behind-the-scenes persuasion." His voice cracked as he tried to keep it under control. His passion for his subject was obvious and Shelley dared to look up into his eyes, which rolled wildly as he spoke. For the first time she was able to see the madness behind Bauer's normally composed demeanor. "Our numbers are small," he said, "but our power is strong, and growing stronger."

Shelley sipped her brandy. "It seems so incredible. How many of . . ." could she dare say "us" . . . "how many are there?"

"Fewer than twenty-five who have made the conversion. We do no more than two each year, unless, as in the case of Jefferson, there are extenuating circumstances. There are fewer than fifty others who are aware of the process. Some, because it is necessary that they be told in order to protect the children. Others, like Andrew Petersen or yourself, because of the influence they can wield in certain important areas. Obviously we must jealously protect our secret. If it were widely known or even suspected, the whole concept would be ruined. It must of necessity be limited to a small, elite group of special individuals. There are those who would find our transformations totally unacceptable. There are always those who claim that this process should be available to all. And others who would claim that it should not be available to anyone." He shrugged. "For these reasons our secret must be ruthlessly protected." He gave a short, uncomfortable cough. "Until now, we have been able to deal with those few who, through one method or another, found out about us." He watched her carefully. "Even the ones like your friend Chandler who don't really know what it is they have discovered."

Shelley looked sharply in his direction and Bauer gave a brief shrug. "We must be willing to accept a new concept in morality. A morality in which the first principle is the preservation of our secret. Those of us who are chosen to join the most elite society that mankind has ever known must be willing to accept the fact that we cannot be subject to the laws of man . . . or of God."

"You mean you reserve the right to kill anyone you choose?"

Bauer's tone was flat, his face expressionless. "One of the things we must learn is that we are no longer like other people. We must be willing to cast aside former colleagues. We must forget about former loved ones: children, parents, husbands, wives, friends. They will soon be gone and we will remain." His tone was gentle now, persuasive. "We must learn to forge new relationships—lasting relationships—without the restrictions of obsolescent moralities." He placed his hand on her leg just above the knee and gave her a reassuring squeeze. "I've had your things brought to my rooms." He looked into her eyes, his power hypnotic. "I'd like you to stay here with me tonight, in my quarters." He waited expectantly.

Shelley swallowed hard. She knew that Bauer was watching her every gesture. Finally she spoke. "I'd like that, too," she said, forcing a smile.

Bauer smiled back and Shelley struggled to keep her gaze steady. Her only thought was about how to warn Chandler in time to save his life.

*   *   *

Sitting by a window in the hotel bar, Chandler nursed a beer and waited. Each time the cable car made its way back across the ravine, he went outside to watch the passengers disembark. With each fruitless trip, his apprehension grew.

There must be someone I can talk to, he thought. Someone who knows something.

Finally, in near desperation, he went to the desk clerk and asked, "What room is Mrs. Jefferson in?"

Karen Jefferson must have been deliberating on whether to answer the knock on her door, Chandler thought. Finally she called, "Who is it?"

"Mark Chandler," he said.

Mrs. Jefferson opened the door slightly, keeping the chain on. "Who?"

"Mark Chandler."

"What can I do for you, Mr. Chandler?"

"Mrs. Jefferson, I'm a reporter from New York. I wonder if I might speak with you."

"Not now," she snapped, anger flashing in her eyes. "You people are unbelievable."

Chandler spoke quickly as she was about to close the door. "It is vitally important that I speak to you now. I'm not here to write a story about your husband. That's merely a coincidence. I'm investigating an entire series of cases, just like your husband's. Other men have died in exactly the same way that he did."

Karen Jefferson's face went white and her eyes looked left and right as if she were expecting eavesdroppers. "I think you'd better go away right now, Mr. Chandler. What you're talking about could get us both in a lot of trouble."

"Where is your son?"

Tears sprang to Karen Jefferson's eyes. "He is being taken care of," she said, as if repeating something learned by rote. "His father's death came as a terrible shock to him, and he is under medical supervision at this time."

"But where is he?"

"That is none of your business. If you don't go away I'll . . ."

"Is he still over there?"

Karen Jefferson's eyes widened with fear.

Knowing he had struck a vital chord, Chandler went on. "Do you want me to give you the names of the other men who died like your husband?"

She opened the door and pulled Chandler inside. "You don't know what you're doing. You could ruin everything. Mr. Chandler," she said, "I never wanted this. I loved my son. I know I wasn't supposed to grow attached to him— 'Stay distant,' they told us—but I couldn't help it." She sobbed. "Even Lawrence loved the boy. Oh, he tried not to show it, but my husband is a good man, not like some of the others. Not like the people who did this terrible thing. If it hadn't been for Lawrence's illness, he would never have let them do it."

The tears were streaming down her face now as her voice rose in hysteria. The words came in a torrent of expiation and Chandler knew that she was not really talking to him. She was talking to herself to somehow relieve whatever terrible pressure she was under. "These people," she said, waving her arms wildly, "have no heart; they have no soul. They care only about wealth and power. My husband was afraid, so afraid. He didn't want to die. It happened too suddenly. He never would have gone through with it."

Chandler was bewildered by her frenetic monologue and puzzled that she kept referring to her dead husband in the present, and her live son in the past. "He would never have gone through with what, Mrs. Jefferson?"

She buried her face in her hands, her body racked with sobs. "David," she moaned. "Oh, my poor little David."

Chandler looked at her blankly. "David?" he said softly as if testing the word. "Why do you . . ." he began, and then it came to him. From somewhere in a dark recess of his mind where the impossible idea had been shunted each time it had run across his brain, the thought exploded like a starburst. Without knowing it, he had been accumulating evidence to prove the impossible, and now the jigsaw pieces were falling inexorably into place.

It all fit: the dead men, the strange wills, the memory drugs, Harrison's experiments, Dr. Bauer's spa and clinic, and, finally, the children. He knew it now, even though he was reluctant to say it. Every fiber of his being screamed that this was not possible, but he knew, finally, that it was true.

The fathers had become the sons. Man had finally devised a way to cheat death. "Is it true?" he asked.

Her anguished look told him everything he had to know. "But the boy," he sputtered. "David. He is your son. Your own child. What happens to him?"

Karen Jefferson, her hands covering her face, slumped into a chair, sobbing. Chandler stood there helplessly, not knowing what to say. There was nothing he could do for her. Finally, as if in a trance, he backed across the room to the door. He could hear her wrenching sobs follow him as he raced down the hall.

Chapter 46

Shelley sat by the fire in Bauer's study, mesmerized by the flames. She was alone. The flames seemed to dance in cheerful mockery of her predicament. She shook her head in disbelief. These people actually wanted her to join them, to help protect them. The rewards she was promised were enormous, but all Shelley could think of was the contorted face of David Jefferson. They had taken a beautiful child and turned him into something, neither child nor man, that was monstrous.

How could they expect her to be a part of that?

She checked her watch, knowing that Bauer could return at any moment, then got up and stood by the fire as if warming herself. Leaving her brandy glass on the mantel, Shelley moved cautiously to the French doors to the right of the fireplace.

She carefully tested the handle on the French doors that led to an outside terrace. They opened. She closed them quickly and returned to her seat by the fire. Bauer had left her alone, saying that he had a few hours of work to do and promising to return as soon as possible.

Shelley knew that if she were to escape, it had to be done before the cable car stopped running. Otherwise she would be stranded till morning.

They trusted her, or seemed to trust her.

How long would it be before they saw through her ruse of acceptance? Could she keep it up long enough to get away? What if she were again confronted with the specter of David Jefferson? Could she pretend acceptance in the face of that?

She shook her head, trying to clear her mind of the vision of the boy that like an icy chill, invaded her every thought.

She went to the door again. No one was on duty; the courtyard was deserted. From the door it was only a quick dash to the gate, then the downhill run to the cable car and safety. If she could get to the gate unnoticed, they would never catch her.

Taking a deep breath, Shelley opened the door and stepped out onto the terrace. The cold burrowed into her bones, and she shivered as she quietly went down the steps to the courtyard.

She hit the courtyard running, racing for the unattended gate. Thirty yards—no sound of alarm. Twenty yards—no voice raised in protest. Ten yards—I'm going to make it.

Even if the gate is locked, she thought, I can be over it in no time.

It was locked.

Just as she put a hand on the top rung and a foot on the railing, a form stepped out of the shadows.

"Good evening," said the guard, and Shelley stopped frozen in her tracks. "Dr. Bauer thought you might decide to go for a walk tonight." He smiled. "May I escort you back to the house?"

Dr. Bauer was waiting in his study. His face was dark and dangerous, but there was a note of sympathy in his voice. "I'm truly sorry that it has worked out this way for you." He shrugged. "You didn't think we'd accept you so easily, did you?"

Shelley said nothing.

Bauer shook his head sadly. "You could have had everything. You could have replaced Petersen as our media contact. You could have gone to the top just as he did. We eliminated his superior and placed him in his position of influence. We would have done the same for you. Now he too will be replaced. I suppose I should thank you for pointing out what a fool Petersen was."

Shelley looked up. "Was?"

"He was of no more use to us."

Shelley's shoulders slumped.

"Take her to the cellar room. I'm afraid we can no longer trust our guest," Bauer said.

As the guard led Shelley away, Bauer called to her from his chair by the fire. "Don't worry. You and I will still have our little rendezvous later. I wouldn't miss that for the world."

At eleven o'clock the last cable car was due back from the restaurant. Chandler, dressed in his warmest clothing against the evening's biting chill, stamped his feet in mindless rhythm as he waited outside near the lower station for the car's arrival.

Finally the machinery revved up and the cable began to move. Soon the car would be here and perhaps Shelley would be on board. If she were not, he was uncertain as to what he would, or could, do. He watched his breath, like cigar smoke, swirl around him in the blustery winds that whipped across the ravine.

As the car approached, he counted heads. There were very few passengers, only the last group of the crew from the restaurant. Even before the car docked he was sure that Shelley would not be on board. He looked carefully at the faces as the car approached. She was not there.

He waited as the passengers filed off the cable car, half hoping that Shelley would appear from some hidden corner and laugh at his worried expression.

She did not appear.

The last man off the car was talking to one of the young women who worked in the restaurant. She seemed to be trying to persuade him to stay. He kept shaking his head, sadly but firmly. It was obvious that he wanted to stay but was duty bound to return with the cable car.

Chandler watched the two talking quietly on the platform. After a minute or two the woman tugged at the man's sleeve, and they disappeared around the corner of the hotel for what Chandler was sure would be a lingering good-bye.

Chandler stepped forward to look inside the cabin. There was no place where he could conceal himself on board. His eyes ran the length of the car, then up to the roof where the car was suspended from the cable by an inverted Y-shaped series of metal braces. This suspension arm, attached to the middle third of the roof of the cable car, was painted a bright yellow in contrast to the deep red of the car itself.

Attached to the side of the car was a narrow maintenance ladder, and Chandler, without a moment's hesitation, clambered up the ladder and spread-eagled himself across the icy roof. The car rocked gently with his weight: he secured a strong grip with both gloved hands on the support superstructure and pressed his feet firmly against a metal ridge that ran around the outside of the roof.

He lay there facedown for a few moments, trying not to think about what he had done and trying to reassure himself that his handhold was adequate to maintain his weight for the journey.

"Just hang on tight," he whispered to himself. "Nothing to it. Just hang on tight."

He felt the car sway slightly as the man stepped on board. Then the door was slammed closed and the handle lock clicked into position. At some silent signal from the man inside, the car moved slightly forward, then swung out, clearing the platform of the lower station.

Chandler felt the bottom drop out of his stomach as the car cleared the rock face and swung out over the ravine. He buried his face in the snow on top of the car, his eyes squeezed desperately shut. His hands were clamped vicelike around the steel support, but his feet kept slipping from the metal ridge. He could feel the cold of the metal through his gloves and wished now that he had down mittens instead of the woolen gloves he'd worn.

Every swing and sway of the cable car seemed exaggerated one thousandfold. If he had thought that the ride from the inside would be gut wrenching, from the outside it was absolutely terrifying. The car swayed from side to side in long pendulum sweeps across the night sky, and Chandler found himself sliding back and forth across the ice-coated roof.

As soon as the car left the protective shield of the mountain and was traversing the open ravine, the wind hurtled at him, screaming in his ear, damning him for his foolishness, buffeting his body with frigid blasts. Chandler tried to protect himself by burying his face in his arms, but wherever he hid, the wind found him. The icy blasts penetrated his body with frozen fingers, and it was as if he were naked.

The steel support was too thick for him to wrap his hands around. His grip was mostly in the fingers—and his gloved fingers were already numb from the contact with the frozen metal. He knew now that he could not possibly maintain his grip for the entire trip. With each sway of the car he was less and less secure.

In a few minutes he had lost feeling in his hands. As he slid across the roof with the swaying of the car, he knew that he had to do something soon or he'd go off the edge. Timing his move to the rhythm of the car, he released his left hand and, sliding himself forward until his shoulder touched the suspension arm, wrapped his left arm around the supports. Then, again carefully timing the sway, he released his right hand and with it grasped his left wrist. Now, at least, his fingers were relieved of the terrible numbing chill of the metal.

He clung there, arms wrapped tightly around the suspension bracket, feet struggling to maintain a foothold, as the car swayed its way across the crevasse. For one brief terrifying moment he chanced a glance to see how close he was to the other side, but as he lifted his head the wind caught the car; the nose dropped precipitously, and Chandler found himself staring down into the ravine below.

The cable car seemed to stop and start, jump and jolt like a balky horse racing across the sky. There was little pattern to the motions. For a few seconds the car would move slowly and steadily upward to the upper station and then, buffeted by a sudden blast of wind, it would swing crazily in any direction. Then just as suddenly it would be steady again.

The strain on his left arm was incredible, and he realized that he was holding on too tightly, but his right hand, apparently with a will of its own, refused to relinquish its death grip. Pain, traveling like an electric shock, raced up his left arm and down his left side. Under his rib cage, he was beginning to cramp.

Shifting his weight to relieve the pressure, he ventured another peek across the ravine. The rock face of the other side seemed immeasurably far away and all sense of time and distance was distorted. He seemed farther from the upper station now than when he'd begun this nightmarish journey.

The cramp in his left side was now unbearable, and he had lost all feeling in his arms and hands. The icy wind, as if it were alive and mischievous, darted in and out in mad attempts to loosen his grip.

Just as he had begun to accept the fact that he was not

going to make it and to wonder what the long fall into oblivion would be like, the howling wind diminished and the wild swinging lessened. He looked up and miraculously the upper station loomed ahead. Soon the car slowed and then jerked itself to a halt, rocking gently front to back as it sat at the upper station.

With disbelieving eyes, Chandler looked up. The car had indeed reached the other side, and he was still in one piece. Frozen, but in one piece. He waited while the man below left the car and slammed the door shut. Keeping his head down, Chandler watched the operator leave the small building at the station and the two men begin the short trip up the path to the château.

After lying exhausted for a few minutes, Chandler scrambled to the edge of the car and tumbled off onto the platform.

He pulled himself up and lumbered up the path, walking carefully. Slowly, he approached the gate; it seemed unguarded. After a momentary pause to look around the courtyard, he gave the gate a small, tentative push, and it swung quietly open. Obviously, after eleven o'clock the doctor felt that his château was secure enough from unwelcome visitors.

Chandler made his way through the shadows along the wall until he was well past the front entrance. He crouched down low, his back against the wall, and listened for any sound that would indicate if his presence had been detected.

In the wing to the right of the front door every light seemed on. Selecting the narrowest distance between the outer wall and the château itself, Chandler sprinted across the courtyard and hid among the shrubbery surrounding the building.

He went to the nearest window and lifted himself up to look inside. It was the dining room and it was empty. He moved to the next window. He could hear the low murmur of voices from within, and when he cautiously raised himself to peer inside, he saw Dr. Bauer and another man sitting by the fire engaged in earnest conversation.

Chandler was now at the back of the château, and the next room was dark. He turned a corner and moved to the next window. As he did, he heard voices and saw lights coming in his direction from around the building.

Chandler crouched low and dashed back across the courtyard. He pressed himself against the outer wall and listened carefully for the sound of movement. He heard nothing. For a split second, he allowed himself to think that perhaps the voices and the lights had not been after him, and he had panicked for nothing. That hope was dashed when he heard a voice say, "Don't move. Put your hands over your head and stay right there."

A lantern flicked on and caught him in its glare, and Chandler slumped back against the wall, his hands on his head. Squinting, he could make out the silhouetted shapes of three men. At least one of them was armed with a rifle.

One stepped forward into the circle of light, aiming a handgun directly at Chandler's midsection. He was short and powerfully built. "You will follow me," he said in a foreign but unidentifiable accent. "There will be two men behind you, and I do not want you to doubt that they will shoot you if you attempt to run."

Chandler nodded wearily, his hands falling to his sides, and the man slapped him viciously across the face. "You will keep your hands on your head until told to do otherwise."

Standing at the open front door of the château, Dr. Bauer waited as the small column arrived. They stopped in front of him, Chandler defiantly dropping his hands to his sides. The man who had slapped him stepped toward him again and Chandler balled his fists, prepared to defend himself this time.

Bauer interrupted the impending confrontation. "Just a moment, Franz," he said to the advancing man, "it's all right now. We want our friend Mr. Chandler to be comfortable." He eyed the intruder from head to toe. "It is Chandler, isn't it?" he asked, and when Chandler shrugged noncommittally, Bauer smiled. "I thought so," he said. "I suppose we've been expecting you."

Chandler stuffed his hands into the pockets of his jacket. He said nothing.

Bauer shrugged. "Take him to my study and let him warm himself in front of the fire." He pointed to the two who had followed Chandler up the hill. "One of you stand guard outside the door, the other outside the window." He turned to Chandler, smiling. "I want you to see how well armed they are. They will shoot you if you attempt to flee. You are trespassing on private property."

"Why don't we just call the police and have them pick me up?" said Chandler.

The smile slipped from Bauer's face. "Take him inside. I will follow in a moment."

Chandler was led into the château and down the hall to Bauer's private wing. The man called Franz opened the door and pushed him inside. Chandler went to the fire, opening his jacket to get the full benefit of the heat of the flames.

"I've really done it now," he told himself as he warmed his frozen hands at the fire. His mind raced through the gamut of escape possibilities, but other than a simple dive through the window and a run past a man with a rifle, he could think of nothing. Even if he could run, even if he made it past the rifle, where would he go? Until 6:00 A.M. there was no way off the damn mountain. Somehow he had to find Shelley and get them both away from this place.

His only chance was to stall for time. Stay alive until morning, he told himself, then maybe . . . maybe what?

He'd have to cross the bridge when—and if—he came to it.

The door opened and a smiling Bauer entered the study. "Perhaps you'd care for a drink, Mr. Chandler," he said pleasantly, as if this were a social engagement. Without waiting for an answer he poured two glasses of brandy at a small desk top bar and then came to the fireplace and gave one to Chandler. "You can sit down if you like," he said, indicating one of several chairs around the fireplace.

Chandler went to a chair and sat, and Bauer selected a chair directly across from him where the two could face each other.

They stared at each other for a moment before Bauer spoke. "Why don't you tell me why you are here?" he asked.

Chandler made a face. "You know why I'm here."

"No, tell me."

"For Shelley. I came for her."

Bauer seemed surprised. "Miss James has decided to remain with us for a while."

"I don't believe that."

Bauer shrugged. "It's true."

"Why don't you let her tell me that to my face. If she does, then I'll leave quietly—no questions asked."

Bauer laughed. "I'm afraid your leaving us is not quite so simple as all that."

Chandler decided to play the innocent. "Why not? I don't know—or care—about anything that goes on here. My interest is merely with the girl."

A small flicker of doubt spread across Bauer's face; then

he smiled. "Come, come, Mr. Chandler. You don't give yourself nearly enough credit. I'm afraid you know too much about us."

Chandler said nothing.

"You probably think that I am a cruel and heartless creature; but actually I am not without compassion."

"Tell that to the people you've killed," said Chandler. "Tell it to the children you've destroyed."

Bauer smiled, displaying rows of impeccably uniform teeth. "See. You do know a great deal about us." He sighed as if what he was about to say made him indescribably sad. "We can't be like other people," he said. "We have so much more to protect than ordinary people. I find no great joy in the elimination of others, but sometimes it is a necessity—just as the slaughter of livestock to provide food is a necessity."

"A marvelous analogy," said Chandler. "You think of people as livestock."

Bauer shrugged. "An unfortunate choice of words perhaps, but nevertheless true." His tone grew serious. "You would understand better if you knew what it is like to be able to extend one's lifespan for an indefinite period." He sipped his drink. "Surely someone who is in the precarious position that you are now must appreciate what it is like to be allowed to defeat death." His eyes grew fiery and his voice trembled as he spoke. "To be able to stand up and say what men have dreamed of saying: I will not die!" He took a deep relaxing breath and turned his gaze on Chandler. He spoke softly. "How would that make you feel?"

"Like a monster. Like a vampire. Like someone who lives by sacrificing the flesh and blood of innocent children."

Bauer shook his head sadly. "I didn't expect you to understand." He made a motion as if to rise, and Chandler, fearing that his moment of respite might be over, blurted a question.

"I would like to know how you do it."

"I'm afraid you wouldn't understand that either."

"How about a simple explanation in layman's terms?"

Bauer sat back in his seat, and Chandler knew that he had judged him correctly—the doctor enjoyed explaining his discovery. "In simple terms, we transfer memory from one person to another."

"I gather that, but how?"

His impatience showing, Bauer said, "By a process known and understood only to me."

"That makes you pretty much indispensible around here, doesn't it? Without you the whole crowd is nothing."

Bauer nodded matter-of-factly. "Quite true."

"It's just the idea of being able to transfer someone's memory that seems so incredible. It doesn't seem possible."

Bauer leaned forward, staring intently into Chandler's face. "The brain, you see, is a vast repository of images stored in cellular fluid. Recall takes place when we are able to stimulate, through electrical activity, certain of these images which then travel across this fluid, like fish swimming through water, to a point in the brain where we can bring them to the surface of our consciousness. Every single fact or image that we have ever seen or heard is stored in various parts of our brain. Think of your memory as a chamber where fluid drips into a receptacle. All of the important memories are contained in a central chamber ready for instant recall, things like who are you, names of friends and family, and other important data. Others might be spread around in smaller deposits, things like memories of people you have met only once or knowledge that you rarely use. I can transfer nearly all of the important memories and, by the use of an enhancer, many of the unimportant ones. It remains merely to find the key to gathering all of that data into what I call the transference point, where the fluid, which is virtually teeming with information, can be collected. Then it is removed from the donor and over a period of several days transferred to the host. Is that simple enough?"

Chandler nodded. "But why children? Why not adults?"

"Because adults have too large a reservoir of collected information," he shrugged. "Their memories are too great. Children, particularly around five years of age, are fertile ground for transplantation. Their own limited memories can easily be invaded and supplanted by the new information. Otherwise a battle ensues between conflicting memory patterns. The usual result is schizophrenia. Many of the test cases during the war resulted in such severe mental disturbance that it was obviously impractical to continue." Bauer grinned wickedly, and his eyes sparkled. "We are still working on completely eradicating memory in the brain of an older host. It would simplify matters if we could transfer to an adult."

Chandler shook his head admiringly to demonstrate to Bauer how impressed he was by this technique. "But how can the donor be sure that this process works? He's taking quite a risk."

Bauer stood up and drained his glass. He smiled triumphantly, and Chandler felt the full malevolence of that smile. "I," he said, "am living proof of my own research."

"You?"

He laughed. "Yes. No doubt you followed the trail of Dr. Harrison and his colleague Dr. Stokes?" Chandler nodded, stupefied. "You need search no more, Mr. Chandler. Although there were many failures in the camps where I conducted my experiments, there were a few successes. When it became obvious that the war was lost and that I would be regarded as a war criminal, I selected a perfect host for myself. I took him and his family to Switzerland. They never knew why. I am Dr. Stokes. I was born in England in 1897. I made my transfer in 1946." He chuckled at Chandler's openmouthed stare.

Chandler sensed that the lecture was coming to a close. Desperately he tried to stall. "What about the wives? I don't understand about them."

"They are very carefully selected. Most of them are women who were very beautiful in their prime, movie starlets, models, beauty queens. None of them, however, was ever very successful in her chosen field. This combination of failure and fading beauty makes them ideal. They are desperate for another chance at youth and beauty. They will sell their souls for another opportunity."

"When are they transferred?"

Bauer laughed. "When they have outlived their usefulness, they are discarded." He stood up. "And now, Mr. Chandler, I think it's time that you retired for the evening. I have an exquisite creature—whom I think you know—waiting anxiously for me."

"Do I get to see Shelley?"

Bauer smiled. "For a brief moment. You will take her place in our cellar storeroom. She will be brought to my bedroom." He smiled obscenely. "She *is* an exquisite creature, isn't she?"

"And what happens to me?"

"You're very lucky. We've just had one death on the slopes, and I don't want to draw undue attention to the clinic or the hotel. I told you that our experiments continue and that we are trying to completely obliterate the memory of an adult host. You will be privileged to be a part of that experiment. Sometime tomorrow you will be found after an unfortunate head injury, perhaps a climbing accident. Physically you will be fine, but, I'm afraid, much of your memory will be gone."

"A vegetable?" asked Chandler.

"I wouldn't go that far. You will probably be able to be retrained for simple tasks. Intellectual capacity will unfortunately be greatly reduced."

Bauer stood and pressed a button on the mantel. Instantly the door opened. "I think you have already met my personal bodyguard," he said, indicating the man in the doorway.

For the first time Chandler took a close look at the man who had captured him. Franz was in his late thirties and obviously a devotee of body building. In spite of the cool temperatures in the château he wore a tight-fitting short sleeve shirt to better display his bulging biceps, and the top three buttons of the shirt were left open, revealing his massive, hairless chest. His hair was cropped so short that it was difficult to tell what color it might have been. The man was short and bull-necked and gave the impression of tremendous power under minimal restraint. He saw Chandler inspecting him and his muscles flexed in response.

"Franz," said Bauer, "take our friend here to his temporary quarters and post a guard outside his door for the night."

Franz motioned with the pistol, and Chandler moved toward the door.

"Mr. Chandler," called Dr. Bauer. Chandler turned slowly. "Have a pleasant evening," said the doctor, smiling cruelly. "I will see you in surgery in the morning."

"And Franz," said Bauer as they crossed the threshold, "tell the guard to check on him frequently. I don't want him to harm himself. There's been enough killing lately." He smiled. "And bring the girl to my quarters."

Franz smiled a thin-lipped smile and marched Chandler down the hall to the stairs leading to the cellar.

Chapter 47

While one of Bauer's men held a gun on Chandler, Franz took a key from his pocket and opened the door to the cellar storeroom. He stepped inside and a moment later emerged with Shelley.

Her eyes popped open when she saw Chandler. "Oh God," she said, tears springing to her eyes. "You followed me."

Chandler nodded. "I missed you."

Shelley broke away from Franz and threw herself into Chandler's arms. They kissed. Chandler wanted never to let go.

"How the hell did you get here?" she asked.

"I came over on the last cable car," he responded matter-of-factly.

"But how?" she said, looking up at him. "They always send a guard over."

"I rode on top. You should try it sometime."

"I don't believe it," she said. He merely shrugged as if such things were commonplace. "Now I know you're crazy," she said. "You could have killed yourself."

"I was sure that you were still here," he said as explanation. "I knew you wouldn't just run off."

"You know about the children?"

"Yes. Then you know too?"

Shelley nodded. "What now?" she said.

"I'm going to get you out of here."

"How?"

Franz pulled Shelley away from Chandler. They held hands till the last possible minute.

"I'm going to get us out of this," called Chandler as the other man led Shelley down the hallway to the stairs.

Franz laughed derisively at Chandler's remark and pointed toward the open door. "Inside," he said.

The basement room was small, windowless, and dimly illuminated by a single bulb hanging from the low ceiling. Against one wall was a cot, but other than that, the room was bare.

"Do you have anything with a better view?" quipped Chandler.

Franz sneered at his attempt at humor. "Tomorrow you won't be worrying about the view," he said, pushing Chandler into the room.

Chandler whirled to face him, and Franz drove a massive fist into his midsection, exploding the air from his lungs. Gasping for air, Chandler crumpled in a heap on the cold, stone floor, and Franz, a contemptuous scowl curling his lips, stood over him, daring him to rise.

Clutching his stomach, Chandler stayed where he was.

Franz, flexed his biceps once to punctuate his performance, then turned and left. When the door closed Chandler crawled to the cot, hauled himself up to a sitting position, and made a quick survey of his situation.

The walls were thick masonry and afforded no obvious avenue of escape; the door was the only exit. A series of pipes, which brought heat to various parts of the château, ran across the ceiling, providing the room's only source of warmth.

Chandler struggled to his feet, still gasping for breath, and paced off the dimensions of the room, five paces one way, four paces the other. The door was of heavy wood construction and obviously a formidable obstacle. Nothing short of a battering ram could break it down. The hinges and doorknob, both of ornate design, were heavy brass and massive in size. In the upper half of the door was a smaller, hinged opening, through which the room could be observed without opening the door itself.

Chandler went quietly to the door and carefully turned the knob. As expected, the door was locked from the outside. His action brought an immediate response from the other side. The small door opened, and a gravely voice commanded, "Get back from the door." A face, so ugly that it might have been a Halloween mask, appeared at the door. The man held up a pistol to the opening so that Chandler might see that he was armed. "If you're thinking of trying anything," he said, "don't."

Without another word the small door was slammed shut, and Chandler was left to consider what other avenues of escape remained.

His mind raced through the gamut of possibilities. How could he escape from a locked, empty room, with an armed guard in the corridor outside? In the movies, he thought, the hero would fake a terrible pain of some kind, and when his jailer entered to investigate, the hero would overpower him. Unfortunately, everybody had seen those movies. After seeing what was on the other side of the door, Chandler decided that even if the man were simple enough to fall for such a ploy, there was absolutely no way that he could overpower such a monster. He would probably wind up missing a few teeth and no closer to the answer to his problem.

He looked up, almost in prayer, and noticed the pipes running across the length of the room. Maybe if he could break one of the pipes and flood the room. What then? Other than drowning or scalding himself, that didn't seem to hold many possibilities.

Then he examined the light fixture hanging from the ceiling. The fixture was an obvious afterthought; the nonmetallic, sheathed cable, a fabric-covered wire, was exposed across the ceiling and ran down the wall to the switch, which was situated at shoulder height next to the door. The wiring was attached to the ceiling by heavy U-shaped nails every two or three feet.

Chandler went to the wall switch—one of those old-fashioned round switches which had to be rotated rather than flipped up or down—and turned off the light. In almost total darkness he groped his way back to the center of the room, his hands over his head, until he brushed against the light bulb dangling from the ceiling.

Taking a firm, two-handed grip on the cable, he pulled down with a steady pressure until the first heavy nail popped loose from the ceiling. He moved a few steps closer to the door, repeated the process, and pulled down the next length of wire. In a few minutes he had pulled down the entire length of wire from the ceiling and stood next to the door. He listened intently to determine if his maneuver had attracted the attention of Mr. Ugly, but all seemed quiet on the other side.

Carefully he reeled in the cord until he was holding the light fixture in his hands, and then taking a firm grip on the cable in one hand and the socket in the other, he pulled them steadily apart until the cord separated from the fixture. Feeling tentatively, he was grateful to find that the line was indeed dead. He carefully placed the socket and light bulb on the floor out of his way. Using his teeth he stripped a few inches of the insulation from each of the two wires which protruded from the sheathing. He then wrapped both exposed ends around the doorknob, twisting them until they were held securely in place.

Working quickly, he fumbled his way to the cot and stripped the blanket and single sheet from the thin lumpy mattress. He twisted the sheet until it was ropelike, removed his jacket, and tied one end of the sheet around his chest just below his armpits. He secured the knot and then slipped it around behind him so that the knotted end was at his back. Holding the sheet so that it stayed above his neck, he put his jacket back on.

He stood on the cot, looped the sheet over one of the overhead pipes, and hoisted himself an inch or two above the cot. He brought his hands to his chest, prepared to accept his full weight, then gave a loud yell and kicked over the cot.

He dangled from the pipe, thrashing his legs in mimicry of agonized throes and almost immediately the small door opened, and the ugly face peered into the darkened room. With barely enough light from the small opening to see what was happening, all that the guard could discern was a thrashing shape, hanging from the ceiling.

"What the hell," he said, fumbling for the key to the door.

The door opened halfway, the man silhouetted in the doorway. Filled with suspicion, he watched for a moment as Chandler continued to thrash wildly. Right hand on the doorknob the man reached with his left for the light switch as he prepared to enter the room.

Instantly he was transformed. He stood straight up, limbs jerking spasmodically, his right hand now anchored to the electrified doorknob.

Knowing that it might be only a split second before the circuit breakers or a fuse cut off the power to the wire, Chandler dropped to the floor and raced to the door. He slammed his full weight against it, crushing the guard between the door and the frame.

Every light in the château went out.

Chandler opened the door, fist clenched, prepared to battle his way out of the corridor, but his guard lay in a heap on the floor. In the almost total darkness, Chandler ran his hands over the man's body, found the pistol tucked in his belt, and groped his way along the wall till he came to the stairs.

At the top of the stairs he opened the basement door. The hallway was in darkness. Voices called out in confusion. "What happened? Who knows where the fusebox is? Are there any candles?"

Chandler went past the entry hall and made his way toward Bauer's private wing. Moonlight was sufficient for him to pick out the door to Bauer's bedroom and he quietly tried the doorknob. The door was locked.

Backing up to the opposite wall, Chandler hesitated a second, then, his pent-up rage propelling him forward, he hurtled himself at the door and smashed it open.

A startled Anton Bauer jerked away from the small group of candles he had just lit. His eyes widened in shock and amazement when he saw Chandler in the shattered doorway pointing a gun at his chest.

His mouth fell open. "You," he said.

"Yeah, me," said Chandler, feeling more satisfied than he ever had in his life. "One move and I'll splatter your memories all over the back wall."

Bauer's mouth twitched, his eyes revealing genuine terror. "Please," he said. "Don't shoot."

Shelley watched them from the bed, holding a sheet up to cover herself.

"Get dressed," said Chandler. "We're leaving."

"I'm not leaving without David," said Shelley. "He's on the third floor." When Chandler hesitated she pleaded, "We can still save him."

"OK," said Chandler. "We'll get him on the way out."

"I'll get him now," she said, pulling back the covers and stepping, naked, onto the floor.

As Shelley slipped out from under the covers, Chandler heard footsteps racing down the hall. He quickly went to Bauer and stood beside him as Franz and another man entered the room. Both were armed with pistols.

"Tell them to drop their weapons," Chandler told Bauer.

"You can't escape from here," Bauer snarled.

"You better hope I do, because the last thing I'll do if I have to stay is blow your brains out."

"Drop your weapons," Bauer told the two men in the doorway.

Franz hesitated for a second, and Bauer shrieked, "Do it!"

Shelley pulled her sweater over her head and turned to face everyone. "You ready?" asked Chandler. She nodded and he said, "Then pick up one of those pistols and let's go."

Obediently, Shelley picked up the smaller of the two weapons, and held it loosely at her side.

"Don't be an idiot," said Bauer. "What can this fool give you? Nothing!" He was almost screaming now, his face alive with fear. "I can give you everything you've ever wanted."

Shelley looked at the gun as if she were in a hypnotic trance.

"Do you know where the boy is?" asked Chandler.

Shelley snapped from her stupor, nodded and looked up at him. "I'll get him," she said. "You go on ahead. I'll catch up."

"I'm not going anywhere without you," he said. "Just make it fast." He waved the pistol at the men near the door, and they stepped aside to let Shelley pass.

"I'll meet you at the front door," she said as she moved past the men at the door and out into the corridor.

He could hear the sound of her running footsteps as she disappeared down the hall.

"Let's go, Bauer," said Chandler, pushing the doctor forward. "You can tell us all about it on the way over on the cable car."

"You'll never get out of here," said Bauer, panic cracking his voice as he spoke. "My people will never allow it."

"Let's keep them busy then," said Chandler. He picked up one of the burning candles and held it to the curtain. In a second a wall of flame raced up to the ceiling. Chandler tossed the still-burning candle onto the bed, where a small brown circle began to grow around the flame.

"Let's go," he said, grabbing Bauer by the back of the shirt collar.

Franz and the other man moved to step aside and let them pass, but Chandler aimed the pistol at them. "Both of you lead the way. We'll need someone to operate the cable, and I'm not about to leave my friend Franz behind. I think I'd rather know where you are all the time, Franz."

They marched down the hallway to the front door, Chandler keeping the pistol low, but in the confusion, no one seemed to be aware that they were leaving.

At the foot of the stairs he waited, the gun trained on the three men in front of him. The seconds dragged on as confused voices drifted down from the upper floors and Chandler expected the lights to come on at any moment.

Finally, Shelley appeared on the stairs carrying the boy who was wrapped in a blanket. "I couldn't wake him," she said.

Chandler's eyes narrowed. "Are you sure he's—" he began.

"Yes," she said angrily, "he's still alive. Let's go."

"I'll carry him," said Chandler, but when he moved toward her, Shelley backed away. "I've got him," she said defiantly, holding David close to her. She glared at Chandler for a moment, then her eyes softened. "I can manage," she said quietly.

Outside, Chandler walked behind the men, with Shelley bringing up the rear. He held the pistol aimed at Bauer's spine, occasionally prodding him with it to let him know it was there. "Tell your friends," he said, "if they try anything tricky you'll be in the market for a new brain transplant."

"Don't worry," said Bauer nervously. "No will do anything foolish." He seemed terrified. "Be careful with that weapon, please. If anything happens to me the consequences are enormous."

"Just keep walking and tell your friends to do the same and nothing is going to happen to anyone."

They reached the cable car station, Chandler taking a quick look back to make sure that no one had followed them. Huge flames billowed from the ground floor of the château, and voices could be heard yelling in the distance. Already the fire had spread to the other rooms and was rapidly racing out of control.

"Fire department is gonna need a long hose for that baby," said Chandler.

"My God," said Bauer his face illuminated by the flames. "You don't realize what you've done. The work of a lifetime— destroyed!"

His eyes grew fierce and for a moment Chandler thought

that he might charge, but his eyes rested on the pistol in Chandler's hand, and he turned away from the sight of the flames.

"Franz, start her up," said Chandler, but Franz merely shrugged as if he could no longer understand English. Chandler turned to Bauer. "I'm losing patience with your muscular friend here. If I start shooting this thing, you're first. He's second."

"Franz, please," pleaded Bauer. "You must cooperate."

"But if he gets away . . ." began Franz.

"Just do it!" commanded Bauer. "The man is insane. Do you think a rational person could do what he has done?"

Chandler smiled. He was feeling good now. "Now you're getting the picture." He turned to look at Shelley. "You still have that gun?" he asked her.

Shelley nodded quickly.

"You know where the safety is?" he asked.

She shook her head as if in a daze.

"Give it to me," said Chandler. "You take this one." They exchanged weapons. "Now you're all set to shoot if you have to."

Bauer looked at her, his eyes glowing fiercely in the reflected flames from the blazing château.

"OK, Franz. Start her up and let's get going."

Reluctantly, Franz moved to the door of the small building which housed the winch mechanism for the cable. He opened the door, and Chandler moved closer to keep him in view. In a moment the motor sprang to life.

"Come out here," said Chandler, and when Franz stepped outside, Chandler peered into the small control room. The mechanism seemed simple enough: two long levers, both with caliper brakes at the top.

Chandler turned to the third man. "You speak English?"

The man looked to Bauer for instructions, and Chandler raised the pistol, aiming it at the man's chest. "Yes," he said quickly.

"You'll operate the controls. The rest of us are going over." He looked over at the hotel. Every light was on, and bells were ringing in the village.

"Looks like everyone is coming to the party, Bauer."

Bauer gave him a look of unmitigated hatred. "You'll pay or this," he said.

"Let's get on board," said Chandler, and Franz opened

the rear door of the cable car and stepped on. "All the way to the front, Franz. I want you as far away from me as you can get." He pushed Bauer forward. "If your man at the controls stops us halfway across, I'll shoot Franz and dump you over the side."

Bauer looked into Chandler's eyes and knew that he meant what he said. "All the way across, Klaus. No mistakes."

They stepped aboard, Bauer working his way down toward the front of the car near Franz, where he huddled as if for protection. Shelley came on board last and Chandler slammed the door shut. Chandler held onto the handrail and waved to the man in the control hut.

The man called Klaus engaged the gear lever all the way forward, released the handbrake, and the car vaulted forward precipitously. Inexpertly handled from the controls, the car swung wildly front to back, and Chandler had to help steady Shelley as she struggled with the weight of the child.

"Put him down on the floor," said Chandler. "It'll be safer."

Reluctantly, Shelley agreed and lowered the boy to the cabin floor where she tucked the blanket around him to keep him warm.

Franz stood in the front of the car, rock still, immobile, only one hand on a support pole. Everyone else was swaying back and forth, and he was rooted to the floor. He glared at Chandler, his hatred obvious, the biceps in the one arm he used to hold on, rippling in anticipation of his move.

"There is still time," said Bauer, and Chandler realized that he was talking to Shelley. "You have a pistol. Use it. You'd be a fool to give up what we can do for you." His eyes were wild. "Those things I promised you—they can all be yours. Wealth, power, youth. It can all be yours . . . forever."

Shelley looked at the gun in her hand as if it were some alien creature. She looked up at Bauer. "I despise you," she said.

"Don't be a fool," snapped Bauer. "Do it! We can dump him over the side, and no one need ever know anything about it."

Shelley aimed the gun at Bauer and was about to say something to silence him when a sudden gust of wind pushed the car's nose down. Chandler staggered, and Franz, using the pole to launch himself feet first, landed a vicious blow across Chandler's chest.

Chandler lost his grip and went tumbling to the front of the car, landing at Bauer's feet; Bauer lashed out savage kicks at Chandler's head and upper body.

The weapon landed on the floor and went sliding to the rear as the car swung back in the other direction. Chandler rolled away from Bauer's flailing feet as Franz dove for the gun on the floor. Franz rolled over and came up triumphantly, the pistol in his hand.

Both hands on the handle, Shelley started to raise her gun, but before she could aim at anything Bauer grabbed her by the wrist. "Give me that, you stupid bitch," he screamed and tried to wrench the pistol from her grasp.

Chandler, at the front end of the car now pulled himself erect, balancing himself against the swinging of the car but in a low crouch at the other end, Franz grinned savagely as he tried to aim the barrel down at Chandler's chest.

The car pitched to the side and Bauer momentarily lost his balance. Shelley gave him a shove, and the doctor stumbled backward between Chandler and Franz, who spun around to aim the gun at Shelley. Her finger twitched on the trigger, and the thunderous noise of the pistol filled the cabin.

Franz, more surprised than hurt, clutched at his stomach with his free hand, then began to raise the pistol again as Shelley, mesmerized by her deed, stood motionless.

Chandler sprang forward, driving a shoulder into Bauer and pushing him toward the rear of the car. Franz had started to straighten up when Bauer smashed into him, both of them slamming into the heavy metal rear door, flinging it open. The wind hurtled into the car and in an instant Franz was gone.

Bauer threw out his arms in desperation and managed to grab a handhold at the top of the open door. He screamed in terror as the door swung wide, carrying him farther away from the opening and the safety of the cabin.

For a moment, seemingly defying gravity, the door stood open at a ninety-degree angle to the car. Bauer's feet thrashed wildly as he fought to hold on and bring the door back. But the heavy door swung farther away, gaining momentum as it moved, and slammed into the rear of the car.

Bauer screamed as his fingers were crushed between the two metals. Horrified, Shelley and Chandler watched as Bauer's battered fingers released their desperate hold.

In a split second he was gone, his face sliding down the

glass, his long scream echoing down the ravine and across to the blazing château on the other side until it was lost in the howling wind.

Chandler and Shelley slumped to the floor in the front of the car. Shelley pulled David to her and held him in her arms as Chandler put his arm around her shoulders. They held each other, neither saying anything, both content to know that the other was there.

Shelley took a long, deep breath that was almost a sigh. "What happens now? What happens to them?"

"With Bauer gone it's over. There will be no more transfers."

"What about the children? Those already transferred?"

"I don't know. They'll have to be found. Then the police or the government will have to decide what to do with them. Maybe putting them away for the rest of their lives would be appropriate. I don't know."

"I love you," said Shelley, and they held each other tight until the car docked at the lower station and someone opened the front door.

"Can I carry him now?" Chandler asked, taking the blanket-wrapped boy from her arms.

"Be careful with him," said Shelley, touching David's face and securing the blanket around him.

Chandler helped Shelley to her feet, and they walked out to a throng of mystified observers from the hotel and the village.

"What's going on over there?" a voice yelled.

"Did somebody fall from the car?" screamed another.

Chandler ignored the questions. "Are the police here yet?" he said to no one in particular.

"They're on their way," replied a chorus of voices from the crowd.

"We'll be inside," said Chandler. "We'll need a doctor for the boy," he said as they moved through the crowd.

They walked to the steps of the hotel, and halfway to the door Chandler stopped and looked back. In the distance the château blazed, and Chandler watched for a moment, fascinated by the flames which now engulfed the entire lower floor and were visible flickering through the second-story windows. The wind fed the flames, causing them to dance and leap from window to window as if the fire itself were anxious to escape the place.

Shelley tugged at him. "Come inside," she said. "I don't want to see anymore."

Together they went up the steps and into the hotel.

Epilogue

It was two weeks later when Mark Chandler sat on a park bench across from the Heckcher Playground in Central Park. The sky was a pallid gray, and the air was crisply cold. Leafless trees, their branches dark scratches across the gray background, ringed the concrete playground like naked sentinels.

There would have been no color if it had not been for the children.

Hands deep in his coat pockets, Chandler watched the children at play. In their multicolored parkas, they ran and jumped and climbed and swung and laughed. Their color was everywhere.

Their mothers, some with still-younger children in baby carriages, sat together on the other benches that dotted the perimeter of the playground. Occasionally a voice would ring out and a child at the top of the monkey bars would look over and reluctantly begin his descent.

Chandler checked his watch. As usual, Shelley was late.

Inevitably, watching the children made Chandler think about his daughter. She would be here in about three weeks to spend the holidays with him, and he couldn't wait to see her. Couldn't wait to have Shelley meet her.

From behind him Chandler could hear the music from the Central Park carousel which lay just beyond the playground. The music, in contrast to the day, was bright and cheerful and floated across the park, bringing memories of other days. Without knowing that he was doing it, Chandler began to sing softly with the music. "Roll out the barrel. We'll have a barrel of fun . . ."

Finally he saw Shelley making her way toward him. She

wore riding boots and a tan coat with a long, school-striped scarf wrapped around her neck. She waved when she saw him, and Chandler smiled as he watched her.

"Couldn't we have met someplace where it's warm?" she asked, sitting next to him.

"Everywhere I go, people want to talk to me," he said. "I can't stand it."

"You'll get used to it."

"I doubt it."

Shelley smiled. "You're a celebrity now. People want to know you."

"Yeah. Until the next story comes along."

In the two weeks since their return from Switzerland, Shelley and Chandler had appeared, together and separately, on no fewer than ten television interview shows and three magazine covers. Shelley, being in her element, was enjoying it immensely; Chandler, a beached whale, felt distinctly uncomfortable in the camera's glare.

"I talked with the doctors this morning. David is doing well."

Chandler nodded.

"So what happened at the network meeting this morning?" Chandler asked.

Shelley sighed. "Mrs. Gresham still denies any involvement. Claims that she was merely a patient at the clinic and knows nothing about these so-called transfers. Those were her words," added Shelley. "She has, however, relinquished control of her stock in the company. Until this matter is resolved, she won't have any say in network decisions."

"Relinquished control of her stock? Now, that certainly seems like adequate punishment for murder and attempted murder, doesn't it? And what about sweet little Todd and the others? What happens to them?" Chandler shook his head sadly. "Do you think that these people will ever pay for what they did? Not only did they murder Carruthers, Romanello, Petersen, Greenfield, Jeanette Nielsen, and who knows how many others, but look at what they did to the children. That's murder too."

Shelley nodded. "It is," she said softly, "but no one knows quite how to categorize it."

Chandler went on. "I talked with the attorney general yesterday. He told me that the investigation is proceeding cautiously. Cautiously!" he exploded. "I asked him if the prominence of some of the names mentioned had anything to do with his caution."

"I'm sure he appreciated that," said Shelley.

"By the time the Justice Department comes up with anything—if they really *want* to come up with anything—these people will have invented some new cover story."

"I doubt that," said Shelley. "Now that some of the wives have come forward and admitted that what we've said is true, I don't think anyone will be able to escape. Sooner or later they will find them all."

"Then what? Even if they identify them they don't know what to do with them." He shrugged helplessly. "What do you do with children who aren't really children, but who are guilty of murder?" Chandler shook his head. "How many of them are there?"

"No more than twenty-five. Bauer told me that himself." She saw the look on his face. "Don't worry," she said, touching his arm, "they'll find them."

"They're parasites," Chandler said. "In the truest sense of the word. They invaded the minds of ordinary children and turned them into something monstrous. They destroyed their hosts and were willing to destroy anyone who stood in their way."

Shelley looked down at the ground and for a while they sat without speaking.

"I got a call from a Bob Witherspoon this morning," said Shelley.

Chandler turned to look at her. "Who's he?"

"He told me that he had worked for Howard Hughes and that he was on board the plane that brought Hughes from Acapulco to Houston."

Chandler's eyes narrowed. "And?"

"He is willing to testify that our friend Dr. Anton Bauer was in the limousine with Hughes Corporation chairman Daniel Colhoun when Hughes arrived at the airport. Jason Arnold was in the car with them. Witherspoon told me that none of what happened that day made any sense to him until he read our story. Now he's convinced that Hughes was going to be transferred like the others—only he didn't live long enough."

"I suppose that answers some questions," said Chandler, who had never taken his eyes off the playground. He seemed anxious to change the subject. "My daughter will be here on the twenty-first," he said.

"I know. I'm looking forward to meeting her. I hope she likes me."

Chandler laughed for the first time that day. "How could she not?"

A ball rolled across the playground toward them, and Chandler stood up to retrieve it as one of the children disengaged himself from the group to run after it. Chandler picked up the ball as the boy approached. He was a small boy, about nine, with large, sparkling eyes and a wide smile that spoke volumes about the joys of childhood.

The boy reached out his arms for the ball, and Chandler hesitated for a moment. He wondered if he would ever see a child without thinking of what had happened to the others— without wondering if all of them had been found.

"Hey, mister. Can I have my ball back?" said the boy.

Chandler flipped the ball to him, and the child caught it with the casual proficiency of a born athlete, before turning and running back to his playmates.

Chandler sat back down next to Shelley, the silence growing between them until she put her hand on his arm. "Don't worry," she said. "Everything will be all right."

The carousel started up again, and the music drifted over to them as they watched the children at play.

Shelley pulled up her collar. "It's cold here. Can we go now?"

Chandler put his arm around her as they made their way toward Sixty-fifth Street and Central Park West.

The music from the carousel followed them out of the park.

As they left, two of the boys disengaged themselves from the rest of the group. They stood without talking, their eyes following the two adults. Finally the one who had retrieved the ball from Chandler said. "That's them all right. I've seen them on television."

The two boys grinned impishly at each other as if, like all children, they knew something that no one else did. Then they ran back to join the other children.

ABOUT THE AUTHOR

CHARLES ROBERTSON was born in Glasgow, Scotland and emigrated to Stamford, Connecticut with his parents and sister in 1954. He continued his education at the University of Connecticut, where he earned a B.A., and later received an M.A. from Fairfield University. In 1967, Mr. Robertson married the former Ann Escott, and they now have two children, Jennifer, born in 1970, and Scott, born in 1974. Mr. Robertson taught English at Rippowam High School in Stamford for ten years. *The Elijah Conspiracy* (Bantam 1980) was his first novel and he is now at work on his third.

DON'T MISS
THESE CURRENT
Bantam Bestsellers

☐	22580	**PEACE BREAKS OUT** John Knowles	$2.95
☐	22740	**HALLOWEEN** Curtis Richards	$2.95
☐	20922	**SHADOW OF CAIN** Vincent Bugliosi & Ken Hurwitz	$3.95
☐	20822	**THE GLITTER DOME** Joseph Wambaugh	$3.95
☐	20943	**THE EARHART MISSION** Peter Tanous	$2.75
☐	20924	**THE PEOPLE'S ALMANAC 3** Wallechinsky & Wallace	$4.50
☐	20558	**THE LORD GOD MADE THEM ALL** James Herriot	$3.95
☐	20662	**THE CLOWNS OF GOD** Morris West	$3.95
☐	20181	**CHALLENGE (Spirit of America!)** Charles Whited	$3.50
☐	14894	**FIRELORD** Parke Godwin	$3.50
☐	13419	**THE CHAINS** Gerald Green	$3.50
☐	20581	**FROM THE BITTER LAND** Maisie Mosco	$3.25
☐	01368	**EMBERS OF DAWN** Patricia Matthews	$6.95
☐	13101	**THE BOOK OF LISTS #2** Wallechinsky & Wallaces	$3.50
☐	20164	**HOW TO MASTER VIDEO GAMES** Tom Hirschfeld	$2.95
☐	20560	**CHIEFS** Stuart Woods	$3.75
☐	14716	**THE LORDS OF DISCIPLINE** Pat Conroy	$3.75
☐	20476	**THE UNBORN** David Shobin	$3.25
☐	20387	**THE COMPLETE MONEY MARKET GUIDE** William Donaghue	$3.50
☐	20134	**THE PRITIKIN PROGRAM FOR DIET AND EXERCISE** Nathan Pritikin w/ Patrick McGrady, Jr.	$3.95
☐	20356	**THE GUINESS BOOK OF WORLD RECORDS 20th ed.** The McWhirters	$3.95
☐	14594	**MORE OF PAUL HARVEY'S THE REST OF THE STORY** Paul Aurandt	$2.75

Buy them at your local bookstore or use this handy coupon for ordering:

Bantam Books, Inc., Dept. FB, 414 East Golf Road, Des Plaines, Ill. 60016

Please send me the books I have checked above. I am enclosing $_____
(please add $1.25 to cover postage and handling). Send check or money order
—no cash or C.O.D.'s please.

Mr/Mrs/Miss_____

Address_____

City_____ State/Zip_____

FB—10/82

Please allow four to six weeks for delivery. This offer expires 4/83.

Coming December 1982 . . .
A horrifying new novel
by the author of
GHOST HOUSE
and
GHOST HOUSE REVENGE

GHOST
LIGHT
by Clare McNally

Fifty years ago, pretty little five-year-old Bonnie Jackson died horribly inside the Windsor Theatre. Now she has returned to perform her showstopping act of revenge.

We Deliver!

And So Do These Bestsellers.